YOU MAKE ME TINGLE

MITZI MILES

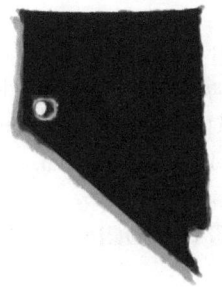

MMK BOOKS

2023 MMK Books

Copyright © 2023 by Mitzi Miles-Kubota

Book Design and Cover Art © Mitzi Miles-Kubota

Published in the United States by MMK Books

PUBLISHER'S NOTE

LIBRARY OF CONGRESS CATALOGING-IN-PUBLICATION DATA

Miles-Kubota, Mitzi

You Make Me Tingle

ISBN 979-8-9862958-2-4

Fiction—20th century—Crime—Humor

Set in Bodoni 72

*With love and gratitude always
to Ron and Ivan, my main men,
and my new main little man Enzo*

Chapter 1

Do you feed a baby 2%? What if you're not really sure how old the baby is? The one with me could be six months, could be a year and a half for all I know about kids. Bad, bad, Auntie Flack. I forgot to ask her mother, my dear, old – probably departed – friend Mona. Bad, bad friend, Flack Murrow. Or Susan Anne, as Mona still calls, or used to call, me. She never did get used to my nickname. She didn't like it. Too butch. She and I go, went, way back to childhood when she was Sheryl Crawford, before she got a bitchy stepmom named Cheryl.

Anyway, this kid with me – Pioche, Mona's baby – is at least young enough not to be able to tell me herself what the hell she wants to eat, but for the last fifteen minutes or so she's making it pretty plain that she's HUNGRY.

We pull my perfect, ruby red '67 GTO into a trash strewn parking place in the otherwise empty lot of a 7-Eleven that I hope is not the garden spot of Oakland off I80W. Drunks and junkies, passed out or in the process of passing out, slouch against the front wall. Your more wired and fidgeting druggies with droopy drawers pace and flick cigarette ashes around like the ashes might be something that bites.

Enter me and my Halloween mask and fright wig of no-sleep, drove-half-the-night red frizz, and Pioche, her skin a rosier shade of her natural brown from the intensity and duration of her bellyaching. Man, the mild-mannered little angel I met a few days ago, and who can sleep through an air raid, sure woke up in a bad mood and fast. I shushed and shushed and sweet-talked her on the freeway til my mouth went dry, and the sun came up orange out of the Bay Area smog, and I finally spotted the haven of 7-Eleven lights right by an exit. Little did I know that not just any 7-Eleven off the freeway would do. Wish this could've been a little better neighborhood. Wish the baby would stop screaming. I'm too tired for this shit.

So, is it 2% for the kid or 100% moo juice? Or is it formula? How long should you feed one of these critters formula? And do I have to heat up what I give her to drink? That'll be a good trick. Maybe teeth could tell me something about what to feed her? I wait for her to cut loose with a long howl and look into her mouth. Four teeth. Little bitty ones. I don't think she's going to chew much.

"Hungry, isn't she?" a fine specimen of a young or old woman in a pea coat with no buttons says to me. "Ought to feed her. Hungry. Hungry's what her problem is. Spare some change?" She smiles with the few brown teeth she's got left. Everybody in the parking lot is looking at me, expecting me to shut "my" kid up. It's too early in their morning or too late in their night to put up with a screaming brat. From the nasty looks I'm getting, I can tell they blame this all on me. Rodney was right: I don't know nothing about taking care of no baby. I pick her up from her nest on the floor and make a casual dash through the rabble to the door.

"Okay," I say when I get inside and to no one in particular, "this is my sister-in-law's kid. Dumb bitch's been gone all night and stuck me babysitting. Said she'd only be a couple of hours, and that was around ten last night. Everything was cool while the kid was sleeping, but now I don't know what to do. I got a bottle, but which stuff do I give her?"

Immediately four tired-looking but well-painted and decorated women group around us. They're all in platform shoes, towering over me, their sequined and satined boobs in my face. One in an overstretched tube top gets a pint of whole milk out of the cooler, takes the bottle from me, and fills it.

"Here, Estelle. Put this in the last of that old raggedy coffee so it can warm up." She passes the pink bottle from her long purple fingertips to Estelle, who's chewing gum 90 miles an hour, behind the counter. Estelle pulls the coffeepot out, sets the bottle in the sludge, and blows and pops a huge pink bubble.

"She dry?" asks a beautiful girl in lime green hot pants.

"Uh . . ." I say intelligently. The girl rolls her eyes at me, unbuttons the bottom of Pioche's sleeper, and pokes a finger into check.

"Ugh, girl. She's soaked. How long she been sitting in this mess? Delilah, get us some diapers over here now."

Delilah, a massive Amazon of a woman with a huge 'fro covered in glitter, trudges quicker than it looks like she could on her unreasonably high silver platforms down the aisle to the diapers. She rips open a box of Pampers with her teeth,

7

not wanting to ruin her nails, takes out a diaper, and shoves the open box to the back of the shelf.

"Milk's near ready," says Estelle. "Here. Lay her here." Estelle makes a space in the displays of NoDoz and rubbers and candy by the cash register, and everyone crowds around to give me instructions. There are a few more trips down a few more aisles for Wash-n-Dries, Desenex, powder. There's a lot of pointing and a little bit of bickering about the best way to accomplish our task. Meanwhile, Pioche is sucking down the warmed milk and staring with her deep, dark eyes at the woman with the purple fingernails who's holding the bottle and humming the most beautiful non-song. Pioche's breath catches a time or two as her body goes off cry-mode and on to chow-mode.

The women are asking separate questions all at the same time: the baby's name and how old she is (which I'm putting at just shy of a year, judging from the tag in her sleeper suit and the fact that she doesn't walk yet) and what's my sister-in-law's name (guess who? Gladys Newberry). There is much speculation about what my sister-in-law could be up to out all night. The stories get wilder and wilder, ranging from sis taking off to Alaska with a pipeline worker, to ménanges of all sizes and configurations, to a suicidal leap off the Golden Gate, which makes each one shake her head sadly and knowingly. Pioche is studying the garish costumes and one set of false eyelashes after another as she continues to drink.

"Girl!" Estelle nearly screams, "what the fuck happened here?"

With all the fussing over Pioche, no one had noticed my blood-stained cowgirl shirt and the dried blood on my neck.

"You best let me take a look at that," Estelle says as she comes around the counter. She grabs my cheeks so hard with one hand that she gives me fish-face.

"Uh-huh," she says once, twice, examining closer and closer. "Who done this shit?"

"Um, I . . ." I mumble. How could I have driven so long with nothing to do but think and not come up with a story to explain the cuts Johnny made on me?

"Never mind that," says Delilah. "What he cut you with? It's raggedy."

"He had this, um, dagger . . ."

"Uh-huh, we got to get this cleaned up 'fore you come down with tet'nus or some kinda contagion or 'nother."

The women are off like a shot, looking for soap and antiseptic and bandages and who-knows-what. They strip off my shirt and bra and make a thorough inspection of me. I'm getting poked and wiped and pinched and sanitized within an inch of my life.

Estelle asks, "Who got a change of clothes?"

It appears they all do because the counter is filling up fast with piles of sequins and lace and feathers and whatnot. These are mostly some pretty big ladies, but they manage to pull together a costume for me: a glittery pink crop-top and a red pushup bra. Like I have anything to push up. The safety pins come out. They do some on-site mending on my body, alterations that keep the straps and bands and neck openings closed to a barely — I mean, barely — acceptable level. To cover up the cotton gauze they've wrapped around the slices on my neck, I am given a fluorescent green feather boa with metallic threads sticking out all over it.

"Them pants, too," orders Estelle. I look down at my blood-encrusted Levis and give them up.

"Here, this'll work." One of the robust women hands me a yellow boob tube that turns into a perfect miniskirt. I keep trying to pull the hemline down and make it longer, but no dice. My cowboy boots are an especially nice touch. Tooled leather design of phoenixes in gold and red on black alligator.

They all start laughing. "Girl, somebody gonna turn you out you go around looking like that!" They're doubling over with delight at my clothing dilemma.

"Thank you. Really. Thanks for taking care of us."

"That's what we do, hon. That's what we all gotta do," says Delilah. She shoves my bloody clothes into a paper bag and sets it down too close to Pioche for my liking.

Pioche has sucked down the whole bottle, and Estelle sits her up – a little too quickly – and part of the milk comes out the way it went in followed by a big burp. The women go nuts for this – laughing, doing little happy dances. One of them hands me a roll of paper towels, and I get the privilege of cleaning up. Pioche looks delighted with all this attention and colors and activity. She starts shaking her arms and kicking her legs.

"She's strong," Estelle says, holding the baby while I try to soak up the rejected breakfast.

"Yeah," I say. "Like her mother. Listen, I ought to change her clothes. She's pretty messy. Could you hold her while I go out to the car?"

"Oh sure, honey, sure. You go on. We got her."

Outside, the woman who panhandled me is trying to talk one of the drunks out of a cigarette. He's got the pack clutched to his chest like a kid trying to keep another kid from taking his candy. She keeps trying to grab one out of the pack, and he's slapping her hand. Finally, he pushes her down. She kicks at him from her seat on the pavement before he staggers away, waving her off with his free hand. She flips him the bird with both hands and calls him a lot of things he no doubt is.

It's been hours since I've had a smoke, so that first one goes down in a couple of puffs. It's chilly as usual down here by the Bay – especially dressed like this. It's May and feels like

December, for crying out loud! May in Reno isn't exactly bathing suit weather, but here? My teeth are starting to chatter. I'm glad all these people who live here don't seem to mind lousy weather much. Keeps them out of Nevada. They have the nerve to feel sorry for us living in a place they think is nothing but dirt-brown hills and sandstorms. And casinos, though that part they do like. Chalk it up to spending too much time indoors to escape the cold and damp. I could never trade our continuous sunshine. My brain would turn to mush down here with the fog and slugs and mold and constant cold. And crowds and traffic jams. And. And. And. There's nothing these people have to put up with every day that I would ever want for love or money.

I light another Lucky and open the trunk of my car to dig out some of Pioche's suspender pants, shirt with a ruffly collar, a sweater, and some socks with duckies on them. Pink and pink and pink. I'd have thought Mona'd show more imagination dressing her kid, but I guess having a baby does strange things to you. Made Mona, of all people, want to turn into a square. She sure dressed Pioche like a typical baby girl.

The fishnet stocking, with the roll of naked, dead Michael's money in it, rolls out of my bag — which I'm thanking myself for leaving in the trunk and not on the front seat, given my current location. I grab it quick before it attracts the attention of the parking lot crowd, and peel off a handful of cash to share with the women who are saving my ass in so many ways. I don't care what kind of work a working girl does. She's always going to welcome a little extra appreciation with no strings attached.

The gruesome thought of the body count at Johnny Ruggerio's — and my role in it all — tries to weasel its way to the front of the line of shit I have to think about, but I hold it off with all the denial I can muster at the moment. I know of one body for sure, the one that's my doing. Then there's Mona's. And Rodney's. I'm sure the Reno cops are still knee-deep collecting evidence. I can't let myself wonder what they're digging up about me at the scene. Nothing I can do about it from here anyway. But those kinds of annoyances do make a girl worry about her choices.

Then out of the blue I start wondering if I locked the door at my office. What is it about me, always thinking about locks? Wonder if I've been evicted yet. That slumlord Felix has been itching for a reason. Pretty sure the mess – in more ways than one – of dead, naked Michael ought to give him just the right amount of ammo to kick me to the curb. Flack Murrow Investigations definitely will be changing headquarters when, if, I get to go home.

Inside the 7-Eleven I let the professionals take care of changing Pioche's clothes. There's more simultaneous commentary about how cute everything is. One of them notices a label that says Joseph Magnin, and we all go "ooooh" and express our amazement that Magnin carries baby clothes. Then the topic changes to what my brother does for work that he can afford clothes like these for his baby. Does Pioche's mom work, too? Where do they live? And I'm making shit up right and left about how they work for one of these new computer companies and how someday we'll all have one of the things in our house . . . and thank god the donut man arrives. I save myself from further interrogation by springing for a round of donuts – including for the motley crew outside. We wolf down everything the man brought in so fast he goes out for more, and we put a pretty good dent in those, too. We're all drinking milk out of cartons (I'm not making a big deal out of it, but I'm not sharing mine. Cooties, you know.) Drinking coffee out of paper cups as fast as Estelle keeps it coming, licking supremely greasy sugar coating off of many colors of fingers. I let Pioche have a lick of my glazed doughnut, which she ends up gumming happily. What little doesn't end up smeared all over her face seems to be staying down okay. Estelle has turned up the store radio, and Marvin Gaye's telling us how sweet it is to be loved by us. Looks like we all think so, too. We're just loving ourselves — all full of milk and sugar. This hasn't been such a bad place to stop after all.

Until Estelle spots one of the drunks swiping a bottle of Night Train off the shelf and trying to hide it in his coat. Before we can get out of her way, she's marching down the aisle with a baseball bat clenched in both hands. Then she's raising it like an ax over her head. Everybody ducks. The drunks and junkies nearest the door vanish. The thief is rocking back on his heels from concentrating so hard on how he's going to hide the bottle, but then he sees Estelle bearing down on him and drops the bottle and puts his arms around his head. She starts hammering at him but is not as good at beating him as I thought she'd be. Could she be giving this sorry so-and-so a break? I make a move to help her, but Delilah holds me back.

"Let them be," she says.

Estelle keeps whacking the man as she chases him across the back of the store, up the magazine aisle, and out the front doors that swing back and forth and catch the bat on a down stroke, momentarily jerking it out of Estelle's hands. It thuds to the floor. She picks it up, goes outside, and runs the whole grimy crew out of the parking lot with her roundhouse swings. I cringe as she gets to near the GTO, but that's where she runs out of steam, calls them all a last, long string of my favorite words and some new usages I must be sure to add, and comes back inside sweating and still mad as a wet hen.

"I'm going to kill that motherfucker. Some one of these days, I'm going to kill him dead. Don't none of you think no, neither."

"Oh Estelle, chill down," says the girl in the green hotpants. "You ain't going to kill your own husband."

"Lord, I am. I'm going to kill that man." Her breath is huffing in and out. Her heavy face is grim, and it strikes all of us as funny at the same time. The women are falling off their platform shoes, holding their sides. I'm hoping their night's work is over because makeup is being ruined at an astonishing rate as they have the best laugh at Estelle, who hangs right in there, determined to stay mad.

"All you all bitches can just go to hell!" she yells. Which makes them laugh that much harder. They got me laughing til tears come to my eyes, too. With the rough couple of days I've had, the tears and the giggles too quickly mixed together into something I completely lose control over. No one notices at first, but when Delilah puts her arm around me and then the rest of them, including Estelle, are touching my hands or patting me on the back and telling me it's okay, I realize that every bit of the noise I hear now is coming from me. No laughter left. I am sobbing. Crying harder than I have in years, here in a strange 7-Eleven with all these strange women whose voices are so soft now, whose used-up, young bodies are holding Mona's baby and me. Letting me cry. Telling me to let it all out, honey. Let it go. And I do. And it's making me so tired.

I'm so tired I slide down to the floor in front of the counter. My legs just give out on me. I cover my face. The women crouch down by me, and I smell the way they've spent their night coming out from under too-short skirts and too-small shorts. Too much perfume, too much sex.

I don't have to explain, and they don't bother to ask. Heard it before, something like it anyway. They know it's not a lost-my-man cry. It's something worse when crying sounds like this. Something so gone for good you can't put it into words. I can't and they can't, and we'll leave it like this for as long as it takes.

Pioche starts up her crying again, too, catching the drift from all of us snivellers. Her baby-bawling blends like a little flute into our over-smoked exhales and runny noses. No one says a word. A crowd is reassembling outside the windows, looking in like mosquitoes you can't chase off for long. We must be a colorful sight. Something you generally don't run into on a regular day at the Sev. Or do they?

I finally get it together enough to say, "This is ridiculous," and try to get myself into a standing position. I get more helping hands than I have body parts. Estelle hands me a pillow-shaped wad of powder blue Kleenex. I soak it pretty good by the time I get done sopping off my face.

"Whew," I say and try to shake it off. "What time is it?"

"Just after seven, honey," says Estelle.

"Man, I got to go. I'm sorry about all this. I just . . ."

"It's okay, whatever it was," Delilah says. "We all get like that. No harm. Besides, the donuts was good."

There are big smiles again around the ring of mascara-smeared faces. The girl in the lime green hot pants says, "I don't know about y'all, but I'm going to go get me some sleep. Some real good sleep."

"Yeah, nothing like a spell of waterworks to get y'all loose and relaxed," Delilah says, passing Pioche back to me. The baby's her usual happy self. Back to normal, whatever that is.

I take a fifty out of my red bra and toss it on the counter. "For the donuts and milk and all."

"Now, you know that's way too much," Estelle says.

"Doesn't matter. Here, take this, too, and split it." I toss out the rest of the wad. "From the baby's mom. She'd appreciate you taking care of us. Oh, and I'll take a pint of Jim

Beam. Better make that two."

"You sure you all right? Estelle asks. "Not thinking of heading to the Golden Gate?"

I think about it for a minute. "Can you tell me what 'all right' is?"

Someone – more than one voice, in fact – says, "Amen."

Chapter 2

Mona lost her virginity before I did. No real big surprise — she was always the expert. Anything you wanted to know about sex. Anything you didn't want to know about sex. She was really only a few months older than me, and I remember that she "lost it" when our ages sounded like we were a year apart. She was still only 14, 13 years, two months and 16 days, if you really wanted to be specific. She was precocious in every way that could get one or both of us in trouble. It would've been so much easier on the world if she'd have been a piano protege or a spelling whiz kid. But her gifts ran to the darker side: thief, liar, drinker, and seducer at an age when, for most other girls, baton twirling was the big turn-on of all turn-ons. I myself? I'm not sure: I was either the world's biggest dumb shit to associate with Mona at all, or I was lucky to have quite possibly the world's most interesting best friend.

I saw my first fully naked adult man in a nudist colony magazine Mona swiped from under her dad's bed. She was actually looking for vodka at the time. As I gaped at the bodies at play on the volleyball court and tennis courts, at the wangling and dangling of parts that screamed for the restraint of clothes and lots of them, Mona described for me in great detail the changes the fully naked adult male's body will go through in an encounter with a fully naked member of the opposite sex. Why these changes weren't going on between the fully naked players on the nudist pages seemed like a sensible enough question.

"Because you have to be alone, in a house, in a bedroom, in a bed with the lights off. It doesn't work if it's day or there's other people around. The man can't concentrate on making it big and stiff."

The expert.

Sounded messy to me, what she described. And sweaty. And a little bit interesting but not enough to run right out and do it. But she had to. Mona has — had — the curiosity. I always felt like the most dull person on the planet for never having dreamed possible the kinds of mysteries Mona poked her nose into and the stories she brought into my life.

So the story went that one of her dad's friends was kind enough to satisfy Mona's quest to get her "cherry popped." That's the way she put it. The way she told it, the poor man didn't have a chance. She laid it right out on the table for him. Literally. That's where they did it, she said: on the kitchen table. In broad daylight. Showed me the exact spot. Reenacted it for me, which I could've done without. No bed, no dark, so a few parts of her original theory were wrong.

"What'd you think?" I asked her.

She had been pretty excited while telling the story,

giggling about the clank of the man's belt buckle against the metal table leg and about the kinds of faces he made and the whimpering and the shuddering, agonizing groans at "the end."

"The end?"

"Yeah. This hot goo comes squirting out of his thing. Like snot."

"Eeeeeewwww!"

Mona stood with one bare foot on top of the other and picked at a scab on her elbow. "I don't know. I guess it was kind of more boring than I thought it would be. So, oh well. That's it."

When my turn came, when Red and Edie's son Clyde started my sex life for me one night while his little sister and my little brother slept in their bunkbeds on the opposite side of the room, when he dragged me out of bed onto the floor so the springs wouldn't squeak, when his big sticky hand over my mouth blocked so much air from getting into my nose I almost passed out, I wondered if Mona would've called it boring, and I wondered why anyone in their right mind would volunteer to take part in such a thing. By then I didn't know where she was, so I couldn't ask her what she thought. Couldn't say anything to anyone else either. Clyde had a few suggestions about what might happen to Timmy if I did. Oh well, that was it. Never did see Clyde fully naked. I guess Mona got proven wrong about pretty much all of it.

Chapter 3

My teeth are ground down to the nerves by the time I make it through San Francisco and check us into a Motel 6 just off the Bayshore Freeway near the airport. Those fantastic ladies at the 7-Eleven stocked me up with pilfered baby crap, several packs of Luckys, a poor boy sandwich, and – get this – two fifths of Jim Beam! Aw, I only asked for a pint and fully intended to pay. My heroes!

Delilah offered to take us home with her, but that idea sounded like a good way to get no rest and possibly get the GTO stripped. I thanked her for the offer but said I had to meet some people, which I do but not until later. I mostly need to lay down on some crispy, white motel sheets in a place where I'm positive no one knows where I am.

Takes me a couple of trips to drag our crap up the stairs to the third floor. Should have thought to ask for ground floor. New to this lugging around baby crap, you know? For someone so little, Pio sure comes with a lot of accessories. I'm finding out she actually needs them all. I leave my saddle and tack and a couple of things I normally haul around and slam the trunk down with my elbow.

Pioche and I play patty cake and got-your-nose. She's kind of young, so I have to make her moves for her. I'm trying my damnedest to hypnotize her into taking a nap with me. The whole time we're playing, I'm running through what's gone on the past few days. Thinking about how old the baby will be before she'll ask about her mother, and her dad for that matter. Who's going to be the one to tell her? Kids can figure out if there's something different about their families easier than they can learn to tie their shoes. By the time Timmy and I lost Mom and Pop, we were old enough to know all too well what happened: Pop killed in the fire; Mom killed by booze and pills and her lost love. I know for a fact that Pioche hasn't got the genes — at least on her mother's side — to ever say "what's done is done" and go on with her life in any kind of usual way. There's a lot of ways this kid could react to the truth, if she ever learns it, about her parents. I know from experience that some of those ways might not be too pretty.

But we have years before any of this becomes an issue. The biggest deal now is delivering Pioche, who I'm really starting to like, into the hands of people who are supposed to take her out of the country. What do I say to them about Mona? Who the hell are "they," anyway? What about the kid's dad?

I wasn't thinking too clearly, or maybe I was, when I loaded us into the car and took off for The City just because Mona told me to. And because I wussed out on coming up with anything better at the time. I have a policy against hanging around a murder scene, with all indications a triple murder, sitting like a cute duckie waiting to be arrested or at least questioned within an inch of my sanity. The smart part about taking off was that it got me out of there — way out of there. The not-so-smart part is that I'm not sure what to do now. I can't keep this baby. No way. Can barely take care of myself and tolerate my own company let alone deal with a kid. But where is she going to go? These people I'm supposed to meet, they're just supposed to be temporary, too. What then? Pioche is part evidence, part baggage, and probably all trouble. And she doesn't even know it. She just smiles and makes cute baby sounds. Right now she's finally sleeping, sucking on her whole fist. Looking at her so comfortable and out of it, I kick my boots off, curl up around her soft-sleeping body, and go out like a light . . .

. . . unusual for there to be fog at Lake Tahoe. Can't see across. Can just see out a few yards onto the still, steel-gray surface of the water. There is snow on the beach. I've never stood on the beach in winter. Most of the time the Lake is the color of a Phillips milk of magnesia bottle held up to the light. Never foggy. Never, that I've seen. Complete silence and stillness. The water doesn't move. I should have shoes on. Bare feet in weather like this can't be a very good idea. Neither is this yellow sundress. I know this dress. It's my mother's. I'm surprised it fits, tiny as she was. I'm surprised it's keeping me warm. A deer glides out of the fog, stands at the Lake's edge, watching me for a long time before she lowers her head and drinks. A doe. Her two babies come out of the fog, too. Come and rub against my bare legs. Soft. I kneel in the snow, and they let me pet them. They sniff my face. I feel their little puffs of breath. Hear them breathe. They smell like spring.

Out of the dead silence: ROAR! A machine. A powerful machine. We can't see it, but it's there. Overhead? On the water? Behind us? I look, the deer look for the same thing that came up on us so fast. The deer vanish. I can't hear where they went because of the snow. The machine is louder. Approaching. But where? Where? A helicopter . . . A helicopter . . . A snowplow . . . A sound I know I should know, but where? I stand up, brush the snow off my knees. I can't see but I think, I think . . .

. . . I know that sound! The fog is gone, the dream is gone. Sunlight sneaks through the narrow slit between the closed motel room curtains. And I know that sound. I roll off the bed. My still asleep legs let me down. I crawl to the window, pull myself up, and the curtains open just in time to see my beautiful GTO fishtail out of the parking lot. Son of a BITCH! In broad daylight. I yank open the door, run down the outdoor hallway to the stairs, fly across the parking lot in my hooker suit and bare feet. I see whoever's got my car run a red light, bounce over drainage dips on both sides of the intersection and disappear over a little rise. I can still hear the engine but not for long. It's gone.

No gun, no shoes. Tugging the boob tube skirt down to cover my butt. Yanking the boob tube up over my boobs to cover the red bra, I watch my pride and joy run perfectly out of my life. I'm left standing in the middle of an urban nowhere street, disoriented, underdressed, and unarmed.

"Hey, lady. What the hell?" A police cruiser stops beside me in the middle of the street, and a California-blond, movie star-jawed cop wearing mirror sunglasses has his head stuck out the window.

I interrupt my cussing long enough to yell, "They took my car, sons a bitches!"

"Stole your car?"

"My car," I say weakly, pointing as weakly in the direction it went. I have run out of swear words for the moment.

The cop looks down the street at the same nothing I'm seeing. Looks at me, parading around half-naked in my "work" clothes. He turns on his flashers and cherry tops, gets out of the car, and leaves it running in the middle of the road. He adjusts the 48 pounds of cop equipment adorning his wasp waist as he comes toward me. He holds up an official hand and makes a hippie in a ratty blue VW bus stop for him. This fashion model cop takes his official time crossing the street, then he waves the guy through with a pompous gesture.

"You, uh, staying here?" He points his powerful chin in the direction of the Motel 6.

"Hm? Oh. Yeah," I say. I'm deeply distracted by the kidnapping of my car. Need to pull myself together and come up with a story for Barney-Fife-on-Steroids. Don't need him finding out more than he needs to know. This guy has "real law by the book" written all over him. I figure I could take him in a match of wits, but I also know I'm not in Kansas anymore. Just like Dorothy and Toto, Flack and Pioche have got themselves plunked down where the rules as we know them might no longer apply. California is Oz to me under the best circumstance, which this is not. Between the billboards after billboards and six-lane freeways and hippies on every corner and rich people in black Mercedeses and gay guys in rhinestones and dope smokers with surfboards sticking through their side windows, this really is no place like home. I'm down here feeling outnumbered (by a couple of million) and like I don't have a prayer of keeping up the pace. Rat race, rats winning. That's California: full technicolor lounge act with circumstances beyond my control. And you know I'm all about control. Flack, just plaster on a knowing smirk and try to fit in.

"Miss, I think your attire is a little . . . you know?, much? For daytime? Come with me and I'll drive you back to your room."

Shit! I had totally forgotten how I'm dressed. Barely dressed. And all of a sudden I'm cold. I look at his car and at him and how far it is back to the motel. Naturally, his car's closer — and warmer, and now that I'm all the way awake, I know I'm way overexposed in these, um, clothes. Riding with him has several distinct disadvantages, mostly the fact that I can smell him from here — a lethal combo of hairspray, coffee, and too much expensive cologne. Also, since there seems to be no way around him snooping in my room, I need to get there first.

"Oh gosh," I say, banging myself on the head with the palm of my hand. "I forgot." And I take off running down the street, half out of wanting to give myself a chance to think, and the other half is that I just remembered about Pioche and momentarily picture her having rolled off the bed onto the floor and killing herself.

"Halt!" he commands, and I keep going, hoping he's not also cliché enough to be aiming anything at me. I yell over my shoulder, "Follow me!", and keep going. Funny that I hadn't noticed how rough the pavement was when I was in hot pursuit. I mutter, "Ow, ouch, ouch, ow, shit, ouch," the entire distance. I see also that I've gathered an audience of guests and housekeeping staff along the rails of all three stories. The ones I have to pass by directly on the second-floor step aside but don't say a word. Just stare. I hold my head up and try to walk so that my body parts don't flip and flop too much, pulling down the hem of my fake mini-skirt. I turn into the open doorway of my room and shut the door behind me.

Well, here's another clue about what Pioche is capable of: she's sitting in the middle of the bed sorting through the beads and fringe on my bag. She remembers seeing, and tasting, this stuff before.

"Hi, Pio," I say to her as I make a quick scan of the room for loaded weapons, bloodstained clothes, et cetera, et cetera. Pioche eyeballs me and goes back to slurping leather and beads. I wriggle out of my current costume, grab some Levis I'm glad I thought ahead to bring. Throw on a Western shirt. Man, do I need a shower. And then there's the bandage on my neck . . . I'm trying to force a comb through my hair when I hear the knock at the door that must be Barney Fife. Let the explaining begin.

"Come on in," I yell as I fasten the pearl snaps on my shirt, but since the door locks automatically when you close it, I have to go let him in. Lock problems. Again. But first I pick up Pioche to make a good second impression.

The cop gives my room the quick law enforcement once-over. Looking for clues to the "activity" my previous attire would suggest he'd find. He looks at me now in my cowgirl duds, bouncing a baby. I can see him trying to connect the dots.

"Well," he says, "who's this pretty one?" He reaches a finger toward her and, bless her heart, she lets out a mighty shriek. The cop looks sad from her rejection of him.

I'm shushing her, comforting her, hoping I look like I know what I'm doing. The fruit doesn't fall far from the tree. Mona's life wisdom must have been delivered in the womb. Pioche has created a nice diversion. Now I can do the injured party act: this man has scared "my" baby, and he's going to have to pay.

I say, "Speaking of who's who, let's see some ID."

"Oh, right. I'm Officer Paul Tingle, ma'am. Officer Tingle." He points to the brass nameplate on his pectoral.

If I wasn't supposed to be trying to act upset, I could have some real fun with a name like that.

"And you are . . .?" he asks as he removes his shades. He

points at me with one of the metal earpieces before he folds the glasses and hangs them on his pocket.

I hate when people ask half questions like, "And you are . . .?" "Do you want to come with . . .?" Like these idiots can't be bothered to finish a sentence. Good thing I'm occupied with Pioche. I can hold off a second or two while I come up with a response. Maybe I'll try a half-response in response to a half-question. Truth is always the easiest story to maintain, so I guess I'll have to give him one-tenth of the truth.

"Gladys Newbury. This is my sister's kid, Karen."

"Isn't she a pretty thing?"

"Yeah, she's cute. We've been visiting her grandma in Redwood City."

"But you're . . . staying? . . . out here?"

Oh. Right. The clothes. Think, think, think, Flack. Because he sure is.

"Yeah, Mom's place is pretty small, and the baby makes her nervous after a while. I've stayed here before and liked it, so I figured why take a chance on somewhere else?"

I can see Officer Tingle is still waiting for an explanation, but he says, "I know what you mean. It's not easy being away from home. You want someplace clean. Safe. Convenient."

I clear my throat. "I know you're wondering . . . my clothes . . . before? . . . out in the street?"

He crosses his blond-haired arms.

"It's a long story . . ."

He gives me the universal hand signal for "and?".

"It's, I'm, not what you're thinking. Can we just leave it at that? These are my usual duds. I swear."

"And that?" He points at my neck. "Seeping."

I touch the gauze. Yep, seeping, like the man said.

"Can we not talk about it?"

"We can come back to it. I have time."

Shit.

He looks at his watch. "Sooooo, your car was stolen." He takes out his requisite little cop notebook and pen. I describe my car as it looked before I had it painted red: sea green 1967 GTO, and I transpose the third and fourth numbers of my license plate. And I make it a California plate. Sticking with about one-tenth of the truth, I tell him, no, I didn't get a look at the no-good thief or thieves; I was asleep. Then he asks me for my address, my driver's license, and other info I don't want to give. And I wonder if I still have it in me to create – or if he's straight enough to fall for – The Diversion. I make myself think about Mona and crew, work myself up into some very real tears. I sit on the edge of the bed, looking as girlishly pitiful and madonna-and-child-like as possible until, aha!, he can't stand it and sits down beside me and puts his arm around me. Rookie. I look up at him with Those Eyes, those sad, doe eyes. His eyes are lovely blue at this range, I might add. My accomplice, Miss Pioche, also gazes up at our savior with perfect timing.

"When my husband finds out about his car," sniff, sniff, I say, "he'll kill me. He forbid me taking this trip alone, but Mom's getting so old now . . . Seeing the baby means so much to her. So, I just . . . left." I touch the bandage for effect.

I've done a lot of sniveling today. Getting good at it, I think. Officer Paul Tingle holds me with one arm and rubs my shoulder with his other hand. I make myself lean against him, and it feels good. Safe. For a second, I let myself believe that's how things really are. It's okay; he thinks I'm crying about something else anyway. He knows men are pigs. Feels sorry for little old me having to face my abusive supposed husband and tell him about the car.

Paul Tingle is rocking Pioche and me just a little bit. He's taken his hand from my shoulder and put it on my hair. Cops

28

really treat you good in San Francisco. Next thing I know, he's kissing my hair, then — the inevitable: he kisses me all the way down the side of my face until he gives me the old smackeroo right on the lips. Not bad. Sometimes my playacting is too good for my own good. I stand up.

Paul Tingle says, "I'm sorry. I don't know what came over me."

I do, but I'll save his pride and not tell him. Instead I say, "Look, Officer . . ."

"Paul," he says.

"Officer Paul Tingle. You see the trouble I'm in here, don't you?"

"Kind of a lot?"

"You can say that again." And, boy, do I mean that! "I need a favor: Before you round up a posse, would you give me a day to figure out how I'm going to tell Melvin?" Melvin?

"Your husband?"

"Yes, my husband Melvin. I mean, you and I both know how much chance you have of recovering enough of Melvin's car to get me back home, right?"

"Let's think positive . . ."

"Stop, please. Don't you see?" I'm going to lay it on thick. "You want to know why I'm really here?"

"To take the baby to her grandma's."

"Let's just say that's what Melvin thinks. For the time being, anyway." I give him a conspiratorial nod.

"Oh, I get it. You're leaving him."

"Correctamundo. If the police start poking around, he's going to be mad as hell about his car. I'm scared to death about how mad he'll be that I left . . . him. Tonight, when he gets back from work, all hell's gonna break loose. And he has guns." I touch my neck again.

Officer Tingle has to think this over. He's got his job to

do. He's got a maiden in distress. He's kissed some woman he doesn't even know in a motel room on the day she, dressed like a hooker, left her husband. I have him sufficiently tied up in knots so far.

"Okay," he says, folding up his notebook, "I won't report it. Yet."

"Thank you. Thank you." I touch his arm for effect.

"Can I take you two anywhere? It's the least I can do."

"Oh no, we'll be fine. I'll call Mom."

"Right."

He looks pretty confused, sitting there on the rumpled, plaid bedspread in his crisp uniform. He's staring me down with those blue eyes. I could break easily. Tell him all my woes. All. What good would that do? Sure won't get my car back or make Johnny and Mona and Rodney any less dead or get Pioche to her rendezvous on time. I really wish I had some backup firepower for that meeting. Paul Tingle would make a good one. Then afterward we could . . . Now there I go, not finishing sentences. Focus, Flack, focus.

"You're sure there's nothing I can do?" he says finally.

I use my best sexy movie star voice, "Kiss me again. And let me know where I can reach you."

He stands up and walks toward me. I shift Pioche over onto my right hip so Paul and I can have maximum body contact. He doesn't smell so bad to me now. I think before, I might have projected a lot of my regular cop stereotypes onto him, but now, goddammit, I'm seeing him for who he really is. Physically anyway. Tall, solid, right in front of me.

We kiss. Again. He pulls me close to him with one arm. I could really use an afternoon of this action, but duty is still calling. When we finally unlock lips, he digs a card out of the pocket he's got his sunglasses hung on.

"I'm writing down my home phone on the back." He lays

the card facedown on the bedside table and writes. "Call anytime," he says. "I have a phone answering machine."

He's really cute and so far not too dumb or conceited. Why couldn't I have met him about a week ago? Before this Johnny thing came up.

"Why don't you give me your mom's number?" he asks.

Think fast, Flack. I kiss him. "You don't think I'll call?" I ask in my sexy voice, batting my eyelashes for effect.

Officer Paul Tingle touches me on the tip of my nose. "You better," he says.

Pioche starts to wiggle and fuss, bringing me back to my senses. "Must be lunchtime," I say.

Paul Tingle looks at his watch. "Just about. Hey, do you want to . . .?"

This not finishing sentences thing is his only noticeable flaw so far. Wonder how long it would take for that to drive a girl crazy. Wonder why I'm letting myself wonder.

"Thanks, but she's had a rough morning. I think I'll just feed her and put her down for a nap here."

"Yeah, kids need a lot of rest." He adjusts his beltful of equipment, takes the shades out of his pocket, points at me with them again. That could get annoying, too. "Gladys . . ."

"Gladys Newbury, at your service," I say.

"Gladys, everything will work out. Really. I have a good feeling for these kinds of things."

"Must be handy in your line of work."

"Would be, except I usually know when things are not going to work out, too. I have a good feeling about you, though."

I'm thinking, glad you do. I'm going to need all the help I can get.

"Got a good feeling about us?" I say, just to carry on with the routine.

He looks up at the ceiling, pushing up his lower lip which is an awfully nice gesture on his perfect face. He looks back over at me. I mean, he glues his eyes on mine. "Gladys, I hope this is the beginning of a beautiful friendship.

Ah, Casablanca. Shit.

Chapter 4

I mean, really, a guy like Officer Paul Tingle is not my type. Honest. It was a weak moment. Should never have happened. And I'm over it. I mean, who needs a pretty boy? And a Californian to boot? Pul-eeze. Probably surfs. Takes his board down to Santa Cruz on Sundays and plays like shark food. Probably a vegetarian, too. A macrobiotic, ginseng-sucking, only-if-it's-organic, tofu head. Wonder if my room smells like smoke. He probably drinks protein shakes made out of bananas and soy powder and a little algae. I wonder if I tasted like smoke. But I'm over it. Wonder if he sleeps naked. I'm over it. Really I am.

Pioche likes the Gerber plum goo from the jar. She scarfs the whole thing except for what ends up on her face and my sleeves. The other yellowish goo that's supposed to be turkey and strained carrots is an instant reject. Can't blame her – it smells like something that had seen better days. I end up pulverizing some of the roast beef and cheese from my poor boy sandwich for her just as an experiment, and she likes that. I keep squishing up more and more til she stops eating. I have to trust her judgment. Hope I'm doing the right thing.

After lunch, I get her settled on the floor with some toys I've rounded up from her things. In the process of dumping out assorted pink bags, I come across a black plastic videotape buttoned into one of those footed baby pajama outfits. Heard the thing clunk when it hit the floor amid all the Ivory Snow softness. The tape has no labels or markings on it, but I know this is "the one."

And seeing it jolts me into doing a mental inventory of what all was lost along with my car. My saddle! Shit! Had that thing custom made to fit my short self. Added a couple of silver conchos. Nothing gaudy. Cushy seat made of maroon rough-out. Not much tooling on the leather: just my initials on each side of the pommel and some double lines tracing the curves. Hard to find a saddlemaker these days who knows when to quit with the goo-gaws. I was really pleased with the simplicity my guy managed to restrain himself to. I wanted a saddle, not a piece of lace. Now, it's gone along with Pioche's phonograph and a bunch of rock'n roll records, her mobiles, her car seat, more clothes. Nothing that can't be replaced. Oh no, it's just me who ends up losing stuff like that.

I sit down on the bed and suddenly don't feel like doing anything. Just sitting here, not watching TV or drinking or smoking or playing with the kid or figuring out what to do next. Planes fly over headed for the airport, one after another. Cars keep whizzing by. Just a few but unnecessarily hauling ass. People opening and closing doors to their rooms. Kids run by, yelling, "Where's the pool?" They're at Motel 6, for crying out loud. Pool? The pool's at the Holiday Inn. Housekeeping carts on squeaky wheels roll by, women speaking English with a black curve to it or Spanish that's trying to be English. They know what to do today, and they're doing it. I'll wager most of the people staying here would rather be anywhere else. Not a lot of happiness to go around. And I'm just sitting here on tilt. Stranger in a strange land getting stranger all the time. Me or the land. Take your pick.

It's all too much, and I'm tired. I don't want to play anymore. Everything I touch turns to shit. Everything I try blows up in my face. Can't even catch a break when I get out of town, end up with my car stolen. Brings to mind the age-old question: what the hell did I do to deserve this? Then I have to think which thing?, which time?

I'm hoping I didn't leave my Jim Beam in the trunk and practically have to force myself to gather up enough ambition to search for it. As I'm rummaging around, I turn up the paper with Mona's instructions for the baby on it and toss it on the bed. One more thing I refuse to think about right now, not til I've had my drink. I find both bottles and have to smile about how I got them and who from. I turn the TV to whatever's on and flop down on the bed. Pioche looks like she's okay with what she's doing. Lucky kid. Keeping on keeping on like a champ. The TV blathers in the background, Pio squeals as she discovers making fart noises with her lips. Planes fly over, kids run by. So what?

The whiskey's burn and bite has that medicinal flavor that never cures me as well as I think it ought to but is still as close as I can get. There's cartoons on the tube. A cat and mouse who can't talk but who fry each other's fur off, flatten each other's faces with frying pans, that sort of routine. Pioche and I are in our little lifeboat, floating for a moment above the sea of shit but still very surrounded by it. The numbness is settling into the front of my thighs like it does with the first few drinks, and I'm thinking for the forty millionth time that I should've gone to work at the phone company. I had the chance. Good pay, regular hours, benefits. Should've done it before that first casino security job got me. I'd've made a good Washoe County groundskeeper, too, I think. Switch off the brain. Be outdoors. Mowing, spraying, picking up trash, shoveling snow. Alone, squandering time on a government payroll. Cruising around in a white Ford truck with my elbow out the window, rakes in the back, and a county emblem on the side. Every night, 5 o'clock, yabba dabba doo. Weekends off. Vacations. No wonder those people like it. Might be cool to have a job that's easy to ignore.

And then that thought fades like it always does. Officer Paul Tingle in a G string struts through my mind. My car speeds by with five teenagers in it, mooning me. People from Hong Kong turn out to be Boris and Natasha from the Bullwinkle show. What to do? What to do? Then Pioche makes up my mind about my immediate future. With a grunt and a sound like the last squirt of shampoo out of the bottle, she introduces me to the new feature of guardianship I'd been dreading. I turn my head to look at her. She's so satisfied she lets out a little squeal and flings a rainbow striped zebra behind her clear over to the door and falls over backwards.

"Good arm there, Pio baby. How's your fielding?" But at least now I have a purpose. My life has meaning. Meaning in the form of a spreading stain on the leg of a pink romper suit. I roll off the bed and start searching for diapers and powder and the rash ointment that Delilah the happy hooker said would save my life one day. I can't say I'm jazzed to undertake what I'm about to undertake, but it's honest work. Not clean but honest. For a switch.

I'm tossing clothes and toys out of my way with both hands now, trying to find the powder. Don't know how our room got so screwed up so fast. Could be those three trips up and down the stairs to get all of this up here, heaving stuff into the room and keeping an eye on Pioche simultaneously. How does anybody take care of these little human things day after day without going nuts?

This diaper-changing ordeal turns into more work than I thought. If a kid starts flipping around while you're doing it, let's just say "stuff" gets everywhere. Pioche and I end up in the bathtub together, and the Motel 6 bedspread ends up by the door. I have to refill the tub twice to get us clean. Then I lotion and powder us both until we're fresh as a damn daisy. New undies for the both of us. I give her more milk and more of my mooshed up sandwich.

This baby thing is becoming too much like a full-time job. Can't do anything about my car or the million and a half other problems I've got on my plate or even go out on the spur of the moment to buy smokes if I have to spend all my time in the bathtub. But I'll only have her for the next couple of hours. After that, she's on a big bird to Hong Kong.

I take another look at Mona's instructions. Says to call Mr. Chan — Charlie? — in the afternoon. I look at my watch. It's two, so that qualifies. I dial the number.

"This Mr. Chan?" I ask the over-loud male voice that answers.

"This is Chan," he yells.

"Okay, this is Flack Murrow. Er, Susan Anne Murrow."

"Yes, Miss Murrow. How was your trip?

"Fine, fine. We just got in."

"Good. Where are you staying?"

"Out at the airport."

"Ah, The Hyatt."

"Not exactly. Listen, I have a little problem. My car was acting up on the way down here, so just to be on the safe side, I called the shop, and they're coming to pick it up."

"You're at the airport. Get a rental from Hertz."

Duh, why didn't I think of that? Rent-a-cars. Never had one in my life. Duh, Flack, you hick. Call a cab, go to the airport, rent a car.

"Right," I say. "Now, we're meeting tonight at . . .?"

"The Mark Hopkins. You know it?"

"Sure," I say as I think to myself, Well, I've heard of it.

"7-ish?"

"Yeah, fine. How will I recognize you?" Because being Chinese in San Francisco, unlike white-bread Reno, doesn't automatically make you findable.

"I'll have on a gold Nehru jacket."

"For real?" It slips out in place of laughing out loud as I picture the Charlie Chan actor with his bowler, his specs, and a gold Nehru jacket.

And Chan doesn't say anything for a few seconds. Then he says, "And you? How will I know you, I mean, besides the fact that you'll be carrying a baby?"

My brain goes straight to the wet mop that is starting to frizz into its usual unruliness on my head.

"I have red hair," I say. "Really red, really hair."

I don't want to think about the picture of me he must have running through his mind. The usual is pleated, plaid skirts, kneesocks, and freckles to go with all the hair. The only part guessing gets right on my whole Irish deal is my capacity for drinking whiskey and getting into fights, not necessarily in that order. And the red hair. Stereotype's right on there.

"All right. We'll see you at seven. You will join us for dinner, won't you?"

"Of course." Of course: I'm going to check these people

out up, down, and sideways before I turn Pioche over to them. Mona's taste in people isn't always the best. I don't think she ever gauged a person by any criteria other than how much money or how many favors she could expect to extract from them. Don't blame her. That's all I figure most people are worth anyway. But in my business, it's not such a one-way street as it is for her. I'm always having to decide who's doing what to who for what reason and behind whose back. Mona had a genius for doing it to them before they could do it to her. Pretty much a straight line. The patterns I encounter are always the proverbial tangled webs.

I hang up from Mr. Chan and call a cab. Stick the five grand Mona gave me and the rest of Johnny's fishneted stake into my bag. Tidy up the motel room as good as I feel like. Hide a few pieces of evidence and get Pioche ready to leave. I bring Johnny's address book along for light reading. Got to go buy a dress. The Mark Hopkins is a pretty swanky place, I hear.

Chapter 5

The perky, gum-chewing Hertz girl rents me this big, white Chrysler tuna boat — an "upgrade" because they were out of the medium-price model that sucked enough as it was. The tuna boat, or Moby, has power steering and power brakes and needs them. Automatic transmission on the floor. How cute. Power seats and windows. Air conditioning! AM/FM radio with an eight-track built in. Blue interior. It's a plush road hog I'm happy not to own. But it'll do the trick. I'm just not myself without wheels. This'll do for now.

Miss Doublemint draws me a map from the airport to the Mark Hopkins. I ask where's a good place to buy a dress, and she draws me another map to Market Street and draws little boxes along with names Macy's, Joseph Magnin, Lerner's, Saks. She seems to know the precise location of about twenty clothing shops in a six-block area. She wants to draw more maps of other parts of town, but I tell her this is plenty. I'm going to grab the first little black dress that fits and be done with it.

I navigate Moby into the heart of San Francisco, and I hope to hell I never have to do such a thing ever again in my life. I get honked at, flipped off, sped around — all of which would be fun, except I have a baby sliding around loose on the front seat, and I'm trying to find a place to park. I wish I had that car seat now. But it's gone with the wind. It's a good trick to keep this monster car headed straight with one hand and keep Pioche from falling over with the other. And flip a few people off as they gun past my window, flipping me off.

After the saleslady at Macy's stops gaping at my jeans, boots, and Western cut shirt — and the bandage around my neck — she holds Pioche while I try on one dress from the five she picks for me. It fits. Fine. She sets me up with black pantyhose, black pumps, and insists on a few accessories: a black satin handbag which I agreed to because it looks innocent enough but is big enough to hold my .357, rhinestone clip-on earrings that I'm sure will make my head throb before the evening's through, and a rhinestone pin that's just kind of a square. I like the pin. She also adds, without editorial comment, a black silk scarf that she arranges delicately around my neck. Guess she's seen this kind of shit before. She gets me all presentable, steps back, and smiles at the miracle she's worked. Then she encourages me to visit their beauty salon for hair and makeup, but I draw the line at that. I don't need to get decked out for another couple of hours, so I take off my fancy duds, pay, and shove all the bags into the backseat. I'll find somewhere to make the transformation. From Clark Kent to Superman. Sort of.

We have some time to kill so I drive around the city,

checking things out. People are getting off work. Lots of traffic and pedestrians, and even they flip me off. Everybody's in a big stinking hurry, looking as cranky as Archie Bunker. Must really be hateful to live here with everybody in your way all the time. Can't go anywhere but home under the covers to not have to see another human face. If there is a hell, it's a city. Any city. Cities look to me like a kind of mind control if you ask me. Cram everybody into one place, and let the TV and the radio and the newspapers and the billboards tell them what to do. Go here, go there. Buy this, buy that. Fun, fun, fun, because you're where it's happening, baby. All you need is money, money, money so work, work, work for it. If it's so much fun, how come all the people I see here look like they're either going to cry or go homicidal? I know I'd end up killing someone if I had to live like this.

Pioche falls asleep dangerously close to the edge of the seat, so I pull over when the crowd lets me and lay her down in a safer position. Cars in motion actually do have the effect of putting kids asleep. She's zonked like last night. I'll keep driving.

I turn on the FM radio and hear a bunch of songs I've never heard before, played by a black deejay who slurs like he's on reds. After he plays about eight weird tunes in a row, he shuffles some papers around and says he has to stop the music to do the goddam news.

Antiwar this, protest that. Gas wars. Another sit-in at Berkeley. The students throw office furniture out of the window of the chemistry building, protesting Dow Chemical's manufacturing of napalm that the military drops on innocent Vietnamese villagers. Way to go, students, I think. "Right on, brothas and sistahs," says the deejay. "Puttin' that bourgeois, white bread, overfed education to good use."

Then comes the item I ought to have been expecting but

which catches me by surprise anyway: ". . . and this just in from the Biggest Little City. The body of Gianni "Johnny" Ruggerio, son of Vittorio and Filipa Ruggerio, the casino robber barons, was discovered early this morning in the living room of his posh mansion west of Reno. Ruggiero had been brutally stabbed to death. The fuzz offered no comment when questioned about possible motives for the slaying — and the killer or killers remain at large and are heavily armed and dangerous. Bolt them doors, brothas and sistahs in the Silver State. Don't let the bogeyman get you. Here's one from Taj Mahal to mellow out your drive home."

The news story didn't give many details — which is either because the deejay was more interested in music than current events or because the police aren't talking because they have a suspect in mind. Gulp. Or because they really don't have much of a clue what went on. Based on the kind of associates Johnny and his family do business with on a regular basis — not that anybody's been able to prove these "associations" legally, the police may be going through their list of the usual suspects for quite a while before they come up empty. Before they get to me. I'm on the list for damn sure, but I've got to think there are a few juicier prospects. The hard guys. The racetrack boys. Most people who ever met Johnny. I wish I could find out more about how the investigation's going. General curiosity, of course, but also how close are they getting to me?

Moby's been climbing the hill to Coit Tower — one of the few landmarks I actually know. Up here, it's a little more peaceful. Less crowded. Good place for a nap. I park Moby and curl up around Pioche. She smells so nice, makes little sucking sounds. I go out like a light.

I wake up to a nice, nice view of the lit-up Golden Gate bridge and the twinkly lights packed tight as far as you can see over everything that's not water. On the water, there are still lights – just farther apart. Time for me to get into my Supersnoop costume so I can blend in at the Mark. The backseat of this cruiser is so big I can work my magic right here.

I apologize to Pioche for the bottle I've given her being cold, but she doesn't seem to care. I prop her between my coat and her diaper bag and climb into the back seat. I wiggle out of my Levis and into my new pantyhose. Good thing I bought two pairs because, sure as shit, I run the first one. I drop the little black dress over my head. Bolt on the earrings. Fasten the flashy pin smack in the middle of the dress's V-neckline. Wish I had the boobs to really show it off. I run my fingers through my hair just to fluff it out to its most ridiculous volume. I'm done in the space of two minutes. All that's left is to wrap the scarf around my neck. I take a quick peek under the bandage that starts the cut bleeding again. I tape the edge back down and realize I should have paid better attention to the saleslady's handiwork. My scarf thingy looks like crap the first three times I try it. The fourth time's good enough. I climb over into the driver seat before putting on the shoes that are going to be a bitch to walk in while carrying a baby and all her necessary items. I give my lips a quick coating of ginger frost. Slap a little mascara on my eyelashes. Put my gun inside the dainty black purse. Voila. Can't really see much of myself in the rearview mirror, so I'll just have to hope everything's covered in the right places. Pioche dropped her bottle and is contentedly sucking on her whole fist. Now to find the Mark Hopkins.

• • •

Since I'm bucks up, I pull under the canopy and let the valet take Moby out and park it. This mere child in charge of taking care of the Mercedeses and Rollses and Cadillacs grimaces at the tuna boat, but he opens my door and takes my hand to extract me from my humble mode of transportation. I go around to the passenger side, gather up Pioche. I feel that she's wet, and her face looks ready to work up some loud complaints about the speed of my service. I bounce her around like I've seen Mona do, which doesn't seem to be helping. The valet has to shout over her as he hands me my claim ticket for the beast. He's glad to get away from us in anything – even something as hideous as Moby.

I'm trying my best to look composed as Pioche lets out wails I would never have guessed something so small would be capable of. This is the most pissed I've seen the kid since I've known her, and it has to be one of the worst possible times. These Hong Kong people could hear this and run.

A red-coated doorman ushers us into the huge, echoing polished wood and brass and chandeliered lobby, and I'm glad I took the trouble to change my clothes. This is one classy joint. There's marble and oriental rugs on the floor and a real live wood fire in the fireplace. People aren't just walking through, they're floating through on their way to the bar – excuse me, cocktail lounge – the dining room, or the spit-shined elevators. They look at us and the disturbance we're making "askance," which I read somewhere and seems to apply to this moment. Pioche is pushing away from me with her little hands, arching her back, which is throwing us totally off balance. Her pretty face is covered with tears and snot, and she's beginning to gulp for air between screams. I guess this is her Mr. Hyde side. Had to happen, I suppose. She was just too perfect a kid.

"Miss Murrow?" It's a British accent coming from a stout

woman dressed all in beige, including her hair and her sweater with a chain holding the two sides of the collar together. When she's in front of me, her hands clasped at breast level, she says, "I am Miss Ludden, the governess. Cecelia Ludden."

I don't know why but I look around me to see if anyone else thinks this is a put-on. Nobody seems freaked out, like this sort of thing happens every day right here.

"And this is Mr. Chan," the governess says.

"How'dya do?" comes the loud voice I heard over the phone. All American West Coast. He's great looking for a Chinese guy. Not all skinny and squinched up like you'd think. Tall, lots of thick, black hair, high on top, greased flat on the sides. He's wide across the shoulders but not husky. Long legs in tight, white Beatle pants. And, yes, the gold Nehru jacket.

His volume gets people's attention since Pioche's seems to have bored them, and they suddenly jerk in their smooth-flowing course through the room to see who the hell is yelling besides the baby. Mr. Chan's a six-footer, give or take, who looks surprisingly great in metallic gold. Striking is the word that comes to mind. But the crowd seems to see him as just another fashionable Chinaman like the city's full of, so they go on their way. The hand he puts out to me has long fingers that don't seem the least bit delicate. I can't shake his hand because I'm currently managing about ten tons of baby crap and a screaming, contorting brat.

"Do let me take her," says Miss Ludden.

And now I know how Rodney felt handing Pioche over to me. I tighten my grip on the kid.

"Miss Murrow, really. Permit me," she says, just barely parting her clasped hands.

So far, I haven't said a word. Just stood there like an idiot, not knowing what to do with the baby or how to act in this fancy-schmancy place, or how I'm going to shake hands with a guy who still has his hand sticking out at me. I'm going to have to give Mona the benefit of the doubt for picking these people. I'm not sold yet. I still need to see how everybody acts. Especially Pioche.

I say, "Okay. Your funeral." I'm classy that way. And I hand the baby to Miss Ludden, whose pillowy boobs — more like her mom's — put the kid at ease. The screaming becomes sobbing that becomes sniffling that becomes the little breath-catching thing that comes at the end of such a fit.

"Now," yells Mr. Chan. "That's better. How'dya do? I'm Mr. Chan."

I shake his hand. "Murrow. Flack — er, Susan Anne — Murrow."

"Charmed," he says and kisses the back of my hand like in the movies. These city slickers have some kinky ways.

"Has she eaten?" asks the governess.

"I gave her a bottle in the car on the way over. It wasn't much. Cold."

"Gracious. The poor little thing must be famished. And she requires a nappy change. I'll take her up to our rooms now if you'll pardon me."

"Hold up there, lady," I say. "That kid's not going anywhere without me until you cough up some ID and any other bullshit I think I might want to see."

"How quaint," says Miss Ludden. "She reminds me of Mona when she first came to us. Doesn't she though, Roger?"

"You hit that one on the head, Cece," says Roger. "Let's all go up. We'll be dining in our rooms. Does that satisfy you, Miss Murrow?"

"It'll do."

The weight of the gun and the extra ammo I'm carrying in the purse under all of Pioche's gear feels very reassuring as we step into the elevator and Roger Chan presses 8. Pioche is playing with the gold chain that holds the governess's sweater together. Miss Ludden takes a lace-trimmed hanky out of her sleeve and starts working on cleaning up the baby's face. The kid, of course, hates it and starts to sputter again, but the face cleaning is over almost immediately — I mean, the kid's face is really spotless — and the baby fixates on the chain again. Miss Ludden professionally stuffs the soggy hanky back up her sleeve. Yuck.

At the eighth floor, Mr. Chan holds the elevator doors back as all of us girls pile out. He has not offered to help carry a damn thing. He steers us to the right, down the hall clear to the end, and opens the double doors to 800, which turns out to be a massive suite with plenty of plate glass and snazzy furniture. A little fire's going in the fireplace.

"I'll take the baby to her room," says Miss Ludden.

"Hang on there, Cece," I say. "Let me get a look around." She seems offended by me calling her by her first name, but, hey, she's the help, right?

This place has three bedrooms and two bathrooms. Both bathrooms have two toilets each. The closets are bigger than my whole trailer. One closet is half full of men's clothes, some straight business suits, some peacock-colored, hep cat playwear. In this room, there's a TV, an exercise bike draped with white hotel towels, and a monster king-size bed. In the next room, there are the makings of about six outfits of women's clothing — all shades of beige and black. One pair of shoes. Black with laces. There is a stack of books on the night table with a pair of half-lens reading glasses on top. Except for these items, you'd think no one was using this room. It's immaculate.

The third room is fitted out for the baby. A crib with fluffy toys arranged on the blankets. A changing table. A rocking chair. A portable refrigerator and a hotplate. These people thought of everything.

I make sure there are no other doors to the suite, no false walls in the closets. That there's no fire escape from any of the bedrooms. Call me paranoid. I'll call me paranoid anytime. Once I'm satisfied that no one is going anywhere without me noticing, I turn Miss Ludden loose with the kid and go back to the living room. Mr. Chan is on the phone talking food. We're having the game hens with currant stuffing. (What's a "currant?") A couple bottles of some kind of French wine. And torte, whatever that is. There's a tannish leather briefcase open on the table, turned towards Mr. Chan so I can't see into it.

"Is there anything you'd like to add to our order, Miss Murrow?"

"Yeah, have them send a bottle of Jim Beam and a couple packs of Lucky Strikes."

"Lucky Strikes? Quaint." He rolls his eyes at me and orders what I asked for. "Anything else?"

"No," I say. "That'll do 'er."

He hangs up and takes a black cigarette case out of the open briefcase. He flicks the lid open with his thumb and offers me one of his cigarettes.

"Dunhill?" he asks.

"Dunhill," I repeat, taking one of the smokes. I sniff it before lighting up. Can't be sure what people smoke around these parts. He gives me a light from a slim, gold lighter he takes from his front pants pocket. The metal is slightly warmer than usual when I touch it to guide the flame to my cig.

The Dunhill hits the spot. Maybe bites the head right off the spot. Strong. Likable. Mr. Chan arranges himself in an armchair to my right and gives me the look that says he's settled in and prepared for the third degree.

"So," I begin. "You live in this hotel?"

"Here? Heavens no. But we do keep the place. I like to have the space available. For us. For visitors."

"Visitors like . . .?"

"Oh, people with business in San Francisco."

"What kind of business?"

"Finance."

"Finance?"

"Finance."

"Okay," I say. "That how you know Mona? 'Finance'?"

He takes a long drag on his Dunhill, blows smoke rings at the ceiling and smiles. "I financed a project for Mona in '68. We've done quite a lot of business with her since."

"What kind of business?"

He stubs out his half-finished cigarette. Bends the crap out of it. Clearly not saving it for later. "Come on," he says. "You know her. You know what she was into. You're her closest friend."

Yeah, her closest friend who would love to have seen her behind bars any number of times, just to get her to use her brains for more constructive – and less criminal – enterprises. I'm also her closest friend who knows she's dead.

I puff at my cigarette and try to look knowledgeable. I never knew the specifics of any of her shenanigans. Sometimes I could figure out the who but not the what; sometimes the other way around but never the two together.

"She says you've been friends many years."

"Grew up together," I say, leaning forward to flick an ash into the crystal ashtray, trying not to think about recent events. "Reno."

"Quaint." He sure likes that word.

"Yeah, we're ass-deep in quaintness. How about Miss Ludden there? What's her story?"

"She has been governess for the child of one of my

colleagues. That child is going off to boarding school now. Cece is quite excellent. Fluent in four languages. Trained in the classics. Pioche will be in excellent hands until Mona is free to join her."

How could he – they – not have heard? Aren't these big shots supposed to have secret sources and grapevines? Hell, if they just turned on the radio. Johnny Ruggerio and an unidentified woman? How hard could that be? The evening just got uncomfortably warm, even in this skimpy dress. They don't know; that's great. I just hope I can get done what needs to be done here and get out before they find out.

I say, "How about those IDs?"

"Oh, surely," he says. He tosses his two passports to me over the open top of the briefcase, one Hong Kong, one American, and two for Cece, one British and one American. Covered with stamps from all sorts of of places. Both of them.

"You guys get around," I say.

"International travel is the nature of business more and more these days."

"Yeah, I gotta do it all the time." I slide the passports back to him.

"Here's a letter of introduction from Mona. I'm sure you will recognize her handwriting. I assume you have a document wherein you are similarly introduced?"

These folks even talk like her. Must have all bought the same Berlitz tapes. I open my little black bag, pull out the crumpled up piece of paper, that is Mona's letter about me, from under my gun. The letter Chan hands me is all nice and neat and sealed in an envelope. He smooths the creases out of my letter over his knee, and we both are reading what Mona has written when there is a polite knock at the door. Good thing. Just holding this paper, looking at her big slanting loops has got me ready to spill my guts to Roger Chan about the fate of the woman who's brought us together. I feel like crying.

"Ah, dinner has arrived," says Chan, getting up. He flips Mona's letter down on the table and takes a gold pen out of his briefcase.

Dinner is rolled in on one of those cloth-covered carts pushed by a busboy, who looks about 90 years old, followed by a waiter, who looks about 13. Both in spotless white uniforms. All of the plates are covered with those silver, domed goodies, just like in a Rock Hudson movie. A centerpiece of real flowers. All white. Whatever you're used to, I guess. The busboy stands aside at attention while the bowtied waiter ushers the cart to the location Mr. Chan indicates and gives me a sneaky wink. He takes a corkscrew out of his jacket pocket and opens the wine. Hands the cork to Chan, who smells it and pronounces it good. A good cork? Then the guy offers Chan a tiny taste of the wine. Chan swirls it in the glass, holding it up to the light, then swishes the little taste around his mouth and pronounces that good. I'm getting quite an education here. Don't know that I'll ever get to put it to use, but at least I know how to act if anyone sticks a cork and a sip of wine in my face.

"Shall I serve the lady?"

"Yes," says Chan.

And I say, "I'd appreciate if you'd just pour me a healthy shot of that bourbon."

"Mixer?"

"Neat. No ice."

The guy winks at me again. Glad I'm not the one in charge of the tip. He's getting on my nerves. He sets my drink down on a silver coaster lined with a paper doily. I said a healthy shot, but he must have misunderstood. I down the smidgen he's poured me in one gulp.

"Barkeep, hit me again. A double," I say. I hold the glass

out to him, and this time I get a healthy shot. And the rest of the bottle.

Chan signs for the bill and dismisses the men over the waiter's objections. He pulls two twenties out of the briefcase and sends the winking bastard and his grandfather on their way.

"Pardon me," Chan says. "I'll go tell Cece that dinner is here."

Come to think of it, I haven't heard a peep out of Pioche or Miss Ludden. I follow Chan to the baby's room, and we find baby and governess calmly rocking in the rocking chair. Miss Ludden is reading to Pioche from some big, fat book with no pictures on the cover. It's not fairy tales or Cat in the Hat so I'm lost, but Pioche looks like she's paying pretty good attention.

"Kipling," says Miss Ludden, setting the book down. "Every child should know Kipling."

Can't argue with that because I wouldn't know what book Kipling wrote that a kid can't grow up without.

"Pioche likes it. How about that," I say. I'm a little bit – a lot – jealous that the baby has dumped me just like that for the favors of a stranger.

Miss Ludden's laughing, well chuckling, at me. "What a quaint pronunciation," she says.

"What?" I'm feeling quainter by the minute.

"Pioche with a hard 'ch' as in 'chair' rather than a soft 'ch' as in 'chaise'. French. Hence the soft 'ch'."

"News to me. Never heard it any other way."

"It is incorrect, my dear."

"Hell, the whole state of Nevada's got it wrong then."

"Of course, if they can't say the name of their state properly, how can they be expected to be correct about Pioche? What, by the bye, is the context from which her name is drawn?"

"Little town out by the Utah border. Nowheresville."

"Oh, how very interesting."

Chan says, "Let's eat, ladies.

Miss Ludden sets Pioche up with a highchair and some kind of hard biscuits to gum while we sit down to about the best meal I ever ate. I eat everything in sight. Damn, if it wasn't some good grits. And that wine! I usually can't stomach the stuff. I don't think I said two words through the whole meal. A torte turns out to be cake, real good cake. Couldn't tell you if Chan or the governess carried on a conversation. I "um"ed a few times but mostly kept my nose in that old feedbag. Sure made me sleepy.

Chapter 6

I feel filled up with warm air between my skin layer and my meat layer all over my body, keeping every outer sensation from messing with my comfy reality and making me feel all floaty. I'm a giant cloud of a woman who can go anywhere, do anything – as long as it doesn't involve moving. Hell, I don't need to move. People find their way to me. Mom. Pop. Timmy. Red. Mona. Laughing. Happy. Glad to see me. But when they get close enough to touch, they disappear. Don't fade out, just all of a sudden aren't there anymore. But they turn up out of the distance again, and we laugh and talk til they get too close and zip – gone.

Technicolor. Brighter than life. Sharper than life. Better than life. Clear. Every word. Every thought, clear. I could get used to this. It makes sense, except for the part where they disappear. But, hell, they come right back, so no big deal.

We're all in the house I grew up in. Nighttime but the house is full of light, and lots of people are over, visiting. Lung and Pop are playing Hearts. Mom's making that good popcorn in the pot with the turny thing that comes out the top. She's melting butter in a little yellow pan with a black handle and a black ring painted around the top. She always melts the butter in that pan. There are green bottles of Coke in the fridge and blue and white cans of Hamm's beer.

A few big, rainbow-colored fish keep flying or floating through the room, but they don't seem to mind us being in their way so I don't mind them either. Mom's playing a stack of 45s. With all these fish around, you think she'd cool it on "Mack the Knife" so as not to scare them, but the song plays over and over while Bobby Darin leans in the doorway to the kitchen, dressed in a blue velvet tux, grinning and snapping his fingers to his own tune. People walk through him from time to time. He keeps singing and smiling and snapping.

I myself can't get off the couch. I'm way too heavy or have no bones. Can't tell. I'm just kind of watching. Nobody tries to make me move. I don't want to move. I'm in an okay place: home, warm, light, noisy with people, alive with fish, good-smelling popcorn. I'll stay and stay. I want everyone to stay. I can control all of this, have what I want, give everyone what they want. This is where we like to be: under the sea in an octopus's garden in the shade. Happy and safe.

But some damn thing in me thinks, "Wrong decade, stupid. The Beatles were mere babies in 1950-whatever. Or is that now? Bobby Darin and the Beatles in the same room on the same day singing their new hit tunes? Grow up. Wake up. Wake up. Wake up."

That's what I start to do because I feel weird, and I don't

like weird. The Beatles and Bobby Darin don't belong on the same sheet of music at the same time. That wouldn't make sense. And what's all-important and all-powerful is sense. I command the warmth and color to fade. For the too-simple happiness to get out of my sight because I know best what reality is. Timmy's in prison. Red's in prison too. Mom, Pop, and Mona are dead. I'm alone, that's reality, babe.

As the airy feeling begins to leave my body, a throbbing pain begins in my head and travels downward. When it gets to my stomach, I'm awake enough to be violently nauseous. Getting up – sitting up – is out of the question, so I just turn my head and . . .

I drink a lot. I've done my share of barfing. I've had hangovers in this 100-pound body that would kill most 200-pound men. As I get older, I have the shakes a bit if I've really overdone. That's all. But this? Is this food poisoning? The flu? And where in the hell am I anyway?

There are slits of blinding white light coming in from spaces between thick curtains. Goody, goody – it's day. Which day? I momentarily go back to my mother's kitchen. She's walking towards me, smiling, with popcorn in a white bowl covered with big red polka dots. She comes only so close then disappears, and I come back to the dark room with the terrible light cutting through. I try to stay in that other place, but I keep getting tossed back to razor blades of sunlight, a vise squeezing my head, and the fragrance of the little puddle of puke next to me on the floor.

I sit up. Might as well. Have to walk on two legs eventually although I dread the prospect at the moment. Everything on me hurts but nothing as much as my head. I feel like I've been in a fight for my life, but it was all so pleasant until now. The room swims into focus. I'll figure out where I am. Just give me a sec."

Memory reassembles in bits and pieces: a baby, a British accent, a tall Chinaman, dinner under chrome. Where is all of that now?

I really have to pee. Which way? I switch on the table lamp beside me. The light hurts. I remember this layout. Three bedrooms. Bathrooms with two toilet setups. I stagger, holding my head in both hands, to the bedroom on my left.

Such a long walk. I start to get sick again as soon as I see the two toilets. One doesn't have any water in it but does have a stopper in the bottom and faucets like a sink. Ah, this must be a bidet. Heard of these contraptions, but a clean crotch is the least of my worries right now. I go for the flushable receptacle. Sit and rest for a second before braving my way through the bedroom back to the living room. I recall that this bedroom was the woman's, the governess's. There were a few clothes in the closet. Some books. Everything nice and neat. All of that is gone now. The place looks like no one's ever been here. Even in the bathroom, the towels are folded in that perfect way new towels are in hotel rooms. I'm in the Mark Hopkins. That's right. Downtown San Francisco.

I cross the living room to check out the second bedroom. As immaculate as the other one. Even the exercise bike is gone. And then it really starts coming back. I rush out of the second bedroom as fast as my head lets me, remembering the nursery. I try the knob, which turns but the door won't budge. I push against it with my shoulder. Too much effort. I see that the door has a keyhole for an old-style skeleton key. An easy one for my Swiss Army knife.

I'm praying for aspirin or a quick death — whichever comes first — as I try to get my eyes and hands to work together to fiddle the door open. Locks! I swear to gawd! This lock's insides are smooth and oiled and slide into neutral easily. The nursery is still a nursery, but it looks like a store display, everything perfect, never lived in.

This sucks. Really sucks. They knocked me out and took the kid! I hope I had decided she'd be safe with them. I honestly don't remember. What the hell is this drug thing about? Did my sense of the bad in people let me down? Jerks.

I'd cry if I could. I'm just too dazed, too sick, too out of it to think straight. I'm all done up in my basic black and rhinestones at 10 in the morning, sitting here knock-kneed, stocking-footed, and cotton-mouthed, wondering what the hell kind of mickey they slipped me. Then I see a piece of paper on the otherwise empty surface of the writing desk between the two big windows. I stagger over, sit down, and force my eyes to focus on the few sentences on hotel stationery – a message for all appearances thoughtfully written and in pretty penmanship that the writer must have to practice every day:

My dear Miss Morrow,

We do hope you will find it in your heart to forgive us. We can only assure you that all of this has been in accordance with Mona's wishes. She was concerned with your propensity for second thoughts. The baby will be fine and reunited with her mother very soon.

As if I couldn't figure out who left me this gem, it was signed, "Yours very truly, C. Ludden."

I'm not sure how long I sat with that piece of paper in my hand, but I had time enough to relive the horrible night at Johnny's. I remember Mona running into the darkness. I remember looking for Johnny, for vengeance. Somewhere in all the haze of the past and the real pain of the present, I hear a light knock, the doors opening, and a woman saying, "Maid." She doesn't say it loud or anything, but I jump out of my chair, stars crashing into each other behind my eyes. The maid jumps back through the doorway and collides with her supply cart. She puts her hand to her chest. I put mine on my forehead.

"Sorry," I say. "You scared me."

"Me, too," she says. She's breathing hard.

"Come on in. I was just getting ready to leave."

"I can come back."

"No, really. I'm going. They sure left the place in good shape for you."

I can see she's not too sure she wants to be in here with me. She glances both directions down the hall before gathering up towels and sheets and pushing aside her cart in the event of needing a possible narrow escape from a crosseyed woman with hair like a haystack. She leaves the doors open, keeps her eye on me as she goes into Miss Ludden's room.

My little black purse is on the coffee table. Miraculously, my .357 is still inside. Still loaded, too. Also inside is a new big wad of money, rolled up and rubberbanded. Thanks, Chan. I'm going to get rich if this keeps up. I don't count it; I just register that it's there and wish it was a big bottle of Excedrin instead. I take out the keys to my rented tuna boat, put my shoes on, and head for the door.

"I'm leaving now," I call to the maid.

"Okay."

"Want the doors shut?"

"No way. I mean, no."

"Well, bye, then."

"Okay, bye."

On the second shelf of her cart, next to the portable radio she'll come out to get after I leave, is a bottle of Anacin. I empty about eight of them into my shaky hand, pop them into my mouth, and start chewing. Things can only get better as long as I don't barf. Again.

I left my sunglasses at the Motel 6, so of course this has to be one of those rare mornings when the sun is shining in San Francisco. All of the buildings and the sky seem too close. I can barely stand up straight as I wait first for the valet parker guy to put down his comic book. Then as I try to take out my ticket, my .357 falls with a loud thud. The kid's out of there like a shot, pardon the pun, to get Moby back from wherever it spent the night. For the sake of my headache, I crouch rather than bend over to pick up my gun.

The valet holds Moby's door open for me to get in and get the hell away from him. I cram a wad of twenties into the hand he has forgotten to hold out for his tip. Hell, it ain't my money. At this point, I'm not sure if it's Johnny's or Mona's or Mr. Chan's. I touch my finger to my lips to indicate he shouldn't mention my gun and all. Which I'm sure he will. To everyone who'll listen.

What happened to San Francisco in May? It's painfully warm and sunny outside, but the car must have been inside somewhere. It's decently cool on the vinyl seats though that won't last long. I'm not sure where to head from here. Reno? Motel 6? Swandive off the Golden Gate seems like an option. Can't sit here at the end of the Mark Hopkins' driveway for long. I make a right because it's the easiest way to go and head down the hill towards the pins and needles of light glittering off the bay.

Long-haired, paisley-printed hippies. Glittery men in tight shorts and tall shoes. Your average Japanese tourist huddle. Business suits. A balloon seller blowing bubbles. School kids passing a joint. San Francisco's got at least one of everybody. When you get sick of who you are, you make up someone new with the name and a change of address to go with it, and you end up here. It's practically required, I think. Outrageous is the name of the game these days, so I'll bet that guy in the blue business suit's wearing a wig over his hip-now-

and-wow, evening-and-weekend long hair. Probably wearing a tie-dyed undershirt and has a pack of ZigZags in one of the picture compartments of his wallet. It's cool to play it straight — as long as it's not really what you're feeling. The only thing that isn't okay to be around here is normal. Father Knows Best, martini-at-6 normal. Or military. Or a cop. Other than that, let it all hang out. Unfortunately for most of us, some of the parts hanging out here ought not to be.

I'm going to run out of the road down at the piers in another couple blocks, but at least my head's a little clearer, the aspirin taste in my mouth is pretty much dissolved, and I'm starting to get hungry. I stop at a red light at the intersection of California and Battery. California is an obstacle course with all the electric buses and whatnot. Probably because it's lunchtime. A hippie chick about 14 years old, hair hanging in blond rats, reaches suddenly through my open passenger window, shoves a daisy at me and says, "Peace. God loves you, sister." She's about to lose an arm when I grab her by the wrist and twist her forearm towards the elbow. The flower falls on the seat. "Hey, fuck you, man," she says as she pulls away. A colorful, barefoot group of patchouli-reeking delinquents gather around her as she starts crying, looking all confused about how mean the world can be. They all look confused. I feel like I did what any red-blooded American would do if a stranger reaches into the car: inflict physical harm. Fast and firm, but now a couple of her cohorts are crying along with her pain. I'm studying this display of innocence, hoping all this emotion might get to me and prove I have a soul when I notice something that gets to me deeper and quicker. Stuck in the intersection right in front of my face is something I never thought I'd see again: my car. My sweet GTO. I kid you not! It's, like, 20 feet away. With two slouched-down teenage punk boys sitting in it, their heads just barely at eye level to see out of the bottom of the windshield. Smug punks with cigarettes hanging out of their disgusting lips, undoubtedly raining ashes and burning embers on my beautiful upholstery.

I slam Moby into park, grab my Colt Python out of my black evening bag, and run into the traffic jam as fast as these stupid excuses for shoes will let me. The boys — and everybody else in the vicinity — see me coming with a gun drawn, and there starts to be some sideways commotion in the cars as drivers decide they might as well make new lanes and get the hell away from this crazy woman. There are a few crackups, but no one involved sticks around to complain. Then, amazingly, holes begin to open up in the congestion, and cars start taking to the sidewalks, making new lanes. I've started a free-for-all, and I don't care. My whole focus is on the two brats who had the nerve to swipe my pride and joy.

The driver's cigarette drops into his lap at some point, and he's moving around fast, trying simultaneously to get out and put out his pants. The other kid opens his door and disappears into the crowd. So much for honor among thieves. I hit the remaining knucklehead on his temple with my gun, not really, really hard — just enough to make a point. He says, "Ouch." I open the door, haul him out of the car by his sleeveless Levi jacket. "Eat the pavement, asshole," I say with all the delicacy the moment deserves.

He's face down and has linked his fingers behind his head. Apparently, this is nothing new for him. It is for me, but I won't tell him that. The cigarette is lying on the driver's seat, scorching a nice dimple into my black vinyl. I sweep it out fast, embers flying all over, which all go out in midair and won't cause any extra damage. But I'm pretty damn mad about that dimple. I turn around and kick the kid in the ribs with my pointed proper black pumps. He cringes but doesn't make a sound other than letting the air go out of his lungs all at once.

"That's for burning a hole in my seat, you punk." We're drawing a crowd by now. I kick him again. "That's for swiping my car." I kick him again. Hard. "And that's for not having any goddam manners."

One of these brats has hung a leather shoelace attached to an iron cross on my rearview mirror. There are a couple of Oly cans on the floor. Empty cigarette packs. I rip down the iron cross and toss it on the street next to the kid's head. Toss all of his own garbage out on him. Along with keys to Moby.

"See that piece of shit over there? That's more your style. Go on. Get out of my sight."

He drags himself up painfully. Picks up the cross.

"Hey, man," he says. "That car's a fucking rental."

I'm climbing into the GTO when I remember that my real clothes are in Moby's back seat. I can hear the sirens coming. The crowd is beginning to get bored and wander off since it's apparent no one's going to get shot.

"Hold it!" I say to the kid's back as he's running to the rental car. He puts his hands up, doesn't turn around. Doesn't want to see the Python again. I walk past him, open the back door and get my jeans and boots and Pioche's crap.

Okay," I say. "She's all yours."

"You ain't going to report this?" he asks.

"If you want to stay out of the slam for a few more hours this morning, I suggest you get it in gear." I point up California Street to where the lights of the cop cars are bearing down on us.

"Holy shit!" the kid says.

I say, "Hertz. Airport. Leave it off after hours. Keys on the front tire." I aim my .357 at him one more time for emphasis. "Don't disappoint me."

The kid jumps in behind the wheel, slouches down, and eases more coolly than most people would've been capable of out into the anonymous flow of traffic. Does the speed limit, incognito in the kind of car his mom probably drives. I let him get away. Good riddance to Moby. That kid will see it home safely.

Meantime, the cops catch up with me, which is a drag. I show them my license and registration. Tell them the car stalled out. One of them suggests I try again, and of course it starts right up. I look convincingly surprised. No one around seems to want to volunteer the information that this is more than a stalled car. Don't seem to care that I pulled a gun on a thief and then kicked the crap out of him. As one cop directs the traffic around the GTO, the other has me rev the engine a few times to make sure everything's really okay. I can tell he's impressed by the way it sounds.

Then, like nothing happened, I'm on my way back to Motel 6. In my own car. My pride and joy I never thought I'd see again. The only good thing that's happened in the last two days. I don't want think about any of it. I just want to lay down and sleep through this drug hangover. Want to clear my head so I can decide what to do next. Want to take a shower. And definitely get out of these pantyhose.

Chapter 7

Overnight. That's how fast the puberty hormones took Timmy away. One day, he was as happy as a little kid could be under the circumstances we were living in, and the next morning he woke up as an angry bulldog I couldn't for the life of me ever remember letting into our room. The carrot-topped, easy-going, wide-eyed little smartypants turned into a mouthy, bad-tempered, belligerent rebel bent on saying and doing not just whatever he damn well pleased but whatever would hurt, annoy, or frighten. I was frightened. He was my sweet little buddy and my brother and my responsibility. He was why I got us our own place and worked so hard and worried so much. He was the reason for everything I did. I doubt I'd have ever gotten out of bed if I hadn't needed to take care of him. I sure wasn't motivated by anything I thought I could get for myself out of life. But I could do something for Timmy. Make sure that the badness in his life went no farther than our folks dying off like they did. He was too young to know much about what happened to me while we were living with the Larsons. Wasn't any of his concern in the first place. I was just doing what had to be done. And what happened to Red, well, all Timmy knew was that Red didn't die, and that seemed to be enough. Timmy studied on that quite a bit. What he came up with, I don't know. Maybe his conclusions blew up on him that one morning I blamed on puberty.

After that, nothing I tried had the slightest effect on him. Couldn't get him to laugh or cry or even to treat me like a person. I could yell, I could joke, I could tell him I loved him, and he'd give me the finger or knock me down. Or both. I felt lucky when he just ignored me.

He – or one of his friends – started stealing from me, what little I had. I'd come home from work, and our room would be trashed, reeking of stale cigarette smoke and spilled sickenly sweet booze. I knew he wasn't going to school, or that he'd go there just going long enough to hook up with his party buddies. Our lousy pad became their usual hangout. It was only when I noticed something was missing or broken or when the whole place smelled like a bar that I knew he was still around. Eventually, when there was nothing left to break or steal, our place – my place – never smelled like cigarettes again.

I guess that might've been my first solo investigating job: find Timmy. Finding out where he stayed, who he was with. What he was doing for money. Reno's not a big place. With kids you'd think it'd be easy. But when you're dodging parents, cops, and truant officers all at the same time, you get pretty good at keeping out of sight. I have since tracked down

YOU MAKE ME TINGLE

adults who didn't want to be found in a tenth of the time it took me to find Timmy. When I did, I was relieved that he was still alive, but I was also a little bit sorry.

I guess everybody's got their ideas about dope dens. Guess what? It's all true. The place where I found Timmy was like something from a bad movie. Crap-stained mattresses, no electricity, cardboard taped over the windows to keep anybody from looking in and to keep out the daylight. Rotting food in filthy takeout boxes in the sink. Mice. Junkies lolling all over each other, not for warmth or sex or anything practical. They just landed where they landed and couldn't move. Yeah, all of those things were there, except they had electricity because through a space in the taped-up cardboard I could see they were watching Hollywood Squares. Or maybe it was watching them. Looked like there were eight. Six guys and two girls. It was hard for me to tell. Didn't matter. I had followed Timmy and another guy from Circus Circus to their den on Washington Street, a dilapidated old house we used to scare each other about being haunted. Somebody lived there, used to anyway. Mail that piled up would eventually get taken in. You'd see the screendoor closed, then a few days later not closed all the way. Maybe a window partly open. Wanting to think the best of people – one of the last times I've bothered – I decided someone too old to live there wanted to stay put even after money and oldness made that a bad idea. Might have been true once. It might. Sure wasn't the truth now.

I watched from across the street, not sure what to say or do, mixed up about how I felt now that I had found my brother. The guy Timmy was with had to shove the door with his shoulder a couple of times to get it open. Flickering TV light flashed around in the opening. Then they shut the door, and I stood there spying on a dark house.

The kid hated me now. At least, that's what he said. From

the way he was acting, I was supposed to believe all that hate was real, but I just couldn't see why or how. What did I ever do to him but protect him and feed him and keep him healthy and try to keep him from becoming exactly the type of person he seemed bent on becoming? It didn't make any sense. If anything, I should be the one. I was so tired. I had so much guilt and humiliation and anger wrapped up inside me, and no one trying to help me make it go away. Who could I trust? Who could I turn to when I wanted to give up? Who gave me a break?

I crossed the street and shoved the door open. Inside it was dark except for the TV and a dim light coming from an open doorway on the other side of the room. I stepped around and across bodies. A couple of the kids lifted their heads and looked at me and then flopped back down without a word. I pushed open the door on Timmy kneeling by the bathtub to fix up his friend, who sat on the edge holding out his scarred-up arm. Timmy glanced over his shoulder at me and went back to looking for a vein. I felt like I could've been anybody. I also felt like I could be sick. I'd never seen anyone shoot up before. They're just kids, I was thinking. Life sucks, but how can shit be so bad that someone this young has to do this?

"What you want?" Timmy finally asked.

"Just to see how you are. Been months."

"So?"

"So, how are you?"

"Peachy," he said as he drew the needle out, loosened the belt tourniquet, and his friend slumped forward. Timmy held him up with one hand and set the syringe on the back of the toilet where the spoon and the dope and a candle were sitting. He stood up, holding his friend.

"Look out," he said as he took a step toward me. I backed into the hall to let them by. Timmy dragged the guy into the living room and unceremoniously dumped him onto the pile of bodies. There was a small amount of groaning and shifting. Then it was silent except for the TV

Timmy came back into the bathroom, took off his coat, and rolled up his shirt sleeve. His arm was marked but not as bad as his buddy's. I wasn't sure if I could watch this.

"Timmy, don't do this to yourself."

"Why? You want to do it for me?" He had gotten his sleeve up to where he wanted it and belted his arm, which he held out to me, a smartass smirk on his face.

"No. I don't want you to do this at all."

"Try and stop me." He continued with his preparations, tapping the dope from a scrap of paper into the spoon. Dripping in a little water. Holding the spoon over the flame.

"Timmy . . ."

"It's Tim, goddammit. Tim."

"Okay, Tim, then. Stop this."

"Shut the fuck up," he said slowly as he refilled the syringe he'd just used on his friend. As he touched it to his skin, I grabbed his hand and pulled it away. The needle dropped into the bathtub. He immediately got to his knees and snatched it up. Then he stood and faced me and punched me with all his force straight in the nose.

"Get out of here!" he screamed. And then almost whispering, "Leave me alone."

My face stung. I couldn't tell which was running faster: the blood from my nose or my tears. I wiped my eyes with my coat sleeve, and by the time I could focus, he'd done it. All the rage was out of him. Everything – even his eyes – went slack. He pulled the needle out of his arm in slow motion and went to set it back on the toilet, missed, and I heard it tinkle on the tile floor. Tomorrow or later tonight or however this druggie business works, someone would pick that dirty thing up off of the floor and use it again.

"Gimme a hand," he said slowly, beckoning me with a loose wave. I helped him get up. He was so heavy. All top-heavy. We stumbled to the pile in the living room, and I let him drop. A black dude and his black puppet were hamming it up with an answer to some ridiculous Hollywood Squares question. The audience was laughing. Peter Lange, the tuxedoed host, and the two contestants were laughing. The puppet was rolling his eyes, and however it was done, the black dude made the puppet look completely disgusted with all the laughing humans. I had to pull on the front door a few times to get it open. There was a commercial on for minty fresh Scope when I left.

Chapter 8

Back at the Motel 6, I rip the pantyhose off and chuck them into the wastebasket. Nothing wrong with them. I just don't like them ever, period. I only wear them if I have to look civilized, and I'd been wearing these for almost a full 24 hours. I scratch my belly, my butt, my legs trying to get the circulation going again. Take off the little black dress, which really wasn't all that bad a thing to wear, and hang it on one of those motel hangers some genius designed to be not worth stealing, making the bent-over part and the hanger itself two detachable but separately useless pieces. I shake a cigarette out of the pack on the table, light it, pour a flimsy Motel 6 water tumbler full of Jim Beam, turn on the TV to some hokey black and white, sweet-girl movie, and get the hot water running for a good long soak.

I always have to remember Kid Brother at the most inconvenient moments. Hell, I guess there really isn't any good time. Those two punk car thieves were all it took today. Looking at that one, lying on the pavement, just expecting – and accepting – trouble? I'll never figure it out. Life is no bed of roses, I'll grant you that. But I keep thinking . . . I keep thinking . . . And it seems to be enough. I've got my bad habits, too. Smoke way too much. I can tell by what I spend on Luckys. I might drink too much, too, if the hangovers are any indication. But that's it. When I have to have it together, I'm together. When I don't, nobody's looking over my shoulder. But you have to be at least a little bit ready all the time. Things just aren't like they used to be in the olden days. Or like they are now on TV. No wonder everyone's hollering for peace and love. I'm not the only one who knows we don't have it. Nowhere. No one. Not for longer than a few minutes now and then. Long enough for you to notice that things are peaceful for once, and then BAM! Someone – always someone – comes along to make sure you stay stuck in the little rat trap of your thoughts.

What amazes me is how fast and how often shit rains into my life. I don't think this much is supposed to happen to one person on a continuous basis, although I've never asked. Who am I supposed to ask? Pop? Mom? Red? Mona? Timmy? Three of them are dead. The other two in jail. Who else do I know? And besides, a question like that? You're likely to have to explain why you're asking in the first place, and that gets into all kinds of mush and junk I'd rather people didn't know about me. I'll just watch, thanks very much. I don't actually expect it, but it would be sort of refreshing to run across a really happy person. Everything hunky-dory. Knowing myself and my life the way I do, if I did meet that person, they'd get run over by a bus within 15 seconds. I seem to have that effect.

Don't even have to try. I've got this nasty talent for spreading trouble. Flows from me like the fumes from those gas refineries in Benecia — all those pretty pastel-colored gas tanks, stacks of Necco wafers plopped on the hillsides. And stink . . .? That's how you know you're getting close to San Francisco: the fresh-fart stink at Benecia. It's all kind of downhill from there. Just another lovely byproduct of people on the planet.

"Jesus," I say to myself out loud in the too-shallow Motel 6 bathtub. "Aren't we pleasant tonight?" But I get this way when something brings up Timmy big time. He's always there, don't get me wrong. He's the only family I got left, even though he won't let me see him. Probably a smart move on his part. He knows what kind of karma comes off of me. Sometimes, like with that car thief today, Timmy's presence is bigger and makes me feel more useless than ever. I go over all the things I know I did wrong, a lot of them because I was too young to know any better. Blame myself again for making him the way he is, for my part in putting him where he is. Can't change the past, but you also can't stop yourself from wishing you could or had. And I don't even have a chance with Timmy if he won't see me. He can hide behind those granite walls of the state pen and just hate me. I screw around out here, playing private eye, and have to know every minute of every day how bad he hates me.

I love that kid. He's 25 now. February 2nd. I celebrate his day in the usual manner: Make myself a box of macaroni and cheese. Put ketchup on it, which I don't dig but he did. A side of barbecue potato chips. Glass of Hawaiian Punch. Hostess apple pie for dessert. Though cherry is my favorite, I celebrate with his favorites. The favorites I remember.

I lost him at 14. By 16 he was in prison for life, but with possibility of parole, thanks to the compassion of the Nevada state penal system. Timmy's crime was bad — murder's always bad — but it was also just a screwed-up kid's hopeless mistake. That cabby he killed needed killing, preying the way he did on kids. He sold them drugs; that was bad enough. But the sex part was what did me in. Boys, girls, groups — no waiting. A lot of them wouldn't know what had happened until the next day. Until the soreness and blood and this other odd wetness gave his activities away. The ones who knew also knew what letting this creep do whatever he, or his "customers," wanted with them would buy: drugs, drugs, and more drugs. The very thing that lured them to him in the first place.

I made up a story for Timmy where what he did was heroic. That when he came to from his drug haze long enough to realize how that perv degraded him and his friends, he was going to step up and put an end to it. But then there was the matter of 75 bucks the cops say the cabby had on him. I hold on to the idea that Timmy, deep down, was still a good boy. He would need more reason than money to kill someone. So he went a little off-track. Don't all kids? I didn't. I couldn't. But I don't buy the cops' story. Or maybe I don't want to be the sister of a cold-blooded killer. We were raised better. Our Pop was a fireman, for Christ's sake. He saved people. Once me and Timmy were on our own, I kept telling him every single day that his life was precious, and he was special and he was going to do great things. Just like our parents had told us. And I have to believe that's what Timmy was trying to do. I just wish he talked to me now. I want to tell him that I know the truth. I've known it all along. I'm on his side — even when I led the police to him. I was trying to help him get help from the kind of people our Pop always said we could count on. Man, was he wrong.

• • •

The water in the tub is downright cold by the time I break the spell of trying to re-write the past. Bad habit, another one of mine. Can't seem to help myself. If I'm not concentrating on work, I tend to drift off into refiguring how I could have made things turn out better. Never works. I never come to any new conclusions, just manage to make myself feel crummy for several hours or several days until something comes along to distract me.

I drink down the last of the bourbon while the water drains out. Then I crank up the shower and stand under the blazing water until I'm warm again. My fingers are all wrinkled up. Must have been in here a long time. My head feels better, clearer and not throbbing so much. I dry off, yank a comb through some of my hair. Go out into the other room and realize the change of clothes I brought is in the trunk of my car. Rats! I throw on my traveling jeans and shirt and go down the stairs barefooted.

I didn't figure on being stuck in San Francisco for long, but luckily I have my emergency overnight kit with me. I've been known to go home on a wild hair with some pretty face or another who thinks he's picking me up. Or sometimes I work late and crash at the office. And there are a couple of other occasions when I don't make it home, so I keep toothpaste, toothbrush, pit stop, soap, shampoo, and a change of clothes in Mom's old olive green Samsonite in my trunk. Be prepared. I would have made a good Boy Scout. Made a lousy Girl Scout. Flunked my bird-watching merit badge. Didn't know you weren't supposed to shoot them and make dinner out of them. I thought my Quail Surprise would have earned me two merit badges. Instead, the troop mom asked me never to return and to take that hideous plate of "food" with me. The quail were delicious, I might add. Pop's recipe. The secret is baking them in tin foil with a couple of juniper berries in the body cavity. For quail, one or two is plenty.

I open the trunk. There're my saddle and tack and a few odds and ends of Pio's. A lavender plaid elephant staring at me, nagging me for not knowing where the kid is now. Giving me the evil eye for letting my guard down and getting myself drugged. I rummage under the saddle for the green suitcase, and right before I shut the trunk, I decide to take the little elephant with me. A reminder that I've still got work to do down here. I've got to find Mona's baby. I don't care if these were the people she thought she could trust or not: nobody drugs me, takes off with a kid I'm in charge of, and gets away with it. I'm going to track them down and make Mr. Chan and Miss Ludden sorry they ever crossed paths with me.

"Okay, you damn elephant, where's the kid?" I ask the button-eyed toy. "Hunt. Hunt. What do you think you got a nose like that for?"

"You always talk to stuffed animals?"

I turn quick to my right, and there's trouble: Officer Tingle in his civvies, spinning a pair of wire-framed sunglasses by the earpiece between his thumb and forefinger. He's changed out of his uniform into creased khakis and a maroon turtleneck. He irons?

"Hey, isn't that the car you were describing to me? The one you said was stolen? Green. Two door. 1967 Pontiac GTO. License number W23380? California?"

Guy's got an annoyingly good memory.

"Not stolen?" he asks.

"Yeah, it was. I mean, it was for a while. They, uh, brought it back."

"No kidding?"

"No kidding at all. Walked out and there it was."

YOU MAKE ME TINGLE

"And it turned red and got Nevada plates?"

"Well, there's something that doesn't happen every day."

"Just my luck," I say, smiling my cheesiest.

"I'll say. No damage. Nothing missing?"

I shake my head.

"Good. That's good. Here," he says. "let me help you with that."

My mind's working so fast, coming up with explanations that I think he means the elephant – which I hold out to him – until he reaches for the handle of the suitcase, which I hold onto until he peels my fingers from it with his other hand.

"Shall we?" he says with a courtly bow and a wave of his hand toward the stairs.

"You're coming up?"

"If it's okay with you."

No, no, no! my brain screams at me for a lot of reasons.

Yes, yes, yes! my body says just to annoy me. How do I get rid of him? Do I want to?

"Did I mess up?" He puts the suitcase down. "I thought you wanted to see me again."

I'm standing with one bare foot on top of the other, hugging Pioche's elephant with both arms.

"I thought you said to call," I say lamely.

"You're right. I guess I did. Do you want me to leave?"

No. Yes. No. Hell yes. No, and that's final.

"Actually," I say. "Now that I've got my car back, I was just going to change and head back home."

"Back to Reno?"

"Yeah. You know, home."

He looks at me without saying anything for longer than I like. "Can I carry this up to the door for you at least?" I laugh at how he keeps trying to get a little closer to the room.

"Sure. Thanks."

He climbs ahead of me up the stairs. He has a very nice butt. Very nice. Very. I admire it moving in front of me for the two short flights up. We get to the third-floor walkway, and he turns so quick I run into him from following too close.

"Sorry," I say.

"No problem," he says. "I forgot which room. 305 or 304?"

"305," I confirm.

I've left the door partway open, the TV blabbing. Officer Tingle sets the suitcase down outside.

"You still have my number?" he asks.

"I do."

"And you will use it?"

"You bet."

"You Reno girls always say that."

"Say what?"

"'You bet.' You know? Bet. Like gambling."

"Oh, yeah, I get it. Gambling. Ha, ha, ha. We sure do say that. Ha, ha, ha." One of the phoniest sets of laughs in my life.

"Please call?"

"You bet. Shit, I did it again, didn't I?"

He's not happy but he's satisfied with that. He says, "I'm going then. Back to my lonely bed. Listen to some lonely Hank Williams songs about lonely whippoorwills."

"You listen to country music?"

"Doesn't everyone?"

"In San Francisco?

"You think I was born here?"

"Where were you born?"

"You'll have to let me in to find out."

"See ya," I say, picking up my suitcase.

"Had to try," he says.

He turns, and I hear him bound down the stairs, taking

them jock-like, two or three at a time before I shove the door the rest of the way open with the side of my suitcase. But maybe I'll just take one more little peek before I wisely let him go out of my life for good. I toss the suitcase onto the bed and turn to go back out onto the walkway when I hear bloodcurdling screams that an MGM starlet would be proud of coming from below me somewhere, followed by three unmovie-ish pops that are the real-life sound of gunshots.

I hit the deck out of instinct before it even registers in my pea brain that, by the sound of things, I'm pretty well out of range. I crawl to the dresser, reach my hand up, pull down my black evening bag, and dump out my gun. Turn again and slither back to the door. The railing along the walkway is only wrought iron which makes it easy for me to see out but is not so good to hide behind. I belly crawl closer to the edge and see Officer Tingle crouched behind an old Caddie with his gun pulled and aimed at one of the ground floor rooms at the other end of the motel. I hit the stairs at a full run in my bare feet. At the bottom I duck fast around the corner of the building to give myself a second to check out the scene before going to lend Officer Tingle a hand. Whoever's doing both the screaming and the shooting must be inside. People are starting to gather on the sidewalk and along the second and third-story railings. A couple more shots are fired, which clear out the bystanders in a flash. I work my way along the side of a Ford pickup and then down behind the backs of five or six cars until I'm close enough for Officer Tingle to hear me without me having to yell.

"Officer Tingle," I say.

He spins around, leveling his gun at me. He registers who it is and his eyes get really big. They get even bigger when he takes in the .357.

"Get back inside!"

"No. What's happening?"

"Go. Damn it," he says. There's another shot, and both of us instantly turn our weapons on the door of the room they're coming from.

"Call the police," he hisses.

"No, damn it. I'm covering you. One of these other assholes'll call."

Officer Tingle really can't believe what he's hearing or seeing. I don't blame him. I just wish he'd get over it before someone gets hurt.

"That's six," I say.

"Might be more than one shooter."

Duh, Flack! Officer Tingle edges around to the side of the piece of crap Toyota he's been hiding behind. I move a couple of rigs closer to where he is. He mouths, "Go back," at me, and I just gesture with my head that he can keep going forward, that I'm going along with him. The lookie-lou's are gathering again. I hear someone say, "Hey, check it out: that's a chick down there . . . with a gun."

That'd be me, and I'm damn glad I have one. The screaming inside the room has turned to hysterical crying punctuated by moans. Officer Tingle is in position crouched under the window to the right of the door where the sounds are coming from. I work my way over to the Toyota, then over to the left side of the door. Officer Tingle looks sick. I level my all-business look at him and mouth, "On three. One. Two. Three." We both get up. Officer Tingle kicks the door in, and the screaming starts again. I jump forward into the doorway. Now it's Officer Tingle's turn to cover me.

I yell, "On the floor! Now, goddammit! All of you!"

Officer Tingle pushes past me through the doorway, and I'm right behind him. Why all these people are assembled in one room is not immediately obvious, but there must be eight or ten of them, and they're squashed onto the floor around and between the beds so thick there's nowhere for us to walk without stepping on someone. Which I decide is my only option, and being barefooted and not weighing much, I stroll across shoulders and butts and rib cages and jump up on one of the beds.

Officer Tingle yells, "Is anybody hurt?"

No one says anything, but a woman continues to whimper.

I locate the sound. She's the body closest to the bathroom, the one with her dress flipped up over her butt and her purple bikini panties and thick, black thighs sticking out for all the world to see. I keep my gun pointed, ready, but kneel on the bed, pull her dress back down and poke her in the leg with my finger.

"Get up," I bark at her. If you can't tell who's the one in the group who's causing a ruckus, it's better to treat them all like they are.

She squeezes herself out of the pile, gets to her knees. Then she puts her hands down on the floor again, probably to push herself the rest of the way up, but, hey, I wasn't born yesterday.

Officer Tingle and I both pull the hammers back. Just those sounds encourage her to start screaming again, waving her arms around all panicky. A jolt of adrenalin pops her up to her feet.

"Don't shoot, don't shoot!" she screams. She's all jiggles now, shaking her hands, kind of bouncing her big body back and forth from leg to leg like a kid having to pee real bad.

"Get up here," I say. I motion with my gun that she should get up on the bed. She steps on someone in the process, and when that person yells painfully, she starts her screaming again and literally jumps from the floor up to a standing position on the bed. This sudden movement throws us both off balance. She's grabbing at me to try to steady herself, and we both fall over. I hear her hit some hard part of her anatomy on the headboard as I'm rolling off onto whoever's laying between the beds who lets out his air with an "oof." I spring to the other bed and get myself resituated.

"Listen," Officer Tingle says, "is anybody hurt?"

A voice from the floor says, "Over there. By the TV. Them two. Them's the two that's hurt. Could be dead."

Officer Tingle nods for me to check it out. I step across the gap between the beds, sit down on the end. One's a man in a dark suit, the other's a woman in leopard print capris and a black satin shirt. I start prodding the bodies with my toe. "Hey. Hey! You okay?" I say. They both move slightly and groan. I relieve both of them of their weapons.

I say to Officer Tingle, "One male, one female. Both armed. Hurt each other pretty bad."

Officer Tingle addresses the room, "What started this?"

Silence. Except for general whimpering.

"You all want to go to jail?"

Nothing.

I hear multiple sirens finally showing up.

"Took them long enough," I say to Officer Tingle.

He shrugs. "It's the neighborhood. Happens out here a bunch of times a day."

"Oh." The way he looks — not bored or accepting but kind of sad — I can tell he's not exaggerating. I can also tell that those sirens are my cue to vanish. Don't want to have to start explaining to them what Officer Tingle's going to expect me to explain to him.

I say, "I think I ought to, uh . . ."

Officer Tingle nods. I climb off the bed and over the bodies and squeeze past him to the outside. I release the hammer on my .357, tuck the gun into the waistband of my jeans. The barrel's cold down there, reminding me of what all I'm not wearing. I let my shirttail hang out over the bulge of my gun.

"Thanks," Officer Tingle says.

Must be the excitement, but I just have to kiss him, which I do quick and hard. We lock eyes for a split second. Then I make myself scarce.

Don't want a bunch of cops and ambulance drivers to see me cruising up the stairs, so I duck around the side of the building while they get busy with the scene. This shady side of the building is none too warm, especially on my bare tootsies, so I stand on one foot and then the other to get at least half a break from the cold cement. Seems to take forever for the police to start leading all of the people who can walk outside so that the ambulance guys can scrape up the wounded. The police assemble everyone facing the wall, hands overhead, and a cop with a pad and pen goes down the line asking each one names, addresses, etcetera. Everyone gets frisked. A paddy wagon shows up. Six men are handcuffed and are being loaded into it. Two women, including the one with the purple panties, are also handcuffed and being led to a couple of squad cars. Then the one who's been doing all the crying faints dead away. Pow! Hits the asphalt just like that. This causes enough of a stir to allow me to finally sneak up to my room without being seen.

I open my suitcase and change into my own, normal clothes: Levis, western shirt. Rub my feet between my hands and on the carpet until they warm up a little so I can put on my socks and my boots. Then I start gathering up everything I own in the room, stuffing it into the suitcase, trashcans, pillowcases, and anything else I can find that will hold a few things. Don't know how I'm going to do it, but I have to get out of here before Officer Tingle shows up on my doorstep.

Always got to go and get myself involved in shit that's none of my business. Last thing I need now is to be in a strange place with a strange, but cute, cop asking a lot of questions. I tipped my hand big, barging into that crime scene, all armed and dangerous. He could have gotten himself killed, though. I really don't need anyone else's death on my conscience to go along with a missing baby who isn't even mine, a dead Reno rich kid whose family's got more killers in it than the Green Berets, and more snoops than the FBI., PLUS a damn videotape with enough bribery and collusion on it to put the entire Nevada State Legislature behind bars. PLUS, I kissed a San Francisco cop on the lips not only once but also not as often as I'd've liked to. Oh boy, Flack, are you in it now.

I walk out to the rail to take a quick look down. There're all kinds of people milling around. Police taking statements. People pointing here and there where they saw such and such going on. Cops dutifully, if not real enthusiastically, writing it all down. I don't see Officer Tingle. Must be in the crime scene, telling what went on. I hope he's leaving me out of it, but there's nothing I can do if he's not.

The crowd in the parking lot has expanded as more and more people want to tell their version of the story or just want to hang out and hear about something exciting that they missed. I can never understand that kind of thinking. Me, if I see a crowd, I suddenly realize there's somewhere, anywhere else I have to be. I don't care if there's flames or blood or a vision of the Virgin Mary, if people are standing around gawking at anything, whether or not they paid money to see it, you won't find me. Crowds like this remind me of a flock of chickens all fixated on the same damn bug: Bobby's staring at it so Betty's staring at it so Debby's staring at it so I'm going to stare at it, too. People. My favorite place to be with people is away. Far, far away. Nothing but trouble, and you know I don't need extra help in that department.

With the cavalry amassed in the parking lot and no back doors in Motel 6 rooms, I'm in a bit of a bind for a graceful exit if I want to take my car and my belongings. Then again if I take off on foot, where will I go? I need to get Mona's baby back — that is, if she's still in the country. This new situation now has thrown a big wrench into the works. Why can't anything ever be easy? Because it wouldn't be any fun, Flack. Since when do you like it easy?

With all the usual city bullshit going on, who's going to notice if I beat a hasty retreat? Even you-know-who is occupied. I pick up my shoulder bag and the rest of my and Pioche's crap, leave my room key and a generous tip on the dresser and close the door behind me. I casually lug everything down the two flights of stairs and across the parking lot to the car, and dump my crap on the pavement so I can unlock the trunk. Now I will calmly place — not frantically throw — everything in. Take my time. Look cool. Walk coolly to the driver's door. Slide in coolly behind the wheel. Coolly start the engine. Then,

"Uh-uh, you're not going anywhere."

Rats, it's you-know-who. I guess you know I'm in deep you-know-what.

Chapter 9

Mom. She used to say that: "You're not going anywhere" because, of course, I was. A high-speed blender of a child. Hit the floor running every day and only stopped when my arms and legs said, "No more."

"You're not going anywhere." Only hers would have "young lady" attached at the end. Good thing Officer Tingle didn't add that or I'd be gone out of here so fast, he'd think maybe he'd just dreamed he met me.

That "young lady" crap of Mom's never stuck. Or maybe she knew it never had a chance and was just making fun of the rambunctious daughter who would never grow into the title of young lady. Not if I had anything to say about it. That, even though I loved her, was part of what made me run from her: the thought of having to get all tucked in and barretted up and bobby-soxed and expected to do what every red-blooded American girl is supposed to do: find a husband. For mothers in the 50s, Job 1 was to get their daughters ready for the altar.

I crossed my fingers and my eyes and spit into water while standing on one leg during full moons for two whole years trying to hex away the evil spirits of impending wife and motherhood. Some kind of shazam or voodoo or witchcraft had to save me from my fate. Almost everybody's mom, or latest stepmom in the series, stayed home, so there was a bountiful supply of supporters who would suggest from their half-open screen doors that I slow down before I hurt myself. The busy-bodies who would narc on me for beating the hell out of the neighborhood sissy Marky Allen. Again. How could I resist? He was an easy ambush, always daydreaming over somebody's flower bed or the cute little birdies in the trees. A kid like that has it coming. I was only trying to teach him to be alert. For his own good.

Running and fighting didn't seem to me like a bad way to spend my time. It sure beat sitting on the sidewalk letting stupid dolls get all the action. I was my own doll. Where the neighborhood girls – except for Mona, thank goodness – could rouse themselves once in a while to skip rope, they seem content as pie to act out their lives through pieces of plastic and cloth that looked like people. Like they were too scared or lazy to be what they were pretending. Then again, when I'd get bored enough to eavesdrop on these wives-in-training, I understood why the dolls were so important to their idea of play: the dolls were grocery shopping and taking care of babies and gossiping over coffee. Like our own moms. Maybe those girls knew as well as I did that being ladylike was a life sentence. Maybe they were trying to keep it away by making the dollies live it for as long as possible. Nope. Wishful thinking.

I never did hear of one of those dollies sticking up a bank or cutting up a cheating husband and his girlfriend. You know? Something interesting? In my jam-packed days, I hunted for Nazi spies and Communists and serial killers. And I caught them. Saved the world. Won medals for bravery and honor. I used to wear two of Pop's old belts crisscrossed over my shoulders and go hunt Mexican bandits like I saw in a movie with Humphrey Bogart. I called the other kids "Pilgrim," which I got from another movie with John Wayne. They never knew what I was talking about. Fine with me.

I never felt weird about saving the world until the day Scotty Stewart told me girls couldn't save the world. Never had, never would. I jumped on his back, knocked him down, and stuck a dirt clod in his mouth. The whole time he was spitting out grit and crying, he was going on and on about how all the good movies and TV shows – the ones with guns and saloon brawls and war – were all about men. Whose were the big names up on the screen? John Wayne, Robert Mitchum, Bogey, Cagney, Burt Lancaster, Kirk Douglas? Yeah, there was a girl's name here and there, but never big or first. Girls were only put in to look pretty and get rescued or kissed. Or murdered. He was saying all of this and blubbering, and when I came swinging at him again, he ran away saying, "Girls can't do nothing. Girls can't do nothing."

I swear that punk Scotty changed my life that day. I swear I never noticed that all the people who got to do cool jobs in the movies were men. I just plain didn't notice. Up until that day with Scotty, all those characters I admired were people. Just people. Then I started to really look and found out stupid Scotty was right. Hell, you couldn't get much spying and crawling through enemy barbwire dressed like Rita Hayworth. Dragging those big boobs through the mud would slow you down so bad you'd get killed. I started seeing what the women in movies were doing: waiting, crying, pleading, serving, lounging. Or batting their pretty little eyelashes and pouting their pretty little lips. Whose idea was it that women in the Wild West wore gobs of makeup and perfect hairdos while the men ran around in two days' growth of beard and a beatup, dirty hat? How could you survive as a frontier woman with a teeny little waist that'd snap like a toothpick? Women and shiny satin and flowery prints and lace, never getting a speck of dirt on them? Goddam Scotty was right: there was not a world saver in the bunch.

I didn't run around much for a while after that. I turned into Marky Allen. All daydreamy. Laying on my stomach in the grass watching ants or on my back looking up at the empty blue sky. I knew I had to be careful where I did it since I'd be a sitting duck for anyone who felt like they owed me a butt-kicking. I knew I had more than a few coming. Weird not to hear mom saying, "You're not going anywhere, young lady," because it looked like she was getting her wish. I wasn't. It's hard to be a badass, gunslinging sheriff and having to be a girl at the same time. Here I was, all absorbed with thinking. How could I have not noticed? Why did I think "young lady" meant every girl but me? How could I have thought all people could do what they wanted, be what they wanted, when the evidence to the contrary was all around me? Who was the fireman in our house? Pop. Who cooked? Mom. Who took care of my new baby brother? Mom. Who went grocery shopping? Mom. Who got his eyebrows burned off fighting a house fire? Pop. Who had a uniform with a badge and a nameplate? Pop.

I was doomed. Doomed to smell nice all the time. Doomed to go to the beauty shop. Doomed to wear aprons. Doomed. Doomed to be a woman and not a person. The world split down the middle into the Us that I was forced into by my plumbing and the Them that my plumbing cut me off from. I listened to and watched my own neighborhood with the astonishment of my new discovery. The whole place changed on weekends. I never noticed this before. Power lawnmowers came out. Cars got worked on in driveways. Boards got hammered. During the week, there were sounds of sprinklers and kids mostly. A few cars going past on errands. Sounds of TV soap operas and music from radios inside houses where women slopped around in shapeless housedresses, curlers, and cold cream in order to escape from their ironing boards at about 11 o'clock in shirtwaist dresses, nylons, high heels, and hairdos to meet up for coffee klatch gossip.

I noticed these things. And worst of all, I started to wonder how someone like Pop, whose days were full of danger and excitement, could stand the company of Mom whose life was full of dirty diapers and dirty dishes. What the hell did they have to talk about? What could he possibly want to know about her day? And this whole thing was repeated in every house on my block, on all of the surrounding blocks, and possibly the whole entire world.

This could not be all there was for me to look forward to. Needing to prove myself wrong, I got up from the grass, got on my bike, and went out investigating. I planned to keep looking for as long as I had to until I found some girl somewhere doing something interesting.

It made for a long week full of many bummers. One neighborhood after another just like mine. No women cops, no women firemen. No spy hunters, men or women. Not even any women mailmen. Scotty was looking more and more right.

Then I went downtown.

I stashed my bike in some weeds on Commercial Row near the train tracks and headed for Virginia Street on foot. In Nevada by the time you're ten, you've figured out the location of the bathroom in every casino in town. From a kid's point of view, casinos are places to pee, eat, and mark Keno tickets for your Pop to play for you while you're eating. You can sneak in for a bathroom break or a piece of pie if you're by yourself and you act like you know where you're going, trickier if you're part of a bunch of kids. At least in the old days, you could get away with it. Having been on the side of casino security, I can tell you they don't put up with kids wandering around like that anymore.

The Primadonna was my favorite club because of the giant showgirl statues out front — I mean, GIANT. And painted to look like real people — I mean, women. Damn, all this man/woman stuff was confusing. The statues were all decked out with all the feathers and sparkles and fishnet stockings. The middle statue was on a pedestal that rotated side to side. She had her arms raised over her head and held a martini in her white-gloves-to-the-elbow left hand. She was my favorite. All fancied up but with a drink in her hand. She had her priorities straight. These statues had serious legs. Like Superman's sisters in their power costumes. Tights were good enough for him, right? Judging from the outside of the Prim, I figured the girls were in charge on the inside, too, and I had never thought about it.

I knew one of the security guards on the Prim's day shift. Terry. He had worked with Pop for years until he hurt his back one day, rolling up a hose on the station house driveway. Just gave out on him. No warning. Not a twinge. But he was getting up in years. Took his pension, got bored, and took a casino job.

Standing on his feet all day didn't help his back much, but he said it beat sitting behind a desk or in front of the TV. He also liked flirting with the ladies, which he was free to do after his wife ran off with a sheriff's deputy.

Terry didn't bother to make a show of not noticing me when I came into the casino unescorted. He'd give me a hug, ask me how things were going. Ask me how Pop and Mom and Timmy were. Usually, he'd walk with me to the bathroom, talking the whole time. But on the day I began my investigation, one drunk had hit another drunk over the head with an ashtray at the craps table, so Terry had to excuse himself. Perfect timing. I knew the drunks would keep security busy so I could take my time having a look around.

The best I can say is that, yeah, seemed like the girls were better off there than at home. There weren't all that many women dealers at the card tables, but they got to dress the same as the men. Tuxedoes, ruffled shirts, black bowties, pants. Looked even-steven to me. The mini-skirted cocktail waitresses, showing lots of boob and leg, seemed enough like the statues out front to be Superman's cousins. The false eyelashes, the frozen piles of curls on their heads did not take away from the look on their faces that they were in charge. That they could giveth and they could taketh away — even if it was just booze. They looked powerful to me. Then it hit me: they had their own money. And that got me a new revelation: maybe the women in my neighborhood toed the boring line because they didn't have their own money. Pow! That was the lesson. What you needed to do was make sure to always have your own money, and you'd never have to wait for it or ask for it or be trapped in the house. The women at the Prim looked pretty damn in charge to me. In charge of themselves and their futures. Of course, I'd find out later that most of them were on manhunts because the man they had been with had run off or because they wanted what they thought would be the luxury of being trapped in the house. Regardless of what they wanted, I decided that day I wanted my own money. I wanted all the say about what went on in my life. I'd go out there and change the world for myself even if I couldn't do it for anyone else. All the Scotty Stewarts in the world couldn't stop me.

I went home and kicked the crap out of Marky Allen for a warmup. The couple of weeks I'd spent moping had made me soft. Then I went looking for Scotty Stewart and sent him home crying, too. It felt good to be back. It felt good to know what I knew about what women "couldn't" do. Mom was disappointed. She thought I'd grown out of my wildness and had seen the delicate light of ladyhood. But I rejected it with a vengeance, and no amount of her lecturing me about it or Pop asking me to please go easy on her changed my mind. "Young lady," my ass!

Two months later, Pop was killed fighting that fire in Sparks. I could never have guessed that the formula for independence I'd been playing around with would be put to the test so soon and so permanently.

Chapter 10

I'd say it's probably not a good sign when the man you've been making goo-goo eyes at suddenly says something that reminds you of your mother. Not a good sign at all.

Officer Tingle is leaning with one arm on the top of the GTO and one hand on the door handle, talking to me through the closed window. Rats. He opens the door before I get a chance to lock it. I could just slam the car into reverse real fast and split, but there's no sense in giving him anything else to wonder about. I'm sure he's gotten enough weird impressions about me as it is. And it looks like I'll be filling in a few blanks. The ones I feel like filling in, that is.

Then there's that thing about him sounding like Mom. Sort of got my back up. It's not his fault — how could he know that phrase is like fingernails on a blackboard? Or, more accurately, a knife in my belly. He opens the door wider, and he's still standing behind it, which means I could easily take off. But he is a cop, and I don't need him finding out anything about me from, say, other cops. Say, out-of-state ones. He's got all the information on my car. Has my real name. A couple of phone calls, and I'll be answering to him through some iron bars while we wait for the Reno posse to show up.

I turn off the engine and just sit there trying not to look at him. He leans his chin on the arm he's got slung across the car door. He's going to try to outlast me. He's staring at me. He's not going to say a word until I do. Hell.

I fish through my shoulder bag on the passenger's seat for a Lucky and my Zippo. I offer him the pack. He takes it.

"'Lucky Strike,'" he reads. He tosses the pack down on my lap. "Might as well suck on a tailpipe."

I light up and take a deep drag. "How original," I say, still keeping my eyes off him. If he's going to play a waiting game, I guess I'll have to get nasty. I've got things to do — like find a new place to stay — and the sun's going down.

"What do you want?" I ask.

"Well, I guess I want to thank you for your help back there."

"You're welcome. Can I go now?"

"I guess I want to ask where you learned your procedure."

"TV."

"Oh, yeah? Me, too."

"Good. We're even. Can I go now?"

He sighs, but he's not giving up.

"Was this car really stolen?"

"Yep."

"And it really just showed up back here?"

"Nope."

"Did you find it?"

"Yep."

"Who took it?"

"Didn't ask."

"Where'd you find it?"

"Downtown."

"Are you a cop?" he asks.

"Nope."

"Military?"

"Nope."

"Vigilante?"

"Close."

That stops him for a few seconds. The fingerprint and photo squad pulls up. He waves to them but doesn't hassle the uniforms doing their jobs.

Officer Tingle says, "You were good in there. Good as I've ever seen."

I put out my cigarette in the car's ashtray and say, "Well, you know, everybody's got to be good at something." I look at my watch and start drumming my fingers on the steering wheel.

"Got a date?" he asks.

"Nope."

"Buy you dinner?"

I look at him now and think, I don't owe this guy nothing. No explanations, no pleasure of my company, no male ego strokes. He's pushed himself into my room twice; now he's practically pushed himself into my car. Won't take "nope" for an answer. He's becoming more and more my type every second.

I say, "Little early, isn't it?"

"Yeah, I guess you're right. How about a glass of wine and a nice, long Jacuzzi soak?"

YOU MAKE ME TINGLE

"Haven't got a bathing suit."

"The Jacuzzi's at my place. You won't need one."

"I don't drink wine."

"I'm sure I'll have what you want."

God, I hate this guy for being so right about me.

I say, "I'm driving myself."

He says, "Okay."

Trusting soul. A minute ago, I was ready to high-tail it, and he knew that as well as I did. Now he knows I'd follow his cute butt and snappy come-backs clear to Redding. I am intrigued and feeling pretty guilty about taking a detour off the Mr. Chan/Miss Ludden trail. For all I know, they're driving down Main Street Hong Kong by now with Pioche in her little car seat, learning the words to "London Bridge." I ask myself, what would Mona do? Answer: she'd chase this good-looking cop all the way to his bedroom. My job with the baby ended back at the Mark Hopkins for all intents and purposes. The way it ended bugs me, but I know — I knew — Mona. She was crooked, no doubt about that. There also never was a more self-serving, self-protecting broad on the planet. Things were bound to go haywire for her at some point, but I have to believe she set things up for her baby with people she trusted. For once I have to remember I'm not responsible. The baby's okay, the baby's okay, the baby's okay. Keep telling yourself that, Flack. And do not lose sight of the taillights on that sexy guy's car.

Chapter 11

Officer Paul Tingle lives on one of those pastel San Francisco hills where the two-story houses are stacked side by side like 3mint dominos, and you'd have to remember which color yours is, or you might not ever find your place again. He tells me to wait in my car by the curb on the opposite side while he opens his garage door and puts his car in. Then he has me pull into a tiny driveway which is just long enough for my back bumper to clear the sidewalk. I push against gravity to open my door on the uphill side, hit the edge of a brick retaining wall that's keeping the front lawn from sliding down the hill, swear, then heave myself out into a slanted standing position - the uphill knee bent, downhill leg straight.

I examine the edge of my door and wish again I hadn't had

the thing painted. All I've done since then is worry about it and end up in predicaments like this one. I did take off a tiny chip of the ruby red paint just now. Shit.

"Hell of a hill," I say, trying not to lean against the car while I walk unevenly toward him.

He smiles and waits for me to squeeze through the tight space between my car and the brick wall where there's definitely no room for two. It would drive me crazy to live like this: packed like sardines. My trailer park's bad enough, and there're only eighteen of us, all camp trailers. We've got more space between our rigs than Officer Tingle's house has with his neighbors'.

He goes up the steps ahead of me to the front door. There are two of those bushes with huge, blue bouquets of flowers on either side of the front porch.

"What do you call those?" I ask.

"Mildred and Hattie," he chuckles at himself. "Hydrangea. Came with the place."

Corn-yyyyy.

He unlocks the door and lets me in first. I instantly step all over his mail.

"Oops," I say, dancing off of the envelopes.

He laughs. "I used to do that all the time myself. Far cry from having to walk clear out to the main road like we do in Yakima."

"Right. You? You're from Yakima? Apple farmer?"

"Dairy. Third generation."

"So you thought you'd become a cop in San Francisco?"

"As fast as humanly possible." He's going through the envelopes. Opens one, looks at the contents, folds it back into the envelope, and tosses the whole works onto a black lacquer bench next to the door.

He says, "Gets pretty tiresome doing the same things at

the same times every single day, 365 days a year. Dad'll never give it up. Both of my brothers either. Cows are too damn demanding. Tell time better than people can. And they're louder and smellier."

He drops his keys and his wallet on top of his mail. Turns on a table lamp. Closes, locks, and deadbolts the front door. Shuts the curtains on the lights of the city that are just coming on. "Now, you said you don't drink wine . . ."

"Yeah, had a bad experience once." Yesterday.

"Name your poison." He walks away from me into what I assume will be the kitchen. I haven't come much further than the front door, gathering information from the room about what kind of character lives in this house. Tidy, I'll give him that. And not much for decoration. The walls are empty. Tabletops are empty. The furniture's good but there's damn little of it: a tan leather couch, three matching black lacquer tables, and a beautiful, red oriental carpet. Against the far wall in what ought to be a dining area, there are stacks and stacks of books, no bookcases. The rest of the space is empty. No TV. No stereo. It'd be my guess he hasn't lived here long. The place is so bare our voices echo.

"So what is it?" he calls from wherever he is.

"Bourbon. Jim Beam if you've got it," I echo back to him.

Go sit down, Flack. You're here. Quit acting like a teenager.

"How do you want it?" he says.

"In a glass."

"Hardcore."

I sink down into the couch and the rich smell of new leather. I really dig leather. And I can tell the difference between new and what people've been using for a while.

Leather picks up the smells that it comes in contact with the most, which can be good or bad. Pop's old jacket? Canoe, a hint of cigarette smoke, on the back of the collar, Brylcreem. One of the pockets smells like Doublemint. His whole personality is in that jacket. All of my memories of him. Still. This couch, on the other hand, has no history yet. No permanent creases, no stains. It's shiny and perfect and new. Hasn't settled into itself or Officer Tingle. In fact, nothing in this house seems to have settled itself. It all seems to be floating just above where it is, waiting for time and use. I deduce that he just moved here. Or he never spends any time here. Or maybe it's just this room. The couch, all of this, just for looks? For company? And he really lives in his den or his bedroom?

"Here you go," he says, handing me a nice, heavy highball glass with a modest shot of whiskey in it. He took me at my word: no water, no ice.

"Cheers," I say and touch my stout glass to his generous red wine glass.

I take a sip. "This is scotch."

"I know. I'm sorry. It's all I had."

I take another sip. It's scotch, but it's good scotch.

"I think I can suffer through."

There's no music, no TV. Just the sound of the occasional passing car, revving like mad to get up the hill or brakes squealing going down. The room is dark except for the one table lamp.

He clears his throat. "Well, I'll start: What do you do in Reno?"

Here we go. "Personal services." I'd have never guessed that phrase would come in useful.

"Uh-huh."

"That's what I do. Honest."

"Like you did today?"

"Sometimes."

"What's that piece you carry?"

"Colt Python. Inheritance from my great-aunt Ruth."

"That's a lot of gun."

"Thank you."

"Use it much?"

"Not as often as I feel like."

"Hey," he says all of a sudden, snapping his fingers. "Where's the baby? God, I just happened to think . . ."

There he goes, not finishing sentences again. Arrgggghhh.

"My sister came and got her right after you left yesterday."

"Boy, you had some trip. First your car gets stolen, then you find your stolen car, then your sister comes for a visit, then you practically get into a shootout."

You don't know the half of it, I'm thinking. Ever meet a six-foot-tall Chinaman in a gold Nehru jacket who slips you a mickey and takes off with your best, old, dead friend's kid? What you don't know about my day . . . Now I'm doing it!

I lean my head back against the soft leather and close my eyes.

I really don't feel like talking, but he's a cop so him asking all of these pain-in-the-ass questions comes with the territory. I've given him a lot of details to piece together, but I still wish he'd quit. I wish he and I were two regular people who met by accident in a bar or somewhere normal and were proceeding to get all hot and bothered for a quickie. He got a load of me in action, and he ain't seen nothing yet.

He touches me on the top of my head. "Tired?" he asks.

I nod like that's all I can muster the energy to do. He strokes my hair, and it feels very good. Then I let him take the drink out of my hand. I know what's coming. I'm ready. Boy howdy, am I ready. He kisses me. I remember the way he smells, the way he tastes. The texture of his tongue.

"I know what will make you feel really good," he says between lip-smacks.

Corn-yyyy. If I've heard it once, I've heard it a million times. They all think they know what you need, and it has one eye and a bald head and theirs is superior to the next guy's or the last guy's when they don't even know who those other guys are or might be. I'd love to meet the man who knows it's going to take his whole brain and his whole anatomy to really get next to me. But I figure I'll move this thing on to its inevitable, non-conversational, and briefly enjoyable conclusion before I get too tired to continue.

I put my hand on the significant part of his lap.

And he says, looking me straight in the eye, "Yes, that might work, too, but I was referring to the Jacuzzi."

Well, knock me over with a feather and color my face red. This is a first. I remove my hand as gracefully as possible from The Organ and tuck some straggling strands of my hair behind my ears. I fold my hands together in my own lap then I cross my arms. Then I put my hands between my knees. Then I just go ahead and cover my face.

"The Jacuzzi, of course," I say. "I knew that. Well, hell, what're we waiting for?"

"I'll get the bubbles going." He kisses me and leaves. I gulp the rest of my drink and head off in the direction where I suspect I'll find the kitchen.

The wine and a bottle of Black Label are sitting on a lime green and black ceramic tile counter where the only other thing cluttering up the space is a toaster. No dish rags or soap or plants or empties. A lonely toaster. I pour a big drink, slug down half, and take the rest back into the living room so I can look like I haven't been snooping around. I take a gander at the load of books he owns. College textbooks. Literature, biology, history. Yellow "Used" stickers on some of them. The

Plague. Utopia, Poems of William Blake, Origin of the Species. The man I'm about to sleep with is no ordinary cop. I'd say you probably don't get anything past a guy who reads poetry. I'm going to have to play it real careful if I don't want my goose well done.

He comes back into the room as I'm finishing off the last of the drink I poured while admiring his beautiful red rug.

"I just got that," he says. The hardwood floor creaks under the soft tread of his bare feet. His stunning bare body walks toward me. I hold on tight to my glass. He steps onto the rug and wiggles his toes into the threads. He's too close for me to take him all in, so I settle for piece by piece: the big veins in his feet, the diamond-shaped calves, the little, golden hairs covering his thighs, the . . . yeah, the in-y belly button, the series of muscles across his stomach, the large, pink nipples on the nearly-hairless chest.

Grapefruit-sized biceps. Long bones in his forearms leading to the thick-fingered hands. Baby, this is a man. This one I'm going to remember.

"You like it?" he asks.

I'm speechless.

"The rug. You like it? Got it at this antique shop near Golden Gate Park. It's over a hundred years old but just look at the condition." He crouches down so he can run his handsome fingers over it. The muscles in his shoulder and back flex as he moves his arms.

And I'm thinking it must have been a long time for me. Either that or this one is beyond exceptional. Let's see: how long has it been? There was, no, he passed out while we were necking so he doesn't count. There was the guy who stayed in his Coachmen overnight in my trailer park. No, that wasn't the last one. Might have been that guy who fixed us his favorite breakfast – oatmeal – the next morning. What the hell was his name? Started with a "D." Lives over on Plumas Street. Yeah, he might have been the last, and that was . . . Let's see. I hadn't had the car painted yet because it was too cold. I think it might have been around Thanksgiving. That'd make it, whoa, six months. That's too long for anybody to go without.

Officer Tingle says as he straightens up, "Like my place?"

"It's beautiful. The rug." You. "I can't believe it. It's beautiful." You.

He gathers me into his arms, and I know the next part is coming: the part where I take off my clothes. He lets me go, and I shove my empty glass at him.

"Oh, another drink? Okay," he says. He downs the rest of his wine and hunks away into the kitchen, leaving me staring at the air.

He's back in a flash with the two bottles and our two drinks and says, "Shall we?" I follow him down a narrow hallway with built-in drawers and cabinets on one side and a series of shut doors. At the end, a faint bluish light casts quivering shapes on the wall. We walk through a small bedroom with nothing in it but a bed, basically a mattress on the floor, and out to a glassed-in porch where the Jacuzzi is churning away. His clothes are laying on one side of the bed.

"You can toss yours there," he says. "I'm getting cold, so I'm going in."

I take a drink, then look around me for a place to set the glass down, end up setting it on the floor. Then I sit down on the bed and take off my boots. Getting naked doesn't take nearly long enough, and I finally have to make my appearance.

He smiles as I step into the blue light. I slide into the water as fast as I can, thinking this is weird. I never have a second's hesitation about shucking my clothes around people. But this guy's physical beauty is intimidating. And tonight, he's all mine. He's mine and . . .

. . . the phone rings.

"Shit, he says. "Be right back." He glides toward me through the bubbles and holds me against as much of his skin as he can. He's warmer than I am and harder and bigger, and I thought I wanted him before – now I'm downright hungry. He steps out over the side of the tub right next to my face, and I see he's pretty hungry, too. He grabs a white terry cloth robe off a hook on the wall and wraps it around him. It won't close over the part of him that's not interested in talking on the phone.

"I'm on call," he says as he leaves the room, completely ignoring the fascinating sight of his protrusion still protruding.

The water feels great. Now that these Jacuzzi things seem to be everywhere, I wish I had the space for one. But that would mean getting a house and having a lawn, and everyone knows that leads to dogs and other time-consuming domestic habits. Maybe I'll work on picking up a few friends with houses and Jacuzzis who go away a lot on weekends and need someone to watch their places. I could do that.

"You're going to hate me," he says, hanging the robe back on the hook. "I have to go for a while." He comes over to me and squats down near the edge of the tub and kisses the top of my rat's nest of curls. The view from my angle is terrific. "I don't know how long I'll be, but dinner's probably out. Can you stay?"

"What's going on?"

"Small riot. Golden Gate Park."

I'm quickly changing my mind about what's interesting tonight.

"Yeah?" I say, turning around and leaning my arms on the edge of the tub.

"Wait a minute. Don't even think about it. This is official

police business."

He walks away to the closet, gets out his blues, and lays them on the bed. Goes out into the hall and comes back with underwear and a V-neck t-shirt.

"You know, I can be pretty handy in certain situations," I remind him.

"Right. I was going to ask you about that once you were sufficiently liquored up."

"Oh, you cad."

He's dressing fast, so I climb out of the tub, grab a towel, and start drying off fast.

"You're not coming."

"Am, too. It's my right as a citizen." I drop the towel on the floor, and Officer Tingle watches it fall.

"Unsanitary," he says.

"Sorry." I go to hang it back on its hook.

"Not after it's been on the floor," he says.

"Well, what the hell am I supposed to do with it?"

He gets up from the bed so he can zip his pants. "Give it to me."

He drapes it neatly over the top of the bedroom door. I guess nobody's perfect.

I'm jumping into my clothes with every intention of seeing my very first riot. Seen them on TV. Race riots. Anti-war riots. Wonder what kind this one is. So I ask.

"Gay."

"Gay?"

"Gay."

"A gay riot."

"That's not how it started out. Some kind of pride rally. Rednecks showed up. Things got out of hand. You're not coming, you know."

"Hey, I'm ready. All I have to do is tuck in my shirt. Didn't know you had rednecks in San Francisco. What are they? Imported?"

"Believe me, we have our share. You're not coming."

"Aw, I promise to behave." I bat my baby greens at him.

And in a totally anticipated turn of events, he says, "Okay then, let's roll."

"Goodie," I say. "I'll drive."

"You'll drive?"

"I'm parked behind you, remember?"

Yee-haw, I'm on my way to a gay riot with a gorgeous, overly fastidious patrolman in my own car. Things are getting curiouser and curiouser.

Chapter 12

Riots are more exciting on TV. Closeups of bloody heads, pissed off faces. Granted, this riot was nothing compared to what's been going on here. Still, I couldn't help thinking that a few well-timed camera closeups and a news guy's running commentary would have made this whole thing more interesting.

It's winding down by the time we get there. The paddy wagon's pulling away empty. Since nobody acted up bad enough, the gay boys are walking or running away arm in arm. The rednecks are dragging their knuckles back to their trucks and hopped-up Chevys. Reminds me of home, of Boomtown after work on a Friday night. That's the rednecks. Gay guys? If you live in northern Nevada, San Francisco is the nearest place you'll actually see them. Nevada's gay guys are "in the closet." I just learned about that. It'd be a real bad idea for a man to wear his favorite rhinestone necklace down at the Zanzibar on Virginia Street. I didn't make the rules – I'm just aware of them. I get "thought-you-was-a-guy" often enough myself to know that in Nevada real men wear plaid flannel and real women don't fish. Helps to have a sense of humor if you come down on the wrong side of the girl/boy fine line. To me, it ain't worth hassling about, but if this little fracas had happened in Reno, the cops would have jumped right in with the good old boys, and the sanitation department would be scraping sequins and eyeshadow off the sidewalk for a month. Here in San Francisco, the cops politely ask everyone to move along. Which they are. Each side still slinging insults but moving on just the same.

• • •

I'm driving Officer Tingle home after he is dismissed by the sergeant. We stop on the way to pick up a Round Table combo pizza, a 6-pack of Dos Equis, and my bourbon. So much for the classy cuisine of The City.

What the riot lacked in brute force we make up for on Officer Tingle's mattress on the floor while the pizza gets cold and the beer gets warm. He's not minding that I make the first move. I was getting damn tired of waiting for him to make it. Besides, the fantasy of ripping off a cop's blues has always been a big turn-on for me. I push him down on the bed a little rough – being as there's not much padding to speak of – and he smacks his elbow so hard it brings tears to his eyes. We don't stop for apologies or an examination of the wound. But I show him how we take a guy to bed where I come from, and I think he likes it.

And now that that part's over – the part where you get a peek here and there, fiddle with this or that, take a nibble here, a taste there – for me anyway, there's not much left to do. Officer Paul Tingle falls asleep with his arms around me, which means that for an hour or so I've been staring at the steam coming off of the hot tub and wishing I was in the water. Never have been able to sleep with someone touching me. Hate it, as a matter of fact. Once the dirty deed's done, I'm ready to go. Got work to do, other fish to fry. The fish that's rolling around in my head right now is named Chan.

That clear, ice water feeling your body gets right after being freshly laid has mellowed to the rosy glow where I start thinking oh so briefly about long walks and candlelight – that kind of crap. I'm not the least bit tired. And I want a cigarette. Bad. And Officer Tingle's arm flopped across my ribs is starting to crush the life out of me like being squished under a freshly killed side of beef. I gotta get outta here.

As much as I've ever talked myself into wanting anybody, I've never been able to make that wanting last. Like this, right now. This is my limit: I came, I saw, I conquered, I came. The end. Now it's just me and this other person who at some point is going to wake up and say something stupid like, "Last night was so wonderful." Or "You're the best." Or – yikes! – "Can I see you again tonight?" Sometimes they mean it, and that's a real problem. Couldn't tell you which one bugs me the most: the ones who say it because they think that's how they pay up before they blow you off or the ones who really do like you enough to want you for their very own private little pet. Officer Paul Tingle's got that pet-person look. If you've got a man who doesn't mind letting you in on the decision about what kind of pizza to buy or who doesn't get immediately pissy if you knock him down on his own bed, that's the man who eventually wants control of the checkbook and who thinks he ought to pick out your next car.

I'm laying here getting worked up as usual. Wondering if my chances are better squirming up toward the pillows or down toward the pile of blankets to get myself out of this mess. If he wakes up, there's too much chitchat to face and who wants that at three in the morning?

I decide on scooting my way up toward the pillows, and it works like a charm. I tiptoe around, gathering up my stuff so I can get dressed in the living room. I find everything but one of my socks. Minor casualty.

Outside, the famous San Francisco fog blots out all of the miles and miles of city lights I know I ought to be able to see from here. The fog's so thick that when I move it moves aside like I'm walking through smoke. And cold — damn, like a wet washrag plastering itself to you. The nice part is that it's so quiet. Same as when there's a big snowfall in Reno. The fog soaks up sound like snow does.

Paul Tingle's street is dead quiet. The curbs and driveways are crammed with cars. Working-stiff pigeons home to roost for a few hours. Bet a person like me could make a fortune down here. I only need to catch the slightest whiff of people whose goal in life is struggling and suffering to move up in the world, and I know all the seedy temptations they're going to fall for. I also know that someone close to them will be chomping at the bit to pay whatever it takes to find out what old Harv is up to so they can divorce or extort or otherwise fuck with him. The ones who make me sad are the ones who hate finding out they've been right all along. Having me to blame for making it real to them seems hardly to be worth the price. I ask if they're sure they want to know beyond a doubt what hubby or wifey is up to. Sure, sure, absolutely, they say. Nail the bum/bitch. I've never managed to talk a single one of them out of giving me money to go ahead and make the hell that they're imagining come to life in technicolor cinemascope on Kodak film. People are strange. Can't see how most of them can stand to look in the mirror. Can't see how others of them can sit across the dinner table from the person they're double-crossing night after night. But it's a living for me.

I bid a fond farewell to Paul Tingle. More like beat a hasty retreat. Nah, it's a fond farewell. I feel a lot like one of my surveille-ees, slipping the GTO into neutral and rolling out of Officer Tingle's driveway by pushing back with my boot. Once I get situated out on the steep street, I let the car coast backward a few hundred yards before firing up the engine because if I'm going to the length of sacrificing one of my socks in order to make a clean getaway, I'm sure as hell not going to let my car get me busted. The new headers are kind of loud for 3 AM even by Reno standards. I start the engine just long enough to back out of the driveway and get facing downhill so I can shut down and quietly coast – which turns out to be about as fast as I could drive. It's so steep, I'm riding the brakes, in fact. When I turn on the headlights everything turns ghostly, solid white. Can't see shit. At the bottom of the hill, I coast through the stop sign I didn't see til I was passing it, restart the engine, and head west at the cross street. Doesn't really matter if I can see much. I don't know where I am anyway.

I float along the invisible street, trying not to hit anything and thinking of breakfast. Bacon and eggs. No, corned beef hash and eggs. No, chicken fried steak and eggs. With a baking powder biscuit. Wishful thinking. I could probably come up with blueberry granola wheat germ macrobiotic pancakes and organic wildflower honey syrup easier.

What I need's a truck stop. A twenty – four hour,

eighteen-wheeler, greasy grits heaven on the Interstate. Of course that would mean I'd know where the Interstate was, and I haven't got a clue. A Denny's would do. A Bob's Big Boy. Sambos. Someplace plain and open all night. You get used to being able to have anything you want to eat any time of the day or night when you live in Nevada. The only enterprise that hasn't caught up with the 24-hour casino lifestyle — and apparently doesn't plan to — is the goddam bank, making it real hard for a big chunk of the population to get anything done with their money. I even know of a 24-hour dry cleaners on Wells Avenue. Never been by there when there weren't two or three people at the counter. And there's a wig shop on First or Second, I forget which, that's open by appointment at all hours. You can buy a marriage license day or night, seven days a week. Have a chapel wedding day or night, seven days a week, with flowers and an organist and witnesses. For all its faults, Nevada's pretty accommodating. Except for banks. They've got all of us by the short hairs. Doubt they'll ever change. Good thing casinos like to cash paychecks.

Paul Tingle's going to wake up with empty arms, poor thing. No note. Just a sock. I'm not big on politeness once I'm done with a guy. Not interested in the long goodbye or even the short one. As a matter of policy, I never never bring a guy back to my place. I know what I want: wham, bam, thank you, man. There are weak moments like I had with Officer Tingle in the Motel 6, but they're like sugar cravings: Ignore them long enough, and they'll go away. Works with men — don't know why I can't get it to work with booze and cigarettes. No staying power at all. With men, once is quite enough, contrary to Jacqueline Suzann's opinion. I mean, what is there after you've done it? It's going to be the same the next time and the next time and the next time. Quite frankly, it's going to be the same with the next guy, no matter how many positions there are. That's the part I never can figure out: If it's so easy for me to walk away, why do I need to walk into it in the first place?

Because it is an animal need. I just need to get laid, and after all these years, I still find that little pestering urge confusing. I've been known to go a year without sex, but then there it is again, and I have to go for it. Must be one of those leftover caveman primal thingies. Like needing to barbeque in the summertime. Mona used to say it was a simple lack of maturity. Mona always stays at least a little while with whoever she picked up. She even went so far as to get married. And get pregnant. And have that cute baby who's godknowswhere right now while I was off being Flack the Cavegirl. Time to come back to earth and to my senses and to the messes I've made over the past couple of days. Honeymoon's over. I gotta get out of this weird city. I think all the pot smoke has gone to my head.

I come up to a stoplight, and the white nothingness of the fog is brighter here, so this must be a main drag. I pick a direction – right – and turn and smack in front of me are the hazy but homey lights shining through red gingham curtains that can only be an International House of Pancakes, and my search is over before it really gets going. I pull into the only empty parking space in front.

The joint's jumping for this hour of the morning. Red ginghamed waitresses soft-shoeing by with steaming pots of great smelling coffee. The real working class of San Francisco in every booth. I take a stool at the counter, re-adjusting my eyes to everything suddenly being in focus again. There's a mug of coffee and a menu in front of me before I have a chance to ask for them. I'm not even quick enough to see who put them there. There's a folded newspaper on the seat next to me – the Chronicle – minus the green sports pages. I open it flat on the stool and read the headlines. Don't see my name in any of them, so I refold the paper.

My foot that's in the boot without the sock is freezing cold from the dampness. I curl and flex my toes to muster up some warmth. Mark Twain wasn't kidding about the coldest winter he ever spent being the summer he spent in San Francisco. I live where it snows, but the cold that comes with it doesn't seem to seep into your pores the way this wet air does. I'm chilled through but especially my one foot.

The gum-cracking waitress comes by, stands in front of me, tapping her pencil on the edge of her order pad until I finally realize she's not going to ask me if I'm ready to order, she's expecting me to hurry up and do it. I pick out hash and eggs and buttermilk pancakes. She refills my perfectly creamed coffee, snatches up the menu, and is off to her next customer without a thank'ye.

The crowd looks ocean-y. Fishing or shipping, judging from all the knee-high, black rubber boots. Lots of men dressed pretty much alike. A couple of tired-looking business types who either didn't make it home last night (tie loosened), or who've got Wall Street rockets in their pockets (tie tight). You've got to get up pretty early on the West Coast if you're going to play the East Coast's game. Those guys who didn't make it home, the loose ties, are going to hate life around nine AM.

Then I notice in the far corner, sitting alone and taking up a whole booth at breakfast rush, a black dude with a huge 'fro, wearing sunglasses at night. He appears to be propping up the weight of his head on his knuckles, his elbows resting on the edge of the table. He's definitely letting everybody know that he doesn't want to be messed with and is going to damn well take his time leaving. He's working on a half-finished strawberry milkshake in a tall soda fountain glass with a straw and a long spoon sticking out of it. He also has the steel

YOU MAKE ME TINGLE

container they made the shake in sitting in front of him.
There's nothing else on the table.

And you know how sometimes you can just tell someone's
staring at you, and you look up right at them and they really
are?

And it's Rodney. With a long line of black stitches running
from his forehead to his chin on the left side of his face. My
mouth falls open. His does, too. He takes his sunglasses off to
make sure he's seeing what he's seeing. He's got a black patch
over his left eye.

Right in the midst of old home week, the waitress drops my
plate of breakfast in front of me with a ceramic thud that makes
me jump. Rodney hasn't budged. He's still staring.

"Tabasco?" the waitress asks.

"Huh?" I answer.

She sighs irritably. "Ketchup?"

"No, thanks."

She screws up my coffee again and leaves.

Rodney stands up, puts his sunglasses back on, and starts
fishing around in his front pocket for money to pay his check.
He's got to pass me to get out the door, but I'm not going to
let him get that far. I pick up my plate and my coffee and move
toward his table. He looks around real fast for another way out
and finally sits back down.

"Hey, Flack," he says as I arrange myself at his table.

"Hi, Rodney. Small world, huh?"

"Yeah."

"You're alive."

"Yeah."

I cut my eggs into my hash. Sprinkle a lot of salt on the
whole works and dig in. Which is sort of hard to do because my
heart's pounding like crazy, partly from Rodney being still
alive and partly because my stomach is doing flip-flops over the

stitches on his face looking so gross. I guess he's watching me eat – his head's facing my way – but it's hard to tell, his glasses are so dark.

"Johnny do that?" I ask finally.

"Yeah." His voice is plenty angry. "Lost my eye."

"What a drag." Stupid thing to say, but there's so much that needs saying right now I can hardly control myself.

He points at the gauze on my neck. "You didn't exactly get out of it easy."

I touch my neck. At least it's quit seeping for now.

"Flesh wound. Handled. By a real nice group of ladies at a 7-Eleven, I might add."

"High tone."

Now eating's impossible. I push the plate to the side. He pushes his milkshake to the side and leans his back against the back of the booth, crosses his arms, and cocks his head like, "Is that all you've got to say?"

"Where's Pioche?" he asks.

I tell him the story. Mona's instructions. Tell him I can show him the paper if he wants to see it. Tell him about being drugged. Tell him that I don't know where the baby is. That I hope Mona was right about these people, but that I'd made up my mind to get Pioche back from them – whatever it takes.

He really looks hurt. He had his doubts about me all along where Pio was concerned, so what do I do but prove him exactly right. I should have kept her. Never kept the arrangement with Mr. Chan and Miss Ludden. I just did what I was told, figuring Mona knew best what to do with her own kid. Now looking at the hurt on Rodney's hurt face, I know I've screwed up. Just can't tell how bad.

He leans forward and points at me and says, "Anything bad happens to that baby . . ."

"Hey, I'm worried, too. But she's Mona's kid. Mona's

119

dead. What would you have done?"

"Sure as fuck not give her over to somebody I don't know."

"I was doing my goddam best, considering." He's starting to piss me off. "Shit, Johnny could have gone back out and finished you off if I hadn't . . . Everything got out of hand."

"I hear ya, I hear ya. I don't have to like it."

"I don't either. I'm working on it." I'm not. Yet. But it's on my list. "What else can you tell me about that night?"

He says, "Fuzz come. Sounded like a couple of them. Then lots more showed up. Lots of noise. Then everybody from the house come back from that Harrah's thing Mona sent them off to. Fuzz hangs out to talk to them. I could hear it off and on cuz I kept passing out. This shit goes on all night. But nobody comes looking for me around the place. Cops must have figured I split with the baby. I held myself together and kept from bleeding to death for a long fucking time until I thought it'd be safe to drag myself into Duke's place."

"Duke?"

"Cat that drives the Mercedes." Ah, yes. Smiley.

My turn. I tell him everything that went on after Johnny came back to the house that night, including the part where I butchered the bastard.

Rodney set his shades on the table. "What you see here," Rodney points at his face, "is nothing compared to what you don't see. But fucking Johnny's dead? Serves him right, you ask me."

"What about Mona? I figure she . . ."

"Fucker laid it on me in detail what he was going to do to her. Right before he carved me up. Heard him going back to the house. Heard him cussing her until I blacked out."

"Man," I say, "I could not find you. Didn't you hear me?"

He laughs a little but tries not to move his mouth much.

"Thought I was dreaming. You passed right by me. Practically stepped on me, but you was looking for someone standing up, not someone on the ground. Thought you was some spirit or a alien or something. Couldn't move my mouth or nothing."

"I probably would have killed you if I'd have found you."

"I wouldn't have let you."

"You'd have killed me."

"Damn straight if Johnny hadn'ta fucked me up like he did."

I take a couple of bites of breakfast.

"You know, I watched you with the baby," I say. "You seem like too good a guy to be mixed up with Johnny."

"Tell me about it. We fell in when he was at Stanford. Him and me made a lot of money off them rich kids. Wasn't no drug they wouldn't pay too much money for. Anyway, til he got his ass kicked out."

"Caught dealing?"

"Nah, man. Cheated on tests. Shit like that. He said why didn't I come with him back to Rancho Spaghetti-O. So, fuck it, I did. I could deal with him being a hothead and a liar. I could chill him out. But when the bullshit started with Mona and Michael . . ."

"She told me nothing was going on."

"Coulda been, coulda been not. What I do know is everything changed. Messed Johnny up big time. Changed him into somebody I did not want to know. But by then, they had put me in charge of Pio. At first I was pissed off about it, Johnny making me a shitty diaper changer. But they started paying me a shitload more money on top of the shitload I already got. And the fucking kid kind of grows on ya, dig?"

"Yeah, grew on me, too."

"I get that Mona was your friend and all. Wasn't like I

liked her or didn't like her. She was trouble come calling, so I kept my distance, right? I watched her like you watch a pet bear cub grow up because you know someday she gone to get too big for the house."

Rodney pulls the milkshake back over to him. Stirs it and takes a sip through the straw. He says, "Be glad when I can chew again." And he tries not to smile. I like him.

I light a cigarette. He motions for me to give him one, which I light for him.

"Where you staying?"

I tell him nowhere. We go together to the register to pay. If this was Reno, a black dude walking with a freckle-faced, redhead, white chick would stop a few forkfuls of food before they reached the intended mouth, but here, even in a place packed with the working class, no one so much as looks up. Or if they do it's to gawk at the scar on his face. It's really hideous, really fresh. Rodney looks like a badass. He's even playing it like a badass. These people will never know how he looked holding Pioche. How protective and gentle and completely uncriminal. For a criminal.

Rodney walked here from his sister's place. We drive back there in my car.

This is so weird.

And I hate weird.

Chapter 13

It's 5 AM. The door's wide open at Rodney's sister's apartment, lights blaring from every window. I can see the fog curling at the doorway, kept out by the heat inside. Sis is talking – more like yelling real fast – into the mouthpiece of a yellow telephone and yanking at the kinks in the knotted phone cord leading to the wall-mounted part of the unit. She's pacing and waving the hand that she's holding a cigarette in like she's trying to address an invisible crowd assembled in her kitchen. Beside the phone is an ivy plant that's growing all up and around the kitchen picture window and is beginning to take over the wall space where there's a torn poster of a Black Power fist on a dayglo pink background. The poster's got notes and photographs thumbtacked all over it. I see the shapes of several models of big and little firearms in the hands of most of the people in the photographs. Sis's hair is bigger than Rodney's and has a red 'fro comb stuck in the back. And she's wearing the biggest, purple-framed glasses I have ever seen. I don't know why it doesn't all shake loose off of her the way she's carrying on.

From the sound of her end of the conversation, someone needs to be bailed out of jail but apparently the legal defense fund of whatever civil rights organization this poor soul expects to be saved by has been raided by some unscrupulous comrade-in-arms, who also made off with a few prized pieces of office equipment and the Mr. Coffee.

Doesn't take long to find all of this out as fast as she's talking, but it takes even less time for her to size me up and decide not to like me. She turns her back on us with a disgusted sneer, and Rodney says we can go talk in the room she's letting him crash in.

"What's her name?" I ask after Rodney closes the door behind us so I can hear his answer over all the screeching expletives coming from the kitchen.

"Who? My sister? Euella."

"Oh. She carry on like that in the wee hours often?"

"All the time. Always in a uproar over something or somebody. Got to be when you're a big-shot urban guerrilla. She's a soldier in the army of the BAJP - Black American Justice Party. This week, anyway. Switches up a lot. Nobody minds. They all glad to have her as long as she wants to stay around. Somebody pisses her off and she's on 'fuck you' and her Black fist is in the air. Can't figure out why anyone puts up with her shit, but she's managed to make herself damn near as famous as Angela Davis."

Rodney's fountain of information dries up long enough for him to lick and stick the joint he's been rolling. He winces, putting it between his lips on the undamaged side of his face, and lights up. I go ahead and light up a cigarette to drown out the obnoxious pot smell, and between the dueling flavors, pretty soon we've got the small room so thick with smoke Rodney can't take it. He makes a couple of comical attempts to stand up on the bed, finally gets his balance on his long, skinny legs, and opens an almost useless slit of a barracks window high up on the wall. I can see daylight just hitting the green siding of the building next door that looks to be about an arm's length away.

We finish our smoke-out. Rodney lays back against some wild, op-art pillows and takes a bottle of pills out of his pants pocket. He tosses one at his mouth but his aim's off. He rummages around til he finds it and places it firmly on his tongue.

"Antibiotics," he says. "First time I had any." He smiles/grimaces. "Lousy high."

I get comfortable on my side at the end of the bed with my head propped up on one hand. I start picking at a purple thread that's coming loose from the bedspread. "Hey, you know," I say, "I've been wracking my brains trying to figure out what Mona's connection to someone in Hong Kong was. Never got to ask her. Never got to ask her about Johnny til it was too late, and look how that turned out. I'd feel a lot better if I knew she'd been importing Kewpie dolls or firecrackers or booking people on honeymoons with this Chan guy. I don't know. Just the sound of 'Hong Kong' gives this small town girl the creeps."

"Know what you mean. All James Bond and shit."

The raving in the kitchen had done nothing but intensify since we arrived. Now Euella's pounding on the kitchen table in between "motherfuckers." Finally I hear her slam down the phone, and she comes stomping up the hall, cussing all the way. Throws open the door to Rodney's and my little boudoir and stands there with her arms crossed, glaring at us.

"Thought you was done with white bitches," she says.

"She ain't my bitch. She's . . . She's a buddy of Mona's."

"Bitch."

I'm not sure if that's meant for me or for Mona, but Euella clears that up.

"Bitch buddy of a bitch."

Just so I know where I stand.

Rodney picks up a little hand mirror from the fruit crate that serves as a bedside table and moves it in front of him so he can survey the damage to his face in sections. He says, "Still can't get used to shit not being where I think I see it. Keep dropping shit and knocking shit over. Practically put my other eye out trying to comb my hair last night."

"What you get for fucking around with whitey," says Euella. "I told you, didn't I? I said you mess with whitey, they gone hurt you. You ought to be dead, umm huh. Ought to be dead."

"You mean like that brother last week who those cats in the BAJP beat near to death for forgetting the secret handshake or whatever bullshit he done?"

"Hey! Hey, professor. You don't fucking know what went down. Wasn't the same as you-know-who. You the one laid down with dogs." She fixes her fiery eyes on me, then glares back at him. "And you the one woke up with fleas." She leans toward me, and a little fleck of spit hits my forehead when she says "fleas."

"On and on," says Rodney. "On and on." He's still examining his face in the mirror. Euella smacks it out of his hand. It hits the wall, and the mirror pops out of the plastic frame but lands softly on the bed without breaking.

Euella says, "This is some shit. I give the man a place to

crash and look at the disrespect I get for my trouble. Bringing white women into my home. Spread her filth around my home. Well, you two go on, do what you want. Don't mind me. I just pay the rent here. I paid for the goddam bed you lounging on. And now I got to go waste my day with the jive-ass, honky pigs who got Muhammed Jones' black ass in jail for no reason but he got a black ass. It's oppression, man. It's the motherfucking honky establishment, man."

"What's the charge?" I have the stupidity to ask.

"Charge? Charge, she want to know?" Euella screeches. "Listen here, Miss Pasty-White—DAR-Cocktails-at-Five-Driving-a-fuckin'-Mercedes bitch, the charge is all the same for the Black man: you black, you go to jail, dig?" She looks satisfied with this explanation, but apparently the look on my face tells her I'm not sold.

"Gone be a revolution," she says. "A armed revolution so quick you whities won't know what hit you. You gone to pay for two hundred years of black slavery and oppression. Pay in blood. Malcolm and Huey and Bobby gone to lead us in the fight for freedom, and just like that every last one of you Wonder Bread motherfuckers is wiped off the face of the map. Then, THEN, we get liberty and equality and justice for everyone forever, amen."

I am so moved, I burst into furious applause. Rodney just lays back, half-smiling. I guess he's heard all this before. Times two. Same as everyone these days. Euella's stringy body is quivering with the intensity of her performance, her skinny chest heaving. All in all, not bad entertainment for 5 in the morning.

I say, "Can you tell me one thing before I die?"

"What, Miss White-Gloves-and-a-Matching-Handbag?"

"Aren't all those dead bodies going to make a hell of a stink? I mean, that's a lot of corpses to be getting rid of all at

127

once. I mean, if it's going to happen as fast as you're hoping, well, not to mention the stink, you've got your flies and your maggots, vultures, wild dogs. The usual. Have you made provisions for that?"

She crosses her arms. "Just like a honky. Don't care about nothing but the black man taking out the stinking garbage. When the time comes, sister," Euella says to me, "you mine. You going first."

"Thanks for the warning. I'll be expecting you."

She turns and stomps out of the room, grumbling about having work to do and no time to be educating simpleminded, no-lifers like myself and her race-traitor brother. Rodney sighs, spreads his hands apart in a gesture of futility.

"That's Euella," he says.

"Charming," I say. "Just like on TV."

"Yeah, TV," Rodney sits up and says, "TV . . ."

His thought fades off. I'd chalk it up to him being high, but he looks serious.

"What about it?"

"TV. The Betamax. You know about the Betamax? The camera?"

"Yeah, I have it. Mona stuck it in with all the baby stuff."

"She give you tapes?"

"Uh, one for sure."

"You watch it?"

"How am I going to do that? I have to have some kind of player-thing, right? What's on it?"

"Johnny, he used to make tapes. Had a bunch of them. Watched them all the time."

"Mona said that's how Johnny got the idea that she and Michael were getting it on," I say. "He taped them talking once."

"Oh, didn't know that. Figures, though. Johnny always

believed the first thing he believed about everything. Couldn't talk him out of a wrong idea. After what you been telling me, I wonder if there's something about what she done with Pioche."

Shit, why didn't I think of that?

"We have to get a look at that tape. Those tapes? Wow," I say.

"I know how to watch'em. I'll hook it up."

"Right on! Man, am I glad I ran into you!"

He takes another hit and almost smiles, but I can see how bad that hurts.

"It's coming back to me now: Chan said his company holds the suite where I met them for their private use. The hotel's got to know quite a bit about what goes on up there. I'm going to swing back by there, get a look at the register, maybe. Ask around. Somebody there has to know what goes on."

"You best be careful, super spy."

"I have my ways. Got to find Chan and Ludden."

"Gonna kill them, too?" he says and laughs a little bit from inside his throat.

"If I have to," I say.

He laughs again. "I think I'll give Duke a call. See if he got to the videotapes before the fuzz."

"Rodney, you sure about him? He didn't strike me as the cooperative type."

"He's pure pussycat if he likes you. He just don't like too many people."

"I think I'm one of them, so you might want to casually not mention my name."

"I won't. But I gotta get Pioche back."

"We'll get her. We'll get her." I stand up to leave, all pumped up with Rodney's new news.

"You need anything?" Rodney asks. "Food? Switchblade?
"

"No. How about you? You set?"

"I sort of left with the clothes on my back. Got plenty of money in Reno but not a goddam dime on me here."

I pull out the wad of bills Mona gave me, peel off an inch or so, and hold it out to him. Actually, I have to take his hand and put the money there so he doesn't miss and end up with a couple of grand flying all over the room.

"I'll get this back to you," he says.

"Don't bother. Isn't mine, anyway."

He nods, looking kind of sad, then he says, "Where you want to meet up later?"

"Not here." I've had all I can take of Euella's noisy politics.

"I'm hep." He throat-laughs again. "Just your luck I grew up here."

We go into the kitchen, and he draws me a map to the hotel and another one to this killer Italian food joint he knows on Green Street. We agree to meet at 7. He looks tired. I don't even want to think about the pain he must be in.

"Okay," I say. "See you there. Good luck with Duke."

"Good luck yourself." He tries to pat me on the shoulder but is way wide to the left. The way he sees the world, literally and probably figuratively, is all changed.

All new. He's the strangest bodyguard/babysitter I ever met. He's probably the only one who ever lived. I can't imagine him on defense mode, but I know damn well he's done it. That he's good at it. And I'd for sure want him on my side in a bar fight.

Chapter 14

Strolling into the Mark Hopkins lobby in my cowgirl outfit at 9 AM gets me way more attention than my sexy little black dress did last night. Who is this hick entering our fine establishment and offending our upper-crusty clientele? Wish I had my hat — my good white felt Stetson. That'd stir them up. Wish I had on my good Levis, too, but you can't have everything. I square my shoulders and pull myself up to my full five-foot (and a half) and stride to the front desk, swaggering like John Wayne, still trying to get my story straight in my head.

"May we help you?" asks the unfriendly friendly man, with perfect skin I might add, behind the front desk.

"Yessir," I Texas-drawl as best I can, "I'm lookin' for . . .

Hold on, pardner."

I pat every pocket I have and come up with my receipt from the House of Pancakes. I unfold it, pretending it's a note.

"Ah, here 'tis. I'm looking for Miz Ludden, Room 805. Might be 809, can't quite make it out."

"I'm sorry, I really can't give out information about our guests."

"Pardner, I 'spect you can't. Lotta shady characters 'round these days, yep'er. Listen, you ever heard of the Reno Pro Rodeo?"

"Well, distantly."

"See, I'm Virginia Oakley, Annie Oakley's great-great-granddaughter. You heard of her?"

"She's fictional . . ."

"No sir, she most certainly is not. She's the gunslingingest woman to ever, uh, sling a gun. Shoot the tip off a cee-gar in a volunteer's mouth at a hunnert paces."

I'm laying this phony accent on so thick I'm ready to crack up. The desk jockey looks ready to crack up, too. So, I'll lay it on a little heavier.

"Anywho, my mama met this Miz," I look again at the slip of paper, "Ludden at a soiree over ta the mayor's house in Reno a month or so ago. Two of'em really hit it off, can you feature?" I shake my head for emphasis. "I know: hard to believe, just durn hard to believe. Make a long story short, Miz Ludden told her that any old time any of us all was in Frisco, we should come on by and set a spell with her at this place. Or if we needed a place to stay when we's in town, why, she said y'all'd be obliged ta have us as her guests. Here I am then."

"Ma'am," the fresh-faced clerk begins in a whisper, leaning toward me, "I was not born yesterday, and I am far too busy to listen to your nonsense. I suggest you take your fake twang, turn right around, and leave before I call security."

I look aghast. I look mortified. I look stunned. I lean toward my nemesis. "Sir, we Oakleys don't take kindly to insults. No, we do not. Now, I'm gonna pick up that there phone and get Miz Ludden on the line. Got a coupla numbers here to try."

I grab the desk phone. He snatches it out of my hand like he's saving its life.

"Ma'am, you'll find public phones on the wall to your right."

I look over. Fancy. Gold booths. But I say, "Lobby pay phones?" I raise my voice. "What kinda outfit you running here? Pay phones for PAYING GUESTS? Why, that sounds like a load of horse-twaddle to me."

Horse-twaddle? Flack, you are outdoing yourself.

"Please lower your voice . . ."

I turn to the passersby in the lobby. "Y'all hear that? This slicker, this," I turn and read his name off his ID badge, "Mr. Kendrick's makin' a scene over me tryin' to use this here phone. Me, a paying guest."

I get a bunch of blank stares from the real guests. The hotel employees are looking at me as if they know my pain from experience, and also probably can't stand by-the-book Mr. Slickface Kendrick. It's enough of a divide between the haves and the have-nots to start a bit of murmuring, one side restless to get far away from me, one enjoying the show and discreetly taking my side. I hitch my thumbs in my belt loops and stride to one of the shiny gold phone booths. I pose for effect at the door before entering and shutting it behind me. Mr. Kendrick cradles the phone he saved from me and starts a rapid conversation, most certainly to security. I'm dialing and gesturing like a woman possessed and listening to the dial tone when a bellhop wheels a full luggage dolly over to me and motions for me to get on between a couple of long fur coats. I sneak on and am whisked away to a freight elevator.

"Thanks, man," I say.

"Don't mention it. I hate this fucking job. Where you want off?"

"Eighth floor."

"Groovy. You really related to Annie Oakley?"

"Nah."

"Far out."

We ride up the rest of the way in silence. When the doors open, he says, "Which room? I got master keys."

"Far out," I say. "805."

"Cool."

He lets me in, and I fumble through a hippie handshake with him. He flashes me the peace sign, tips his hat so the hat and his wig both come off, and long blond hair streams to his shoulders. We both laugh. I slip him 50 bucks, and he smiles, tucking his real self back in.

How lucky am I?

I extra-lock the door behind me, and when I turn around, expecting the place to be empty, I'm greeted with a sinisterly large handgun pointed at me by a woman in a black beehive hairdo and huge dark glasses.

"Susan Anne!"

"Mona? MONA?!!"

Chapter 15

You know that phrase, "You could have knocked me over with a feather?" Well, you could have. I'm so damn glad to say you could have. First Rodney, now Mona? How lucky am I?

We say simultaneously, "YOU'RE ALIVE!"

We run to each other and hug and both start crying.

"How did you . . .?"

"How did we . . .?"

"Where . . .?"

"What . . .?"

"I never expected . . ."

"Fuck!"

"Shit!"

"I hate you!"

"I hate you more!"

"I can't believe this!"

It's stupid, I know, but that's about all we can say at the moment. Then she notices the bandage on my neck.

"Johnny?" She touches it.

"Yeah. Nothing serious."

"And he's . . .?"

I nod.

"You?"

"Yeah."

She bows her head. She liked him. Might have loved him even. She pulls off the wig and sunglasses, shakes out her massive blonde mane. She's not wearing a stitch of makeup, which is a first since she started at age nine. She looks great without it. You can see her freckles, which she hates but I think, have always thought, make her all the more beautiful. So are the tiny crow's feet starting in the corners of her eyes.

"How did you find me?" she asks.

"I didn't, knucklehead. I thought you were dead. I came here looking for Chan and that Miss Ludden. And your fucking baby."

"I'm not even going to ask who let you in."

"I have my ways."

"I need a drink."

"Ditto."

I plop down on the plush velvet sofa and stick out my hand. A very generous portion of what I hope is Jim Beam is thrust into it. I down the whole works and stick my hand out again so Mona can refill me while she's still up.

"Lazy ass."

"Just taking advantage of a rare opportunity."

Mona flops down right next to me like she has to reassure herself that I'm real and in the flesh. She's drinking at a more ladylike speed.

I swallow my drink in one swig. "I saw Rodney this morning."

"You WHAT? Oh my God!"

"Yeah, we had breakfast together. Supposed to get dinner later."

"Oh my God! How is he?"

"Johnny cut him up good. Lost an eye but breathing."

"Oh. My. God." Mona drains her drink, gets up for more, and I wave my empty glass at her.

"Jesus, Susan Anne, are you trying to kill every brain cell?"

"What brain cells?"

"So, where is he? Rodney?"

"Staying with his sister, one of those Angela Davis types. Barrel of laughs."

"They have a point, you know."

"Another time, Mahatma. Where's the kid?"

Mona gets up and walks to the window, sipping her drink. "Mo?"

She comes back, sets her drink on the table, sits down with a sigh, and cradles the sides of her face on her fists. Her smooshed-up face would prompt a sarcastic comment from me usually, but now is not the time.

"Florida," she says, though it sounds more like "Floo-da."

"Not Hong Kong?"

She shakes her head.

"Chan and Miss Ludden?"

She shakes her head.

"MO! Seriously! Where is Pioche?"

A sigh. She leans back into the couch cushions.

"With her dad." She closes her eyes.

We've never really discussed him. I figured if he didn't matter to her, he sure as hell was none of my business.

"Shamar. Shamar Cook. Used to be Danny when we were married. Before he went all Haile Selassie on me. All Jah love."

"All what? Who? Jah?"

"Rastafarian."

"Rasta . . . what?"

"Never mind. Pioche is in Florida with her dad."

"Is she okay?"

"Of course she is. I knew Chan would help. He owed me. I knew I was in deep with that Johnny thing. I'm still in deep — especially with him gone. I never told anyone at Johnny's who Pioche's real dad was. Said it was a one-nighter. Some guy I picked up at a disco in Martinique. Truth was, we were married. Tight. Danny, Shamar, is a pilot. Back then I had connections from, uh, another, uh, partner you don't want to know about. I made the deals, and Danny flew the products in and out. You don't need to know from where. Went along like clockwork. We were making money hand over fist. We were great together. Then I got pregnant. And we had a, a little skirmish with the cartel. If it had been me by myself . . . But there was the baby. Our baby. I stayed put to put on a show like everything was as usual."

"Yep. Hey, what's a cartel?"

"You don't want to know that either."

Mona refilled her drink.

"We had everything going along just fine. Then x, y, and z happened, and I fled back to Reno, where I at least knew my way around. I had plenty of cash, so we — Pioche and I — kept mobile. In comfort, of course. I have more aliases and more passports than I can count. And a baby is great cover. People either fell in love with her and ignored me or compared her skin color to mine and gave us a wide berth. Then Johnny. You saw him. How could I resist?"

"I could give you about ninety million ways . . ."

"I mean, he had it all. Money, power, charisma . . ."

"A big dick?"

"Well, duh. I'd rented the penthouse suite at his casino in Tahoe. The Tah-Win? Pioche and I had the hotel staff wrapped around her little finger. Babysitting at a moment's notice. I was a countess visiting from Austria at the time. It was so much fun being her. All the jewels and furs. Fake accent. I was playing faro one night when Johnny stopped by the table. We immediately bonded."

"I think I'm gonna be sick. How stupid, Mo."

"I know, I know. It had just been Pioche and me for months. I needed . . ."

"I get it. I get it. I don't need technicolor."

"I let him sweep me off my feet. I saw what I wanted to see. I believed what I wanted to believe. Things moved fast around him. Intrigue. Excitement. Money. Famous people always at his house: Sinatra, Bobby Gentry, Tom Jones. It was fun. And glamorous. Eventually, I told him who I really was, where I had come from, but not about Shamar or any of that. He loved that I was a real Nevadan — you know how we all are."

"Home means Nevada. Battle Born."

"Nevada is like a drug: dangerous, bad, and so sexy."

"Gotta agree with you there." She was starting to make me homesick. And I've only been away three days!

"But then," she said, "I started to see an assortment of suspicious characters hanging around, as well as a fairly big contingent of politicos. They would have these closed-door meetings that went on all night sometimes. Quite often there would be arguments and shouting and doors banging and cars peeling out on the gravel. All I could think was, 'Oh no, not again!' I just seem to have an instinct for trouble."

"Ya think?"

"Susan Anne . . ."

I hold up my hands in surrender.

"Sorry," I say. "Go ahead."

"And it brings us here: My baby is thousands of miles away, and I'm stuck in a hotel room with you."

"Mona, is Pioche safe?"

"Safer than with me. For the moment."

I know that wasn't saying much, but I decide to keep my mouth shut.

"I haven't had contact with any of them – Chan, Shamar, Miss Ludden. They'll let me know when things are safe." She slumps further into the couch. "I'm exhausted. So fatigued. I don't know what to do, whom to trust – except you. I'm so glad you found me."

"Me, too. I'm glad you're not . . . you know."

Mona laughs. "Thanks."

I stand up, clap my hands, and muster up my best phony positive attitude.

"What do you say to some Italian food? Supposed to be the best in The City."

"What would you know about good food – especially in The City?"

"A little birdie told me."

"A little birdie missing an eye?"

"You got it."

Mona's face brightens. She stands up from the couch and stretches.

"Just one little minute while I put on my face," she says, sashaying out of the room.

I kick off my boots and lie down on the couch. Might as well catch some shut-eye. She can wake me in the hour and a half she'll waste on her already beautiful face.

• • •

I know I keep saying how I hate weird. I mean it. But all my life, just breathing seems to draw more weird in on me. Mona and Rodney are still alive! That's weird. To find them both on the same day? Double weird. I'd never believe half the stuff that happens to me if it was somebody else's story. I'm telling you: You can't make this shit up. It's just too, well, weird.

Chapter 16

From a very young age, Mona had a city girl's taste for comfort and convenience and, above all, cleanliness. She didn't ride horses or take off walking up a hill just to enjoy the view or swim anywhere but in a hyper-chlorinated pool. She wouldn't drink out of a garden hose or catch grasshoppers or eat snow. She could keep her tennies white-white, which, with the Nevada dust and wind, is a near impossibility. I couldn't even get her to eat jerky. Dirty peasant food, she claimed. No toasted marshmallows for her. No proximity to a campfire ever, for that matter.

Me? My family were desert rats. We took off any chance we could get for some dry camping anywhere off-road. We had this beat-to-death, used-to-be white '51 Chevy pickup with holes in the wooden bed you could watch the pavement through when you were riding in the back. My pop put up side rails made of old barn wood on it so we could pile in supplies – water, tents, camp chairs, cooking stuff, food for us and a horse or two, guns and ammo – and go out to the empty desert and pick a direction. We got stuck a lot. Part of the fun. Getting stuck in the sand or sometimes in the water gave us a puzzle to solve with teamwork and muscle. Bagging quail or sagehens or cottontails (never jackrabbits, filthy things) gave us sport and dinner. We dug latrines, built fire rings, and cleared every scrap of anything flammable in a wide circle. We sat out watching blazing sunsets as the day cooled into night, singing "Don't Fence Me In" and "Tumblin' Tumbleweeds" by the fire as the stars came out. As the Milky Way streaked over our heads. Then we slept in our zipped-up tents to keep the rattlesnakes from slithering into our sleeping bags to keep warm.

We'd come back to town in a cloud of dust, every inch of our clothes and our bodies and all that we had taken with us covered in fine sand. The only clean-ish skin on us was around our eyes from rubbing the blowing sand out of them. We'd be tired and sunburned and totally happy and hungry. Our welcome home dinner was always Dinty Moore beef stew with a fried egg on top. Tabasco to taste. We'd eat and fall into our beds and sleep like the dead. In the morning we'd start talking about where we wanted to go next.

I invited Mona a couple of times. No way. She just could not see that in all that dust and desolation there was indescribable beauty. I tried to explain it to her, but there really are no words. I told her so. That you just had to be there.

"YOU," she said, looking up from her latest crush in the latest Tiger Beat, "just have to be there. I'd rather lounge by the pool at the Beverly Hills Hotel and have the cabana boy bring me mai tais."

"Mai tais?"

"It's a drink. A booze drink."

"Oh."

I figured that's what happened to a person who read too much. She was definitely one of them. She knew about so much she really knew nothing about because she'd read about it somewhere. She could make it sound like she'd done and seen a lot. But I could never feel it. That's the thing about reading: No matter what the subject is, it stays at a distance, out of reach of smell and touch and taste. Knowing about something from reading is like swimming in that chlorine pool. Sure, it's water, but it isn't adventure. There's nowhere to go, nothing to step on that may or may not be pleasant, no hidden treasures to find. With words, you get to find out what something's about but not really what it is. That's why I don't read. I don't have time to sort things out from words. There's so much actually happening to take in with my senses that adding a layer of paper over the top seems like too much work.

Chapter 17

To put it in today's slang, Rodney was "blown away" when he saw Mona again. He stood up so fast at the restaurant that he knocked the table completely over, setting candle wax on fire on the tablecloth. A waiter ran over with a red fire extinguisher and sprayed it out. I was thinking he could have just stepped on it. Leave it to a city slicker to go to extremes. Rodney didn't seem to notice any of the hubbub going on around him – the alarmed patrons, the scurrying staff. Rodney lunged over the mess and squished Mona in his arms. The two of them had a tremendous cry. I just stood there wondering who I had to blow to get a drink in the place.

We settled in for, I have to say, another one of the best meals I have ever eaten. Mona caught him up on her news. I

145

drank. Rodney caught her up on his news. I drank. Now we're back in the Mark Hopkins, getting ready to see what's on the Betamax tape.

Rodney hauls this big metal suitcase up to the room and starts unpacking. There's a big black doodad with a bunch of dials and junk, and what I recognize as a camera like the one I got out of the pawn shop with the ticket I got off murdered Michael in my office. Rodney takes out a bunch of wires and hooks A into B and C into D or something along those lines.

"Where's the tape?" he asks.

"Oh, right." I rummage around in my bag and hand it to him.

He turns all the crap on, slides the tape cartridge into a little slot that pops up on top, and pushes it down. A staticky image comes on the little screen on the camera. Then in a blink of an eye, there's Johnny in his game room rolling a cue ball around on the pool table. He's talking to someone we don't see yet.

"Man," he says, "I'm getting tired of all this fucking around. Let's get this goddam thing handled and handled pronto."

Another voice says, "We're working on it. Honest to God. He's just . . . he's coming up with one excuse after another."

"Think I give a flying fuck? Get it handled!"

"Johnny, see, there's all this legal . . . What you're trying to do, see? It's, it's complicated."

Johnny heaves the cue ball that lands with a meaty thud.

"Fuck, man, I think you broke my rib!"

"How'd you like me to break your fucking neck?"

He grabs a cue stick and charges out of the picture. We hear many, many meaty whacks and curses and grunts and screams and finally nothing. Johnny comes into focus, wiping at blood splatters on his face. He reaches out, and the screen goes dark then back to static.

"Whoa!" Mona and I say together. Just as we're catching our breath, the picture comes back on, this time in a bedroom. A door opens at the back of the room, and in walks Mona, stark naked.

"Uh, WHAT?" she cries.

Rodney looks at her and smiles. I can't help giving a little tee-hee.

Mona spreads her beautiful body seductively out on the bed, adjusting her blonde hair to partially hide one side of her face and one breast.

"Do we HAVE TO?" She's covering her eyes.

"YES!" Rodney and I exclaim in unison, grinning from ear to ear. Mona covers her face with a pillow.

Without going into all the gory details of a nicely orchestrated bit of pornography that has nothing to do with any crime in question, Rodney and I both whistle and clap and yell "ENCORE!" at the end. I'm not trying to be difficult, just sticking with the facts of the case. But Johnny does have a nice ass. And now I have proof of the big dick as well. The screen goes to static again.

"Wish I'd thought to bring popcorn," I say to which Mona hits me repeatedly with the pillow. I light a cigarette and pretend ecstasy.

"I hate you," she says.

"I hate you more."

"Pour me another drink, jerk." Holds her glass out to me.

Rodney stops the tape, takes a joint out of his vest pocket, and lights up.

In the first two movies the camera stays in one spot, but in the next one, someone must be holding it and walking because there's a lot of jiggling, and we're outside somewhere. Doesn't take long to recognize that we're at what is not-so-affectionately known as Carson Bridge. For reasons that must be known to someone, when they widened Highway 395 through Washoe Valley to four lanes between Reno and Carson City, they — whoever "they" were — decided to build an overpass complete with on- and off-ramps across our spanking new freeway. It's a nice one, the overpass. Swankiest bridge in all of Nevada, maybe.

Here's the thing: the bridge goes nowhere. The east end dies out on the shores of that lovely mud puddle we call Washoe Lake; the other side stops at the fenceline of the Steens Ranch. All that concrete and steel for what? AND the thing fell down! School kids sang, "Carson Bridge is falling down, falling down on the new freeway." Then they, whoever "they" are, rebuilt it. The only thing I know it's ever been used for is to teach driver's ed students how to enter and exit a freeway because there are no other on and off ramps anywhere for hundreds of miles.

As non-political as I am, I just thought Carson Bridge was a dumb joke. I didn't think about the millions of dollars it cost or whose pockets it lined. Those kinds of things are way over my head. And boring, too.

Now here it was on the Betamax screen. The cameraman is moving toward a group of men in suits standing around talking at the west end of the bridge. They see the camera and start yelling, "TURN THAT THING OFF!! WHAT'S THAT FUCKING THING FOR?!! ARE YOU CRAZY?!"

"Here, take this." The picture goes all sideways and screwy.

I know that voice.

Johnny comes into the viewscreen.

"Got it?"

"Yeah." I know that voice, too: naked, dead Michael.

Johnny walks over to the men. "It's just ME. Cool it!"

"What's the fucking camera for?"

"Hobby, man, hobby," he says. "You know me, you know Michael. We're just screwing around. Making home movies. Want copies?"

He's blowing them off big time. They're not loving it, but you can tell they know better than not to buy it. "Anyway, hi guys. Hey, Bud. Tom. Steve. Good to see you." Et cetera.

"So," Johnny continues, spreading out his arms, "this is it. From over there then to that white fence post way over there. This is the last piece of dirt we need, and, goddammit, Steen won't budge. Neither will Anderson."

The group nods, looks all concerned and serious all of a sudden.

"We're going to need you fellas to call in your markers, circle the wagons, bust some kneecaps — joking! — whatever it takes to get these last 10 acres or there's no easement. You all know what this racetrack will do for your cities and counties. Hell, for Northern Nevada. Fuck Vegas. Horse racing — top quality, high stakes . . . I don't have to tell you what kind of money we're talking about.

I'm thinking I recognize faces, but the screen is so tiny I'm not entirely sure. And like I said, politics bores the boots off of me, so I can't definitely tell the players without a scorecard. Looks to me like Johnny-boy is holding court with the Ormsby and Washoe county commissioners, state representatives, gaming commission muckety-mucks, and I'm guessing a Laxalt or two.

"El Washoe Downs is this close to being a reality. Permits are in the pipeline, thanks, guys; contractors are set. All we're waiting for is this last puny bit of land."

A bunch of voices talk over each other: "You can count on us." "We're on it." "We'll get them." Blah, blah.

"In the meantime," Johnny says, then reaches for

something outside the picture, "have a little taste of what's coming."

He walks toward the group carrying a briefcase that he sets on the ground and opens. He takes out a pile of thick manila envelopes and hands them out. The men joke around, pretending to be checking the weight of their haul.

Johnny looks back toward the bridge and waves. The camera makes a too-quick, nauseating turn, and we can see a black stretch limo coming over the bridge. The camera swerves again, and Johnny's face comes into focus. The men notice the limo, and suddenly look real uncomfortable. He's already scared the shit out of them with the Betamax, so they're edgy.

"Hey, hey," he says, "it's cool, it's cool."

The limo pulls up in a cloud of dust and stops, and out steps a rainbow of slinky, mini-skirted, ultra-bouffanted, long-legged showgirls carrying a bottle of champagne in each hand. The girls are shrieking and giggling. The guys are cheering and whooping.

"Party favors!" says Johnny.

Everyone's getting down to business, boys being boys, money and women giving them amnesia.

Johnny says, "Let's cut it. Those worthless pricks make me sick."

The picture wobbles around, goes to static, then black.

We're all quiet for a minute.

"Did you two know about this?" I ask.

Rodney says, "The plans, yeah. The videotape? Nah."

"This, this . . . this is . . ." Mona sputters.

I know what this is: Time for me to get my ass back to Nevada.

Chapter 18

Oh. Boy. What a revoltin' development. Wish I wasn't such a freak about truth, justice, and the American way. I should just let this go. It's none of my business. Is it?

But, you know what? I take "Home Means Nevada" way too seriously. Never lived anywhere else — never want to. I am Battle Born to the soles of my size 7s. Cut me, I bleed Nevada blue. I was born with a CC mint silver dollar in my mouth. The one-armed bandit is my friend. Dust devils and chapped lips and Model Dairy milk. Awful Awfuls at the Carson Nugget where they claim to send out winners to get players. My halo is neon. The Friday all-you-can-eat seafood buffet at Harrah's is my altar. And I can't stand it when crooked politicians are only too happy to take payola to help scum like Johnny screw up the beautiful countryside that is Washoe Valley. With all the desert sitting there empty that a racetrack wouldn't hurt a lot less, why Washoe Valley? Besides, the wind out there whips like a banshee, affectionately known as the Washoe Zephyr, just a normal 40-mile-an-hour evening breeze. Yeah, there's rattlesnakes and scorpions and red ants and tumbleweeds. No big deal. Yeah, Washoe "Lake" is pretty much a mudhole of wild levels of full or empty. Some years there's one big lake, some years one big and one little. Some years just mud. And the catfish? They're little, but the spiny, fanged bastards will rip you to shreds in a heartbeat. They do make good eating if you're up to the task and bring pliers and leather gloves.

None of these things make the Valley any less beautiful. On the east side, the tan hills make the sky look bluer. On the west side, the pine trees come right down to the valley floor. Bowers Mansion is over there. The Bowers built it with a massive silver mining fortune in 1863. Now it's a county park with a swimming pool. A really nice one. Out of the wind just enough. Tucked away just enough. The west side is the "good side." Big ranches with actual grass. It's sort of boggy out there, amazingly. Slide Mountain looms all grey granite and snow in the background. I'm sorry, that land is too pretty to get the Johnny Ruggerio treatment. I can't be in possession of the information on this Betamax tape, not turn it in to the authorities, and still call myself a Nevadan. I can't let that happen.

I'm deep in my revery when Mona finally forms a coherent sentence.

"This is what he needed the money for."

"Come again?" I ask.

She lights a cigarette, takes another swig. "Now, stay calm. Just hear me out . . ."

"I'm not liking the sound of this, Mo."

"No, you're not going to like it. Or me, for that matter . . ."

Now I need a smoke and a swig. Rodney is sitting with his hands in here's-the-church-here's-the-steeple position, just waiting for the fireworks.

"Shortly after Johnny and I met — well, shortly after I moved in with him . . ."

"Which I'm sure was shortly after you met."

"Cute."

"Well . . ."

• • •

Right here, I'm going to skip ahead. Blah blah blah, Rodney and I headed back to our respective residences to grab our crap for a probably dangerous and certainly unwise road trip back home. I don't want to have to tell the story twice because, as it is I've got a lot of explaining to do to a lot of people, and I definitely wouldn't waste your time on all of it. Have patience. I'm pretty sure this is going to get good.

It gets good right here at the Motel 6.

The door to my luxury suite is crisscrossed with yellow crime scene tape.

Shit.

Chapter 19

Crime scene tape is not a good thing to come across in any circumstance, but it's kind of really extra super-duper-scary when it involves you. At least there's no chalk outline or signs of smoke or shrapnel. The door and window aren't broken — which is good — and there's an official-looking note on hot pink paper taped to the wall.

I've been invited to the police department.

Goodie gumdrops.

I rip all the festive wrapping down. My key still works. I let myself in. Slowly. Carefully. Hand inside my bag, finger on the trigger of the Python. A quick recon shows no evidence that anything has moved since I left. The bed is still unmade. A towel and my underwear are still on the floor in the bathroom exactly where I left them.

I turn to close the door. Guess who's standing there with the light gleaming off his blond hair and his mirrored sunglasses flashing at me where his eyes should be?

"Officer Tingle, I presume."

He takes off the glasses, hangs them on his pocket in that way that is so individually him.

"Um, wanna come in?"

He shuts the door behind him, crosses his arms over his chest, and I fully expect to hear him say, "Where have you been, young lady?"

Which he doesn't. He takes a cop notebook out of his pocket, flips through the pages. He looks more like he's buying time to collect his thoughts rather than looking for information.

I'm right. He puts the little black book away.

"Susan Anne Murrow, aka Flack Murrow. 28. 5 foot no inches. 101 pounds. Hair, red. Eyes, green. Social Security number 530-22-5667. Birthday November 17th. Private detective. Merry Wink Motel, Space 6, Reno, Nevada. Phone number 702 . . ."

I sit down on the bed. "Awright already, you can stop now."

He sure looks like he lost his best friend. "Gladys Newbury. Right. You are a person of interest, you know."

"Sure, I know you're interested."

"Cut the crap."

Oops, not funny.

"Where's the baby?"

Wow, I'm pretty jazzed not to have to lie. "With her father."

"Who is who and where?"

"I am not at liberty to disclose them or their

whereabouts."

"I'm going to ask you again: where are they?"

"They're fine. Really."

"Where?"

"I'm not at liberty . . ."

Boy, is he unhappy with me.

I get worked up into the best huff I can manage. "Look, I don't have to tell you anything. I'm not under arrest."

"Yet."

"Okay, yet. All the welcome home confetti out there, was that your doing?"

Paul Tingle shakes his head. "Oh no, but I was lucky enough to overhear an interesting story in the precinct house. About a missing Reno woman who may have information about a pretty grisly murder. A woman matching your description who may have fled to San Francisco. With a baby. Baby girl? Brown skin, black hair, black eyes, about a year old . . ."

"Not quite a year . . ."

"They're looking for you, Susan Anne."

"I prefer Flack, and I can explain. Soon. I think."

"You don't have to explain to me, but you do have to accompany me to the precinct."

I crisscross my arms. "Not unless you arrest me."

"I can do that," he says, removing the cuffs from his duty belt.

"Oh man! Really? After all we've been through together?"

Think fast, Flack. Rodney's waiting.

"Can I get my one phone call?"

"Sure. After you're booked."

"On what charge?"

"Resisting arrest."

"Arrest for what?"

"Give me a minute."

"Give me my phone call."

Mona and I made up a bunch of codes when we were kids so we could alert each other of changes of plans because of parent avoidance or whatever, depending on the severity of the situation and the level of emergency. If things were just generally sucking, we'd say, "I got a C on the test." If we couldn't get away, we'd say, "Laugh-In was pretty funny this week, huh?" If we needed to escape and meet immediately, we'd say, "I'm wearing the jeans jacket I got at Sears," where neither one of us would be caught dead shopping ever. This code meant, "I'm fucked. Stay by the phone. I'll call when it's safe." Of course, as we grew up the codes grew, too, so now I could say, "Mom, you're just going to have to trust me."

As soon as I call her "Mom" when she picks up the phone, Mona knows what's coming and plays along, waiting for it. Paul Tingle has not taken his eyes off me for a second.

"Hi Mom. Yeah, I know you're waiting for me. Something's come up. No, nothing bad. I'll just be a little late. Mom, you're just going to have to trust me. Okay? Love you, too. Bye."

Not great, but what do you want on the spur of the moment? I stretch out my arms for the cuffs.

"Or," I say, "do I look dangerous enough to put them behind my back?"

Chapter 20

He's so damn cute. And nice. I kind of like him. And there's that other thing he's good at. Plus, we've barely met and already gone on a couple of cool adventures together. If our lives weren't totally oil and water, you know I'd give him a run for his money he'd never forget.

Help me out here: I'm trying to be a big girl and talk myself out of my attraction. All the good parts I mentioned? Oh, it gets better.

Officer Paul Tingle let me go.

I know, right? It was real neighborly of him. I didn't even have to cry or shoot him or anything nasty. Now he's got a lot of heat to deal with. I'm touched, I truly am, that the silly sap is doing this for me. Turns out he does have that dash of the criminal mind that drives a man into the police force rather than turning him into a car thief that robs liquor stores for fun and profit.

There's a lot to be said for the silent treatment. He put me in the back seat of the squad car, and I clammed up, mostly because I couldn't come up with a good reason for him to turn me loose. I was thinking. Appears he had a chance to do some thinking, too. He turned the car around, drove me back, opened the door, and stood aside looking at the pavement. When I tried to give him a hug, he held up his hand like he was directing traffic to stop. Never looked up. What could I do but go inside, lock the door, and call Mona to tell her I had a close call that I'd explain later.

I literally throw my belongings over the rail into the parking lot. Back the GTO up to the stack and toss it willy-nilly into the trunk. Now to grab my henchmen and get the hell out of Dodge.

I like being on the road. Mostly I like the leaving part of most trips better than the arriving. The drive is that step into the future. Whether the destination is fun and frolic or drenched in blood, there's something new on the road mile after mile. This part now, leaving San Francisco, borders on thrilling. With that one hunky exception. Shake him off, Flack. He deserves better than your unreliable, lying ass.

I swing by the Mark Hopkins and pick up Mona and all her shit – which is a lot – under the schmancy awning. The red-coated, gold-trimmed doorman tries to help her with her mountain of necessities and is turned away with an elegant display of firm dismissal and a wad of cash. He backs away, bowing. I see him counting. He turns around for just a second, his jaw hanging open. I swear if we were anywhere else, he'd jump up and click his heels. But he is a professional through and through. With Mona's cash steaming in his pocket, he's now offering his services to a woman in a white fur coat who hands him the reins of two giant wolfhounds.

Mona throws her mountain of luggage and crap in about as sloppily as I did, but it takes up so much more room. I watch her try to close the trunk. Then the two of us try sitting on it.

"We'll have to use the back seat," I say. We start unpiling and repiling until the mess is off the sidewalk, into the car, and there's barely room for us.

"Where're we going to put Rodney?" I say.

"Oh, that's right!" She has three makeup cases piled on her lap and four gigantic purses blocking the stick shift. I can't see out the back window and get honked at when I pull out in front of a limo. The side mirrors on my car are so small they're pretty much useless for letting me know what's going on back there.

Rodney has only a small gym bag, a green, yellow, and red striped backpack, and a real talent for squeezing himself into tight spots in spite of his long legs and giant hair. He doesn't seem all that surprised at the clutter, just lights a joint and rolls down the window.

And we're off.

Mona says, "Are you going to tell me what held you up?"

"Some day."

"I hate you."

"I hate you, too."

"Like a drink?"

"Thought you'd never ask."

With this, we leave The City. The sparkling Bay. The Transamerica Building. Coit Tower. The Bay Bridge. Left on I-80 toward home. Rodney's asleep with his head on a pink satin pillow before we're out of Oakland.

"You have a look about you, Susan Anne."

"Oh yeah?"

"You look freshly fucked."

"Oh yeah?"

"Around the eyes . . ."

"I don't want to talk about it."

"A-HA! You did!"

Ever seen a redhead blush? It starts at the neck and climbs right up the old kisser. I am whiter than powdered sugar. The only color I ever pick up is freckles. And the freckles? Well.

"My god," says Mona, "you are transparent."

"Gee, thanks."

"Tell or I'm jumping out of this car."

"Have a nice fall."

Dammit! I've gone and made her sad. Never have been able to stand that. I don't even have to look at her to feel any worse than I already do, so . . .

I take a deep breath. "He's tall. Blond. Looks good in blue. A police officer, actually. Paul Tingle. Officer Tingle. Officer Paul Tingle. He was arresting me when I called you."

There is a brief pause while she collects herself before cracking up so wildly she gives herself a coughing fit and ruins her makeup crying. A false eyelash dangles. I hand her the flask. And a Kleenex.

When she can finally speak, she says, "Susan Anne, you never fail to delight me! Tingle! Indeed! Rodney, did you . . . oh, he's still asleep. Tingle! Let's see: he was taking you in for indecent exposure . . ."

"Well, he could have . . ."

"Or kidnapping . . ."

"He could have done that, too."

"TINGLE!" she says again and sets herself off. "I really do wish you'd get a life, my dear."

"Who needs a life when you have a sense of humor and such a fine audience?"

"Tingle!" She's running out of steam finally.

The first thing I'm going to do when we get home, after I sleep for twenty or thirty hours, is saddle up Rockalee and ride out into the desert for a day or two. All this company over the past few days has gotten under my skin in a big way. I'm used to being alone, and with all this bullshit going on, I have not had one moment to myself. Not one quiet, uninterrupted, soothing moment. At this rate, someone's going to die if I don't get some peace.

"If you're done making fun of me," I say, "I'd like to know where I'll be dropping your annoying ass off."

Mona waves her hand to shush me and takes the last drink out of the flask. She reaches into the black leather Dior bag on the console between us and pulls out another flask.

"Wow, talk about being prepared," I say.

"Boy Scout through and through," she replies. She takes a deep, cleansing breath. "Clearly, I'm not going back to Johnny's."

"Crystal."

"I had thought I'd check back in at the Mapes."

"Could."

"Or the Riverside. It's really improved of late."

"Okay."

"What about you?"

"My trailer's at the Merry Wink, but Officer Tingle told me they're looking for me over the Johnny thing."

This sets her off on a new spurt of laughing. And drinking. I feel like it's just as well she keeps thinking I'm kidding; both of us are in so deep.

"I'm thinking we need to be as undercover as possible for now, Mo. I'm thinking good hotels are out."

"No matter what you say I am NOT coming with you to that dismal bucket of tin you call home. I need a long, hot bubble bath, a massage, and room service."

"You need a hideout."

"Aren't we just the Babyface Nelson."

"Seriously. We have to keep our heads down while I get the lay of the land."

"How do you intend to do that, Sherlock?"

"I'm a private detective, remember?"

"Right you are. Such a comfort."

Rodney snorts himself awake.

"We there yet?" he asks.

"Not even to Auburn," I tell him.

"Groovy," he says, plumping up his pillow. He's out like a light again.

"That man has a heart of gold," Mona says.

"And lousy taste in friends."

"Loyal to a fault, that one."

"Sure is. Sure loves Pioche."

"I hope I'm doing the right thing by her. I miss her."

"Me, too."

"Me, too," Rodney says sleepily.

This is one car-full of trouble. But it's a nice day for a drive. May. Summer just waiting to blast us. Hot days, blue skies, cool nights. I keep trying not to think about what all could be, probably is, waiting for us back in Reno. I'm retracing my steps, trying to remember what I said to who, who saw me where. Who's on first. I'm hoping Grady is still a pal. Going to need him. Got to get this Betamax to him. Someone I can trust.

"Susan Anne?"

"What?"

"I . . . there's . . . I have to tell you . . ."

"Oh shit."

She goes quiet, looking down at her frosted orange

fingernails.

"Out at Johnny's. I left something out there."

"Oh shit. What?"

"Um, I sort of left a scrapbook. I think. I've looked everywhere, through everything."

"Oh shit. What's in it?"

"Um, me. Johnny. Rodney. Michael. Um, you."

"ME? What about me?" I nearly swerve into the other lane and receive a blast from a semi for my troubles.

"Sorry, sorry," I tell the trucker who can't hear me.

"You. And me. When we were kids. And your dad, your mom, Timmy, Red."

The whole goddam stroll down Memory Lane.

"Where'd you see it last?" is my obvious question.

"Um, Johnny's room?"

"Jesus H. Dogpaddling Christ, Mo! How sure are you?"

"Not very?"

I shake a Lucky out of the pack and smash in the car's lighter and hurt my thumb. I give it a medicinal suck before lighting my cigarette. Mona holds out the flask. I shake my head.

Mona says, "I thought I had everything that would connect me to him, but it wasn't easy to discretely pack up with everybody around. Always somebody lurking. I knew things weren't right. I couldn't think why; they just weren't. When Johnny wasn't raging, he was stone-cold silent. I had trouble getting him to even look at me, and you know I'm good at that. Then for a while, it felt as if he was coming around, loving me again. We were talking, screwing, like normal — normal for being around Johnny anyway."

"Why would you have such a thing? Why would you keep that kind of crap?"

"Sentimental fool, I suppose."

"I'd think that was sweet if it wasn't so stupid for someone of your skills."

"I'm still human."

"Now she plays the human card! Next you'll be telling me about your diary."

"Um . . ."

"No. NO! NOOO!!"

"Just kidding. My word, you're so serious all of a sudden."

"I hate you."

"I hate you more."

"But you're not kidding about the scrapbook, right?"

"Unfortunately, right."

"I'm sure by now the cops have it in their hot little mitts. Wait'll I present them with the tape. We'll be public enemies #1 and #2 AND local heroes #1 and #2." I snuff out my cigarette and reinjure my thumb.

"I could use a pitstop."

From the back seat, "Me, too."

Pains in my ass.

Chapter 21

Who knew the infamous and nefarious Mona Crawford would have the mushy, girly-girl flaw of keeping mementos. A scrapbook? A fucking SCRAPBOOK? Not only is it off-the-charts girly-girl, it's dangerous as hell. All this time I've tracked her, waiting for the slip-up I need to nab her, put her behind bars where she belongs. Because I want her to knock it off with being a goddam criminal already. To put her brains and shifty ways to positive use. You know, like I do. A genius criminal mind is a terrible thing to waste on crime. Using such a gift to catch the bad guys, while not as moneywise rewarding, is pretty exciting. If you don't get caught for the criminal things you do to get your man. Mona. She is diabolical when she's on her game. Which is always. Ruthless and seductive. That "come hither" look of hers disarms even the gnarliest outlaw. For her, it's always about money. I don't think she's been directly the cause of some lowlife's bitter end. I'll have to remember to ask. Or have I asked? That's how scrambled my brains are. Johnny, Mona, the baby, Officer Tingle. The hell of two days in San Francisco. The hell of driving Moby. Ick. I wonder if those two punks that stole my precious GTO got nabbed for stealing Moby. Serves them right if they did. Should have given Officer Tingle the heads up. Easy bust. They probably had weed, too.

Mona's "qualities" bring to mind that my Timmy had a thing for her when we were kids. I mean, like, she was 14 and he was 11. Little brothers are a pain in the ass on a good day, but to have one all moony-eyed over your best friend? Sneaking up on us, hanging around, asking what we're doing, can he come with us. I couldn't beat him up often enough to make him stop. We wanted him to leave us alone, but I mostly wanted to save him from his first heartbreak. Even at 14, I knew what Mona could do. She egged him on, practicing the skills that would get her anything she wanted from men later on. The kid didn't stand a chance. She worked him for money, for little errands, for swiping booze and cigarettes and Ding Dongs. I told her to knock it off, but she couldn't. Using other people – especially men – was/is in her blood.

Just between you and me and the wall, I think she might have taught him a thing or two I REALLY didn't need to know about. One day he just seemed . . . different. A little taller. A little straighter. Bigger somehow. I was pretty sure it wasn't because he won Stevie Baker's favorite purie marble, though it could have given him the balls to win Stevie Baker's purie.

Ah, Mona. My Sheryl. How do I let you get me into these things? And for a goddam, sissified, totally incriminating scrapbook.

Chapter 22

California has the best rest stops. Clean. Shiny. Mirrors, hot water, the whole works. The butts and bladders of I-80 get the royal treatment. Showoffs. But thanks all the same.

I get out, stretching. Touching my toes, working out the kinks while Mona and Rodney head for the cinderblock bathrooms. The Sierra Foothills are bright green with signs of spring. This is where the elevation starts to suit me. Couple thousand more feet and my smoker's hack will return to normal. Getting above the Sacramento smog is a good thing, too. I can see it blanketing the valley below us. All that flat land. All those flat-landers. If there's one thing worse than San Franciscans, it's flat-landers. Not much imagination there; everything laid out in a grid like a checkerboard. From up here it looks like it makes sense, but I'll be damned if I can figure out how they find their way around without mountains or even the ocean to get a fix on. All those straight miles and miles of houses and strip malls get my inner compass spinning all out of whack. Even the path of the sun doesn't look right to me down there. Directions like "Go east on such and such" mean nothing to me once I get down from the foothills. Up here, I start to know exactly where I am.

Man, is my back tired. And my neck is a mess of tension. I roll my head around, listen to the snap, crackle, pop of stiff muscles.

"Can I help you with that?"

I whip around with my fists up.

"What the FUCK! You're FOLLOWING me?!"

There is Officer Paul Tingle, resplendent in an aqua blue golf shirt and khakis that still have sharp creases down the fronts after driving two hours. And the son of a bitch is SMILING?

"WHAT THE FUCK?" My vocabulary is running away as fast as I want to.

"Turn around," he says.

I do turn around. And put my hands behind me to get ready for the cuffs. He puts his hands on my neck and starts rubbing with his thumbs. I'm mad as a wet hen, but damn, that feels nice.

"Mmmmmmm," I say accidentally before I shrug him off and turn around. I feel like Alice on The Honeymooners with my hands on my hips, leaning forward at the waist, and glaring at him like he's Ralph, who deserves to catch an earful.

I say — and if I was accurate I'd say I spit, "What the fuck are you doing here?"

"Miss me?"

"No! I do not! I DON'T. What are you THINKING?"

Of all the things I didn't think I'd have to worry about . . .

169

• • •

He wipes the smile off his face. Suddenly he's Officer Tingle again. But he has to go and say, "You're in a heap of trouble, young lady."

It is at that point that I jump up and punch him right in the schnozz.

"Ouch!" I say, rubbing my hand.

"Ouch!" he says, rubbing his nose.

"Asshole!"

"Bitch!"

I'm shocked! He called me a bitch?!

And we both burst out laughing.

"I HATE you!" I spit.

"You do not," he says. I'll have to teach him the proper reply.

"Seriously," he says, "I've got more news for you. It couldn't wait, so I . . . followed you."

"You stalked me. You tailed me. You, you sneaked up on me."

"I didn't know what else to do."

I lean against the car and light a Lucky. "That bad, huh?"

"Yeah. Bad."

"Shit."

"Deep," he says.

And of course, just about this time, here come Mona and Rodney. The Mod Squad: Mona in her silver mini skirt and white go-go boots, Rodney in purple polyester and several strands of beads. And that hair. Let's not forget the hair, which now has a 'fro comb sticking out the side and a rainbow headband. And an eyepatch and a creepy row of stitches. They're both taking in the scene: this straight, white, Ken-doll-looking dude chatting me up.

Rodney speaks first, "This honkey botherin' you, Flack?"

Paul Tingle is taking in all the details of my gang. I can't do much but nod. Then I see the wheels turning behind Mona's eyes. I try to stare her into shutting the hell up, but here it comes.

"Officer Tingle. Officer Paul Tingle. City po-lice."

Rodney's about to run for it when Mona spews laughter all over us. She's turning red and starts to choke. She leans on Rodney to hold herself up, and he's patting her on the back like he would with Pioche. Mona points at Paul Tingle and goes into another spasm.

"It's okay, Rodney," I say. "Mona! Fuck!"

"I don't get you white people no how," Rodney says sternly.

Paul Tingle offers Rodney his hand. "Hi. Paul Tingle. Guess you know that."

Rodney tries to give him a brother handshake that goes completely wrong. Officer Tingle ends up just kind of waving.

"Cool," says Rodney.

"And you are?" Officer Tingle asks.

"Rather not say."

"Fine."

"And you are?" he says to Mona.

She can't straighten up for a single second to tell him.

"Mona," I say. "Friend of mine. I wouldn't even try to shake her hand just yet."

She's shooing him away anyway.

"Damn," she says. "Pardon me." She turns and heads back to the bathroom, laughing all the way.

"What's so funny?" Paul Tingle asks.

"It's just the way she gets when she meets new people," I explain.

Which leaves the three of us standing in a rest area

parking lot with weary travelers and screaming kids and semis and barking dogs all around. With Mona's gleeful outburst, it's a carnival atmosphere. Wouldn't surprise me a bit if the next VW that pulls in unloads about eight clowns. Nobody knows what to say until Rodney says, "Gum?"

He offers us sticks of Fruit Stripe. We each take a piece. Paul Tingle trades me his orange for my green. Smart guy.

"How you know each other?" Rodney asks.

Paul Tingle takes the bait. "We, uh . . ."

"Met in The City," I butt in. "Yeah. Just met."

"And now you here?" Rodney glares at him.

"Oh, hey, it's not, I'm not . . ." Paul Tingle sputters.

"No, he isn't, we're not . . ." I sputter.

Rodney chews his gum thoughtfully, looking us both over.

"White people," is all he says, and wanders off shaking his head.

"I like your friends."

"Gee, thanks. I was hoping you would."

Officer Tingle stretches, gazes up at the blue, blue sky. "Pretty out here."

"Yeah, real bitchin' rest area. What do you want? We need to get going. Chop chop."

"You can't go back there."

"Plan on stopping us?"

"No, plan on talking some sense into your beautiful head."

"Nothing wrong with having a plan."

"Be serious, Gladys, Susan Anne, or should I call you Flack?"

"Flack."

"Station grapevine says Reno might not be too safe for you."

"Which I will not substantiate."

"Here's the thing: it's a reward. Put up by the . . ." he takes his stupid cop notepad out of his back pocket, "Ruggerio family? Think I heard about a son getting murdered? Want to tell me what that's all about?"

Uh-oh, Ruggerio trouble is worse than the police by about a thousand percent.

"Um, no. Nothing I can think of."

"Just locker room gossip, maybe. The details I overheard sounded definite. They're looking for you."

"And you thought the thing to do was pursue me for 150 miles to let me know? I'd find out sooner or later when I got home."

"Susan Anne . . . Flack . . . whoever you are, this sounds very serious. You could be in danger."

Ha! Think so, lover boy?

"It's just Nevada. Rough, tough, and hard to bluff."

"Would you be serious?"

"Seriously?"

He comes over and tries to take me into his arms.

"Stop. The neighbors will talk."

Paul Tingle throws up his arms in despair. I expect him to go all Andy-Taylor-on-Barney-Fife: "You beat everything. You know that? You just beat everything!"

He turns back to me, running a hand over his forehead. He's so cute when he's angry.

"I'm coming with you."

"What about your job? Who will protect Gotham?"

He grabs me by the arms. Kinda sexy.

"Listen to me for one minute. You don't know what you're up against. These people are dangerous. Don't you get it?"

"Yeah, I do get it. I'm a hometown girl. I worked for the Ruggerios. Where do you think I learned my trade? And, Mr. Smarty Pants, I have friends on the police force, the fire department, E Klampus Vitus, and the Kiwanis Club. I know how to take care of myself, thank you very kindly. I don't need any help from you. Mona! Rodney! Let's va-moose."

They've been standing almost out of earshot, pretending to take an interest in the architecture of the bathrooms. They turn when they hear me. I dearly hope Mona can conduct herself as an adult now.

"You can't stop me from coming, you know," Paul Tingle says.

"Free country."

He's in for it if he tries to follow me now that I know he is. The GTO is souped up with massive horsepower, and I can drive every hoofprint of it like Sterling Moss. Or Steve McQueen. Take your pick. I'll lose him once we get over the summit. If I haven't driven most of the side roads, I've ridden horseback over them. Not that my car is for off-road, but it's got to be beefier than whatever he's running.

Mona grinds out her cigarette with the pointy white toe of her go-go boot.

"You love birds make up? It looked a little heated."

"Well, you know how it is."

Rodney opens the passenger door for Mona and offers her his hand. She offers the seat to him, pointing out their differences in height and build. He sweeps his hand at the seat with a charming smile and helps her in. That guy.

He looks at me over the top of the car. "Just say the word. Just say the word."

"Thanks," I say. "You got it."

Rodney folds himself into the back and resumes his oneness with the pink pillow. From across the parking lot, we hear a VROOM!, and here comes Officer Tingle in a stunning '65 Mustang convertible. Black. Black interior. Top down. His hair gleaming like a crown. He pulls up behind us, takes a snappy British racing cap off the passenger's seat, adjusts it most dapperly on his head, puts on his mirrored sunglasses, and gives his beast another nice rev.

Sure hadn't counted on that.

I think I'm in love.

Shit.

Chapter 23

And then there were four. For someone who really, really hates company, I sure am gathering up a whole bunch of it. At least one of these two doesn't talk much. Mona's alternately fussing with her fingernails and rummaging through the contents of the six purses.

"Hm," she says, examining a gold glittery thingie that's practically blinding me. "This one isn't mine. Such a tawdry fake. Oh, lookie, party favors!" She shakes the little vial of white powder at me before dabbing a bit on the end of her pinkie and rubbing it over her gums. "My, my." She taps a bit onto the side of her hand and snorts it up. Taps a bit more and holds her hand out to me.

"What the heck." Sure, there's only one cop following me. That I know of. I snort it up sloppily, mostly all over my cheek,

176

trying to keep my eyes on the road. Lovely. Numbing and invigorating at the same time. Mona wipes the excess off of me and applies it to her gums. Then takes another big sniff.

Rodney perks up at those familiar sounds. Leans forward and snaps his fingers. Mona closes the vial and hands it to him. One of the strings of beads he's wearing turns out to have a tiny spoon hanging from it. He takes it off the string, serves himself, and hands it and the vial back to Mona. I'm awake now. I'm buzzing now. I'm ready to drive fast and take lots of chances. I'm ready to . . .

"Dish," says Mona, checking her nose in the mirror of a red compact she's found in whoever's purse.

Not exactly what I had in mind. I shove in the 8-track tape that's in the player, and Tammy Wynette blasts out of the speakers. "Stand by Your Man."

Mona and Rodney both scream and cover their ears and start bitching in unison.

"What are you DOING to us? MAKE IT STOP! MAKE IT STOP! I'm begging you!"

Whiners.

"Okay, okay." I turn off the player. There's rustling in the back seat. I look in the rearview and see Rodney digging in his backpack.

"Try this one," he says, tapping me on the shoulder with a battered tape with no label.

"What is it?" I ask.

"Try it."

Since I have offended them with mine, it's my duty to try his. I eject Tammy and get ready for whatever's next. Mona holds the spoon up to my nose. This time, with a new utensil, I have better luck.

"Harder they come, harder they fall one and all . . ."

Nice beat. Lively. Growing on me. Not bad. Not bad.

Mona is bopping her head and smiling. She looks like she's getting misty but happy at the same time.

"What is this?" I ask.

"Dig it?" asks Rodney.

"I might. How 'bout you, Mo?"

She just keeps bopping with her eyes closed. And now a little tear is running down her beautiful face.

"Jimmy Cliff," says Rodney. "One love. Rasta. Reggae." He settles back in his seat and lights a joint.

"Mind opening the window?" I ask, waving away the cloud.

"Righteous," he says, holding his breath and cranking his window down. He passes the joint forward to Mona. She takes it and pulls a couple of long, long hits that have her coughing her brains out. I'm waving away smoke like a madman.

"Window! Mo! Jesus!"

"Smooth," she says when she can breathe again. She hits it a couple more times – lightly – before offering it to me, which I wave off, before handing it back to Rodney. He's one gigantic grin. He's in the groove.

"You can pass me what's in that flask, though, if you don't mind," I say, mostly so as not to come off as too much of a square. I just don't like marijuana. Makes me too fuzzy, and if there's anything I've learned about being me, it's that I've got no time for fuzzy. Plus, it makes me think about myself, and you know I hate that. Jim Beam and I get along just fine. Him, I got down to a science. And Lucky Strikes? Cut my teeth on those.

"You okay, Mo?" I ask after I've had my belt.

She's wiping her tears on a paisley scarf. "I was just thinking about Pioche. Her dad is a reggae freak. It was all he listened to. It's how he became Shamar. Now he's playing it for her. She's hearing it, soaking it up in its birthplace. Next time I see her, she'll be in dreadlocks. Like her father."

"Dread what?"

"It's a hair thing. A black thing. Forget it."

"Learn something new every day."

"Righteous," says Rodney.

I keep checking behind us to see if Paul Tingle is still there, but I guess I don't need to bother. He rolls up alongside me, waves, and fades back. Smart ass. Good thing for me that my passengers are into their music and their high. I'd have taken a terrible amount of teasing if they'd seen that little stunt.

Closer we get to Reno, the more I start wondering – make that realizing – this might be a real bad idea. Whatever they think they know, Ruggerios are a family that does not fuck around. Learned that working for them. They were on top of everything all the time. I really admired their standards, but there was not one iota of wiggle room in any of them. Cocktail waitresses were weighed every three days. Two pounds over and you were history. Keno writers could expect random searches of themselves and their lockers at any time. Slot mechanics? Practically had an entourage, there were so many security personnel watching their every move. I was one of them; I should know. It seems like small potatoes to be looming over guys wearing toolbelts, fiddling around with machines full of nickels, but we're talking thousands and thousands of dollars from each machine every day in a busy casino. A slick change girl/slot mechanic/security team can do all right and rip off the place for a long time since the card and craps table take up most of the attention. I took down one such crew of slot robbers. They had hit the Ruggerios of upwards of $20,000 before I caught on. Nowadays, there's not just one security guard watching a repair but three: one for each person involved. I got a promotion for that bust. Put me up in the catwalk with binoculars. Boring. So, so boring. I like the personal touch. Especially if it involves handcuffs and the occasional bit of blood.

Did someone actually see me take out Johnny? Someone I hadn't accounted for out there? Was this another Candid Camera kind of thing? Am I on Betamax? Was Mona's headcount right when she bought everyone at Rancho Spaghetti-O that limo and VIP seating to see Bobbi Gentry at Harrah's Tahoe that night? Did someone see me drive off?

I think the coke is making me paranoid, so I take another slug of whiskey. Or whatever this crap is in Mona's flask. Reno's going to be a mess. I don't even have a trailer to call my own. I hope Rockalee's okay. I did see The Godfather and all. I've been worrying about where Mona and Rodney were going to end up; now I have to worry more about me. And Paul Tingle. Gotta figure out how to shake that cop.

The next time he pulls up beside us, I flip him the bird. He looks crushed and fades back. Poor guy. He deserves better than me. Everybody does. If I don't piss you off one way, I'll piss you off another. It's not my job to make you love me; it's my job to do my job. To get the bad guy. To get your lying, cheating spouse or business partner or employee. Low-down things people do make me crazy. Makes me who I am. Makes me do what I do. Liars and cheaters? Damn. Nevada's got them in spades, pun intended. Small time, big time. Gangsters. Shills. Snakeoil salesmen. Crooked bankers. Crooked pawnshop owners (big wow). Even crooked cops. I really hate that. Johnny Ruggerio's Betamax stunt just brought me a new category to hate, one I don't want and never had as a client or person of interest: crooked politicians. I mean, I'm not stupid. I know they exist. I know Nevada is sick with them, just like the seedy underbelly of the gaming industry is sick with gangsters. I've just managed to steer clear of them. That whole political world shit? Too far beyond my get-your-man mentality. The ins and outs of their doings is a bigger mystery to me than why space is dark when the sun's right there. Yeah, I have thought about it. You can't spend as much time sleeping under the stars as I have and not think about it. I'm way out of my league where it comes to politics. Why they do that, how they got there, who listens to them, and who they listen to? I vote for President, but that's where my interest ends. I punch the ballot card going eeny-meeny-miney-moe for all the rest of the shit I've never heard about. A bunch of guys killing themselves and each other to get the job of sitting in a room talking and talking and talking and talking? Puts me to sleep. Never have managed to sit through a single one of their boring speeches without getting a sudden urge for some garlic eggplant from Lung Fung's. Once that happens, there's no getting my attention back.

But I saw that tape. Now I need to figure out who to give it to. All of a sudden, I'm not sure who in my tiny inner circle I can trust. No police captains, no d.a's. Flack, you are severely fucked on this one. Other than the people in the car with me now, I don't know who to trust. And that's saying a lot since Mona is one of them.

"Know what we need to do?" Rodney pipes up from the back seat.

His voice startles me out of my coke and booze haze. He has not opened his eye, though I can't for the life of me figure out how he can rest under the influence of this coke that has set my teeth on edge.

Then he goes quiet.

"What?" I ask.

Nothing.

"Rodney! What? What?!"

"Oh shit. Did I say something? Thought I was dreaming. Let's see . . . Can't remember. Shit."

181

This is why I don't smoke marijuana. Can't afford to space out. I stay sharp on Jim Beam. Like I said: science.

Jimmy Cliff on the 8-track is sittin' in limbo, sorta like Rodney. But if he's got a plan, I sure would like to hear it.

I look at him in the rearview. He's got his eye closed, digging the music.

"Rodney!" I yell.

"What?"

"You said you know what we need to do!"

"I'm thinking on it. I'm thinking on it."

We've passed Donner Summit and are in the home stretch for Reno.

"Soon, if you can manage it."

I see Officer Tingle's Mustang in my side mirror right behind us.

Rodney says, "First off, we need to hang onto Wonder Bread boy back there to help us figure out what the fuck."

Do we?, I'm thinking.

"See, no one knows him, ya dig? Just another one of them honkey white boys in a crowd. We can scuff him up some so he looks Nevada enough. He might could be our secret weapon."

"Oh no. That's a terrible idea. That's . . . it's . . ."

"You know you busted, Mona. Semi-busted. I'm black as fuck. Who you think they gone listen to? Let into the good ole boy club?"

Man's got a point. A point I don't love and doubt Officer Paul Tingle is going to love. That man has straight-shooter written all over him. Then again he did let me go when he didn't have to. Plus, he is one great lay, the kind I've only gotten off of bad boys in the past. Officer Tingle just might go along with us.

"Flack, check it: Big city cop? Thinking of joining the Reno PD? Girl, they will suck his limp, little, lily-white dick, bunch of shit-for-brains honkeys."

Mona says, "Rodney does make some interesting points."

"Shut up, Mo. Don't encourage him."

"No, no, think about it. Ivy League-looking white boy wanting to bring justice to the frontier? Tell me you don't think that mentality isn't still alive and well in Reno."

They're both right. There are zero black police in Reno. There's not all that many black people in Reno, so they still scare the living daylights out of everybody. Paul Tingle is the white guy's ideal of perfection in every way. Lamb to the slaughter. Our decoy. A whole number of clichés. All of which I do not like.

"I barely know the man," I say.

Mona speaks first, "He met Pioche?"

"Liked her, too. And she liked him. Well, not right at first."

"That's saying something," Rodney says. He knows that kid. He loves that kid.

"Here's the other thing," Mona begins. "He clearly likes you. What did you do to him?"

Rodney laughs.

"Well, there was my car . . . And then we had to duck between two cars . . . Shots fired . . . Then the gay riot thing . . . Then . . ."

"In one night?!" they both say simultaneously before laughing their asses off. Man, these two.

This is stacking up to be three against one. I have to get rid of these people. No, not THAT way. Just away. I can't think with all this talking and talking. All these schemes. Trouble to the left and the right and up and down. Worst thing is they think it's funny. We are in deep shit. Deepest I've ever been in, for sure. Can't say the same for Mona. So, I guess I could ask:

"Mona, have you ever been in deeper doo-doo than this?"
Her laughter vanishes. She turns her face to the window.

"In Jamaica. There was this guy Raoul. I was five months pregnant with Pioche. Shamar had just changed his name. We were moving a lot of product for Raoul. Ganga. Mary Jane. Grass. A lot. Things were going along great. Everyone was making tons of money. I still have a place down there. Right on the beach. Eight bedrooms. We'll have to go sometime.

"Then Raoul gets into dealing with the cocaine mob. Now we were really making money. It was going fine until Raoul got way too friendly with the product. He turned all paranoid. Never slept. Thought everybody was out to get him.

"He decides that I've been talking to the Federales. That I'm setting him up. He's not saying this to me, of course, but everybody he's telling is turning around and telling me. Shamar is fearing for my life, our lives. He plans to smuggle me onto the plane with the next shipment to Miami. I just have to lay low, stay out of Raoul's way without acting like anything's going on.

"But things were becoming tense. Raoul was behaving crazier by the minute. One by one, his key people were 'disappearing.' His whole crew was taking on a new demeanor. I mean, there are thugs and then there are thugs. The scruffier their appearance, the tighter the lockdown became until no one was allowed to leave the compound without three or four armed escorts. If we got permission to leave at all.

"I was lying by the compound pool one day. Acting natural and scared witless. I was accustomed to the place being surrounded by armed guards, but this was different. The old timers were feeding me information. They were watching out for me.

"It happened so fast. Raoul came out of the house, smoking one of his nasty cigars. He was wearing thongs and a blue Speedo and an open white linen shirt blowing in the breeze. He commented on the beautiful day right before he shot me in the side. Guards came running. I heard more shots.

"I woke up in an i.c.u. four days later. Shamar was there. Two of Raoul's guards were with him. I was hooked up to every machine and i.v. and monitor imaginable. I immediately put my hands on my belly. Still round. Shamar showed me which blips and bleeps were the baby.

"I was in and out of consciousness for a few days before finding out we were in Miami. Long story short, I lost my spleen and part of a lung. But not the baby. And it left me this."

Mona pulls up her shirt and pushes her skirt down to reveal a real mess of scars. I have to keep my eyes on the road, so I only catch a glimpse. Rodney's leaning over the seat. He pats Mona on the head and slumps back onto the pink pillow.

"So yes," she says, "I've been in binds before, but this one was the worst."

"Damn, Mo, that's horrible."

"But it did get me out of Jamaica. And Pioche survived. Shamar put together a small army that took out Raoul and his goons. Took over Raoul's house and his business."

"Aren't you worried about Pio in that kind of place?"

"I told you: Shamar's in Florida. Actually, a private island. He got out. We had already made more money than we could spend in three lifetimes. All cash. Of course, he still has to maintain a security force that rivals the Secret Service – some of them are ex-Secret Service – and he lives quietly, painting, playing dominoes, reading, listening to reggae. For now he's a dad, a good dad. We split because we decided I was staying here with Pioche to keep her safe, and he wanted to go back and 'settle' with Raoul. I'm not clear on the outcome of that. He refuses to tell me. I know she's all right. He'd do anything to keep her safe, just like I did when we were with Johnny.

"A person in my 'line' can't stay single for long, you know? I figured, gaming family? Three measly casinos? How ferocious could they be? Most of them aren't. They're cagy, but not killers. At least they don't seem so. But I had to go and pick Johnny."

"I did, too," Rodney says. "He wasn't always such a bad dude. Testy, maybe. High strung. He sure changed."

The mood in the car shifted fast. The next time Paul Tingle pulls alongside us, it takes me a minute to notice. He's smiling, trying to act goofy like he's challenging me to a race, but the smile stops when he gets a good look at my face. I'm too rattled to put up a fake front. I really need to get rid of all these people.

"We'll be home in about an hour," I say. "Better think quick about where you want me to drop you. Mona, the Mapes or any place like it is out of the question. Think harder. Rodney?"

"I got friends."

"Good friends?" I ask.

"Yeah, they good. Leave me downtown. I can get there."

Mona rummages through her many purses, extracts several rolls of bills. She tosses two of them back to Rodney.

"Nah, you keep it."

She turns and growls at him, so he thanks her and puts them in his duffle bag.

"You could come shack up with me, Mona," he says.

"Dahling, are you sure you can accommodate a woman of my tastes and temperament?"

"What you think? Cool cat like me? Shiiiiit, woman. Who do you think taught Johnny about art and all?"

"Interesting proposition. What do you think, Susan Anne?"

"Sounds like the beginning of a beautiful friendship."

"Okay, then, it's settled. I will need my own room. White décor. With ensuite bathroom. With Jacuzzi. With separate access. With private telephone line. With . . ."

"Lord, what have I done?" Rodney laughs.

"Whoa, pardners," I say. "Mona, you've got about half the Gray Reid's women's department right here in this car, remember? Not exactly traveling light."

"Oh, well, it's not like I need ALL of it. Just this. And this. I can't go without this . . ."

Rodney pipes up, "Mona, you got more money than God Almighty. Score you some new crap."

Now it's my turn, "No, you don't! I'm not keeping all of this shit for you. No, ma'am."

"It would only be temporary . . ."

"What part of Officer Tingle telling us I don't have a home did you not understand?"

"Right. Let's see, this is a dilemma."

"YOUR dilemma."

"Rodney, be a dear, would you?, and hand me that and those and maybe not that."

Rodney tosses armloads of clothes and bags and who knows what onto her lap. Mona is busy examining labels and fabrics, then she rolls down her window and starts tossing her precious items out.

"That was a Chanel. That was a St. Laurent. Those were Guccis."

"Gee," I say. "You named your clothes?"

"Very funny. Oh, I must keep this one. I was given this in Monte Carlo when I was with the count. And these were given to me by Mick Jagger . . ."

"Mick Jagger? THE Mick Jagger?" Rodney says.

"There is only one, darling."

Expensive doo-dads flip and fly behind us. Glorious colors. Furs. Sparkly whatevers.

"Can I keep the pillow?" Rodney asks, snuggling its pinkness to his face.

"Certainly."

She keeps tossing but admits defeat before even half of what's on the back seat is gone. It's just too much for her. She takes a long drink from the flask, emptying the last of it.

"I can't do it," she says. "It's like murder. My beautiful, beautiful things. It's criminal."

Rodney and I get a good long laugh out of that one. Mona crosses her arms and frowns like the spoiled child she is.

"Okay, okay, Mo, you can leave your crap in the car. I won't be driving it for a while."

"Why? What are you going to do?" Mona asks

"Drive out to the stables, stash this rig, grab Rockalee, and go."

"Go where?"

"Camping, baby."

"How perfectly disgusting."

"How perfectly quiet, you mean."

"Whatever float your boat," Rodney says, holding in a hit and hugging his pillow.

"But you're coming back, right?" Mona asks.

"Oh, you'll never see my lily-white ass again. I'm done with you two criminals. Once I drop you off, you're dead to me, got it?"

Mona and Rodney go quiet.

"Come on, you two! I'm kidding. We got work to do. I just need to clear my head for a week or so, if you don't mind."

They go bantering back and forth over who minds and who doesn't til I have to tell them to shut the fuck up.

"Dammit! I'll come and find you when I'm ready."

"And how will you do that, pray tell?" Mona asks.

"Flack Murrow, Private Investigator. Jesus, Mona, a little credit here."

"Right you are. Oh, look, there's your boyfriend again."

"'Again?' You guys saw all that?"

They look at me like "duh."

Paul Tingle's alongside of us. Has a worried expression on his puss. I blow him a kiss before I blow him away with my horsepower. Nothing like a road trip. Nothing like it.

"Hey now, was that nice?" Rodney asks, giggling into his fist.

"Really, Susan Anne, you should be kinder to your boyfriend," Mona says, not even attempting to hide her evil smile.

"Paul Tingle is not my boyfriend! See him back there? No way he can keep up with me. On or off the road. No fucking way."

Rodney asks, "How come you don't just call him Paul? It's Paul Tingle this, Officer Tingle that, Officer Paul Tingle the other?"

"Distance," I tell him. "Keeps him at a distance, just like I'm doing now."

The black Mustang is a tiny speck in the rearview. Couple more slick maneuvers, and I'll be free of his ass.

His tight, smooth, powerful ass.

Shit.

Chapter 24

I heard somewhere that the desert and the ocean have a lot in common. Sounded fishy. Tee hee. But think about it. Both are huge, blank emptiness. Hostile. Too dry in the desert, too much salt in the sea. Wind and weather that tears everything to pieces. Too much sun, not enough rain, too much rain. All kinds of creepy crawlies, carnivorous beasties, deadly poisonous killers. Land or sea, these are tough places for anything to try to survive. Growing scaly, tough skin works. Fangs and poison are nice. Expecting and accepting only the bare necessities works. Relying on yourself and yourself alone works. Being as prepared as you can will save your life.

Camping desert rat style is a whole different ballgame from campground camping. No friendly pine trees for shade and ready-made stacks of firewood. No friendly, trickling brooks.

190

Instead, you get wind that will turn a tent into a sail in nothing flat. Out on the desert, you are exposed, plain and simple. You can be spotted for miles. You will leave tracks. I've heard that people also lose their way, but it's never been a problem for me. I know the northern Nevada desert like the back of my hand. It's been my playground, my hideout, my teacher since I was little. I always know where and who I am out there. It's not romantic – it's reality. Harsh but beautiful reality.

You can see the Milky Way almost every night. When there's no moon, you can hardly see the hand in front of your face. When there's a full moon, you can read by it. And you can hear the rustling of critters you can't see. That's kind of the eeeewww factor. And then there's coyotes. I have great respect for keeping those bastards at a distance. They are sneaky and don't play fair at all.

Sunrises and sunsets are positively psychedelic. Intense oranges and reds and purples. Then the blue sky takes over and looks so close you could touch it. It looks solid like it's a giant cutout shape parked on top of the bare hills. Everything is so in focus, so clear. Times when I've been at my lowest and most confused, the desert has straightened me out. More than Reno or my trailer or my office, that is my home. I don't care how bad my nose peels or how many new freckles I get, I keep coming back to the safety I feel when I kick back against my saddle on the ground, watching Rockalee find little bits to munch on as the sun goes down. She knows to stick around. She's like a dog that way. She's also reliable when it comes to giving a snort at the presence of a small invader – a snake or a lizard or a jackrabbit, and a whinny to warn of a bigger enemy – a coyot, a fellow desert ratter, a wildcat. Usually I can get them to turn tail and run just by yelling, but if that doesn't work, a .357 shot across the bow does. And if that doesn't work, well . . . snakes are good eating.

The secret to staying in the desert for more than a day or two is to know your hermits and respect their privacy. They're out there. They're out there for a reason, and when you run across one of them, you need to keep your distance or win his heart quick: a bottle of Jim Beam, some jerky, a book or two. They're touchy about the way you're traveling. They hate dirt bikes and sand buggies and such. You show them who you are by how you're outfitted. How you got there and what you're packing goes a long way to win their cranky old hearts. If they can see you don't intend to dig in and get all fucking neighborly, you're all right.

I know one crusty old guy, well, not sure if he's old or not – just scaly – named Pete, who dug himself a maze of tunnels that he covered in plywood and piled sand and sagebrush slash on top. He's been there so long the sagebrush has grown back over his home. He even dug an underground parking garage for his rusted-out pickup. You'd never know he was there. And come to think of it, he's the guy who told me about the ocean and the desert being the same. Pete knows more about the ocean than anyone I've ever met. His dirt walls are covered with tacked-up star charts and maps and calculations. He sleeps on stacks of books, sits on stacks of books, eats breakfast on stacks of books. Unlike the other hermits I know, he invites me in – down – and talks my ear off about tides and doldrums and water spouts and currents. Black holes and gas giants and moons and comets. Shows me illustrations. Points to spots on the maps. I'd like to say it's fascinating, but he talks so fast and skips around so much I can never keep up. After a while I have to say I need to get moving, and he goes up the ladder with me, talking all the way. He insists on filling my canteen with water I know he can't afford to part with. Can't argue with him; he won't shut up long enough. I say thanks and ride off, and I'll still hear him behind me going on about finding water on Mars. He's a character. Exactly the kind of desert character that's born, not made.

Out here, with so much space and so few people, you're your own self and your own fun. You have to be interested in the tiny details. A rare, tiny flower hidden under the brush. The quick blooming of different kinds of sagebrush flowers. Itty bitty flowers that smell better than any perfume. You might find the occasional purple bottle or green glass insulator peeking up out of the sand. It ain't excitement you come out here to find. You sure as hell don't go letting off fireworks or throwing big parades. The rootin' tootin' Nevada thunderstorms are plenty flashy. Real Nevadans respect what we do in the desert because we know we're going to leave a mark. A scar. Tire tracks linger. Roads don't heal. The desert is mean, but it's also fragile. Holds itself together by the narrowest threads and is bare naked. And shy.

I have always come out here to get myself together when I start wanting to give everybody a black eye. Reno's growing. Makes me sad to hear newcomers bitch about how ugly the landscape is. Every time I see another batch of tract houses going up, I cry. Seriously. That's what's ugly: more crappy boxes on paved roads with sidewalks and a spindly tree or two dying from the sand and wind. Scars, more scars where I used to walk out to breathe and get away from everything. I don't know what I'm going to do when there are no empty spaces left. I don't kid myself that it won't happen. Guys like Pete? He'll be worse off than me by a long shot. Some people are just not made for neighbors or streets or Dairy Queens.

Maybe he'll end up going out to sea.

Chapter 25

I managed to shake Paul Tingle just outside Truckee. His Mustang could have had me, but I'm a better racer. Plus I know the territory. After dropping off Mona and Rodney and what was left of her fashionable shit, I grabbed some provisions and went immediately to the stables out in Lockwood. Parked the GTO in an empty barn and covered her with a tarp and some scatterings of hay and crap. I even leaned some old rakes and shovels against her – which hurt me but added atmosphere. I covered my tracks and split.

And tried not to think about his bod. Poor lost soul, wandering around Reno, looking for a friend.

I'll keep the details of my campout to myself, if you don't mind. It'd bore you to tears anyway: I rode, I slept, I ate, I thought. I didn't talk to anyone but Rockalee, and she'll never tell. A week. A whole week of no disasters or murders or murderers or bullshit. A week of not looking over my shoulder, of not having to tell anyone to shut the fuck up. Of not having to be clean or on time or pay attention. Of letting things start to sort themselves out on the back burner. It might have been easy for another person to roar into town and let things fly, but if there's one thing I've learned in my line of work, going Wild West only makes MORE work. And that means more people and more explaining and stories to make up. I know when I'm plumb out of ideas and energy and tolerance. Heavy on the tolerance. Many lives have been saved by me going camping. Including my own.

I snuck back into town last night, stashed the GTO in Harrah's parking garage waaaayyyy in the back at the top. From there I could get a look at the area around my office before checking in at the fleabag Capri Motel, an excellent choice for those who do not want to be found. They're used to clients showing up without luggage or cars or real names, and paying in cash. I was so tired and dirty and sunburned I looked like a regular. They didn't even blink. Not even when I paid for a month rather than a couple of hours. Cash is king.

The shower. The bed. The shower. The bed. The 14 hours I slept. The TV I didn't turn on. The window where I could hear the Truckee River and get a tiny bit of breeze to clear out whatever the hell that smell was. It was sort of month-old baloney combined with rotten cantaloupe, if that makes any sense. I know it could have been worse.

I laid low and cased my office for a couple of days. No sign of Mona or Rodney, smart kids. They know I'll find them when I'm ready. That sneaky Paul Tingle would be doing the same thing as me, guaranteed. That is, if he knows where my office is. Maybe he does? Or maybe he left? Not sure what I think about that. Either way.

195

Today's the day, though. Time to get a look-see. I take the precaution of a bit of costuming: hooded sweatshirt, plaid flannel shirt with the sleeves cut off, and a toolbelt slung over my shoulder. Goddam building is a constant repair job. I'll pass for one of the guys easy. If runty.

No tenants around. After 5. Couple of new names on a couple of doors. A "finance" company. A shrink. A vocal coach (good luck with that). And a remarkable decrease of patchouli stench. Guess Felix finally 86ed the "artists."

I get to my door and, big surprise, my key doesn't work. Bastard! I jimmy the cheap Kwikset in nothing flat. Love it that my landlord spares no expense to keep my space secured. I'm not really sure why I'm here, what I expect to find, but since my home is MIA, this is about as close as I can get to a place that's sort of mine.

There's a pile of mail that came through the door slot. Surprised Felix didn't abscond with it. At least he respects the U.S. Mail. Flyers, catalogs, a couple of bills, a couple of my invoices marked "Return to Sender." Shit. Deadbeats. An invitation to a slot tournament. That's a hoot.

Geez, glad everyone missed me so much. "Occupant" and "Resident" got a lot more mail than me. Not one thing of interest in the whole she-bang. I toss the shit into the round file, then figure I'll "set a spell," as Granny Clampett would say. Just take in all the sights I love about my office. Basic, private eye shabbiness I got out of movies. The lack of personality and interior decorating ability. Except for my window. Those big ass, beautiful letters. My name. Come on up and see me some time. I just knew the jilted and robbed and otherwise abused masses would be knocking down my door to solve their problems. True, I do okay. Especially "for a girl," since my male clients always have to add that remark in order to maintain their swagger and feel less fucked for stooping so low as to hire me, because they're too embarrased to have to tell another man about their woman problems. To that I say, "Poor baby. Give me your dough." You know I only think it, though, right? Can't let the sorry bastards know how not sorry I am for them.

I hope there's still a bottle of Jim Beam in the bottom desk drawer. Yes, there you are, my friend. And, a-ha, what's this? A gentle reminder that I still have some pretty big fish to fry. The goddam baseball cards. The evidence of how this whole fiasco started. A dead guy with pockets full of trouble. Damn, damn, damn. The calm I found in the desert is evaporating faster than fog on a windshield. Time to go find Mona and Rodney and get this party started.

Shit.

Chapter 26

They say insanity is doing the same thing over and over and expecting a different result, so it must mean I'm nuts to go back to Mona again and again. She's gotten me in more jackpots than I can count going back our whole lives. She operates under some kind of magnetic field I'm a sucker for. Loves living on the edge. Life blood for her. She's addicted to seeing how far she can go and then going a little farther just for grins. I can only try to keep up, just like when we were kids. Back then I used to do it because I needed a friend so much, and she happened to be my age and close by. She'd been through enough herself that nothing I did or told her came as a surprise. Not that she was sympathetic. She'd knock me on the head and say, "Get over it, wimp," and I'd act like I could. She showed me new ways to deal with anger and grief. I'm not

198

sure if I can say I'm better for her instruction, but bad shit rolls off my back like water off of a duck because of her.

I hate her guts as much as I love her.

Down to business. If I was them two desperados, where would I be?

I take a glance out my window. It's starting to get dark. The Cal Neva's lights turn everything completely unnatural colors out there. I zip up my sweatshirt, stuff my hair up under the hood, grab my toolbelt and the baseball cards, and crack open the door to listen and look before I head out into the hallway. Nothing stirring except there's a light on in the vocal coach's office, and some really bad la-la-las coming out of there.

I'm walking softly, keeping my head down, trying to look repair guy-ish. Smoking a cigarette is always a nice effect. So far, so good.

Out on the sidewalk tourists are bumping past me, swilling drinks from one casino while making their way to another. They're loud and happy. Haven't lost their asses yet. I'm not worth noticing. Who gives a shit about a repair guy when you're drunk enough to know you can break the bank at the next craps table? I just kind of slouch along, looking down, looking tired, which is easy because I'm both. Center Street is thick with after-work traffic. Noisier than usual. I'm starting to want to punch a few of these flatlanders in the throat, but I don't have much farther to go back to the Capri.

"Excuse me. Excuse me, sir?"

Head down, Flack, keep walking. Probably talking to some other asshole.

"You there, hey you." And then, "You-hoooo, sailor. Need a lift?"

Oh shit. My life just got easier and harder at the same time. A long black limo pulls up and double parks next to me, causing a bunch of honking and cuss words.

Mona.

She's waving out the window at me like some goofy girl on prom night. Both arms. Making a goddam scene I could do without. To keep her from attracting more attention from everybody for two blocks thinking they've spotted Charo, I slip between the cars legally parked at the curb, open the door of the double-parked limo, and climb in ready to give her more than one piece of my mind.

"Surprise!" she yells.

Which I am when I rip the hood off, ready to rumble, and see she's not alone. Oh no, not Mona. That's not her style.

I was expecting Rodney, sure. In a cloud of smoke, a splendor of purple velvet, a sequined eyepatch, and a green fedora.

Who was I hoping not to expect? You got it.

Chapter 27

"You found them?" I say to Officer Tingle as I pull off my hood, and my hair fills half the car.

"Wrong. WE found HIM." Mona smiles as she hands me a tall glass of champagne. I hate the bubbly, but when in Rome . . . I slug it down, belch beautifully, and hold my glass out for more. At least it's Dom. I'm less likely to barf later. Still going to give me a headache, though.

"It didn't seem hospitable to leave the poor dear adrift in a strange city," Mona explains. "We've been having such a lovely time, haven't we, boys?"

Rodney clinks glasses with me and settles back into his seat with a very satisfied grin.

"I'm going to kill you, Mo," I say.

"Susan Anne, it is unwise to make such threats in the

presence of an officer of the law."

"Hi, Officer Tingle," I say.

"Hi. You can call me Paul, you know."

"I don't know, and, no, I can't."

Mona and Rodney are decked out in flashy evening wear that screams metallic and Day-Glo. Rodney's wearing a headband that looks like it's made of snakeskin, which, upon further inspection, proves to be the truth. It's still got the rattle attached. A gold ankh dangles from his right earlobe matching the one around his neck. Mona is slightly more subdued, but only slightly, and I'm pretty sure the rocks around her neck and wrists are the real thing. Paul Tingle is full-on GQ: creased slacks, polo, hair styled, and, I'm pretty sure, sprayed into place. He's quiet. Just sipping, watching.

"So," I say, "how about those Dodgers?"

Mona knocks on the window that separates the driver from us. The window slides down.

"Yes, ma'am?" He's wearing full livery, including the cap. Of course.

"Excuse me," says Mona. "Driver? One more stop. 370 Mount Rose, please."

"Yes, ma'am." The window goes back up.

"The Redfield mansion?" I ask.

"The very one. You've been there?"

"Sure. Yeah. All the time."

"Then you'll feel right at home. More bubbly?"

"Why not?"

Paul Tingle stares at me steadily. He's daring me to say something about us first. Mona and Rodney appear to be making mental bets about who it will be. I can wait.

"Come on, you two," Mona says finally "Time to kiss and make up."

"Butt out, Mo."

"Can I say something?" Rodney asks.

All of us say, "NO." Rodney snickers and relights his joint. I see Paul Tingle flinch.

"Out of your jurisdiction, sweetie," Mona says, taking the joint when Rodney offers it. She holds it between her index and middle fingers as she would a regular cigarette, puffs it dramatically, nods her approval, stifles a cough, and hands it back to Rodney.

"Smooth!" she proclaims, holding her breath.

We cross Virginia Street and Sierra Street and make a left on Arlington.

The Redfield mansion is on a little rise on the corner of Mt. Rose and Arlington. It's a handsome place made out of giant granite boulders like something out of a fairy tale. I've always loved it. It's so solid and strong. Even though it puts the rest of the neighborhood that grew up around it to shame, it looks dignified rather than hoity-toi like a lot of the glass-and-Masonite crap the casino crowd are slapping down all over the place. Like Johnny's, where square footage is more important than fine craftsmanship. I don't know all the history of the Redfield place. Don't give a damn about how many skeletons are in the closets, but I do know what's supposedly in the basement. Everybody does. I prefer to picture myself in a huge, comfy chair by a roaring fire in the living room, big dogs curled at my feet. Two, maybe more. A velvet robe. Green. Goes best with my hair. Bottle of Beam, pack of Luckys. In sweet, sweet silence except for the crackle of wood. Truly, just the idea of pulling into the driveway gives my heart a flutter. It's the closest me and my kind will ever get to old money luxury like that. Nevada ain't exactly an old-money place.

We turn onto the gravel drive on the left side of the place and park under a roof held up by giant boulder pillars. The driver gets out, opens the door for Mona, takes her hand.

"Just be a moment."

He walks her to the door. A little kid opens it. I see that this is the kitchen door. Only the best kind of company comes in through the kitchen door. And that's Mona? Mona ruffles the kid's hair, and they go in.

Our driver returns, shuts the doors, and waits outside the car with his arms by his sides, engine running. At least I get to peek through the windows at close range. Just as I figured: chandeliers, gold trim, wallpaper. Massive wood furniture. Bookshelves. Tons of books. Paintings. The crackling fire of my dreams in a space where you could park a VW bug.

"Man!" I exclaim without thinking.

"Far out," says Rodney, rolling down the window to take it all in. "Who the fuck lives here?"

"Couldn't say exactly. It's the Redfield mansion, so I guess it's one of them."

"Man," he says as we keep ogling. Paul Tingle is still trying to stare a hole in my head.

"Ahem," he says.

"Stop," I say. "Don't spoil it." I'm living my dream. Rodney pours us the last of the champagne and pulls another bottle out of a small fridge behind the driver's seat. He removes the cork expertly, no geyser, and only a delicate pop. He puts the bottle in an ice bucket on the floor.

The little boy who opened the door walks Mona back to the car, holding her hand. Rich people are different as hell. She bends down and kisses his cheek and offers him hers with a finger pointing right where she wants his lips. He smiles and runs back inside. The driver opens the door and helps her in.

"I'll never forget this, Mo," I say. "Never in my whole life."

"Oh, please, don't exaggerate."

"Really. Thanks."

"I'll introduce you someday."

"No shit?"

Rodney says, "Me, too?"

"But of course! You're family."

"Right on," he says.

"So . . .?" I say.

"In due time. In due time."

Sometimes I wish she'd talk like a regular person. Rodney hands her a full glass. We back out of the driveway and head south on Arlington.

"Where to now, boss?" I ask.

"Huffaker Hills."

Which is another of the prime pieces of real estate in Reno. I'm not being sarcastic. It's green grass fields out there. Can you believe it? Horses, cows. Some places grow alfalfa that is deep, deep emerald green. The money out there is like the money that built the Redfield place. Mostly made in the silver and gold rush. Lots of space between houses. Old cottonwood trees shading them. Little creeks flow through some of the land. All year. Can you believe it? Rare sight, water. I roll down the window and breathe in young, green hay, my favorite smell after sagebrush. The desert can grow just about anything if you add water. Take your Heart of Gold cantaloupes. Grown in Fallon, can you believe it? The season is short, the dirt – well, sand – is for shit, but everybody starts licking their chops when harvest time is coming. Best tasting melon ever. Water is the ticket. It's just so hard to come by.

We round the switchback on Windy Hill, where I know there's a flagstone house that looks carved out rather than built. Blends right in. No paint. Just glass, rocks, and a slate roof. Tucked into the hillside. Built to last like the Redfield place. Another one of my favorite houses. Rocky and I ride as close as we dare just to get a peek now and then.

And guess what? We pull up the driveway in a cloud of dust.

"Who are we not getting to meet now?" I ask.

Mona laughs. "Us."

"Seriously, who is it?"

She laughs again. "Us. You. Me. Them. Us. It's mine."

"Get out of town!"

"Would you like to examine the deed?"

Seems the bubbly has gone to my head. I distinctly heard Mona say she owns this place. I think. Rodney offers to refill my glass again, but I think I'd better stop and let what I've already had burn off. I think the chauffeur just offered me his hand to climb out. I think Mona just dismissed him. I think she and the guys are walking ahead of me. I think she's putting her key in the door. I think I'm gonna barf. I do, then I'm even more lightheaded. Champagne and me don't get along. Paul Tingle comes back for me. Actually picks me up. I feel like he really doesn't have to, but it's okay. It's okay. I'm fine.

I wake up in the dark, not sure where I am. If memory serves, wherever this is I got here by limo. No, that can't be right. I don't own a limo. There's a bit of light coming from under the door, enough for me to cross the room and feel for a switch. I hear voices coming from somewhere. Music. The smells of cooking. I hear Mona's laugh. I'd know that sound anywhere.

I turn on a light that makes my head explode and have a look around. Wow! Tapestry rug over a stone floor, Western art, antique furniture. I've been asleep in a canopy bed covered in a silk crazy quilt. I'm wearing a white satin nightie that's too big and too long, and my clothes are missing. But my gun and toolbelt are on the loveseat near a door that I hope leads to a bathroom. I'm dying of thirst and in need of a handful of aspirin.

I can see enough to make my way to the sink – a hammered brass affair with handles shaped like deer antlers. I gulp down two huge glasses of water, barf, drink another half a one, locate some aspirin, and slowly swallow three. There's also some Pepto. A slurp of that and I'm about as good as I'm going to get. I have a look at my hair in the mirror. I rummage through a couple of drawers and come up with a yellow scarf that looks like shit on me, but I tie it on pirate style. Splash some water on my face. Looking rode hard and put up wet, Flack.

I follow the voices out to the kitchen that is WAY too bright and too full of smells. They all start at once saying hi and asking me if I'm okay. I put a finger to my lips and my hand over my eyes, and they get it and lower their voices. Rodney turns off some of the lights, dims others.

"Here," he says and hands me a cup of coffee that smells like an instant antidote. He leads me to a high-backed chair. "Sit."

Paul Tingle is at the stove, stirring, tasting. He has a white kitchen towel thrown over one shoulder. He smiles at me and carries on.

"Coffee," I say. "This is good coffee."

"Thanks," says Paul Tingle. "There's more."

"Coffee."

Mona sits down with me. "I should have monitored your intake."

"You should have." Paul Tingle pours me another cup.

"Coffee," I say.

"Can I get you anything else?" he asks.

"No, thank you. Coffee."

I hold the cup with both hands like it's precious beyond words. It has certainly taken the words right out of me.

"Where are we?" I ask.

Mona says, "Reno. Huffaker Hills, more precisely."

"It wasn't a dream?"

"What wasn't, sweetie?"

"The house. That house on the hill. You know the one?"

"Yes, that's it. That's here."

"Coffee."

"Relax. We have all the time in the world now. Oh my, that gown doesn't fit well, does it?"

I look at a bare breast that I quickly cover up. How embarrassing. Pretty good of them not to give me shit about being half-naked.

"I'll go see what else I can find," says Mona.

I look around, careful not to move my head too quick, and see that fucking Mona has left me there alone with Paul Tingle. Rodney's outside smoking weed, steam rising off of the lit-up pool, a faint whiff of sulphur. A hot springs? Seriously? This place is turning out to have everything I need – except for the absence of people, even if they are helpful.

Here comes that uncomfortable silence between two people with a lot to say, so I say, "Uh, how do you like the Biggest Little City so far?"

"You know, fine. I haven't looked around much. Mona kind of took over."

"She does that."

He opens the oven door and takes out a roast with all the trimmings. I'm going to want some of that . . . tomorrow. He takes a baster and sprays the meat with pan drippings before sliding it back in.

"Good stove," he says. "Viking."

The kitchen's huge, built around a center island made of a thick slab of some kind of wood that's still shaped like a tree. Lots of chrome and metal and wood all around. Even I couldn't hurt this place . . . that is if I could cook at all. I could go for some of Lung Fung's eggplant about now. Best hangover food ever. This Brady Bunch home cooking thing isn't striking anywhere near the right chord.

Except for the coffee.

"We going to talk about this?" Officer Tingle asks.

"The coffee? It's great. I already said."

He bangs a pan down hard on the stove. "Goddammit! Will you cut the wise-ass routine?"

Whoa. Made him cuss. And that bang? My poor head. He's not looking at me now. He's staring up at the ceiling. I'm trying to keep my nighty from falling open again, but I'd really rather cover the ringing in my ears. Aspirins haven't quite done their job yet.

"You have no idea the risks I'm taking being here with you. And them. I could not only lose my job, I could end up never getting another job. Anywhere."

"Nobody asked you to be here, did they? Nobody said, 'Hey, Officer Tingle, like to get mixed up with a bunch of shady characters in Reno?' Who gave you the right to follow me? What makes you so goddam special?"

Rodney opens the slider, gauges the tension in the air, backs out, and closes the door. Nice and quietly.

"Susan Anne, I found these." Mona. She has clothes draped over her arm. She's still sorting through them and hasn't looked up. "I can't believe I was ever this size. A bad breakup was all it took for me to drop 35 pounds . . ."

She stops about ten feet away and takes a look at us. "I'll just put these in your room," she says as she skedaddles.

I get up from the table. He still isn't looking at me. "Whatever the hell you're thinking, get over it. I don't need your help – we don't need your help. I don't want you here."

I'd like to say I march out like a trooper, but I stub my toe on the chair leg, trip over a carpet, and stagger back to my room, cussing the air blue all the way.

Mona's waiting for me. Thankfully she's found me some jeans. Not Levis, but denim anyway. They're too big around and too long, but I pick an acceptable shirt, tuck it in, and roll up my pant legs.

"I'll get you a belt," she says.

"Thanks."

I sit down on the loveseat and rest my head on the back. With my eyes closed, I feel a hundred times better. I can hear Rodney and Paul Tingle talking low in the kitchen. Can't really hear what they're saying, just the sound of male voices. I've always found that reassuring: the sound of men. I've known some good ones. More of them, at least, than bad ones. I loved to hear my father and his friends laughing and talking after I'd been tucked into bed. I'd fall asleep with the lullaby of their deep tones letting me know I was safe at home. The sounds of men talking in the distance still has that effect on me. I'm on the verge of nodding off when Mona returns.

"Here," she says, handing me a beautiful tooled belt with a silver buckle shaped like a horseshoe.

"Yours?" I ask, inspecting this un-Mona-like accessory.

"Certainly not! I'm not sure where it came from. Keep it."

"Oh, I plan to."

She sits down by me. "Don't be so hard on that poor guy. He genuinely likes you. It boggles the mind why. He told me about your exploits together. I can just see you out in the street in your hooker suit. I must say you do make an outstanding first impression."

"What is it with guys? Pull a gun on someone? Run out into the street half-dressed? And they go and get all moonie-eyed. What happened happened. That's all. He can't be here. I don't want him here. I can take care of myself."

She snaps her fingers. "Now I remember! That belt? Marilyn Monroe was supposed to wear it in The Misfits. My friend Victoria brought it to wear when she visited here. She thought it would help her blend in."

"Did it?"

"It would have if she hadn't topped off her ensemble with the most ludicrously large white Stetson I've ever seen. Movies are one thing, reality is quite another."

I hold the belt up to the light. "Ain't my style, but, damn, Marilyn Monroe almost wore it? You're never getting this back."

"Help yourself."

"Wait, you said your friend Victoria? A friend-friend? One who actually likes you?"

"Ha. Ha. For your information, Miss Smartypants, she's a lead costume designer for Paramount Pictures. She has won several Academy Awards."

"Whoop-de-do."

Mona just sighs.

There's a light tap on the door. It's Rodney.

"Food's on the table."

Mona says, "I'll be right there. Susan Anne, lighten up on Paul. He's a keeper."

Now that I'm dressed all I want to do is get undressed and climb under that crazy quilt and go back to sleep. I get up and drop my drawers.

"You keep him then. I'm going back to bed." I strip off my shirt, lay down, and pull the covers over my head.

"You'll feel differently in the morning, I guarantee it."

I flip her off. She flips me off.

I'm laughing now. "That how you treat your friend Victoria?"

"Most certainly not! She's too much of a lady."

211

She gets a pillow in the face for that. One last thing before I go nite-nite. "Mo?"

"Yes, my love?"

"A hot springs?"

"Oh, that. Of course. And a nice, cold freshwater spring in the summer."

"Damn."

I bury myself in the covers. She quietly closes the door behind her.

And something happens that rarely happens to me: I start to cry. Not like at that Oakland 7-Eleven. No big pitiful sobs or anything, just dribbles. It's the booze, the fight. I don't want a keeper. Or anyone else for that matter. I want to be left alone to do my thing.

Then it occurs to me that I'd also like to know why we went by the Redfield mansion. Damn my curiosity. Damn my stupid tears. Damn Paul Tingle.

• • •

I hang out in my room as much as possible. Got to admit: I'm comfortable. Except for Mona's other houseguests. One in particular. I found some Zane Greys on the bookshelf to keep me company. Rodney drops me food. Leaves it outside the door with a light tap. That guy! He even leaves me the right amount of Jim Beam and Luckys. Clean ashtrays. That guy!

Mona? She barges in and bugs me whenever she feels like it. I can get her to leave if I start reading Zane Grey out loud. Sometimes I have to make it REAL loud for her to get the point. She usually ends up throwing something heavy, but not breakable, at my head. Like one of my boots. I win! Even if it hurts sometimes.

212

Paul Tingle? Why doesn't he take the hint and hit the road? The couple of times I've suggested it at the top of my lungs, he reminds me it's a free country and Mona's house, and she says he can stay as long as he likes. I can't figure out how to make him not like it here. What is it with him?

I have to come out once in a while to do laundry or go for a soak. That hot springs water is just too tempting. When I do poke my head out of my hidey-hole, those guys throw a party. Booze, music, snacks. I'm a sucker for M&Ms. I keep my distance from Officer Tingle, though, dammit, I catch myself sneaking peeks at him. If anyone notices, they're smart enough to keep that info to themselves. They know what's good for them.

So, why am I still here? My trailer is sitting empty. Probably full of mice by now, but it is my home to go to. Any time. I have a car. I can just go.

I have gas money.

It's that damn hot springs water!

That's my story, and I'm sticking to it.

• • •

Tonight's Rodney's birthday, Mona tells me, and we are by gawd going into town to celebrate. It's to be a surprise, so keep my trap shut. I'm told I will dress up, dammit. And don't even try to get out of it, you hear me? (I can hear the dreaded "young lady" on the end of that sentence.) 7 sharp, you hear me?

For Rodney? I shall be on my best behavior. Spit-shined and waiting by the front door at 6:57. Mona's already been in here three times asking me what I'm going to wear. I have told her, "Clothes," three times. She has given me the evil eye

213

three times. I advised her that three times is enough, and threw a boot at her. I missed. She hasn't come back. I still have that little black number I picked up in San Francisco. Wait til they get a load of that!

It dawns on me that this will mean the four of us on a date. That sucks. Small talk. Avoiding eye contact. Making nicey-nice. I'm only good at one of those things. You know what I'm talking about. But it's Rodney's night. I can suffer through a few hours of hideous, dressed-up torture for Rodney. I won't think about Paul Tingle. Not one solitary thought. Not one.

I emerge from my room, yanking down the back hem of my dress and falling off the side of one stiletto.

"Fuck!" I say. Only my pride is hurt. Nobody saw me.

Rodney calls from the kitchen, "Everything okay?"

"Yeah, fine."

"Cool."

Let's see: Glamorous, almost-too-small handbag? Check. Colt Python? Check. Loaded? Check. Money? Check. Ginger frost lipstick? Double check. (Why double check?) Clock on the wall says 6:50, so I'm early. I sit down on the arm of the couch, cross my black-pantihosed legs, yank the dress down closer to my knees, and wait. I know where Rodney is. Those other two must still be dressing, the show-offs. I hear water running, hairspray spraying, closet doors opening and closing. I pick at my ratty fingernails and wait.

Rodney arrives with a drink for me.

"Happy Birthday," I say. And then I say, "Whoops."

"'s cool. I know what's up."

We clink glasses. He is a vision in black velvet with a peacock feather eyepatch and an electric blue turtleneck. Style.

"You look nice," he says.

"You, too."

"Easy when you this pretty," he says, patting his Afro. He's got a ring on almost every finger. I take the hand that's not holding his drink so I can inspect the quality. Yeah, they're all the real deal.

"Nice," I say.

"Better be. Hold up."

Now he takes my hand. He examines my fingernails with a face that looks like he's smelled rotten eggs. But then he takes a monster diamond ring off of his pinkie and slides in onto my right index finger.

"Well," he says, clears his throat, and says, "Well . . ."

What can I say but, "Thanks."

A car pulls up out front. Limo. Naturally. Mona. Same chauffeur from the other night. Didn't know you could special request chauffeurs. Snazzy.

I hear Officer Tingle and Mona complimenting each other as they enter the room. I stand up. Tug at my dress. They both look at me like they've never seen me before.

"What have you done with Susan Anne?" says Mona. She's decked out in gold everything. Beaded, strapless mini dress. A couple of thick necklaces. Paul Tingle is wearing an immaculately pressed navy blue suit with a blinding white shirt and red and black striped tie. I glance at his face and see he's looking all goo-goo eyed at me.

"Man, you look like a fucking politician," Rodney says. He goes over and grabs him by the upper arm. "Come with me."

Rodney's laughing, leading Officer Tingle away.

I accidentally sigh. Mona starts to speak. I glare at her til she shuts her mouth. "I'm getting another one of these," I say. "Want anything?"

"Vodka. Rocks."

"My pleasure." I walk as gracefully — which means slowly — as I can toward the kitchen. I hear her stifling a giggle, so I flip her off.

"You could use some pointers, my dear," she says as I hand her to drink.

"You know what you can do with your pointers . . .?" I tap her glass with mine instead of finishing that sentence. She wouldn't listen anyway.

Paul Tingle returns a changed man. Rodney has ruffled up that beautiful blond hair, and put him in a black satin dress shirt open at the collar, cuffs rolled up. Over that he's wearing a black vest embroidered with vines made out of metallic silver thread. Sounds pimpy, I know, but it's sharp. He really looks sharp.

Mona says, "That's better. Shall we go?"

I open the door and wave them out. As Paul Tingle passes me, I smell Irish Spring and a hint of something I can't quite put my finger on, but it's definitely doing a number on me.

Then I slam the door shut with me inside. Doesn't work. Rodney comes back and drags my ass out.

I get into the limo last. Mona has already broken out the champagne and handed it to Rodney.

"Uh uh! No fucking way! Never again!" I say.

"Oh, I wouldn't worry about that, dahlink," Mona says, and get this: opens the door and slides out. She extends her bejeweled hand back for Rodney, and he gets out, too.

"My birthday ain't til November," he says with an evil smile.

Mona slams the door, bangs on the roof to tell the driver to take off, and she and Rodney stand there arm in arm, waving good-bye to me and Paul Tingle like a couple of parents seeing their little girl off to the prom. I hate her. I truly do.

Trapped.

I muster up all the pissed-off-ness I've been storing up, look him in those blue eyes, and say, "You . . . you . . . you . . ."

But it's clear he's as stunned as I am. "I . . . I . . . I . . ."

He flops back against the seat, crosses his arms. I scoot away as far as I can and cross my legs and my arms. I'd love to know where we're going, but I'm not going to give him the pleasure of wondering first. We just sit there, not looking at each other, riding.

The chauffeur's window rolls down. "Would you like some music?" he asks.

We both yell, "NO!," and go back to being . . . well, in my case, pissed off. Don't know what he's thinking, and I ain't asking.

Chapter 28

The Midnight Mine is made of wood, wood, and more wood. Varnished, rough, carved – you name it. Floor to ceiling. Wood. Little candles flicker on the tables, the lights are low. Waiters are friendly ghosts bringing slabs of steak from the kitchen with barely a sound. The place is a romantic destination, one of those best kept secret kind of places. I've been here on a couple of dates that didn't work out. But the food and the vibes were good.

I love this place for all its outdoorsy-ness in our town of neon. The sign in front – carved wood, naturally – is lit by a single yellow bug bulb. At night, if you didn't know exactly where you were going, you'd pass the place a couple of times before you'd see it. The parking lot is dirt. There are huge cottonwoods surrounding it. And – ahem – there are also a couple of little cottages in the back, same kind of rustic, where newlyweds and adulterors can "rest" after a good meal.

The food? Top-notch. They make what they call a "caesar salad" right at your table. Never heard of that before I came here with a wrong guy. He ordered one for each of us. The showoff. But I was hooked. On the salad. Had my first lobster on that disaster date, too. Likewise hooked. On the lobster. You can keep the turf. Bring me the surf.

I open the limo door before the driver can come around, and start walking to the Mine. I assume Paul Tingle is right behind me. Fuck it, we're here. Might as well eat.

"Good evening. Do you have a reservation?" asks the spectacularly well-groomed and stacked hostess. She takes in my costume, head to toe, and seems to approve.

"Uh, Crawford?"

She runs a long red fingernail down the page. "Yes. Follow me, please."

I follow her swaying butt and her stilettos to a secluded table. She pulls out a chair on the side, but I stop her.

"I'll be facing the door if you don't mind."

"Certainly." She rearranges the chairs and pulls mine out. Not only that, she slides it back under me and puts the white cloth napkin in my lap. A little fresh, if you ask me. She steps back and collides with Officer Tingle, who she takes in head to toe, and really, really approves of.

"Oh, sir, I'm terribly sorry."

Paul Tingle has her by the elbow, which she seems — really, really seems — to approve of because she doesn't get out of his way very fast.

"It's okay," he says. "That's what I get for tailgating."

She's literally gawking at him now.

"May I bring you a complimentary cocktail by way of apology?"

"Sure. I'll have a . . ." I stop myself. Duh, Flack, she's not talking to you.

Officer Tingle lets go of her arm and says, "That's not necessary."

"Oh, but I insist."

She can't take her eyes off of him. I can hear the silent, "Pretty please?"

He smiles that 1000-watt smile. "How can I refuse? A glass of something red and dry as the desert."

Barf, I think.

"Excellent. Back in a jif." She sways away from our table without asking me for my drink order.

Officer Tingle plants himself in the chair next to, not across from, mine and spreads his napkin in his lap.

At one of the other tables a couple, who look like they're celebrating maybe a 30th anniversary, are enjoying coffees, cognac, and desserts, winding down dinner early. The only other couple here looks to be on a first date. They break off eye contact with one another pretty quickly. Glance around the room a lot. I see the man sneak a peek at his watch. Is he waiting to spring the idea of one of the cottages on her? Or wishing she'd hurry up and eat so he can drop her at her house? I love making up stories about people when I'm stuck being out and about. Good practice.

"Here we are." The hostess is back with Paul Tingle's wine. A full bottle, to be exact. "I hope you like it. It's one of our best. Your waiter will be here shortly to uncork it."

"Ahem," I say. "Can you take my order now?"

"Huh?" She looks to have completely forgotten me. "Er, what can I get for you?"

I decide to go classy and order an Old Forester instead of my usual.

"Hurry back, now," I say as she stays frozen in her tracks.

220

"Huh? Oh, right. Coming right up."

She teeters away on her spike heels, then turns back after a few steps.

"May I bring you anything else? An appetizer?"

Before Officer Tingle can answer, I say, "Yeah. You guys still make those, ya know, little crab dealies?"

"Crab cakes? Absolutely."

"We'll take some plates of those."

"Excellent."

I turn my attention back to the anniversary couple. The man motions for their check. He takes a thin box out of his jacket pocket and hands it to the woman. She opens it and produces a beautiful diamond bracelet. She puts her hand to her heart as he fastens it around her other wrist, which already has two or three other humongous diamond bracelets on it. Brother, is she easy to shop for. They kiss sweetly, look into each other's eyes. When the check comes, he takes out his glasses, examines the bill, and pulls out his wallet. He stacks a pile of cash on top of the check, then stands and pulls back his wife's chair. She gives him her hand. He hands her a silver cane. Holding one arm, he helps her cross the room, waving to the hostess who comes to open the door for them. The man kisses the hostess's cheek, the hostess kisses the wife's cheek, and they leave. I see the hostess breathe a huge, heart-filled sigh, putting her hand to her heart the same way the woman had when she got her gift.

Corn-yyyyyyy

"Wow, that was really beautiful," says Officer Tingle, putting his hand on my shoulder and giving a little squeeze.

I shrug him off. "Your buddy the hostess is sure into it. Let's me and you just try to enjoy our food."

I'm asking here: Should I cut the guy a break? Am I the only person on Earth who thinks I ought to run out of here screaming? What is my major malfunction? Hey! Who's side are you on anyway?

A dark-haired waiter with huge white teeth brings my drink, then proceeds with all the wine-opening rigamarole for Paul Tingle, who performs his part perfectly. Showoff. When the crab cakes arrive, my "date" eats his with a knife and fork while I pick one up with my fingers and down it in two bites. These little suckers are GOOD. I could make a meal out of just these, but there's lobster to be had. And ceasar salad. I'll behave.

Looks like the first-date couple isn't likely to snuggle up in a cottage. She's out of her seat and out the door before he gets a chance to pay the check. Not sure what to make of that. Except it wasn't a very hot date after all.

I order my usual surf and surf. Paul Tingle goes for very rare prime rib and a baked potato with extra sour cream. Nothing green. Except some chives. His farm boy is showing now.

When our waiter rolls up a silver cart with the making for my ceasar salad, Officer Tingle says, "May I?"

"Uh, certainly, sir," says the waiter, not entirely comfortable with the idea but also knowing we're VIPs. "Be my guest."

Now, you know I've never made one of these things, but Paul Tingle sure has. He's a goddam expert. I am impressed and having a hard time not showing it. He cracks the egg. He stirs. He whisks. He tosses. He grates. He grinds. He lays out the anchovies just so. Then he sets it in front of me on the tips of his fingers with one hand behind his back.

"Whoa," says the waiter.

"Whoa," I say, holding out my glass for a refill. "Double me up, okay?"

When our dinners arrive, I watch him examine the slab of

dripping beef with his expert eye, prodding it with his fork.

"Angus," I say. "From Anderson Ranch out in Washoe Valley."

"Grass-fed. Good marbling." He slices the oozing meat down the bright red middle and starts eating from the inside out. He nods his approval.

"Excellent," he says. "Dairy beef is about one step up from shoe leather. Sure have eaten my fill of that."

I dive into the lobster, but I can hardly taste it because I'm still all wound up about the salad. Yeah, it's just green stuff, but this one is somehow gooder than I remember. Is it because . . .? Nah. Just keep telling yourself that, Flack. Nah. And take another scrumptious bite.

"Is yours okay?" he asks.

"Mine? Oh yeah. You can't miss in this place."

"Those ingredients were really fresh. I could tell."

"How about that."

The low light, the extra booze, the rich food. I'm feeling friendlier by the minute. A little. A little more. I start telling him the stories I'm making up about the diners coming and going. And guess what? He's pretty good at it, too! Figures. He is a cop and all. Now we're laughing and having to lean in to whisper to each other. He has sneaked his chair closer to mine. Our hands have touched on the table.

Seems like only moments have gone by, and now we're having coffee and splitting a tiramisu – which I've never heard of and he ordered. With two forks. Man, is that stuff good! He has a speck of powdered sugar on his lip. I wipe it off with my finger and lick it. He smiles. Cuts another piece and feeds it to me off of his fork. So I do one for him.

My concrete-and-castiron composure is suddenly shot to hell. I'm having fun now, dammit. Right in front of him! He orders us each a warm Amaretto. Heaven.

Bam! He kisses me smack on the lips. And, dammit, I kiss him back. We get into a serious lip-lock. Feels like it goes on and on and on. I want it to go on and on and on and on. We put our hands on each other's faces. We're glued, dammit.

When we finally come up for air, the big-toothed waiter is standing there looking casually in another direction. He hears us break suction and asks if there'll be anything else he can bring us. We shake our heads no. He takes our bill out of his apron pocket and sets it in front of Officer Tingle.

"Just sign for it."

Officer Tingle has nice handwriting. He reaches for his wallet to leave a tip.

"All taken care of, sir."

That Mona.

"Oh, and there's this." He hands Paul Tingle a key on a gold chain that says "3." Paul Tingle looks confused.

I say, "I'll show you."

Outside, the air feels wonderful and fresh and the tiniest bit chilly. Our limo is gone.

"But how do we . . .?" he says.

"I'll show you."

Remember me saying about those little bungalows out back? 3 has smoke coming out of the chimney.

Chapter 29

It's not that I'm a prude. Shit, you can tell that by the way I talk and the company I keep. I'm just not one for sharing every single detail about what goes on between my belly button and my knees. There's a reason that's called "privates." Besides, anyone's imagination in those areas is better than mine. I'm more of a "Do your own thing" girl, not a "Let it all hang out" one.

I will say this for our night in 3 . . . Actually, no, I won't. Except this:

I think I'm in love.

Shit.

Chapter 30

This morning started this afternoon when we finally got hungry for actual food. And coffee. Coffee. And a ciggy for little ole me. Midnight Mine only serves dinner, but we see the back door of the kitchen is already open, and we go begging. Probably not the first bleary-eyed, messy-haired couple to do that. Officer Tingle promises to stay out of their way if they let him whip us up some eggs and toast. I plop a handful of hundreds on the counter near a pile of chopped onions – and get royally cussed out about contamination by a tattooed mountain of a shaggy man, who scoops the cash into a steel bowl, sets it on a high shelf, and nods at Paul Tingle to carry on.

We carry our breakfast back to 3 and eat in bed between giggles and smooches. I'd die of embarrassment if anyone saw me so romancey.

He says, "I guess we should call Rodney or Mona to come get us."

Gawd, am I not ready to face them. Her, for sure.

Thinking fast, I say, "Hey, you know all that mess with the Ruggerios you were worried about?"

"The what?"

"The reward on me? The one you followed me here about? The place? Where it happened? Johnny's? It's a couple miles up the road."

That immediately took his attention off of both me and the food. He jumps out of bed and starts throwing on his clothes.

"Well?" he says. "Get UP!"

"I ain't getting far in these," I say, dangling the idiotic stilettos.

"Piggy-back?"

"Yeah. Right. I know a chick about a mile from here. I can bare-hoof it that far. She'll loan me something."

This is a very stupid, un-Flack-like thing for me to do, but his fresh eyes could be just what I need. I think. Or am I just showing off like a sex-crazed idiot?

• • •

So, here we are, walking along the shoulder of Highway 40. In any other town, a guy in a black satin vest, a black shirt, and slacks carrying pantihose, stilettos, and an evening bag, kicking up dust with a bare-legged, bare-footed girl in a black mini dress would attract attention. And cops. But, luckily, this is Reno. Drivers fly past us without a glance, stirring up tumbleweeds and gravel we're getting clobbered with. Just another Thursday morning. I mean, afternoon. Ho-hum.

It's my mom's old friend Judith that lives out here. She slops around her flakey trailer and its assortment of add-ons and lean-tos in holey overalls and oil paint-splattered flannel shirts, with too many cats and three old brood mares. After Mom died, Judith and I used to ride together and talk and cry. Before the horses got too old. Or maybe Judith got too old. Or maybe she couldn't cry any more. I still stop her place by now and then. She has one evil sense of humor. I can always use a dose of that.

Sage, Queeny, and Flame whiny at me as we walk up. Wish I had remembered to snag something to feed them. They let me and Officer Tingle rub their muzzles. We let them slime us with snot and spit. He's all smiles, scratching Queeny behind the ears and baby-talking her. His country boy is showing.

Judith comes out the screen door, kicking cats aside. They snarl and hiss, but I know they'll be back. She loves them.

"I swear to Christ there's more of'em every damn day," she says. "Flack, sweetheart! Good to see you."

She crushes me against her massive bosom and twists us side to side.

"Who the hell's this hunka burnin' love?" she asks with a come-to-mama look behind her coke-bottle-bottom glasses.

"Paul Tingle," I say as I, DAMMIT!, blush. "Officer Tingle. Officer Paul Tingle."

"You brought the fuzz to my house?" She tries to act all serious but starts cracking up. "How's tricks, fuzz?"

"Pleased to meet you," he says, holding out his hand. Judith grabs it and pulls him into her pillowy self. Paul Tingle seems shocked at first but hugs her back. She wraps one leg around his, sticks her tongue out at me, and laughs her ass off.

"You two are a pair. Been out all night, I take it?"

"No, we had a place . . ." he starts as he points to where we came from.

I elbow him in the ribs to keep him from spilling more beans. Judith bends over double, laughing at us.

"Ain't love grand? Come on in. Let's have a snort."

Her snort is a Hamm's. Officer Tingle takes one, too. She always has Jim Beam on hand for me. Hands me the bottle and no glass.

"What you working on, Judith?" I ask.

"Oh man, I'm all into broken-down cars and houses and wrecked stuff. Be right back."

She waddles off to the back, cussing at cats, and slinging crap out of her way. Officer Tingle takes advantage of her absence to sneak in a few kisses. I sure do like that too much.

Judith comes back with a couple of canvases she props on the couch.

"Judith, these are amazing," I say. They truly are. Colorful and abstract and gritty. I love them! Then I notice that one of them is of the casino sign graveyard. "Is this one for sale?"

"Shit, sugar, everything's for sale. You know me. But your money's no good here. Take it." She puts it directly into my hands.

You can't fight her, I know that. I also know I HAVE to have this painting. The sign graveyard was one of Mona's and my favorite places to play. All those colors and wires and dead neon. Close as I ever got to Disneyland.

Paul Tingle says, "You really are good, Judith. These are so Kandinsky-esque."

"Canna what?"

"Kandinsky. Mid-Modernism. Early Abstractism."

"Good Lord, Flack. I don't know what he's talking about, but he sure sounds purty." She slaps her thighs, laughing.

"Any chance I might have left a change of clothes around here?" I ask.

"Honey, if you did, they're in the spare room."

"Uh, which one?"

"The spare one. Over there. Shit."

I go the direction she's pointing. Weave my way through canned goods and Frosted Flakes and magazines and boots. I find a box with my name on it under several dead houseplants. I rate my own box? That's really cool.

I don't remember leaving my stuff out here, but they're mine all right. I change out of the little black dress into Levis and a Western shirt, and I'm feeling like my old self again. Wish I'd left some socks. I hate how feet get all sweaty in boots.

"That's better," I say.

"Back to normal," Judith says.

"So, hey, can I borrow a car real quick?"

"Sure, honey. Take your pick." She takes a full ring of keys out of her pocket and tosses them to me. I find one with a Ford logo.

"What's this go to?" I ask.

"Green pickup over by the propane tank."

I look at the heap out the window.

"It runs?"

"Of course it fucking runs. Think I'd keep it if it didn't?"

I tell her we'll be right back. She doesn't ask where we're going, but she insists that Officer Tingle give her a kiss on the lips, which he does. I thank her for the loaner. She kisses me on the lips.

Her yard is full of junkers of all sorts of years and makes and levels of rot. Nothing's up on blocks or crashed to shit, though. She might be serious that they all run.

I'd have bet against it, but the green truck farts and starts after only half a dozen tries and multiple pumps of the gas peddle. We're not going far. It'll make it.

In the daylight, Johnny's place looks even more like a random pile of white shoeboxes dumped out in the desert. Architect must have been on some serious LSD to come up with something this . . . what's the word I'm looking for? . . . stupid.

"There it is," I say. "Rancho Spaghetti-O."

"He didn't really call it that."

"Should of."

"Frank Lloyd Wright gone wrong."

"Uh, I'm not even gonna ask, college boy."

"He's an architect famous for his . . ."

"You can quit there, pardner. I'll never remember."

He's quiet for a minute.

"You sure you want to do this?" he asks.

"Me? Nah, won't bother me."

And as soon as I say it, I don't feel all that sure. Even taking out an asshole like Johnny was a stretch for me. I didn't go there bent on murder. It just . . . happened. Weird how nobody – Ruggerios or the cops – has hassled me. Yet. Suddenly I'm jumpy about the decision to come out here. I was feeling so mushy about sharing . . . stuff . . . with Officer Tingle it just slipped out. I hope I haven't completely slipped up.

I pull the pickup onto a dirt road that doesn't look like it gets used much. I drive a ways down and into a low gully. Yikes! It's softer than it looked. Gonna be a bitch to get out, but us being on foot will make it easier to sneak up on Johnny's. Just in case.

Paul Tingle doesn't ask about this move. He knows. We check our weapons and start walking.

"Place is even uglier up close," he says.

"Got that right. Wait'll you see inside."

I feel sick. Damn.

Officer Tingle's dress-up clothes are getting dustier by the second. Makes me laugh.

"What?" he asks.

"Your fancy duds, city boy."

"Yeah, well. I've been covered in worse."

We duck into some of the taller brush on the pool side of the house to do a little recon. Somebody has painted a gigantic peace sign and some psychedelic flowers on what used to be a big, blank wall over here. There's a pile of garbage. Lots of wine bottles, looks like some clothing, smells like rotten food.

And then, there it is. The tell-tale whiff of patchouli and marijuana. Flashbacks to my former office mates, the "artists" on the top floor. And? Drumming? From inside. Great googly-moogly! Sounds — and smells — like there's a party going on.

We swing around to the deck, crouch down, and look through the bottom of the railing. Here we go: naked people. A whole bunch of'em. Gyrating and flopping their arms around to the beat that fucks up and restarts and fucks up again. Naked people wrapped around each other, some of them in group-gropes. Everybody's got long hair. Hard to tell the chicks from the dudes.

Crud. Hippies. Hippies have squatted down in the snazzy, expensive, out-of-place Rancho Spaghetti-O and turned it into a dope den. I see smoke. I see bubbles. I see . . . feathers? White, fluffy feathers being tossed around like confetti. Looks like someone's dismantling the furniture.

So far Paul Tingle's getting a kick out of showing up at an orgy. He's grinning his goofy, too-white Clark Kent grin.

"Stay or go?" I whisper.

"Oh, stay. For sure, stay. This ought to be interesting."

Good enough for me. It'll be fun messing with these stoners' heads.

"Follow my lead," he says.

232

"Hey, this is my crime scene, remember?"

"No, really. For once just do what I say."

"You're the boss." And I do not mean that at all.

It figures that at least a few of Johnny's best friends would be living it up at the Rancho for at least as long as there's food and booze, but I sure didn't take any of the ones I met as being hippie types. Well, wait, there was Smiley the chauffeur. A-ha. Gotta be. He's partying his ass off in his murdered employer's house, he's so heartbroken. I'm not a betting woman, but I'd take your money, I'm feeling so right. Can't wait to see my friend Smiley! Hope he remembers me.

There's so much noise and shit going on that we slide open the door, slide inside, and go completely undetected. Not bad detectiving. There must be 50 people in various orgies of dancing or eating or — barf — screwing. Or blowing bubbles or frolicking in feathers. Lots of laughing, singing, grunting and groaning, drumming. I see Smiley now. Nekked as a jaybird, lounging back on the gutted couch, a nekked, definitely underage chick on each side of him, his hands on each of their crotches. He seems to know what he's doing. They're loving it.

"Stop," I whisper to Paul Tingle. "I know that guy."

"Which one?"

"There. On the couch."

Officer Tingle stands up and marches his way through the crowd of stinky, sweaty bodies and kicks Smiley's feet off the coffee table.

"Hey! What the fuck, man?" he yells. He makes no move to get up, though the girls — and pretty much everyone else — take one look at my date's slick, blond, establishment haircut and general normalness and beat a hasty retreat.

Paul Tingle nails Smiley to the couch with his cop voice. "Did I say you could leave, asshole?"

What is he trying to pull here?

"Mark Gallagher, IRS," he says. "And you're the owner here?"

"Uh, well . . ."

"Can you tell me where I can find him? He owes the government back taxes since 1970."

"Uh, well . . ."

"Come now, Mr. . . .? I didn't catch the name."

"Hey man, I got nothin' to do with this place. Me and my friends, we just . . ."

Smiley tries to stand up, but Paul Tingle pushes him back down.

"I need to see some ID," Officer Tingle says with authority. "I see you don't have any on you."

"I have it. I do. Gotta go get it."

Okay, playtime is over. Paul Tingle's had his fun. My turn. I walk over to them. Officer Tingle looks disappointed. He was just warming up.

"Hi, Smiley," I say. "Remember me?"

"Should I? Who the fuck are you?"

"A friend of a friend, you could say."

"Look, mama, you need to get the fuck off of my property."

Officer Tingle pipes up again. "Thought you weren't the owner."

Smiley takes a longer look at the two of us – me in my usual cowgirl clothes, Paul Tingle in dusty evening wear. He's catching on. Good boy.

"Hold up, now. You look like a hick, he looks like a pimp. What the fuck is this? Wait. You're that friend of Mona's. Yeah, that's it. Smack?"

"Close enough."

"How's it going?" he yawns and stretches out, putting his

feet back on the table. "Who's your pimp?"

"Uh-uh. I'll be asking the questions."

"Shoot."

"Don't tempt me."

"You're trippin', mama."

"What's going on here?"

"This? Caretakin'. My job."

"Oh, that's what this is."

"Is."

"And them?"

He snickers. "Trainees."

He thinks he can out-smart-ass me? I can't have that.

"Hey, you know where Mona's at?" he asks.

"Dead."

"Bummer."

Officer Tingle looks confused but keeps up the game. He says, "What we have here is trespassing, breaking and entering, vandalism, and whatever else the police want to come up with. Sooooo, I'll go ahead and let the home office know I found a responsible party to collect our taxes from. Where's your phone?"

Smiley's quick for a pothead. He pulls a pistol out of what's left of the cushion he's sitting on.

Officer Tingle and I return the favor, of course.

"What's it going to be? You want to go out horizontally or vertically?" Officer Tingle asks.

"I think I said I'd be asking the questions," I say, moving forward. "What's your fucking name?"

"Puddin'-tane."

I cock the hammer back, so he does, too. So does Paul Tingle. This is getting sticky.

"The lady wants to know: What. Is. Your. Fucking. Name. She'll want to spell it right on your headstone."

"Duke. Duke Bradbury."

"Now, that wasn't so hard, was it?"

Duke says, "I gotta ask one question if that's all right."

"Okay. One."

"What in the ever-loving hell are you doing here?"

"I heard there was some trouble. Thought I'd take a look. Maybe find a clue or two."

"That's hilarious, mama. You ought to know. You was here that night."

"I believe your facts are a little off. According to my sources, you weren't here."

"True, true. So, what do you think, Flack Murrow Private Investigator? Find any clues? And who the fuck is he?"

Duke knows my name after all. Sneaky bastard. I uncock my gun, he does the same. So does Paul Tingle.

I say, "Just a handsome stranger I picked up in a bar last night." I glance at Officer Tingle. "What was your name again?"

"Very funny," the guys say in unison.

Officer Tingle says, "Let's not all get testy. Seems what we have here is just some boring old hippie trying to relive his glory days."

"That I am, that I am. Going out in style or not going at all."

"I believe you're right," I say. "Case closed. Welp, me and Robin are heading on back to the Batcave."

"You do that, Batmama and Robin."

"Gotta ask a favor, though."

"You can ask."

"We need a ride to our car. The Batmobile's due back at the rental place by 6."

"You got it."

"Whoa there, pardner. I'm not done with this place yet,"

says Officer Tingle.

"Are you fucking kidding me?!" I say. I really don't want to spend another second in this hell hole.

"You dragged me out here. I'm having a look around."

"But . . ."

"Sew buttons on your butt," he says over his shoulder as he walks away.

Duke says, "'Sew buttons on your butt?' Where'd you find this guy? Old folks' home?" He laughs himself into a coughing fit. He's turning red. Should I be worried?

"You okay?"

He holds up a finger but keeps choking.

Finally he catches his breath enough to talk. "I'm used to it. I smoke plenty of grass, dig?"

"But you turned red. That can't be good."

"Irish blood. Normal."

"Right."

Here I am with yet another naked guy. I'm telling you: Between naked guys and babies, I have my hands full.

Then KEEEE-RASH! from somewhere.

"I'm okay," we hear.

"What broke?" asks Duke.

"Um, I'm not sure. Big. Ugly. Apparently glass."

"Nice going, slick. I'll have to charge you for that." This sends Duke into another fit. Glad he finds Officer Tingle humorous.

"That boy's a one-man rock fight," he says after he takes a swig of wine out of a bottle.

"How's that?"

Duke pantomimes taking a rock, tossing it straight up, watching it come down, and hitting him in the eye. He spreads his hands like ta-da. My turn to have a laugh. Can't wait for the opportunity to put Paul Tingle down with that one.

We've arrived at the dreaded lull in the conversation. Duke scratches his nuts before I have time to look away. Eeeeewwww. Then he has the nerve to offer me the bottle of wine with the same hand. And the fucker's smiling.

"Pass," I say.

More silence.

"What you been up to, Flack? I mean, other than bumping off homeowners."

"You got no proof of that."

"Might."

"Meaning?"

"Now, you know Johnny liked to make his little movies."

"Do I?"

"Cut the crap, mama. I know you're shacked up with Mona, and I know she has one of the cameras and some of the tapes."

"One?"

"Jesus, Johnny had more money than gawd. Think he'd settle for just one of anything?"

"Guess not."

"You'd guess right. Lemme show you."

Officer Tingle's still farting around, so what the hell? I follow Duke back behind the bar, where we scare up a covey of naked hippies hiding back there. They scatter. A couple of them scream when they come across Paul Tingle, and we hear doors slamming and feet running outside. There they go, off through the brush to . . .?

Duke slides open the mirrored wall behind the bar, exposing a whole bunch of black equipment with lights and dials and wires and screens and crap like a science fiction movie. It's all turned off, which makes it even scarier looking. I half expect either Bob Wilkins or Alan Funt to jump out and tell us to SMILE.

"I don't think he ever knew what half of this junk was for. I know I don't. Don't want to either. He was always futzing around back here like he was some Frankenstein or Einstein or something. Kept him out of our hair, I'll say that much for it. He was so paranoid from all the coke and shit at . . . the end . . . he was positive everybody in the house was out to get him. Took it into his head that he had to know what was going on here every minute, every room. But, like I said, I don't know if this shit works or not."

"You guys!" Paul Tingle yells. "Check this out."

"Where are you at?" I yell back.

"Up some stairs. Game room."

Duke starts out ahead of me, which means I'm looking at his hairy ass.

"Don't you want to put some pants on?" I ask.

He keeps walking. "Why?"

Criminy. I'll check out the floor tiles.

We pass the closed door to Pioche's room. You bet your sweet bippy I'll slide in there before we go.

Paul Tingle is giddy as a kid at Christmas with the stash of handguns he's come up with from inside a dark pinball machine.

"Look at you," I say. "Good job. Can we go now?"

"But this is a lot of firepower for just one guy."

Duke says, "Johnny? He was never just one guy. Nobody in that family is."

Paul Tingle looks like he could settle in for a long review of Ruggerio family history.

"Later, Paul Tingle, I promise," I say.

"Paul Tingle. Pretty formal for you two lovebirds, isn't it?"

Me: "No." Him: "Yeah." In unison.

There Duke goes, laughing and choking again. Officer

Tingle makes a move to help him when he turns red.

"He's okay," I say. "He's Irish."

"But . . ."

"He's laughing because this many guns is nothing to the Ruggerio family."

"But . . ."

"Man, let it go. Come see what we found."

That's when Officer Tingle notices Duke's still clothesless.

"Man, put some goddam clothes on!"

"What's it to you, bub?"

Paul Tingle pulls his gun.

"Fine. Fine," Duke says, walking away, scratching his ass.

Officer Tingle shivers and makes a face. "Can't even stand that in the locker room."

"Guess that's lucky for me."

Which, I guess, is a cue for the smooch that makes my knees wobbly. A little. Not a lot. A little. Okay, a lot.

He lets me go, then checks the stairway for Duke.

"Here," he whispers. "Found this, too."

He reaches into his back pocket, takes another glance at the door, then hands me a little book — a little flowery teenager diary with the flimsy little lock that's still closed but is ripped loose from the back cover.

"Awwww, you broke it?" I say.

He makes his guilty face.

"Shit, all you had to do was push down on the fucking thing. It would have opened."

"I see you have some experience."

"You bet. Mona. Always had to try to stay one step ahead of her."

"And did you?"

"Not often enough. Is this hers?"

He shrugs. I take it from him.

"What is it?" he asks. "Nothing but numbers."

Not many pages are written on. Two sets of handwriting. Awww, his and hers; I recognize hers. I know instantly what they are.

"Keno," I say. "Each game, 20 numbers. See? And this? Time and date."

"So, they were keeping track of keno numbers?"

"10 to 1, they were setting them."

"You can do that?"

"Yeah, if it's your casino, which I'm 100% sure this is from."

I flip through the pages. Paul Tingle, looking over my shoulder with way more body contact than necessary, says, "They didn't do it for long."

"They might have gotten bored and quit. Probably not. Might have gotten caught. Also probably not, but if that's why it ended, you can count on somebody else having to take the fall. Where Mona's concerned? There's something more to it than fun and games."

"Sometimes I think you don't really like her much."

"Sometimes I don't. And I never, ever trust her."

"How do you stay friends?"

"She's interesting."

Duke's back in a bright red velour leisure suit, jacket unbuttoned, bare-chested.

"SANTA!" Paul Tingle and I both exclaim.

"Ho-ho-fucking-ho," he snarls. "You ready to go?"

We follow him down the stairs. When we get to Pioche's door, I take a detour.

"Be right with you guys."

The place has been ransacked by the police. Mona's left-behind froo-froo and Pioche's baby stuff are slung all over the

241

place. Drawers and closets open and empty. Carpets pulled up and flopped over. Black fingerprint dust on the pretty pink walls. I plop down on the sliced-up, flower-upholstered rocking chair, suddenly feeling suddenly sad, and I hear something fall out from under. What is with these people? Does every goddam thing around here have something hidden in it?

I get up and turn the chair over. And I'm getting summoned from the living room. I grab a short metal tube that must be what fell and stuff it down my shirt. Cold! I wiggle around to warm the damn thing up.

The boys are dinking around with the wall of electric crap.

Paul Tingle says, "Look at all these loose wires." He holds up handful after handful. "These ought to do something."

"No shit, Sherlock," Duke says, banging his palm against his forehead.

"My uncle Jed has a ham radio setup. He's a real weirdo for this stuff."

"Uncle Jed." That sends Duke into another fit.

"What's so . . . oh, I get it. Screw you."

Duke chokes out, "That . . . makes . . . you . . . Jethro." And he has to sit down and chug some wine.

"What if," Paul Tingle says, scratching his head, "this is some kind of radio transmitter?"

Duke starts humming the Twilight Zone theme, drinking more wine. A couple of his "trainees" are peeking through the windows. Makes me feel, just for a sec, like I'm in a zoo.

"We're still here," I yell at them, and they vanish. I tap on one of the TV screens. "Radios don't have these, do they?"

"Okay, so what if it's not just sound but pictures?"

"Man, you are trippin'," Duke says, holding in a hit of marijuana. He holds the joint out to us. We wave it off. "Didn't you want a ride to your Batmobile? I got more important

242

things to do than listen to your bullshit."

"You know," I say, "he's right."

"But . . ." says Paul Tingle.

"Come on now. You can come back and play another day. Ain't that right, Duke?"

Duke sighs, rattles his keys. "Bus leaves NOW."

Chapter 31

We pull up to home sweet home just in time for evening cocktails by the pool. Pitchers of something orangish with lots of lime slices and ice. I down the first big tumbler in two gulps. Tequila Sunrise. Not my favorite, but it'll do. Officer Tingle is no slouch in the guzzling department either. We're dusty and filthy and tired but refreshed now. We strip down past our unmentionables and double cannonball into the steaming water.

"Thanks, you two," says Mona, brushing away water drops. "Hope you don't clog up the filters with your filth." She is wrapped in some kind of fur coat. Always cold. Like a snake.

I spit water at her and swim off to the other end. Paul Tingle follows me. We'll probably leave a ring of dirt, sweat, and old makeup around the waterline. This feels great. Right amount of warm. Paul Tingle tries to initiate some playtime, but I give him a dirty look and swim back to Mona for another drink. Rodney, in fuzzy leopard print slippers and a matching fuzzy leopard printed robe, comes out through the slider. Mona motions to him that my glass is empty. When he takes it from me, he gives me a "well?" look. I act like I don't know what he's referring to.

Rodney hands me my glass. "Y'all just getting back." He and Mona smirk at us.

"Fuck you," I say after I down my drink and hold the glass out again.

"You're welcome," he says, and turns away laughing and shaking his massive 'fro.

Officer Tingle's at the other end of the pool, but he's heard everything. "We had a wonderful time. Thank you. Flack even took me to Johnny's."

Mona looks like she's been slapped. "WHAT?"

"Well, we were all the way out there. With no car, I might add." I shoot her the look we've used a million times together, the one that says PLAY ALONG.

"All you had to do is call . . ." she says, getting up and stomping into the house in her white, feathery, high-heeled sandals.

"What the fuck you do that for?" Rodney's clearly pissed. I've never seen him angry before. I give him THE LOOK. Thankfully, he gets it.

"Fuck!" Rodney follows Mona and slams the slider behind him so hard I'm surprised it didn't break the glass.

"So much for happy hour," says Paul Tingle.

"Wow," I say. "I'm used to Mona being mad at me, but Rodney? I feel lower than whale shit."

"What's eating them?"

"No clue," I say. "I'm going in for a shower."

"Want me to scrub your back?"

I blow him a kiss and pour him another Tequila Sunrise.

"Enjoy your swim. I've got girly things to attend to."

Not really, but it always works. Girly stuff makes even the manliest man squirmy.

• • •

I run into Rodney on my way through the kitchen. He's eating cold roast out of the fridge. He doesn't look at me but hands me a big, dripping slice anyway. With a disgusted sigh.

"Thanks," I say.

He flashes me a weak peace sign and keeps eating. How does he stay so skinny, having the munchies all the time?

I motion for him to come with me. We find Mona sprawled face-down on her bed.

"I mean, it was right up the road . . ." I say.

"Reckless! Stupid!" Her voice is muffled in her pillows. She's pounding the mattress with her perfectly-manicured fist.

Rodney speaks up: "What's wrong with you, woman?"

"Heat of the moment?"

"I'd like to 'heat of the moment' your hide!"

"Officer Tingle only knows there was a crime, a murder. Shit, he's police, remember? Remember at the rest stop? The reward he told us about? The grapevine? He still doesn't know it was me, goddammit. I didn't tell him that part."

Now Mona and Rodney are sitting side by side on the edge of the bed with their arms crossed, glaring at me.

"You guys, fuck! He doesn't know about you, and he doesn't know about us."

"This the most fucked up shit . . . ." Rodney's beyond pissed.

"Duke was having a party." Pretty lame attempt to change the subject, Flack.

Mona pipes up, "I am surprised to hear he's still there."

"Caretaking is what he told us."

"Well then, I suppose the family is right to keep him on to watch over the property. He can do whatever he wants in his own place."

"Party was in the main house."

"WHAT?!"

"Muthafuck." Rodney gets up and moves to the open slider like he's in slow motion, puts his hands on his hips, and stares out into the distance. For a skinny man, he can look like he takes up a lot of room.

"You didn't know he was still out there?" I ask.

"I surely did not. Thought they run everybody off," he says.

"So his caretaker story is bullshit?"

"Can't say for certain. I know I wouldn't leave his dumb ass in charge."

Mona says, "I'll take care of this."

"Nah, I'll rap with him."

"Don't you think the family should be told?"

"Why?"

"Well, it's their property, isn't it? Now?"

"Like they give a fuck? Only body who liked the place was Johnny. He was like, you know, the outcast. Born under a bad sign. Nothin' but trouble times a thousand. I tried to warn you, Mona. But you so stubborn. You just would not lay off the dude. And with the baby and all? I's trying to quit that scene. Fuck off back to The City. Then you move in. I had to make sure you was okay, stayed okay. You and Pio, you dig?"

"It looked like such an easy score . . ."

There's Mona's true colors.

"I'll remind you," I say, "it was you guys' bright idea to stick us with Officer Tingle. Consider us stuck. We're going to have to act normal — whatever that is. I think he's seen enough to keep him busy in his cop-brain for a while. He knows NOTHING about us, okay? Truce?"

Rodney nods and pushes me over — not real gently — onto the bed on his way out the door.

"Susan Anne, of all the idiotic, unprofessional, stupendously . . ." Mona says.

"Yeah, yeah. I get it. I keep going over in my mind what went on out there today. I don't think I blew it. Plus, we did find a couple of new clues."

"Fantastic. Fan-fucking-tastic. What makes you think someone won't be missing them or coming for them?"

"True." And we discovered your handwriting on a Keno number scam. I'll save that item for later.

"Why? What made you take such a risk? Oh, I get it: Showing off for your lover. For heaven's sake!"

"We did have a pretty good time . . . And it is all your fault."

"I hate you. Truly. You scare me to death."

"Not yet. Working on it." And I hate you more.

• • •

I have to give those two a lot of credit. Back out at the pool, they're managing to turn the conversation away from Rancho Spaghetti-O with impressive skills. They keep feeding Paul Tingle booze. He's happy. He's warm. He's freshly-fucked. We own him at the moment.

"Hey," I say when a dreaded lull goes on too long. "Just out of curiosity, why did we go to the Redfield mansion?"

Seems safe enough.

"Ding dong, Avon calling?" Mona says.

"Give me a break."

"Okay, not quite Avon. More like Tiffany's."

"Like the jewelry store Tiffany's?"

"You've heard of it?"

"Mona!"

She holds out her right hand and displays a honking big diamond ring.

"Seven and a half carats. Isn't it divine?"

"We took you SHOPPING?"

"Why, yes, in a sense. My friend Victoria I was telling you about? She brought it out from my safe deposit box in New York."

"To the Redfield mansion?"

"Darling, she lives there."

"Holy shit! Wow!"

Rodney says, "Man, that is too cool."

I try to take Mona's hand to get a closer look at the rock, but she jerks it away. Then she laughs and hands it to me to try on.

"It'd make a nice wedding ring," she says.

I hand it directly back to her. The thing weighs a ton. Just to put icing on the cake, I take off one of her froofy sandals and toss it at Officer Tingle in the water. He picks it up and puts it on his hand like a puppet.

"I hate you," I say to her.

"I hate you more," she says.

"I'm starting to hate you both," Rodney says, rolling a joint.

"Well, on that happy note, Mona, I'm going to need you to do some legwork for me."

"I'd rather jump out of a plane without a parachute."

I lean over to her and whisper, "Let's see: Why am I ass-deep in this mess? Who was it came to my office in all kinds of trouble?"

I take off her remaining sandal and toss it into the pool.

"Those were Ferragamo's."

"Now they're little white ducks sitting in the water. You're going to help me, Mo. Really."

"What do you need me to do?"

"There's some stuff at my trailer, for starters. I'm sure I can come up with a couple dozen other errands."

Mona sighs. "Fuck."

"That's my Mona-ba-Bona." I kiss her on the lips.

"Don't smear them!"

"Shut up, slut."

"I hate you."

"Ditto. Anybody else hungry?"

There better be more of that roast left. Paul Tingle's a helluva cook.

Chapter 32

Next morning, Mona raised holy hell at my costume suggestions for her undercover work. We had a huge fight, which I won because I had to. And because I threatened to throw more of her shoes into the pool. She looks the part now, though. The basic Nevada hick that she made damn sure to cover up with her la-de-dah manners and fancy clothes reappeared before her very eyes. Her very grouchy eyes.

"Hold your face just like that," I say. "You'll fit right in."

"I hate you." She looks into the mirror at the horror she has been transformed into. Too large, faded overalls, a ratty gray sweatshirt, holey Converse sneaks. No jewelry, not even earrings. No makeup except for some hideously pink lipstick I found laying around. Worst of all, I dismantled her expensive bouffant and turned her beautiful hair into braided

251

pigtails fastened with plain old rubber bands.

"You'll pay for this, you know." She's really grumpy now.

"It's so worth it." I have to laugh at how completely different she looks.

She sucks in a big breath through her nose. I know what's coming, but I beat her to it. "I know, I know: you love me."

Judith's pickup is perfect camo for Mona's mission. We send her and the truck fuming down the road. Wait til she notices I swiped her Virginia Slims and replaced them with my Luckys. That'll push her right over the edge. She flips us off as she drives away. Damn! Her fingernails are perfect! Missed a spot, Flack.

Rodney and I sit down over cups of his fantastic coffee.

"Sweet on him, ain't you?"

I lean back in my chair. "Not on your life."

"You a bad liar."

"Am not."

"You say."

"I AM NOT."

"Okay. Cool it. So?"

"We have to figure out what we're going to tell him. I mean, he could be useful . . ."

"He could also sing like a goddam bird. He's the fuzz, man. They don't change. I like the cat, but he's too damn close for comfort, ask me."

"You two dragged him into this . . . Hell with it. Right now, I need a favor."

"Like what?"

"Could you get him out of here while Mona's gone?"

"Gonna dig through our stuff? Toss the place?

"Just hers."

"Right."

"Cross my heart."

"Right."

He carries his cup to the dishwasher. "Hey, white boy," he yells, "get dressed. We going to town."

"Thanks."

"Don't mention it. Me and him? We blend right in." He gives my shoulder a squeeze as he goes by. "Wish us luck."

• • •

Rodney waves bye-bye to me the way he would to Pioche. I stick my tongue out at him, put my thumb in my mouth, and shoo him out with my other hand. I let Paul Tingle peck my cheek, though he had moved in for a whole lot more. They are a very dapper pair. Hope they don't get killed. I don't know what Rodney's plans are. Just have to trust him.

So for the first time in what seems like years, I am free! I do a little happy dance, pour myself more coffee, and then get down to the business of sticking my nose in where it doesn't belong: Mona's bedroom.

Chick's got a lot of books. All over the place. Some pretty brainy ones, too, I might add. Real live literature, Shakespeare and whatnot. Atlases. Dictionaries in a lot of languages. Stuff about history and politics. Art. Maybe they were here when she bought the place. Maybe they're just for looks. She's not the intellectual type, she is a quick study. I can see her brushing up for some encounter or other by skimming for just enough vocabulary and atmosphere to play whatever part she needs to play to get whatever it is she's trying to get.

Her most recent reappearance in my life is one of the more outrageous and oddly satisfying since she embarked on her life of crime. Pioche has done wonders for her. Made her more

253

careful. And more calculating. When she disappears again, I'll know all of her reasons, know that her heart is finally in the right place, and that I have to let her go for her sake and the baby's. The straight-and-narrow won't be easy for her, but I think maybe now she's brave enough, and rich enough, to lead a "normal" life. Probably in some castle on the coast of Portugal. Looks like she'll protect Pioche, give her the best of everything.

I go around opening drawers and doors. How can I be finding nothing of interest? The usual clothes and shoes and towels and crap. I have to start thinking like Mona. Where would I keep my secrets? Even the massive desk in her wood-paneled office has only stationery, stamps, and pens. No files. No personal photos. No locked drawers. Her sneakiness is getting on my nerves.

I'm under her desk, tapping around for hollow hiding spots when the phone rings, making me smack the top of my head. Hard. The answering machine blabbers away. Then I hear Mona saying, "Susan Anne? Are you there? Are you listening? Pick up the phone. Susan Anne? Pick up the phone."

So I do. The machine clicks off with a screeching beep in my ear.

"Mo?"

"Oh good, you are there. I found your trailer house."

"You did? Great! Where is it?"

"You won't like this. It's in the impound lot at the police station."

"WHAT?!!!"

"Oh yes. Your landlord at the Merry Wink showed me a receipt and a card from a Detective Rogers."

Rogers and Hammerstein. On the job.

"Shit."

"Want me to go down there? I'm in a phone booth at the butcher shop on 395."

Man, this is a problem. I go through my mental inventory to see if I think they found anything incriminating in there. I hope they've left Pop's jacket and my tack alone, but what else might they have found?

I light a cigarette. A gaggy Virginia Slim. "Nah, I'll handle it."

"Good. Since I'm all the way out here amongst the peasants, how do steaks sound for dinner?"

"Moo. Moo."

"I'll pick up four ribeyes. Ta-ta."

I hang up and kick my snooping into high gear.

• • •

Nothing. I come up with a big, fat zero. Granted, I'm doing a lightweight search. She'll notice anything out of place, the sneak, and it's a fact you can't turn up real dirt without trashing a place. Plus, I'm not all that sure what I'm looking for. "Anything" isn't much to go on.

"Honey, we're home!"

Rats! It's Rodney giving me a heads-up. What the fuck are they doing back so soon? I slip out the slider in Mona's room and grab a magazine out by the pool. I flip it open. It's upside down. I turn it over. All the subscription cards and perfume samples fall out.

"Shit, shit, shit," I say, trying to gather them up and still look casual. I shove them into my back pocket and stroll to a lounge chair, acting natural — except I forgot my cigarettes and bourbon, a dead giveaway that I'm doing a lousy job at it. Add the fact that I'm "reading" Vogue? Hell's bells. I'm so busted.

But they come flying out the kitchen slider all smiling and laughing and excited. Even normally stonefaced Rodney.

"Didn't expect you back so soon." I stretch and yawn and lay that crummy magazine down.

"You're not going to believe what happened," Paul Tingle gushes.

"I can't wait."

"We're driving along – doot-de-doot-de-doo . . ."

He did not say that!

". . . swapping Frisco stories . . ."

Tell me he did not say "Frisco," too!

". . . when all of a sudden NEEEEEE-YOWWWWWW-ERT-ERT-ERT!, this little plane – I swear to gawd – lands on the ROAD! On the HIGHWAY! Cars and trucks are swerving. People are honking. The plane's tires are smoking!"

"It was a trip, man," says Rodney.

"Then, then the pilot and two other people bail out and go running across the field. I go to jump out and lend a hand, you know?, but Rodney here stops me. Which was probably the right thing to do on account of it was a total mess of wrecks and people running around. I'd just be another lookie-lou, so we came back home."

"Trippy," says Rodney, licking the glue on a joint.

"Definitely something you don't see every day. Even in Reno," I say.

They're going a mile a minute tossing around details and what-ifs at the top of their lungs – which is good for me. They're so busy entertaining each other, I split for my room where it's quiet. It's adorable how excited they are.

Pretty soon they run out of steam, and I hear a rackety knock.

"Who is it?" I sing-song, like I don't know.

He throws the door open and sails in. And knocks me over on my back. And rips our pants off. And covers my face with hot kisses. And . . . His legs are almost as fantastic as his . . . Those kisses are . . .

Then he's on his feet, rosy-skinned from all the excitement.

"I'm taking a shower." He slaps my ass – very nice – and heads for the door.

"You can use this one. I could maybe join you?"

"All my stuff's in my bathroom."

"Your stuff?"

"Shampoo? Conditioner? Pumice stone. Nose hair clippers . . ."

Pumice stone? "All I got's Ivory and baby shampoo."

"See? Tootles."

He did not say that!

He dances out of my room, blowing me a kiss I only half-ass pretend to catch.

I'm basking in the afterglow when I hear Rodney. "You decent?"

"One sec," I say, grabbing my Levis and shirt. Smash my hair a little and go out.

I follow Rodney to the dining room table – the conference table. Ah, Luckys and Beam. Right when and where I need them.

"I know that plane," he says.

"You what?"

"Belongs to a smuggler Johnny did a lot of business with. Coke and smack. It's why they ran."

"No shit."

"'nother reason I didn't want to stick around. Don't need them knowing I'm still living. Fuck no."

"Close call."

"Of all the fuckedupness that ever was . . ."

"Wow."

"Damn straight. His people are everywhere."

"Ribeyes have landed!" It's Mona. She had to say "landed." Rodney and I lose it laughing.

"What's so funny?" she says.

Madame Beauty Queen stands there with a thick package in white butcher paper in one hand and two bottles of wine in the other. She still looks like trailer trash the way I dressed her, but she did undo the pigtails and her beautiful hair is puffed out huge and kinky from being braided.

"Good grief," I say, "you look like hell."

"Even on my worst day – this being one of them, thanks to you – I am far more beautiful than you could dream to be, my mousy friend."

She heads for the kitchen as Officer Tingle returns all Irish Spring fresh in a pair of well-worn Levis – button flys, point in his plus column – and a gray sweatshirt unzipped just the right amount.

"Hey, I found this," he says, walking up to Mona, holding out a really dorky scrapbook trimmed in ribbons and lace.

Those two bottles of wine? Ker-smash on the tile floor. That'll stain.

"Oh my God! Where?" Mona says.

"Where?" I ask Paul Tingle.

"I was looking for . . . that is, I needed . . ."

"You were snooping?" she asks.

"Not really, really snooping."

"Meaning?"

"I was looking for . . . baby powder. Got a little . . ." He points to his crotch.

"We get it," she says, covering her eyes.

"I opened a couple of doors in the hallway. I figured since

you had a baby and all, there'd have to be some. Found a diaper bag up on a top shelf. No baby powder, but there was this."

"Thank you! Thank you! Thank you!" she exclaims, rushing over and kissing him all over his face, splattering blood from the meat package all over everybody.

"Eeewwwwww! Mona!!!"

Officer Tingle is laughing. "Reminds me of home!" he says.

"Good lord! Where was home? A slaughterhouse?" she asks.

"Sometimes. I grew up on a dairy farm."

"How gauche."

Rodney wrestles the package from her, she has such a death grip on it. Officer Tingle wipes her bloody hand with a dishcloth he immediately tosses in the garbage can. Rodney steers us to the couch and sets us down side by side.

The scrapbook Mona thought she left at Johnny's! Mona and me at Lake Tahoe with our moms in the sand in the background. Mona and me dressed up in our moms' clothes, pouty-lipping, arms over each other's shoulders. Mona and me hanging upside down from the scraggly apple tree in her backyard — the one that never had a single apple on it even though it got tons of great-smelling flowers every spring. Typical Nevada, the wind rips those dinky flowers to smithereens before the bees can get busy on them.

The pictures go all the way through high school. What started out as two little girls farting around ended with two heavily made-up, micro-miniskirted, cigarette-smoking, grim-faced young women flipping off the world. Our eyes are mean. Our bodies are hard and twisted up. We're looking to party. We're looking for a fight. We're looking to fuck. We're not giving a shit about ourselves or anyone else. We're hurt and angry and alone, wondering when the other shoe will drop. What new load of crap will land in our laps that we're not ready for but will have to deal with because no one's looking out for us.

Paul Tingle leans over us with drinks and assorted munchies. "You two go way back," he says.

We barely hear him, flipping through pages. Going backward over the years like washing away the future.

"Yeah. Known each other a long time," Mona says.

All of those memories. All the things we thought were possible way back then. The husbands we wanted. The children and houses and cars. The German shepherds and golden retrievers. White picket fences, though we'd never actually seen one. The American Dream we expected. We did. Would it have been wonderful to be bored and boring? To live next door to each other? Swap recipes over coffee with the other wives in our bunny slippers and hair curlers? Would we still have wanted to raise hell, drink and smoke, steal and kill, con and cheat? We just had to accept what we had to accept and make up our lives out of thin air as we went along. Did that take courage? Or did we earn courage from our choices? I can't imagine living any way other than I do now. I wouldn't know how.

I hear the two men sweeping up glass and talking, laughing. The kitchen is their territory. They're happiest when Mona and I are somewhere else while they whip up amazing goodies and even clean up after themselves. Lucky us.

Mona snaps her fingers, breaking my concentration. She hustles away and is back in a flash.

"Baby powder," she says as she sets the container on the table, and we go back to flipping through the pages.

We look at our past together, together. Some tears, some

laughs, some gasps. We don't have to talk. We do, however, need booze and cigarettes. We need them quick. As soon as I can think it, Paul Tingle is there with both. Mona points to the powder.

"Thanks," he says, blushing.

She says without looking up, "No rotten crotches in this house.

Chapter 33

Been dreaming about Timmy a lot lately. Haven't seen him in over 10 years. Before that, I mean after he quit living with me, he'd show up now and then. Broke, hungry, dirty, strung out with random "friends" in the same condition. Until I kicked them out for keeps this one, last time. Big mistake. After that, the only way I saw him was by tracking him down and spying on him from a distance. Just to make sure he was still living. Once he went to prison, he banned me from his visitor's list.

Lately my dreams are of visiting him in prison, which is weird because I've only ever dreamed of him the way we were when we were little kids. Before everything. Now I dream of sitting across the table from a freckle-faced, red-headed man with a mustache and – get this – black-rimmed glasses. He's wearing prison grays. "Murrow" on a name patch on the left side of his chest, numbers on the other. He's happy and laughing when we talk and hug. We sit across a table from each other – no cuffs or chains or barriers - which I know, when I'm awake, doesn't happen in The Big House.

In my dreams I bring him socks and See's candy. He gives me leather belts and headbands he's been making. His tool work is fancy. Real art. He gets all excited explaining how he makes his crafts. Loves to see me try them on. We share the candy. We talk for hours. No guards. No one else. Just us.

Because it's a dream.

I have no way of knowing how he is, only that he's still alive and hasn't been granted a parole hearing in at least two years. They let me know about those, but he won't let me come to them. I've tried. I miss him so much. I'm so sorry for trying to help him and for having been so wrong to trust the court to see that he was a good boy who lost his balance but wasn't a lost cause. Nevada is unforgiving in so many ways. Especially where drugs are concerned. You can have all the booze you want. The cops don't even get especially freaked out over catching the occasional underage beer bash out by the river. They just dump the beer and send everyone home. But drugs? No dice. You're going to jail. Down in Carson City if you get busted for grass, you're getting your head shaved, too. No question. You get to be a walking billboard for a couple of months, supposedly to intimidate your pot-smoking buddies about their evil ways. Drugs are the devil. All of them, though speed is a little less likely to get you some time. Too much of the casino industry counts on those little white pills. Just keep them out of reach of the kiddies.

It hurts to say this, but in Timmy's case, the drugs pissed them off more than the murder. They knew that fucking cabbie, yet another distant, misguided Ruggerio kin, was molesting the kids he sold drugs to. Under Nevada's unwritten rules, child molesters have it coming, but there was way more talk about drugs during Timmy's trial than there was about him killing a man. Basically, he got a life sentence for being a junkie. And I put him there. His only family. I've never forgiven myself, and will never forgive the justice system. Timmy was so young when they locked him up. They never got to see him full of life and adventurousness and caring. The man I sit across from in my dreams is the Timmy, with all his good qualities, that I know could have been saved. Should have been saved. How do you do that to a person? How do you not see that living a life chasing heroin has nothing to do with choice and everything to do with pain? How is prison the only solution?

Chapter 34

I've been part of one big, happy family out here at Mona's place for quite a while now. We've fallen into routines: breakfast, lunch, swims, naps, cocktails. Plenty of cocktails. Paul Tingle is a great cook; Rodney's a great cleaner and organizer; Mona keeps the house stocked with groceries and goodies; and I . . . um, do laundry. Sometimes. Keep the firearms cleaned and oiled. Plink the odd cottontail or quail or sagehen. Catch the odd trout. Paul Tingle whips up some gourmet grub out of my hunting.

I brought Rockalee up here from the Lockwood stables. She missed her horse-friends, so she and I would go out riding every day to keep her from being lonely. Paul Tingle, as it turned out, is a helluva horseman. Good roper. We went and got him a beautiful palomino gelding we named Chester from a neighbor down the road. Laid in a supply of nice grass hay from the same neighbor. Officer Tingle and I extended the corral and stable. He was a damn fine builder.

Rockalee took to Chester right off. Now she's barn-shy when I want to go out riding just the two of us. She and Chester whiny back and forth, and she tries to turn back. Eventually she comes around to wanting to explore. She has to for me, because in that house full of people, I'd go crazy if I couldn't get some solitude. Paul Tingle was hurt at first, but he's coming around. And we do ride together an amount of time that I consider to be a lot. Mona and Rodney are a big help in teaching him that me being off by myself as much as possible is in everyone's best interest. Maybe the best help I give the household is to be elsewhere?

Mona's place is big and fairly well-soundproofed between the rooms, but with winter coming on I can feel the walls closing in. Rodney reads a lot. Mona does her nails and fiddles with her hair. Officer Tingle cooks and cleans and bugs the shit out of me the rest of the time, asking if I want anything 90 million times a day.

If I thought I had the bad fortune of being in love with him before, oh brother: Once he dumped his khakis and golf shirts for Levis and t-shirts – that he looks so good and normal in – we all breathed a big sigh of relief. He hasn't asked about Rodney's face. Anyone could tell those wounds are fresh. He hasn't said a word to Mona about Pioche. He doesn't ask questions. It's kind of creepy, ignoring the assorted elephants in the living room. So many secrets, so many questions.

• • •

It's a beautiful evening out by the pool tonight. One of

those classic Nevada thunderstorm skies at sunset. Enormous poofy clouds. Purple, orange, red, yellow, black, bits of blue. Brighter than bright. We can already hear the thunder and see lightning across the valley. All that beauty comes with the price tag of wildfires, which are no fun but pretty to look at. At a distance. Once they get started, the wind around here drives them fast. Then it's all hands on deck. Pop spent many a summer evening fighting fires caused by lightning. Sometimes he'd drag in after midnight smelling like sage smoke and Old Spice, but all cleaned up from the firehouse showers. Sometimes he'd be gone for a couple of days. Either way, we worried. One odd shift of the wind could mean catastrophe. We'd keep reassuring each other that he'd be all right. They'd all be all right.

Wouldn't they?

With the BOOMS! coming closer and louder, we go inside. No sense getting electrocuted in the pool. We separate to our rooms and get our jammies on. Paul Tingle is the first one done and is making popcorn when I come out. He's wearing cutoff sweatpants and a t-shirt with Rat Fink on it.

"Rat Fink?" I ask.

"Not a fan of Big Daddy Roth?"

"You crazy? Who isn't? I just didn't think you . . ."

"You're right. It's my kid brother's. I took off with it by accident. Bet he's pissed."

The popcorn's going to town. Officer Tingle is shaking it for all he's worth. Then he dumps it into a big bowl, pours gobs of already melted butter over it, tosses on a fistful of salt, and fluffs the whole works with his hands. He tosses a kernel into the air and catches it in his mouth, then tosses one at me, which, of course, hits me in the forehead. I pick it up off the floor and eat it.

"Eeeewwww," he says.

"What?" I lick my fingers for spite before I plunge my hand into the bowl for a sample.

"Eeeeewwww!"

"WHAT?"

That's when he grabs me by the waist and kisses the living shit out of me. I'm done for. I'm as melted as the butter as we slather each other with greasy kisses. His hands go under my shirt. Mine go down the back of his pants and pull him against me hard. We're in a mindless flurry of pent-up lust. I want to stop. I do. I can't. I should. I won't. I don't. He backs me around the corner into the pantry and quietly shuts the door. We don't even undress, just make enough space for Tab A and Slot B, and we push and we push. And we kiss and we kiss. And we knock down a shelf of canned goods. And we don't care as we avoid them rolling around at our feet. I feel like . . . I feel like . . . ah, Ah, AH, AHHHHHH!!! He's there, too, grunting into my shoulder blade, shivering. Wow.

"Thank you," he whispers.

"You're welcome," I whisper back.

"Hi," he says.

I look him straight in the eyes: "Hi."

"I love you," he says.

"I need a cigarette," I say, rearranging my clothes and opening the door. Cans roll out.

Mona is at the conference table, lighting candles of all shapes and sizes. Just in case? Or just for romantic effect.

I hate her.

She makes a kissy-face at me, smiles and shakes her head.

I light a cigarette. "Don't."

She keeps shaking her head. We can hear Officer Tingle maneuvering around the cans and muttering. He comes out, smoothing his hair down. A can of chicken noodle soup rolls into the kitchen. He pushes it back with his foot and shuts the door. Mona cracks up.

"Rat Fink? Classy."

Paul Tingle goes beet red.

"A little merlot to go with the popcorn?" she asks.

He sets bowls and wine glasses on the table. The storm is right over us now. The glasses clink together from the thunder.

He says, "I'm going to, uh, check on the horses." Turns and practically runs from the room.

"I think our boy is in love with you," she smirks.

"Shit. I know. What am I going to do?"

"What do you want to do?"

"Hey, can you catch a piece of popcorn with your mouth?"

She tosses a piece in the air and catches it, spreads her hands like "ta-da."

"Figures," I say.

Rodney comes in smoking a joint and wearing his glasses. Glasses and an eyepatch. Interesting combination.

"Rodney, can you catch a piece of popcorn in your mouth?"

"No. Never could. And now . . ." He points to his eyepatch and serves himself a glass of wine.

While Officer Tingle is outside, I take advantage of the privacy to ask the two of them if they think it's time to have The Talk with him.

"I don't know. Like, he's the fuzz, man," Rodney says without looking up from Stranger in a Strange Land that he's squinting one eye at.

"How about this? Let's show him the Betamax. See how he reacts. None of us are in it, right? Wait, you are, right Rodney?"

He nods.

"Shit," I say.

"Yeah, but I'm not legally culpable for Johnny's actions. I ain't hand over the money. I ain't shook their hands. I ain't run the camera. In a court of law, I could be called as a witness for the prosecution, but could not be charged with any aspect of the bribery."

The mix of him sounding like a lawyer and a cool cat at the same time has Mona and me looking at each other.

"Where'd you learn to talk like that?" I ask.

Rodney puts down his book and takes his glasses off. He rubs his face under the eyepatch and laces his fingers across his chest.

"Like what?"

"Like a lawyer."

"I am a lawyer."

Our jaws drop. Here's a guy who looks like a Black Panther telling us he's a LAWYER?

"Oh come now," Mona says, "be serious."

"Just cuz a brotha is hip and pretty as I am don't mean he ain't educated. Or shall I put it another way: Just because I happen to speak and dress the way I do, it would be incorrect to assume I cannot function admirably in The Man's game."

Then POOF. That's when the power goes out. Makes us jump.

"Mona, good job with the candles," I say.

"Lucky me. Perhaps I should go play some craps."

I look at Mona. "He did meet Johnny while they were going to Stanford."

"He did? You did?" Mona stumbles.

"I said he was going to Stanford when we met. Didn't say I was."

"But you were there . . ." I say.

I remember Paul Tingle is still outside, really in the dark (in more ways than one).

"Hold that thought. I have a cop to rescue, and I want to hear the rest of this," I say, grabbing a flashlight.

• • •

"I had this girlfriend going to Stanford. Getting a teaching degree. Affirmative Action and all. I was organizing protests and such on campus when we met. She was so high on getting educated. She didn't talk about much else practically. And she was fine. So fine. I started hanging out in some classes. Hiding in the back of these big old auditorium type rooms where the professor is so far away he looked like a little dot. Nobody ran me off, so what the fuck.

"I went all around. Philosophy. English. Economics. Biology. Chemistry. Archeology. Bunch of different shit. Met Johnny outside the business school where he was going. He comes up and asked me if he could score some grass. You know, the way I looked and all . . . I told him no, so he tried to sell me some! We got a laugh out of that. Next thing, we're in business together. Made sense. White boy, black boy. The dynamic duo of drugs. Made mun-nay.

"Anyway, I was walking down the hall in one of the old, old buildings when I hear a whole lot of arguing going on. I look in the little window in the door and see these two cats going at each other from two podiums. No cussing or name-calling. Nobody threatening to cut nobody. I go inside real quiet. They were hollering about precedent and evidence and cases and so-and-so v. so-and-so. No one stopping them. Students taking notes on what they're saying. Went on for a while til this buzzer goes off. They shook hands and sat down, and two

271

more cats got up and went at it.

"I kept slipping into all kind of law classes. Torts, common law, criminal law, ethics, corporate law. It was interesting to me. Don't know why. It all seemed make sense. Fit together like puzzle parts. What one dude would say that the other dude would challenge. Who would win. Why. It was a game. Same as checkers or chess. More like chess. I play chess. Love it. More wine, y'all?"

Mona and Paul Tingle hold out their glasses, I fill mine with Jim Beam.

Officer Tingle holds up his glass. "A toast to our distinguished Stanford alumnus."

"Hold up, hold up," Rodney says, waving him off. "I didn't get a diploma. I never actually enrolled. But I found out I could take the California bar exam without a degree. So I did. Kind of for kicks, know what I'm saying? I mean, I had the bread from all the drug dealing and all. What a better way to pay for a test to be called a lawyer? I passed the fucking bar first time through. I got my license in '68. Been keeping it up ever since. Never once used it. Just like having it. Rodney X. Franklin, Esquire. Classy."

Now I not only know his last name but his middle initial, too. And the fact that he's a lawyer. Who changes diapers. My mind, as they say, is blown.

"But, you smoke marijuana . . .?" Officer Tingle stating the obvious.

"That I do, son, that I do," he says as he holds in a hit.

"How can you?"

"Like this." He takes another huge toke and passes the joint to Mona. He's grinning ear to ear.

This is pretty cool. I've been thinking I needed a good lawyer. I doubt I could find one I'd trust more than Rodney.

Mona clears her throat. "Well, counselor," Mona begins,

"what's your stance on some show and tell?"

"Show what? Tell what?" Paul Tingle pipes up.

Rodney says, "I know where you going with this. According to California law, ain't no problem. Nevada law? Don't know."

"Officer Tingle has no authority here, though, does he?" I ask.

Paul Tingle says, "Jesus! Will you quit calling me Officer Tingle and Paul Tingle! I have a first name!"

I still can't look at him. "Yeah, but I don't wanna."

"Paul? What's wrong with plain old Paul?"

"Maybe a nickname?" says Mona.

"What do you suggest?" he asks.

"Brutus," I say.

"Get serious!" he says.

"It's Brutus or Paul Tingle and Officer Tingle as far as I'm concerned," I tell him, crossing my arms.

"You . . ." Paul Tingle says.

Mona hugs him. "Let her be. She's so stubborn."

"I hate you," I say. "Guys, what about the Betamax? Yea or nay? Hey, I sound like a lawyer, too."

I don't get a laugh.

"Betamax?" Officer Tingle asks.

"A tape recording only like a movie. Homemade," says Rodney. "'course we gone have to wait for the lights . . ."

And, BAM!, like destiny, the lights come back on.

"Hot DAMN!" This night getting creepy as FUCK!" Rodney says as he goes off to set things up.

"This isn't some kind of smut, is it?" Paul Tingle, who's getting to know us pretty well, asks.

"Actually," I say, "there is that one little hiccup right at the beginning . . ."

Mona's turn to blush. "Oh God! I forgot." She yells,

"Rodney, could you . . . ?"

"Sure, sugar," he yells back, not disguising a laugh.

• • •

After watching the whole Washoe Valley scene over three times, Paul Tingle reacts the way I figured. He wants everybody arrested. NOW. He wants the tape in evidence. NOW. He wants to call the police. NOW. This minute. He wants Johnny behind bars. Immediately if not sooner. He's pacing up and down. Smacking his fist into his palm like it's Johnny's face. Ranting and raving about payola and graft and abuse of power. He wants to go get his man.

Rodney stops him. Physically. In his tracks. "Hold up, now. Nobody getting no man, you hear? Let's calm down and think about this."

"It's right there! The man is guilty as sin! He has to be stopped!"

Rodney keeps hold of Paul Tingle's shoulders. "Um, he already stopped." He looks over at me to see how far I'm willing to take this.

"Whoa a second," I say.

I go to my room and fish a dollar out of my bag. I hand the buck to Rodney and demand a receipt, which he writes on the back of a Yahtzee scorecard. In pencil.

"As my attorney, what do you say?"

"I say you got a strong case for self-defense, is what I say."

"Self-defense? You mean . . . ?"

Here we go.

Shit.

Chapter 35

Self-defense is one thing; what I did to Johnny was carnage. The guy pissed me off, looking for all the world like he had killed Mona and Rodney and had the same plans for me. Not to mention Pioche. I had to protect that baby, didn't I? I got carried away. He's not the first thing I ever killed. I love to hunt. But I don't hunt for kicks or to feel superior. I hunt with the intention of eating what I bring down or of ridding the earth of something cold-blooded and venomous or hairy with nasty fangs and claws. Johnny, unfortunately, fell into the category of "human" despite his violent, savage, psychopathic nature. Human laws take a dim view of humans killing other humans — even if you're doing the world a favor by making them go bye-bye. Rodney and Mona never saw how It went down; they only know that It had. I skimped on the gory details with them, too. Same as I was doing now with Officer Tingle. I wasn't trying to make myself look like a good guy; I was only trying to hold down on the level of blood and guts out of politeness. The cops documented the scene. If these three really wanted to know all the details, they'd find a way.

Now I am a murderer and, while not exactly lying about what I did, a mealy-mouth, detail-leaver-outer, sugar-coater. Not sure which thing bugs me the most. In my line of work accuracy is a valuable skill. Getting called on to testify means you've got to have that story down pat, or some idiot lawyer will rip your client to shreds.

Having to go over this with Rodney and Mona still among the living is something I hadn't realized would be so freaky. I knew they were dead when I took off with Pioche. I just knew it. But here they both are, listening to me tell Officer Tingle about what I did that they didn't see. Come to think of it, I could have laid Johnny's murder off on Duke the chauffeur or any one of the gang hanging out at Rancho Spaghetti-O. Should have thought of that before I opened my big mouth.

What happened to them that night? They were so damn surprised to find each other alive. Rodney never showed after Johnny turned the power back on. Mona disappeared into the dark long before that. I was getting the baby the fuck out as fast as I could. No time to give any of it a second thought. Besides, I've always known Mona can take care of herself. And Rodney? I have to admit I didn't think much about him til I saw him again in The City.

Now that my story's out there, leaving Officer Tingle speechless and frozen to his seat, it's time to hear what happened to them that night.

Mona lights a cigarette and leans back in her chair. "I just . . . ran. Like, away. The other way. Away from the highway. Into the brush. And you know how I despise close contact with sagebrush. That smell. Yuck. I ran until I was completely breathless. I remember I sat down. Just sat down and stayed put. I could see the flashing lights of a cop car reflecting off the hillside below me, so I got up and kept going. I kept falling down. It was so dark. I kept going."

"Yeah," I say. "I passed the police on my way out. One car. Glad to see that. Bought us lots of time. Rodney, what about you?"

"Made it down the tunnel."

I nearly spit out my drink, which would have been a crime of another sort.

"Tunnel?"

"Yeah, Johnny had this escape tunnel. Saw it on some James Bond thing or some kinda spy shit. Had to have one. Goes from under the barbeque pit out to the other side of the highway.

"Wow," I say, "holy shit!"

"Actually got used more than once while I was there. Not running from the fuzz. Just hustling dope in and out mostly. That night, I crawled to it. Just barely got the fucking lid open. Sort of fell in and passed out in there. Woke up all sticky from blood. Still had my flashlight, and when I turned it on, that's when I found out my fucking eye wasn't working. Didn't know yet it was also fucking gone. I ripped my clothes into bandages, wrapped up my head, crawled the rest of the way in. They's a room down there with bottles of water. Food. Rifles and shit. Passed back out. Don't know how long, but til it was quiet, for damn sure. I waited and listened and checked shit out for a real long time before I drove myself to this guy I know. Was a medic in Nam. Stitched me up. Said my eye was gone. Out there in the dirt, I guess."

"Wow," says Paul Tingle.

"I got a glass one somewhere. Like the patch better. More

fierce."

"So, Mona . . .?" I ask.

"After the sun came up, I could see down the hill that there were more police at the house. I could tell from where I was that the road was to the east. I started walking. But I wasn't thinking straight at all. I was scared for my baby. I had nothing: no money, no water, no change of clothes. I must have looked like a lunatic, and of all things I come across these kids riding dirt bikes. They looked at me as if I was something they saw every day. Just asked if I needed a ride. Nevada kids. One of them put me on the back of her bike. I burned the hell out of my leg on the tailpipe getting on. See? Right there. I didn't care. I had to get out of there.

"They took me to that trailer park down by the Truckee. Heated me up a can of chili. Even poured me a shot of Jack and lit me a cigarette. Never asked me to explain a thing, despite all the hubbub at Johnny's. What kid could resist taking a peek at all the action? They suggested it would be a good idea if I was gone before any of their moms got back. One of boys called his sister to come out and get me. It was cool, he said. She had just got out of prison. Armed robbery. She wasn't going to make a stink.

"She showed up in a loud, souped-up car. She skidded into the yard, waved me over. I got in, and we sped back out. She didn't so much as stop to say hi to her brother. She was huge and covered with some of the worst tattoos I've ever seen. Even had two teardrops on her face. The rest? Well, here I am. Alive and well."

"Wow," says Officer Tingle.

I speak up, "All in a day's work, they say." But I'm pretty rattled from their stories.

"And I thought San Francisco was exciting."

"Nothing beats Nevada for cold-blood excitement,

brother," Rodney says.

"We square with you?" I ask. "Not going to turn us in, right? You would so totally miss us."

Paul Tingle paces a bit. I have to say after I heard all of our stories even my brains are scrambled.

"First," he says, "we have to get that tape to the police."

"Mail it?" I suggest.

"We have to get it into the right hands. Who knows who else is involved in this deal. Johnny had politicians, he probably had police, too."

"One of Pop's old friends, Grady, is my insider guy at the department. He's not high up, but he's honest as they come. He's as close as I have left of family."

"You can get it to him?" Rodney asks.

"I can. Off the record."

"Good. Who's thirsty?"

Knowing that there's lots more talking to be done, we gather the popcorn and the booze bottles and lunch meat and cheese and crackers and grapes, and spread it all out on the conference table. And turn the lights back out. The candles are a nice horror movie effect, throwing our huge shadows against the walls. We look like some kind of satanic cult, casting spells over baloney and American singles. The smoke from my Luckys, Mona's Virginia Slims, and Rodney's grass curls over our heads. Mona wants to switch from wine to bourbon, so I pour one for me and one for her. She tosses an ice cube into hers. We clink glasses.

As we're laying out plans, Paul Tingle is silent. Just watching and listening. At first I figure he knows that we have more information and connections than he does, so he has nothing to contribute. Then I start thinking that maybe he's making mental notes for the purpose of ratting us out. I nudge Mona and tip my head in his direction. Now she notices he's

279

been quiet this whole time.

"Penny for your thoughts, Brutus," she says.

"Hm? Me?"

"What's up?" I ask.

"Oh. Uh. I guess I might as well . . ." He looks down at his hands.

"I'm on leave. Disciplinary leave."

Do tell. Mr. Squeaky Clean ain't so squeaky?

"What for?"

"I . . . got involved in something."

"Really. What?"

"This is embarrassing."

"It's just between us friends."

This better be good.

"I mean, it wasn't all me. I got talked into it by a couple of the guys. Then one of them ratted me out. I should have known. He was up for a big promotion. The department was having so much trouble with cops on the take, cops stealing evidence, cops accepting bribes. This guy? He had something on every one of us. Got that promotion, too."

Juicy. And vague so far.

"I was the perfect pigeon. New guy. You know? 'Peer pressure?' All the pop psychology books talk about it."

I would not know. I got problems enough without having to read about them.

"Country boy from Yakima and all? They figured me as clueless as a newborn pup. Which I was. Now? The ax is falling left and right at my precinct. I was the first to go."

"How long have you been on the force?"

"A year and almost three months."

FNG. Fucking new guy. And one from farm country? He was ripe to get worked over.

"What'd you do?" Rodney asks.

"It didn't start like a big deal. There was this hard guy who was getting too greedy up in the Tenderloin. You know the Tenderloin?"

"Heard of it."

"Real bad part of town. Strip clubs. Dive bars. XXX movie houses. Sex shops. Hookers."

"Sounds like the whole state of Nevada," I say.

"Anyway, there was this hard guy. Started throwing his weight around too much to be ignored. Demanding protection money from the businesses, shaking down pimps, robbing drug dealers. A couple of the guys had been staking him out for months. Off the clock, though. I mean, we all knew what was going on. They said we were waiting for our chance to arrest him on something big that would stick."

"You mean like hookers turning up with their throats slit?"

"Who knows? When they laid out the plans to me, I thought we might interfere with his business enough to make him move on. Honest, I was thinking about the people he was hurting. Whether or not I agreed with how they were living, I didn't want them to die. I didn't want it on my conscience that someone was going to get hurt before this guy got what he deserved. That's how I talked myself into it. That and, you know, trying to earn some respect big city style.

"We rousted him every chance we got. Took his money. Split it up. What could he say or do? He didn't dare. He didn't dare turn us down either. But he escalated. And people did start to get hurt. Like, hurt, you know? He brought in more and more muscle, so our 'plans' were harder and harder to carry out. I wanted it to end. I wanted to go back to driving my beat. Handing out tickets, responding to rear-enders, getting to know the neighborhood. Probably sounds wimpy to you, but I thought that's how it would be for me for the first couple of years. At least until I got some experience.

"Then the man finally turned up dead. It was over. We were done with him. I really didn't – don't – care. But, the guy who finked? He made the bad guy come across like a victim. I mean, sure, none of us beat cops gave a rat's ass. He had it coming as far as we were concerned.

"The money did us in. The bribes? That, the bosses cared about. They called in internal affairs and put us on indefinite leave. And . . . here I am."

"Wow," I say.

"That's it? 'Wow?'"

"I'll think of something better. Give me sec."

Yeah, when you think you're talking to Clark Kent and he turns out to be a crooked cop, I'm all ears. Also impressed. He just got way more interesting. He seems as down on bad guys and determined as I am that they get what they have coming to them. If the situation was reversed and I had to prove myself to a bunch of macho assholes in a stationhouse locker room, what would I do? San Francisco is a long damn way from Yakima. Light-years. Lot of pressure.

"How did you end up with SFPD?" Seems like an obvious next question.

"Funny story . . ." he says. "I went to the police academy in Seattle. Like every cop in Washington state. It was my first time in a big city, but there were so many other hicks like me in my class that it didn't seem all that strange. It was like being stationed somewhere, you know? You don't really live there, you're just there for training. You're with the same bunch of guys every day, everywhere you go. The split between the city guys and the bumpkins shows right away. They went their way, we went ours. Most of the men in my class were planning to go straight back to wherever podunk town they were from and play Andy of Mayberry. Easy job, easy pay. Folks who know them and automatically respect them. Family. A high school sweetheart waiting back home. Me? I wanted to get the heck out of all the grapes and hops and peaches and beans and hayfields. I didn't want any part of that life anymore. I wanted a big city life. Whatever that meant. That's how green I was.

"There was a posting on a hallway bulletin board about a big recruiting effort at SFPD. I applied on a dare. Literally. They ribbed me so hard. Never occurred to me that thousands of cadets would be applying for a couple of hundred positions. That I would be screened and interviewed and background checked. That there would be scads of tests. That once all that was over, it would be months until I'd find out whether or not I got picked."

"You got picked." Mona raises her glass to him.

"Can you believe it? It had been so long I had already started looking other places: Portland, Los Angeles, Denver. I was top of my class. Had plenty of choices."

"Naturally."

"After the academy, I went back home to wait. It was spring. Planting time. Calving time. Fertilizing time. Chemicals that stink pretty bad. I went back to work driving tractor for my uncle. He reminded me every day that I was going nowhere, that I wouldn't even get hired on as a local cop. I'd be lucky just to keep working for him."

"Sounds like a swell guy," Rodney says.

"He was that way my whole life. I wanted to make him eat his words. I guess that was one part of wanting out so bad. Then this letter comes. SFPD wants me to come down for another interview. Know what I did? I took it as a sign from God that I would get the job. I gave away everything but my car, my books, and some clothes, and knew I'd never go back."

"And you didn't?"

"Can you believe it? I got the job, rented a place — not the one you came to. Got that later with the money we took. Well, they didn't know I had it . . . I was happy. And busy. The weight of all of those people needing help or needing to be taken off the streets was overwhelming to me. Exciting, too. I wondered if I was really up to it. And I wasn't even in the thick of things like in the Mission or the Castro or the Tenderloin. Yet. They gave me neighborhood beats around Golden Gate Park and the Presidio and Russian Hill. Quieter places but gangbusters for me. Learning how to navigate those streets. Finding addresses. Dodging electric buses and trolley cars. Pedestrians who walk right out and expect you to stop. Try handing out jaywalking tickets. I gave that up right away. They'd just laugh and say, 'Have a nice day' and turn the ticket into a littering violation. One day a hippy lady I was ticketing gave me a smiley face pin and a daisy. I watched her toss the ticket in an actual trash bin. A first! I learned a new level of cuss words from the people I was protecting and serving. Got spit on. Called "pig." I quit telling stories about my day because the guys just laughed and called me rookie. They teased me, pulled all kinds of pranks on me. Called me "pretty boy" until it became my nickname. Pretty Boy or PB. Then there's all the nonsense that comes with a last name like Tingle."

We're all on the edge of our seats waiting for the next big news.

Paul Tingle sighs. "Yeah. Well, the thing is . . ."

Rodney says, "Fuck, man, WHAT?"

"I kind of . . . See, the guys were like . . ."

"You did him, didn't you? And those other guys . . .?" Rodney says.

"Sometimes you don't get a choice . . ."

Holy shit. Officer Squeaky Clean's a killer. In uniform.

I'm really starting to warm up to the guy.

Chapter 36

Grady's been living in the same crappy single-wide in the same crappy trailer park in crappy Panther Valley my whole crappy life. It used to be white and hot pink. Now it's kind of tan and nipple-pink. His bedroom window's covered with tinfoil to keep the light out. A Nevada swing and graveyard shift trick. It's been up for so long that bugs and spiders and sand have built up deep between the foil and the glass. I don't know why he doesn't take it down. He hasn't worked a night shift in 20 years. Creature of habit. Same with his porch roof. There are so many holes in the fiberglass it doesn't keep out the sun or the occasional raindrop. It's green, too, which makes the light inside green. You have to know right where to step on the porch or you might go right through. Handyman he ain't.

His car's in the saggy carport that's supposed to be the landlord's responsibility, but he takes as much pride in ownership as Grady does. I pull in behind. Still laying low. Extra because of who I'm visiting.

He doesn't recognize Judith's truck, so he doesn't answer the door til I call his name. He pulls aside the tattered curtain on the door's porthole window. Sees it's me. He opens the door and hauls me none too gently inside. Then he sneaks a lookout in a Keystone cops kind of way.

"What are you DOING here?" he exclaims.

"I . . . what's up, Grady?"

He takes a few more super-spy looks out his windows before he clears a spot for me to sit in all the newspapers and TV dinner trays piled on his dusty plaid couch. His cat Jaws jumps into my lap and sheds all over me.

"You still have Jaws? What is he? About 100?"

"Never mind him. What the hell, Flack? What are you doing showing up here?"

"I brought you something."

Oops, he doesn't seem too glad to see me. Shit, what does Grady know?

"Where have you been?" he asks. I almost expect him to say "young lady" the way he's jabbing his index finger at me. The one he cut off half of with a Skillsaw, which probably accounts for him not being crazy about home improvement.

"Here. I've been here." Which is true. For the past few weeks. I'm getting better about leaving out details. That's not really lying, is it?

"They're looking for you."

"Who are?"

"Jesus, Flack. The dead guy from your office? Connected with Johnny Ruggerio, who's dead, as if you didn't know?"

"Oh, you must mean the police?"

"Cut the crap, kid. You're wanted for questioning on his murder AND Ruggerio's. Something about a kidnapping. You're a person of interest in, hell, more shit than I thought anyone ever could be. And you show up here?! You weren't followed, were you?"

He takes another circuit around his windows. Jaws starts clawing at the back of the couch, so I smack him onto the floor.

"Hey! Careful!" Grady picks up the scraggly thing and tries to comfort him and gets a nice chomp on his hand for his trouble. Grady tosses the cat to the floor. "Sumbitch."

"I can still trust you, right?" I ask

He plops down on a wobbly kitchen chair. He hates this, I know. I hope he loves me more.

"Kid, I'd do anything for you. You know that."

I lay it all out for him. No, I didn't kill Michael. Johnny arranged that. Yeah, I killed Johnny, but I tell him my lawyer says it was self-defense. Yeah, I kidnapped a baby. At Mona, the baby's mother's, request. I know the kid's with her father and safe.

"Should have known Mona'd be involved. She's a bad seed."

"She's a mom now. It changed her." Momentarily, I'm thinking.

"Where've you been?"

"Probably better you don't know."

"You're okay, though?"

Grady's working up to asking how Johnny came to be murdered so violently. I can see it in his eyes, so I cut to the chase.

"It wasn't just my life I was afraid for out at Johnny's. He was on a rampage. I thought he had killed Mona and this one other guy. That wasn't the worst, though. It was the baby. I was real scared for the baby. I couldn't have lived with myself if she'd gotten hurt. I snapped. You know how they say you see red when you're really pissed? I saw black. It was like nothing mattered except to end that sonofabitch. Permanently. No question. I don't regret it. The world's better off without him."

"His family has gone to war," Grady says, running his hand over his stubbly face. "With each other. With the department. I don't know how much information they have or where it's coming from, but I hear they're offering a $20,000 bounty for you. And, I hear, Johnny was about as unpopular with his family as he was with, well, everybody. So, this level of pissed-off-ness?"

"A bounty? Isn't that illegal?"

"They're calling it a 'reward,' but we know what it really is. Pretty sure it would include 'dead or alive' if their lawyers weren't stopping them."

"Shit." I know they're dangerous. There're lots of them, too. Once you get a train like that rolling, it's damn hard to stop.

"You need to make yourself as scarce as possible," he says. He takes another tour around the windows.

"10-4," I say. "What about you? You safe?"

"Uh, about that. You know Johnny's brother? Vincent? Offered me a bribe — a big one — to let him know if I heard anything. Where you was. Who you was with. Came with a promise that if I held out on him, I'd wish I'd never been born."

"Shit! I'm so sorry. We'll figure out something."

"Tell that to Rogers and Harney."

The Betamax tape I'm about to hand him has all of a sudden taken on a new role. Exposing what's on the tape — to the right people — could be our last line of defense. All of ours.

289

I dig the tape out of my bag.

"What's this?"

"It's a videotape for a Betamax."

"Beta-who?"

"Yeah, it's like a home movie camera, but you don't have to develop the film or nothing. You record, like with a reel-to-reel. Only you get sound and picture. This one's got some evidence on Johnny and a whole lot of pretty important people. Congressmen, county and city counselors, and such. They've been plotting to build a horse racing track out in Washoe Valley, only there's a big property owner holding out. It's all on there."

He turns the tape over in his hand.

"It plays on a special camera. I need you to get this to someone at the station who'll help us. Someone you trust."

"Christ. Give it here. Goddam. Look, kiddo, don't mean to be inhospitable, but get the fuck out. Keep your head down. You're too hot to be hanging around with me. Tell you what: you know Pelican Point?"

"Out at Pyramid Lake? Sure."

"Meet me next Tuesday. 2 pm sharp. I oughta know something by then. Got it? Tuesday 2 pm."

"Got it. Take care of yourself. I love you."

"I love you, too, kiddo. Now get the fuck out. Don't take any wooden nickels."

"Aw, but I love those."

"Okay, here then." He scrounges under the crap on his kitchen table and comes up with a wooden nickel from John Ascuaga's.

I give him a big hug and a kiss. He opens the door and smacks me on the ass on my way out.

"I'm still pissed at you," he says, shaking his finger at me again. "You're not too big to spank."

"Try it, old man."

"Old man this," he says, flipping me off and slamming the door.

I'm scared. For him now more than for me. He's all alone, and he's got that fucking tape. If I was the praying type, I sure would be doing it now. I think watching out for Grady sounds like a good assignment for Paul Tingle. Superior firepower beats prayer every time.

Chapter 37

I hide out at "home" for a few days to get my ducks in a row before I decide my first move ought to be heading out to Hope Springs Stables to swap Judith's junker for one of Anita's just in case. Never know who might have noticed what I'm driving. Given Grady's news, I'm taking no chances.

What seemed like a good idea at the time falls apart in a big hurry as I'm easing down the dirt driveway to the stables. All of a sudden, Paul Tingle comes roaring past me in his monster Mustang and pulls sideways in front of me, blocking the road, cutting me off. I slam on the brakes – which does almost nothing – so I slam on the emergency brake, too, and stop just short of the 'stang.

"RUN!" Officer Tingle yells, standing on the perfect leather front seat of the convertible, waving his arms. He points at the stables. Two black, shiny, unmarked, obvious police cars. I grind the gears into reverse and chug backwards through the exhaust and dust into a turnaround spot. Last I see of Paul Tingle, he's driving down to the stables, into the rats' nest. There's no time to worry about why. I turn east on 80, simply because it's the opposite way from Reno, and plod through the gears, past the truck's limit, to a screaming 52 mph. I feel like I could get out and run faster. Hope this bucket of bolts holds together until I can decide what to do.

I know the cutoff for Silver Springs coming up. Great place to leave the Interstate. Not Washoe County, not Reno. There's not shit out here, but the road will eventually hook up to Highway 50, which could mean Vegas if I can get my hands on a better ride.

The road is a straight shot through miles and miles of foot-high sagebrush. I would be worried about all the exhaust and screeching engine noise I'm making, but there's no one out here. Just space to be driven through. Highway 50 will be my ultimatum: right into Carson City? Left for 400 miles of nothingness to Vegas?

Or . . .

Holy shit! Flack, you beauty! You are soooooo good!

• • •

When the road deadends into 50, I make a right. About 15 miles down will put me on another right turn into the Comstock: that haven for outlaws and misfits and hermits. I'll pass the Craft Guild, where "artists," mostly just potheads and moochers, make a little bit of effort to sell their crappy copper wire jewelry, blobby sand candles, and weed while enjoying (to me it would be enduring) a communal lifestyle.

This crew is not just motley, they're downright moldy, moth-eaten, and damn fun to party with. Parties there always feature The Sutro Sympathy Orchestra playing for a fundraising dance because the residents don't try too hard to do much other than get stoned, screw, and sleep, so they always need money. Also most of Sutro Sympathy lives there. Turn on, tune in, drop out.

I blow by the Guild, head up the hairpin curves of Geiger Grade to Silver City, Gold Hill, Virginia City then down the Yes-Jesus-Loves-Me hairpin curves on the other side of the Grade that'll lead back to 395 and civilization. Only I won't be going that far.

Out on the flats, I turn onto Toll Road – the original Geiger Grade route. Toll Road is a neighborhood mess of trailers, shacks, and other inventive living spaces that house a zoo of humanity ranging from the Born Again to the Flower Children to rednecks to outlaw bikers to hopeless burnouts and drunks. The person I'm going to see is Dirty Dave. He's all of those types combined.

Dirty Dave's place is like being inside a dinosaur skeleton. Like in those fancy museums in New York and such. The insides of Dave's half-buried cavern are a network of old beams and timbers rescued from the Winters Ranch barn when it bit the dust in the '67 Washoe zephyr. Boards from the barn make up the walls. The house is as rough and weathered as Dirty Dave. And burly. And, for both of them, given this new lease on life, hard to knock down. His house is a gigantic splinter factory.

Since he built half of the house below ground level, all the windows look out at people's ankles. You have to look UP from inside to see who's at the door. Then you yell, "Pull the string! Kick the door!" The "string" is a leather strap that sticks out through some copper tubing fitted through the massive barnwood door that lifts a thick metal bar out of a metal brace on the inside. Pull that, then the kick knocks the door open. Whenever Dave wants to lock up the place — which is almost never — all he has to do is pull the leather strap inside. Genius.

Dirty Dave's is a goddam fire hazard if I ever saw one. Pop didn't live long enough to see it. He'd have had a stroke from all that square footage of tinder. Only the front room and kitchen — really just one big room — are heated. By wood. In an old O'Keefe and Merrit gas stove with two woodburning side burners and a flimsy Franklin fireplace from Sears that, even when piled full and the black metal glowing red, barely keep the space from freezing. But the windows grow beautiful patterns of ice inside for a lovely Christmastime.

Once, experimentally, and to keep his wife from leaving him, Dave crammed the Franklin with actual coal, which everybody told him was a terrible idea. Dave says it was nice and toasty, but while he slept, his whole family and half the neighborhood sat up all night, scared shitless that the stove was hot enough to melt. He did eventually install a small electric wall heater in the bathroom as a courtesy to his wife. By then it was too little too late.

Dirty Dave's entire family left him one by one once they realized that the "family" home he almost built for them would never be finished or comfortable, that the family construction business he gave lip service about starting was never going to happen, and that selling LSD and grass out of his Shaklee vitamin dealer bag had become his primary occupation. Minors, too, were served whatever they wanted. This made his family pretty edgy, but no one has ever talked Dave out of anything Dave wanted to do.

The thing about being a drug dealer in Nevada is that every infraction results in a felony. Especially where marijuana is involved. People get locked up right and left for seeds, for smells, for roaches in the ashtray – any little shadow of the demon weed. And selling to kids? You get the picture.

His wife left first, not wanting to end up some prison dyke's finger food. Daughter and middle son next. Youngest son ended up being hauled to juvie because he happened to answer the door to cops who were coming to arrest Dave – who was shacked up in town somewhere – for the scraggly patch of marijuana growing in the dry, weedy vegetable garden. Nothing ever came of it jailwise – only Dave could manage that – but it was the end of the road for the family. It's pretty nuts for me to be thinking about ancient history considering the current events of my life, but the lore of Dirty Dave makes for great entertainment when there's no radio.

Now he lives in the dinosaur skeleton alone. Most of the time. At some point his town ladies get tired of his constant state of stoner poverty and stop letting him in at their places. Then women and girls come and go from Dave's place like motel guests. The lure of Dave is a mystery to me, but there's plenty of chicks that dig long hair, weed, wine, and sex no matter how crusty the guy is. A chick gets comfortable here until she realized she's buying all the groceries and doing the cooking and washing clothes and cleaning house, while he's off on whatever fantasy, money-making idea catches his interest and never makes it off the drawing board. But there are always more chicks, each unique, like snowflakes. Always another one.

That's where I'm going now. Not for the first time, sorry to say. Hippies. Like I need hippies in my life. Especially when I need level heads. Clear heads. I'm stuck. I have to count on Dirty Dave. That's really hitting bottom for me. He's the unofficial grandfather of the hippest of the hip crowd. Dave's never messed with heroin or any hard drug – is against that kind of shit 100% – so the really strung-out kids who take refuge at his place are going to hear his lectures and follow his rules. No. White. Powders. Ever. With most of them, he succeeds, partly because he doesn't draw the line at pot. In all that marijuana smoke and sex and general sloppiness, they find someone they can actually talk to. It matters. They blow in and out of his life like tumbleweeds. Now and then some idiots will trash his house, craving stronger drugs and money to go get them, but they leave when they find nothing. Dave picks up the pieces and moves on. And every now and then kicks some ass. He and the house are rough and sturdy. He knows what to keep away from them and where to keep it. And I know for a fact he tries real hard to get them off smack.

Timmy brought his strung-out, pregnant girlfriend to stay at Dirty Dave's for two weeks after he killed the cabbie. She didn't like the looks of Dave, mostly the way Dave looked at her, so she split. Timmy, over Dave's advice to let it go, frantically went to find her, and that's when he got pinched.

Dirty Dave reached out to me after Timmy's trial. He was a mess. Crying. Saying he was so sorry to have failed my brother. Told me the whole story. He hated himself because he hadn't done better by him. Then he asked me to sleep with him because he was so sad and so lonely. Motherfucker, I thought, motherfucker. Today, I'm over it and can admit to myself that he tried to help Timmy. The Dirty Dave way, but he tried.

So here I am.

I pull the string, kick the door. He's in the kitchen, getting a beer from the 1940s fridge he's been barbwiring together for the past three years. He hasn't even turned around to see who came in. He's buck-naked except for a loincloth that reveals his whole butt to me and the matt of gray hair that covers his entire body. When he turns from the

297

YOU MAKE ME TINGLE

fridge, I see his beard and long hair have beads braided into them. It appears the current lady of the house might be a teenager with crafting skills. The loincloth hanging from the front is only mostly sufficient.

"Beer?" he asks.

"Fine," I say.

"Aren't you . . .?"

"Timmy's sister? Yeah."

"Right on. Flip, wasn't it?"

Close enough. I don't correct him. I need a hideout, not a positive ID

Dirty Dave hands me a Coors and scratches his barrel chest down the beer-belly to just where the loincloth begins.

"How's the boy?" Dave asks, clunking beers with me.

"Don't know. He won't see me."

"No shit. That's a drag."

"A drag."

"I liked that kid. Did you know he taught me — well, tried to teach me — chess when he was here?"

"That right?"

"Don't know where he come up with that. He was sure hot for it. Me? Nah."

He doesn't ask why I'm here, and it's great he doesn't care. We sit down at his massive, Dave-made dining room table, and he starts rolling joints out of a big pile of grass. He lifts up a cheek and farts and keeps on rolling.

"Put us on some tunes, would you? Just flip that stack over."

I flip the heavy stack of l.p.s over and set them back at the top of the spindle. I dink around with a few dials and end up blasting some kind of twing-twang, bing-bong music before I can get it turned down. God, I hope they aren't all like this.

"Hey, let me ask you something, you ever heard of . . .?"

Now, when Dirty Dave starts a question with "You ever heard of . . ." unless you have as dirty a mind as he has or a strong stomach, you may want to tune out. I learned from him about vibrating butt plugs, pearl necklaces, love doll beachball – a good many things that interest him that I could have gone my whole life perfectly fine not knowing about. Thing is with Dave, once he gets talking about sex, you can walk away, and he'll entertain himself. Before he gets started telling me something I've never heard of and don't want to hear of, I'm going to the back of the house to find the extension phone in Dave's room. Right now.

I unearth the phone from Dave's mess and call Mona. I let it ring once and hang up. A signal we made up as kids. Call back and she picks up after the fourth ring. Another signal.

"Hello. Who is this?" she answers.

"It's me. Did you get the watermelon?" "Watermelon" is code for "how fucked are we." You never know who might be listening.

"I got a big one."

"We'll need it." Also code for how fucked are we.

"I'm going to be late. Down in Gardnerville now checking on Mom." Code for "10-4, over and out."

"I'll let Bill know. He'll be here at 7."

"Okay, bye."

"Bye."

That basically means, "Glad you're all right, don't come home yet."

Fuck. What the hell's going on? I need a nap.

When I've been forced to stay out here at Dave's, I take the corner bedroom near the bathroom if it's available. It's got the best windows to keep an eye on Toll Road though it's not much fun when Dave's on the can. He does enjoy serenading his bowels.

Whoever stayed in this room last left the place neat as a pin and fresh as a daisy. Totally unexpected and totally excellent. Person even left me something to read: Jonathan Livingston Seagull. I lay down with the book – just to rest my eyes a second – and make it through about three sentences before drifting off. Seagulls: rats with wings, Pop called them.

• • •

I come wide awake when I hear Pioche cry. Takes me a minute to figure out where I am and that she's not here. But my heart is pounding now so sleep is out of the question. I rummage in my bag for my pack of Luckys. Dirty Dave doesn't allow tobacco smoking in the house, so I head to the courtyard where he's barbequing. Corn on the cob and chicken. Bless his heart.

"Oh hey, Flip. Still here. Food?"

"Yeah. Thanks "

We eat from our laps on lawn chairs held together with black electrical tape. When we're finished, Dave whips off his loincloth, turns on the outdoor shower – orange, sulfur-smelling Grade water dribbles out – and proceeds to wash his pits and balls. I grab our paper plates, cobs, and bones and haul ass through the house to the garbage cans out in the unfinished three-car garage. It's got cement block sides at least. No windows, no doors, no roof. Either his wife's inheritance or his enthusiasm ran out. Probably both.

I have another smoke on the way out to the pickup where I left a bottle of Beam under the seat. One of the neighbors is shooting cans with a .22, another is tuning up a motorcycle. Mike across the street is watering and drinking beer as always. For a desert rat, he grows amazing flowers. A couple of teenage girls coast down the road on 10-speeds with their feet in the air and no hands, whooping it up.

Dave comes out all spit-polished for town. Shoes, pants, more beads, hair still wet but brushed a little bit, the works. He holds his hand out for my bottle, takes a huge gulp, burps, and says, "Later." Climbs into his heavily-decorated VW bus and leaves. I have the place to myself.

I decide to move Judith's truck since I'm not planning to go anywhere any time soon, and it's just as well to take the precaution. I drive out to Kivet Lane and park it behind an empty single-wide with all the windows shot out and all the cinderblocks stolen out from under it so it sits on rusty axles. A nest of wild cats hiss at me – especially the babies. I hiss back. We're friends now.

Walking back up to Dave's, it occurs to me that I'm not getting any exercise lately. Laying low involves a lot of that: laying, sitting. And smoking. I try jogging. That's no fun. Makes me cough. I stretch a little. Gives me a backache. Flack, you are getting old. The walk seems to take forever, but I still think stashing the truck was a smart thing to do.

How should I entertain myself for the rest of the night? Jonathan Livingston Seagull? Dave's questionable record collection? I didn't see a TV, can't imagine he doesn't have one. I think tonight Creature Features is on, too. Don't want to miss that.

I go in and have a gander at Dave's records. The man is all over the place: rock, psychedelic, classical, country. Some of them aren't even yet. Lots of rejects from the cut-out rack. Japanese flute, Gregorian chants, polkas. $1.99, most of them. I'm a Loretta Lynn, Conway Twitty, Tammy Wynette type myself. KVLV radio in Fallon does me a whole lot better than KCBN in Reno that's starting to play nothing but teeny-bopper crap: Beatles, Herman's Hermits, Chad and Jeremy, and like that. Sounds like clanking tin cans to me. "Yeah, yeah, yeah" and "I can't get no" don't do much for me. I like to hear about sweet love and kisses and dogs and pickup trucks, even though most of those things haven't been especially kind to me. I'm a square. Give me "Stand by Your Man" over "Let's Spend the Night Together" any time.

I move on from Dave's music to the pile of books and magazines on his wood-butchered coffee table. Dave told me that when building this table – an 80-pound monster made of four-by-fours – he drank "massive" beers and beat the thing with a tow chain, burnt it with a blowtorch, and hacked at it with an axe to get that groovy weathered look. Said he laughed like a maniac the whole way through the process. Had to rough it up – give it character. He gave it structure then pounded that structure into art. According to him. I have to say the blunted, burnt corners and the grooves beat into the surface definitely scream "Let it all hang out!" Put your feet up. Spill beer. Dance on me. Have a seat and puke on the floor. What other 1973 coffee table gives you so many options? There is – and will ever be – only one. I know because Dave is lazy and distractable, and also because normal people could never dream up such a thing.

Magazines? Reader's Digest, McCalls, Playboy, Teen Beat, Argosy. Books? An avalanche of Louis L'Amour and Zane Grey. Slave Girl: A Brand for Betty. Sinful Sexpot. Madame Butch.

Starting to make that stupid seagull look more tempting.

I find the TV on the floor in the front room between two giant pillows and some kind of gigantic plant that reaches to the ceiling and has leaves as wide as four of my hands. How the hell does it stay alive in the cold and heat and neglect? Creature Features and I are about to have our Saturday night rendezvous as I settle in on the pillows and try to point the

302

antenna in a direction that catches the signal.

The open doors and windows let in the early summer perfume of sage and piñon and juniper pollen. Wish I could bottle it. Warm nights push the resiny–dusty–piney–flowery–sandy smell of the desert past the point of just smell into something impossible to put into words. I could say "perfume," but that's not enough. No combination of aromas in this world can compare with Nevada desert at night. I guarantee. I'd fight you on that.

Goddammit! There are more goddam people under my skin than I know what to do with! Look where I am, for Christ sake. Dirty Dave's? Isn't that about as low as you can go? Aren't I one step above giving up entirely? I don't know what to do, which isn't new, but this mess is much bigger, much closer to my cold, hard heart than anything I've let myself experience in a very long time. Feelings confuse me. I prefer not to have them. I've got a whole slew of them now, coming from every direction.

I sink down into what must be Dave's favorite chair, judging from the burn holes and red wine spills and general grubbiness. Looks like it used to be greenish. Now it's mostly tan where stuffing isn't sticking out. The TV is a cube the size of a couple of six-packs with screwed-up rabbit ears wrapped in tin foil. Classy. I've come a long ways down from the Mark Hopkins, and I have to say this suits me better. I get how to operate at this basic level. That city life? Oh please.

But I can't focus on whatever show's on. I keep thinking about Johnny and Mr. Chan and Pioche's dad. And Mona. All the trouble I should be walking away from. I know, I know, and Officer Tingle, too.

I'm also thinking I need another swig of Beam and to go outside for another cigarette.

I'm thinking, Flack, you think too much.

On this excellent half-moon night on the Grade, I can see Mt. Rose's granite face sparkle like diamonds. The Grade folks are settling into their assortment of bedtime rituals: one more beer while watering petunias; screams of panic and then a mother's joy after finding a lost kid; the neighborhood pit bull growling while being swung around the yard on a hose he will not unchomp; horses and goats and sheep and chickens cheering for their suppers after making their people miserable for hours with their bellyaching about wanting to get fed. I can hear the body grinder and see sparks flying across the street at Ken's. He's working on a '36 Ford Roadster he'll never finish – like all the other scrap metal in his yard.

I stub out my cigarette on the cement floor in the garage and go back with my bourbon. All my worrying starts again as soon as I flop down on the pillows. I'm hoping Grady got the Betamax tape to someone. I'm hoping Grady stays safe, the old fart. I love that man so much. And then there's . . .

I hear a knock – clamor – at the front door. I set the TV and Jim Beam on the loveseat to go and see who's there. And I draw my Python just in case. All I can see from the window are tattered tennies, skinny hairy ankles, and the limp hanging toes of a woman obviously being carried. Rather than yell, "Pull the string, etc.," I go open the door.

A couple of very young kids stagger into Dave's house. The man is a tiny, smelly troll who is supporting another tiny, very pregnant troll.

"Hey," he says. "I'm Glen. Glen Gray. And this here is my lady, Lady Gray."

Thick hillbilly accent. The real deal. Black teeth. Bad skin. Baaaaad hygiene.

"Think her baby's coming."

I look at her and she looks at me kind of cross-eyed, and I say, "Think?"

304

"We waddn't sure what to do, so we come to Dave. He here?"

Oh, shit. This chick's about to pop, and they don't have one single clue. And guess what? Neither do I. And neither would Dirty Dave if he was here . . . or if he wasn't.

"Better get her to a bed," is all I can offer. Poor thing looks like she's been at it a while.

"How long she been like this?" I ask.

"Oh," says Glen Gray. "Couple hours, maybe?"

I take Lady Gray under the arms. "You know how to do this?" I ask him.

"Me? Nah, ma'am. I surely don't."

"Oh fuck," I say. "Uh, get me a whole lot of water and towels and rags and shit. And some, uh, string. Scissors. And call an ambulance . . ."

"We ain't got no money for no ambalance."

"Then . . . Oh fuck! Never mind. Get Nancy! Over on Kivet."

"I know her."

"Go!"

Glen takes off. Me and Lady waddle back to "my" room – the cleanest in the place. I feel sorry for her. I have no idea how to be much help. I keep repeating over and over that everything will be okay while I just know I've got a dead woman and a dead baby on my hands. Glen looks about as reliable as a diaphragm with pinholes. Lady here is so thin and pale and worn out I can't imagine her surviving what I'm told childbirth involves.

"I'm dyin'! I'm dyin'!" she says.

I want to say, "That's what they all say," but instead I say, "No. I won't let you die." Mentally crossing my fingers.

"Glen! I want Glen!" She pronounces it "Gleeee-en."

"He's getting help. He's coming."

305

"Oh, my Lord. My Glen. My . . ."

She gets eerily quiet and spreads her legs. I'm no expert, but here it comes. Lady Gray's baby's whole head is pretty close to out. I don't know what else to do other than press on the sides of her pushed-out puss to keep it from splitting. The baby slides into the room on a magic carpet of gore. Glen still hasn't come back, so I am making up shit as I go along: find something to tie the cord, cut it off. The baby girl takes to Lady Gray's breast right away, though the girl looks so malnourished I can't think she has much to offer. Look at me, talking all maternal-like. I read. I keep up. I know about Lamaze and La Leche League. In the background, but yeah, women have kids. Women feed kids. Kids are a pain in the ass.

From all I can tell Lady Gray's going to live. The baby, a little girl, sounds like she'll make it, too. Lady named her daughter August because, well, it's May. Glen hasn't shown. I'm starting to doubt he will. Good. His teeth were making me sick. She asks for him over and over. She's so young, maybe 14 or 15, and he's got to be pushing 30, maybe more. Dick. Both from Down South. Bama? Looziana?

Lady's telling me Glen's been talking about moving to Oregon where welfare pays the most. Probably a lot more now with the kid. Some guy they met in some shelter somewhere told him all about it, mooch to mooch. Somebody should have told her about birth control.

Baby-having is messy. I am remaking what was supposed to be my bed, looking around for anything that will serve as a diaper for both August and Lady. All hands on deck means: Flack! Handle it! As per usual, I am. Barely. Killing a guy? Cleaning up a dead body? No problem-o. This here? Whole different rodeo.

How can Lady already be calling her baby "Augie Doggie?"

Glen scampers in with Nancy right on his heels. She's carrying what looks like a giant sewing kit. Calm as a cucumber. Says hi to Lady.

"Good to see you, Flack. Been a long time. How the hell are you?" Nancy's taking a real close look at Lady's nether regions, pushing on her belly. "Where is the placenta?" she asks.

The what? Oh, that blobby thing I figured was Lady's liver – at least some of it.

"This?" I unroll the towel it slopped onto. Good thing I hadn't chucked it out yet. Seems important to Nancy, who turns it over and over, prodding it with her fingers.

"Looks like it's all here. Good job. Some women like to eat a bite or two. Helps with their milk coming in."

Okay, everything leading up to now was gross and bloody and messy, but the idea of eating a hunk of raw meat that just popped out of someone's snatch is too much for me. I race to the bathroom and barf peanut butter and boloney and Jim Beam into the bathtub because the toilet didn't look big enough to hold what I felt was coming up. I don't want to know if Lady took Nancy's advice, and I tell them so through the wall.

While Nancy deals with the new parents and their offspring, I clean up the mess I made. I much prefer my job to theirs, despite the chunks. I scrub the bathtub with Comet til it's less barfy and a little less orange alkali-water stained. When I get back to the bedroom, the new parents are missing, and Nancy is sitting on the bed holding August.

"They're in the courtyard taking a shower," she says. "Want to hold her?"

So, it's not b.o. but blood that will get the smelly, new parents into the shower.

Nancy doesn't wait for me to answer, just shoves the baby

at me. I grab the kid so she won't fall.

"Support her little head. Hold her against you."

August is still covered in drying bodily fluids. She's peaceful and small and alive.

Nancy says, "I'm going to get a big bowl of hot water so we can clean her up. You okay?" Then she just walks out, and I better be okay. I have no choice.

Crap. I got nanny-duty. Again. Change my name to Miss Ludden. And I think again of Pioche. We'll get you back, kiddo. We're working on it.

Glen and Lady come back in stark naked and shivering from their shower. He's not holding her up as much as she's leaning on him real hard. She's walking pretty stiff. They climb into bed. I hand her the baby. They form a circle of arms around themselves and the kid. I tuck them in. I wish I thought this little family would have a happy life, but Glen has all the earmarks of a #1, tried-and-true deadbeat. Shifty eyes. The stink. Lady kisses and kisses his gaggy mouth while the baby takes a rest. I may throw up again.

Nancy brings in a stewpot of warm water and plenty of wash rags and towels. She takes a bar of what must be special baby soap out of her sewing bag, puts the sleeping kid on her lap, and begins to wash the past off of her. Doesn't even care if she makes a mess of her own clothes. Nancy's all about the baby. She's singing "Good Morning Star Shine," because, you know, it's the middle of the night.

I can't help thinking this may be as clean as that child will ever get before she ends up in a foster home. The stink of the Gray family goes with the territory of life-by-handout. I back my way out of the room and go in search of cigarettes and bourbon. No one's asked the whereabouts of Dirty Dave. He'd just be in the way. And every other sentence would start with, "Hey, did you ever hear of . . ." who needs that at a birthing?

Nancy joins me in the living room, leaving August with possibly the world's most irresponsible parents.

"They can take care of this," Nancy says. "They have to start figuring it out now."

"Think they will?"

"They have a choice?"

Somehow that feels sadly appropriate. Nancy flops down on the couch with her sewing bag of wonders and extracts a doobie. She sparks up and offers it to me.

"Got mine," I say, hoisting my bottle and taking a slug. She snaps her fingers for the bottle I'm glad to share with her, though I turn down the reefer. "Never got the hang of it," I tell her.

"Right on."

Don't know what makes me wonder, but I have to ask, "Where are they living?"

"Ken rented them a fucked up old school bus on his place."

"'Rented?'"

"I don't even want to know."

We sit quiet for a while. I was right about Creature Features. I'm watching it out of the corner my eye. Where does Bob Wilkins find these idiotic "horror" movies? They're mostly ignorable, but Bob's commentaries are priceless. That skinny four-eyed nerd is the perfect host for black-and-white blood and guts.

Then she says, "Heard you was in The City."

I nearly spit out my drink. As far as I remember, there were six people who knew I was there, and one of them is not old enough to talk. I turn off the TV. She says, "Don't freak out. I didn't tell anyone."

When I recover the use of words, I ask, "Who told you?

What did they tell you? Why you?"

She takes a deep hit and grins. "Sweetheart, everybody tells Nancy everything. I am the High Priestess of the Grade. You know that." She grins bigger. She's so high.

Who else in the entire Comstock could come close to deserving such a title? Nancy's a large woman. Tall, muscular, all female, and absolutely no bullshit. She has long blonde hair starting to go gray early. When I say "long," I mean long enough for her and anyone next to her to sit on. She's always rearranging it forward over her left shoulder where she can keep an eye it. Then she moves around so much that it falls back and she tosses it forward constantly. Her beautiful, round face is full of mischief and comfort. She's always wearing some crocheted vest or scarf or sweater she's made. With two young sons of her own, a trailer house, husband, and the entire Grade to take care of, I don't know how she finds the time for a hobby. I don't know her all that well – she doesn't talk much about herself – but she is one of those 100% trustworthy people you know instantly is okay with whatever you tell her.

"I'm worried about that baby," I say, with a nod toward the new family, trying to change the subject.

"Kids don't get to pick what the fuck adult situation they're born into. We're all here finding our own way. I can't let my heart get broke every time I see a baby land bad. August has her work cut out for her, for sure. Glen won't be around for long, I can tell you that. Probably for the best. Those two little girls'll be raising each other."

"Think Lady'll be a good mom?"

"She might. She just might. Cross your fingers that her taste in men improves."

She flips her hair forward and nestles into Dave's dilapidated couch. "How was The City?" she says, holding a hit.

"What'd you hear?"

"Ah-ah-ah, no way, sister. You first."

"I got nothing to say."

She leans forward points at me with the hand holding the joint.

"I think you do," she says. "I think you got a lot to say about a whole lotta shit."

"Maybe I do, maybe I don't." God, Flack, that was lame.

"Don't jive me. You're in some deep shit."

I feel trapped like the rat I am. The pure trustworthy look on Nancy's face is not only tempting, it's irritating.

I'm going to stand my ground: "Who's been talking to you about me?"

"If it's that important to you: Uncle Elmer. Elmer Grady."

"Grady?" Uncle Grady snitched to somebody? Since when?

Can the fishbowl that is Reno get any smaller? Does everybody know everybody?

"He loves you," she says.

"I know."

"He looks out for you."

"I know."

"You put him in a bad spot."

"I know." I don't say I had nowhere else to turn.

"He laid everything on me in case . . . anything happens to him."

"Why you?" I mean, who is she, anyway? An old, Geiger Grade hippie chick who crochets and delivers babies.

She repeats, "Wanted someone to know. That's all."

She's giving me the creeps. And she's so calm about it. No accusations, just facts. She even goes so far as to rummage a tangle of yarn out of her birthing bag and start crocheting something pink.

"What'd you want me to tell you about San Francisco?"

"How Mona fits into all of this. Your version."

"Why?"

"I don't trust her."

"That makes two of us."

"Where is she?"

"Around."

"She's a goddam menace to society."

"She's changed. A lot."

"Right. A leopard don't change its spots."

"She did. She has." So I tell her about Pio and San Francisco. I leave out the part about getting drugged, and Pioche getting snatched by Chan and Ludden. Since, according to Mona, all is well, I figure why give Nancy information she doesn't need.

Nancy shakes her head. "That woman's going to get people killed. Mark my words. Could be you. She doesn't give a shit."

"What makes you so fucking sure? I think I know her a lot better than you do."

"Then you ought to know what she's been up to."

Up to? She's literally been under my nose for weeks now, but I'm not telling.

"She's buddy-buddy with Vincent Ruggerio – probably more than a little – you know that?"

I'm hoping that it doesn't show that I do not.

"And Vincent is buddy-buddy with our shady piece of shit police commissioner Roy Semanski. You know that?"

I do know who that is. Who doesn't, the piece of grunt. But I did not know about Vincent, so ditto what I said before. Keep up that blank look, Flack.

"That tape you gave Uncle Elmer? Apparently she and Vinnie made a copy of it. The two of them took it to

312

Semanski."

There are copies of the damn thing? Man, hang in there, poker face.

"Oh yeah. Unk walked in on the three of them looking it. He said he had one you dumped in his lap on him. He was on his way to Phil Hamby's office with it, totally not expecting to catch those three together. He said he barely got a peek before they slammed the door in his face. Better believe he beat a hasty retreat with your little Betty-max. Never did give it to Hamby. You're in the clear. For now."

Grady's still got the tape. Which is good. But Mona, that sneak! We've practically been joined at the hip. How did she manage to find time for all this sneaking around with Vincent? I could kill her. Hypothetically speaking. Mostly.

All the interior doors at Dave's slide like barn doors, and weigh as much, so when the hall door slides open with a bang!, me and Nancy get the crap scared out of us. There's Glen dressed in his stinky, shabby clothes.

"Them two is out like a light. I'ma head on home."

He walks through and out the front door without a pause. Not a wave or a thank you.

"Real gentleman," Nancy says.

The way he left and who he left is all I need to know about him. Too bad he'll be back. That new baby's a damn good meal ticket.

"You know, she's calling that baby girl 'Augie Doggie'?" I say, pretty much pointlessly.

"Really? That sucks."

Everything sucks.

Chapter 38

Nancy and I spent the rest of that evening and the next week trying to convince Lady to move in at Nancy's at least for a little while, but she wouldn't hear of it. Glen came and went – never stayed long. Never brought food or clothes or diapers. But he sure ate and drank and enjoyed the clean sheets when he was here. Thank the gods they always stayed in the room when he came by. His reek of putrid sweat hung in the air like a bad reminder long after he left. Even though I hate incense, I burned up every stick I could find when he was around. Almost wanted to put Vicks under my nose like you do when you have to check out a very, very dead body.

We kept the girls as clean as we could. By the end of the week, Lady felt well enough to walk across the street, so she took the baby and went "home" to her man and the gutted school bus. Next thing we know, the three of them stopped coming by to mooch. Days went by. Then Ken said he saw them walking down the street one morning, her carrying the baby and a bunch of bundles, Glen empty-handed with his guitar hanging behind his back, five paces ahead of them, headed for the highway. We haven't seen – or smelled – them since.

Dirty Dave must've found some place comfortable in town since he hasn't been around either. Nancy's usually busy with her family, so I get left on my own with nothing but time to beat myself up for the mess I've put everybody in.

I finally decide to go collect Judith's truck from its hiding spot. Hopefully it'll start. I need groceries and a pay phone. And a carton of Luckys. And a couple of gallons of Jim Beam. There's a little market on Geiger Grade that will serve all those purposes.

I chase a few spiders out of the truck. Wipe the dust off of the windshield with my sleeve. There's tumbleweeds piled around like sandbags against a flood. Lo and behold, the damn thing fires right up in a cloud of black exhaust and a loud backfire, and I'm on my way to get supplies.

From the parking lot phone booth, I call Mona's, hoping she doesn't answer – I'm not ready to deal with her – so I'm happy when Rodney picks up.

"It's me," I say.

And he knows enough not to say my name.

"Where you at? You okay?"

"I'm fine. I am where I am. How's things?"

"Shit. Groovy."

Uh-oh.

"Your girl's been MIA a while. Don't know where. She left a number, but we been waiting on you."

Okay, so she's at large. Good to know.

"Just you and Pretty Boy out there?"

"Far as we know. Here he is."

Before I can say no or hang up, Officer Tingle's on the line. Dammit, it's nice to hear his voice.

"Don't say no names," I hear Rodney say in the background.

"Hi," Paul Tingle says.

"Hi." I'm melting. Pull yourself together, Flack.

"Okay?"

"Pretty much. You?"

"Okay."

"Welp, I guess I got to get going now . . ."

"Wait. Wait. Could you . . .? Could we . . .?"

There he goes, not finishing sentences again!

"No and no. Not yet."

"Sure you're all right?"

"I said so, didn't I?" I try to sound super irritated, put some of my pissed-off-at-Mona vibe on him. "Put Rodney back on."

"Guess I'll see you later then." He sounds hurt.

I get the number Mona gave Rodney, hang up with my finger on the bar, but hold the phone to my face for a few seconds. I wish I didn't miss that man.

Where is Mona? Shacked up with Johnny's brother Vincent? She does love the attention of a man in her life. Or what about her pal Victoria? Or Pioche's dad? Mona's got plenty of options. Plenty of people who will buy – or choose to ignore – her bullshit. Including yours truly. I want to talk to her, check her out, but that'll only result in her conning me – again – and me believing her. Again. What is it about Mona that makes you forgive and forget her over and over for the stunts she pulls? What is so fucking special about her particular brand of bullshit? I know part of it is that whatever she's saying, she somehow makes herself believe is true before she says it. That's how her stories always seem new.

I buy more crap than I planned from the Grade grocery store. Salty, greasy, sweet. Piles of packaged crap. I down a package of peanut M&Ms in the parking lot while I decide this old clunker could use an extra run down the highway to charge the battery.

I turn south towards Carson City after coming to a full by-gawd stop at the flashing red light, keeping one foot on the gas and one on the brake, truck in neutral, to keep from stalling out, or, heaven forbid, rolling out. Wishing the blinkers worked. People get killed at this stupid intersection of Geiger Grade/Mount Rose Highway/395 all the time. The flashing lights are pretty much taken as a suggestion to stop, so there's wrecks out here several times a month. Tow truck drivers' dream.

395 gets busier every year. It's the damn Californians. That's right: damn Californians. Moving up here and bringing their crappy, cranky driving skills with them, so us locals have to drive like assholes, too, out of self-preservation. Damn Californians claim to move here to live a more peaceful, slower, down-home kind of crime-free life, and immediately break every driving law and import every damn department store and fast-food joint they left behind so they'll feel more at home. What is it with people who have to make a new place feel exactly like the tired, old one they say they hate so much? Californians are hell on my blood pressure. Still when somebody's behavior sucks so much it's dangerous, isn't it my duty to say something?

I get as far as the Steamboat Springs post office – the opposite direction from Reno – before I know there's no way around going back. I pull into the parking lot to flip a bitch.

Steam rises up out of holes in the earth here. It's this huge patch of hot springs that makes Geiger Grade water so yucky to look at and so horrible tasting. Won't clean your clothes, stains everything orange, and rots your plumbing in no time flat. The Steamboat post office, a sweet, one-room, alpine ski chalet-looking deal with just enough space for a counter and 24 post office boxes, sits smack dab in the middle of these steaming streams of mineral gunk. Its sweetness is real creepy given the fire and brimstone all around it. You half expect a child-eating witch to be in charge of the place, but it's just a bald-headed, near-sighted, too-cheerful fat man in a regulation post office uniform, starched to a cardboard-y surface. So serious he's comical, which adds to the Halloween atmosphere.

Parked to one side of the building is an ancient blue four-wheel-drive jeep delivery truck with THIS VEHICLE MAKES FREQUENT STOPS stenciled across the back. The postmaster's wife does the delivering. She's the exact opposite of him. Flowered mu-mu. Bluish, ratted-and-AquaNetted hairdo, Tootsie Pop stick dangling from her lips. She lives to honk cars and pedestrians on horseback out of her damn way, cussing a blue streak out the window at them as she impedes traffic without a smile on her appointed rounds.

The ultimate touch of creepiness here is a lone red and blue mailbox waiting out in front, just daring someone to drop something into it. I picture a hairy hand would reach out to grab the birthday card you're trying to mail to your granny.

I love Nevada.

Back to Reno for me. But where? It's been months since I slept in my own bed. Which is in impound. Shit. My car's at the stables. Shit. There's my office. Not too comfortable, but at least it's sort of mine. Who knows? I might have mail. Publishers Clearing House could be looking for me. Ed

318

McMahon could be waiting with my check. It'd be a shame to waste more of his time.

• • •

The old truck spews and chugs down Wells Avenue, and I find a free parking spot next to the topless joint with the sign that just reads "op ess." I'll walk the rest of the way to my office with my sack of junk food, cigs, and booze. All a girl needs. It's a nice night for a stroll. The Truckee River gurgles on my left, the lights of the casinos glow against each other. Ah, home.

I know something ain't right when I get to the street door of my office building, the one that used to be dented aluminum but is now a glossy steel, double-hung affair held open at the moment by a couple of five-gallon paint cans. Hmmm . . . In the entryway – the "foyer" according to the new directory – the smell of fresh paint hits my nose and bright lights burn my eyes. New blue tweed carpet covers the floor and stairs. A blocked-off construction site in one corner appears to be the beginnings of an elevator shaft. The banister and stair rail that I last saw reparied with slapped together 2x4s are now impressive, polished oak.

What?

I take in the new view and then look out again at the address above the door to see if I'm in the right place. This is it, but I am very confused.

On the first landing wall there is a Great Seal of the State of Nevada. Battle Born. I go on up beside powder blue painted walls to the next floor. Here, the new carpet is covered by painters' tarps and scaffolding. Goddam place is bright, bright from new fluorescent fixtures. The door to my office,

You Make Me Tingle

like the other antique wood doors that open to the hall, has been restored to its original glory and is also propped open by a paint can. My name is gone. In its place it reads "University of Nevada Foreign Exchange Program." Then I notice all the doors are claimed in some way by UNR. Shit.

I set my stuff down on a steel desk that is divided from three others by blue-carpeted cubicle walls. The place stinks of new paint. On a ladder in the corner is a painter doing touch up. KCBN is blaring on his radio.

"Hey," I yell.

He whips around. I scared him.

"This is my office. Or used to be in my office. Where is my crap?"

He shrugs and goes back to work.

Fucking Felix sold me out to the state? Just like that? No notice? The paint, the carpets? The little lights glowing from multi-line phones? A copy machine? My beautiful big arched windows that once cast FLACK MURROW INVESTIGATIONS across the wood floor are now bare and have gleaming white venetian blinds and potted plants decorating them. Shit, even this place isn't mine.

Gone. All of it's gone. Back on the street I look across at the Cal Neva, lovely in neon as ever. The whole street is the same – only my part of it has changed. I am erased. Not much left to do but check back into the Capri, eat some cold Vienna sausages and saltines, drink way too much bourbon, wash out my one set of undies, and ponder what's next.

I shower and rinse out my unmentionables in the only real estate that settles for "mine" for now. I've been re-wearing the same clothes for too long. Tomorrow I'll hit Parker's Western Wear for new duds. Tonight I want to forget everything. I know I won't. The business – hell, the life – I slapped together out of emergencies, experience, good intentions, and razzle-dazzle has unraveled before my very eyes. I have nothing left to give. Nothing left to hope for or strive for. No reason to want to take on the world. All that I thought I had to hide means nothing compared to all that I have left myself open to pay for. Being on my own is one thing; being alone is totally another.

Who am I now?
What do I do?
Where do I belong?
WHERE'S MY STUFF?

Shit.

Chapter 39

Mona. I should know better by now. She's unbelievable with her "hate you/hate you more" gameplay. She'll say anything, be anyone, do whatever it takes to get what she wants. She literally has no heart. She treats the world like her personal toy box. People are nothing more than tools.

I'm completely wrong about motherhood changing her. She used Pioche like she uses everyone else. Packed her off to the dad as soon as the going got rough. Now I'm scared to death about that situation. She made me part of it. I fell for her bullshit as usual. I hope I learn my lesson this time. The shambles that is my life is all tied to her.

She's going to pay. She's messed with this "best friend" for the last time.

I shouldn't be doing this because I'm drunk and otherwise fucked up, but I rummage through my pitiful belongings and find the matchbook I scribbled Mona's number on.

"Bon soir," a woman's voice rings out on the phone line.

"Who is this?"

"C'est Victoria. Qui est-ce?"

I'm pretty sure she said it's her and wants to know who the hell I am. "This is Flack Murrow – er – Susan Anne."

"Oh, how nice to hear from you. Mona speaks so highly of you."

Yeah, I bet. "She there?"

"Why yes. Un instant."

How is it that everyone I'm simply asking the whereabouts of is standing right next to the person I'm asking? Just like with Officer Tingle, I wasn't quite ready to do this, but here goes.

After a bit of muffled transferring, she says, "Hello?" Innocent as a kitten.

"Hi, Mo. I called the house. They said they hadn't seen you . . ."

"Taking a breather from the menfolks."

"Really? Well, that's good."

"Where are you? Where've you been?"

"Here and there. You know me."

"Where's 'here?'"

I'm going to tell you?

"Town."

There's a long pause. The wheels turning.

"I have good news," she says finally.

"I could use some."

"I got your trailer out of impound. It has been installed at the park where Grady lives, if you can call that living."

Too close. My trouble is way too close to him.

"You didn't have to do that."

"What are friends for?"

Nothing you'd know about. "Thanks," I say instead.

Another pause.

She says with a bit of an edge, "So, here we are."

"Yes, we are."

These pauses are getting more difficult and longer. I know what I want to say to her, but I also need her to feel like we're cool.

"Susan Anne, is something wrong? Are you angry with me?"

Oh, you betcha, baby. I want to bury you. I want to forget you. I want to kick myself for all the things I've let slide where it comes to you. I hate myself for loving you, for trusting you again and again while you go around hurting everyone in your path. I can't tell which of us is more psycho: you for not giving a fuck or me for thinking I'm the exception to your rule that people are just things to be used.

I finally manage to say, "I'm just tired. The past couple of weeks have been rough."

"Where are you? I'm worried about you. Paul is frantic, you know."

"I told you: I'm in town."

"What's wrong? I insist you tell me."

"Nothing to do with you. It's personal."

"Tell me."

"Not on the phone."

"Then tell me where you are. I'll come get you."

"Not tonight."

She clears her throat. "Paul told me about the police at the stables. He said he managed to stop Anita saying much to them, and talked them out of trashing the place looking for you. The police wouldn't tell her anything, but Paul went all good-old-boy's club on them til they left."

Paul Tingle is either my new favorite friend or an even bigger pain in my ass than ever.

I say, "Tell me again, why aren't you staying at your place?"

She misses a beat in the conversation.

"I, uh, Victoria had some foot surgery. I thought I'd stay with her while she recuperates."

Hmmmm, I seem to remember she just needed some space from the menfolks. She lost track of her lie while making up a new one? Bad form, Mona.

"That's too bad," I say. "Hope she gets well soon."

"She's doing fine now. In another few days I'll be able to leave her on her own."

"Bet you'll be glad to go home and let the menfolk get on your nerves again." Hope she caught that.

This is the weirdest conversation – each of us not saying anything that isn't an absolute truth or flat-out lie – except the part about the surgery, which I sincerely doubt. Since I know A: where she is and B: she's not leaving there soon, I'm going to take my chances and go see Paul Tingle and Rodney. I need to round up a posse and put Mona and her fellow criminals behind bars for a long time. I've got plenty of evidence. I may be outmanned and outgunned between crooked politicians and police and the shady – and very pissed off – Ruggerio family, but I will find a way to bring them down.

Mona says, "Are you sure I shouldn't come and get you? Victoria's got lots of room. She'd love to have some company besides me."

"Thanks, but I'm really dug in and comfortable where I'm at. I'm doing laundry, sorting out my mail. Snug as a bug. I'll call after I'm rested up."

"Can you at least give me your phone number?"

I make up a number with a 786 prefix. It's in a nicer part of town. Then we say our fond goodbyes.

I have to beat feet for Mona's before she does. There's a lot she doesn't know. All of it can, and will, hurt her.

I'll make sure of it.

Bitch.

Chapter 40

Paul Tingle hugs me so hard for so long that he smashes the pack of Luckys I have in my shirt pocket to unusable crumbs that smell delicious. Rodney ends up hugging all of us together in his long, stringy, surprisingly strong arms. We must be a sight: scrawny little me sandwiched between two really tall men, one white, one black. My face comes up to their shirt pockets. I'm starting to feel suffocated.

"You guys! Stop! Give me some air, goddammit!"

They let me go but keep staring at me like they're seeing a ghost. Both of them have little tears in their eyes.

"Awright awready. I'm glad to see you, too," I say, scooping my mangled cigarettes into the trash compactor.

"Man," says Rodney," I need a drink."

"Make that three," I say.

It's late. I woke them up. The house was dark. Chester and Rockalee whinnied and snorted when they saw me, so I gave them a quick nuzzle. Officer Tingle must have heard them because he came to the door with a shotgun pointed at me.

"Don't move!" he commanded.

I put my hands up and turned around slowly. He shined a flashlight in my eyes, and then dropped both the gun and the light when he saw it was me. He picked me up and spun me around and kissed me all over my face and hair. Glad I showered.

He told me he loved me . . . about 90 times.

Shit.

Once we got inside, the stories started flying. We were all talking at once. Things at Casa Dirty Rat, as I came to think of Mona's, were quiet enough, but news was flying hot and heavy. First off, that day at the stables when Officer Tingle engaged the cops in a bit of small talk. Just boys in blue swapping stories like they do. He entertained them with tales from the Tenderloin, and eventually they let their guard down, and he got more than a few tidbits about what they knew. Seems an "anonymous" tip led them to believe one Susan Anne Murrow, AKA Flack Murrow, should be brought in for questioning in regards to the murder of one Gianni "Johnny" Ruggerio. Officer Tingle put on his law enforcement look of concern; they just kept spewing. Knowing as much as he did from what Rodney, Mona, and I had told him about that night, he was able to blow their version of my involvement in events as full of holes as a cattle crossing sign on Hwy 50. They went away scratching their heads.

I thank Officer Tingle and Rodney for their help, grab a handful of M&Ms, and toss one to each of them. Officer Tingle catches his in his mouth no problem. My toss to Rodney goes way wide, so I passed him the bowl instead.

Time for me to lay out my hand. I tell them how at the beginning of all of this mess, Mona had come to me at my office, begging for help. How she got me out to Johnny's, how she got me to take Pioche, how she disappeared that night and left me to get rid of her boyfriend for her. She set me up. I tell them it was not all the way clear what she was getting out of her scheme, but I found out she had taken a copy of the Betamax to the police commissioner Roy Semanski. And that Johnny's brother Vincent was with her. I didn't reveal Grady or my informant Nancy – Officer Tingle may not be totally on my side – but I told them I absolutely believed it was true. The police commissioner was in possession of the tape, and Mona and Vincent were responsible for it. That tape was most likely the reason for the anonymous tip: Mona finked on me.

"Oh, and guess what? I had a baby."

At this point Officer Tingle and Rodney both sit down, mouths wide open, looking like they've been struck by lightning. Twice.

"I mean, I delivered one."

"Girl, you should not be let out unsupervised," Rodney says, pouring himself more wine. Paul Tingle snaps his fingers for the bottle and fills his glass til it overflows.

"Mona's some friend," Officer Tingle says.

I sit down, too. Sure could use a smoke.

"I'm not defending her or apologizing for her," I say. "Can't do that anymore. I feel so stupid, letting her double-cross me my whole life, always trying to convince myself I'm wrong. Then she weasels her way back and always, always screws me over. One way or another. Used to be for money. Then it was for keeping secrets from her folks or some boyfriend. Then she needed me to hide her or cover up for her or hide some 'thing' for her. Then it was Pioche. Here I am, still thinking this will be the last time – she'll go straight now. Especially with a kid. If anything she's just more dangerous. That crooked ass police commissioner owes her big time."

Here we are now. My shit is out in the open for them to do what they want. I am sick and tired of it all, but I'll be goddam if I'm going to let Mona cause me anymore misery.

"She got to get got," Rodney says.

"I agree," says Paul Tingle, making goo-goo eyes at me and missing the point about "got" and who should get it.

"Thanks, you guys."

"You all right – for a white chick."

"Flattery will get you everywhere," I say, tossing a green M&M at him. His mouth opens, but with his eye gone, it hits him in the cheek, and gets lost in the wild pattern of his paisley printed robe.

"I know where she is," I say. "That fancy rock house on Mount Rose Street. Remember? Where we went that night on the way here?"

"No shit? Where we stopped for that ring? Wow, so it's Victoria's place?"

We sit in silence, having our drinks, eating M&Ms. Then Officer Tingle stands up, stretches, and announces he's hitting the hay. Suggests we all do, and we can start fresh in the morning. He holds his hand out to me. Rodney snickers and hauls himself up out of his chair.

"Do what you feel," he says and flips us a peace sign before going off down the hall. I'm left sitting and looking at that extended hand. He sure has nice nails. Wonder if he takes Knox gelatin.

What can I do? I take his hand, start toward the room I've been assigned.

"Uh-uh," he says and instead leads me out by the pool to

the cabana, where a bed is made up with beautiful white sheets and a fluffy cover. The roof is open to the sky and the French doors are all open wide, too.

We strip each other down and pile between the sheets. Then pile back out to sweep out the usual coating of sand. Blows in everywhere.

Frogs, crickets, the pool pump. How do I notice all of this in my delirious ravaging of Paul Tingle? His taste. His textures. His sweat. His . . . How is this all real? How is this all mine?

For now.

Nothing good lasts, Flack.

Chapter 41

It's a good thing cops become cops because they are the criminally-ist criminals that ever looked to commit a crime. They have to think like a crook to catch a crook or whatever sneaky bastard they're after. I suddenly have two cops — Grady's turning into a permanent fixture out here, right down to a razor, toothbrush, and his undies showing up in the laundry — and a lawyer on my "team." These guys are scaring me, they're so ruthless.

Once Grady and Paul Tingle started plotting Mona's demise, I started thinking about locking my bedroom door at night. Their plans take deviousness to a new level down to the ittiest bittiest detail. Rodney and I do more listening than talking. Grady and Officer Tingle are downright diabolical. Crazy. When Rodney and I do jump in, it's only to slow down

332

MITZI MILES

the train before those two can mount up and go slaughter some assholes. Most of them would be good riddance, but Mona? I'm plenty pissed at her, but I don't really want her guts spread all over Virginia Street "by accident," or for her to end up buried alive in the Black Rock Desert. They really do want to go that far. If I stay in this private investigator business, I have a whole new set of skills to put to use just from listening to those guys. I'm even taking notes . . . when I'm not sitting there with my mouth open going, "Holy SHIT!"

"It's the tape, guys, the tape. That's the key to getting all of them," I tell them, spoiling their fun. They know I'm right. My way's just not as much fun.

"Seriously," I say, "listen: Who's on that tape? What are they talking about? Who brought them together? Who has a copy of it? I'm telling you, we could get just Mona, or we could basically get everybody."

We're enjoying a beautiful Indian summer. We spend most of our time out by or in the pool, plotting. Thank you, Mona, you sleaze ball, for the groovy pad. She hasn't tried to make contact. Good for her, or my henchmen would for sure kick her ass. They're having a blast calling me an idiot for keeping/letting her in my life.

"She's interesting, though, right?" I ask. "And she has great taste." I spread my arms to indicate the luxury we live in.

Paul Tingle says, "It's a shame how right you are about both. Can I get either of you some caviar?"

For a hick farm boy from Yakima, he sure has adapted to the finer things in life. Personally, I think fish eggs are for fishing, but the guys are wolfing it down. I settle for M&Ms, popcorn, and jerky around snack time.

Finally I get them to agree that the tape – not murder – is our ticket. How best to serve it up is the next job. How to get the zippiest bang for our buck in true Nevada fashion.

We spent many days head-scratching and going back to the drawing board. And then one afternoon while I was paddling around the pool, doing my best to try not to think at all, BAM!, DUH!, Fern! Fern Howell from high school! FERN!

I streak into the kitchen, naked and dripping and screaming, "FERN! FERN!" The guys don't bother to look at me like I'm crazy. I've been nothing but a whole lot of crazy since this Johnny thing started, so they ignore me again, and keep on doing what they're doing. I grab the phone book off the kitchen counter.

"FERN!"

I scram to Mona's room where there's an extension phone: a pretty pink princess model.

I call Fern.

I explain who I am. I add a little bit about the Betamax.

She remembers me. Yes, she still works at KOLO. Yes, she knows about videotapes.

She's coming to dinner. Thursday.

She's bringing pine nuts.

I'm about the hand her the story of the century. I hope she's open-minded. And doesn't have to be to work too early Friday.

Chapter 42

I didn't know Fern all that well in high school. She was always behind a camera when she wasn't in class or in the darkroom. She made the yearbooks happen. She made little Super 8 movies for fun, and showed them to a few of us in the audio-visual closet. I didn't know how my red-headed ass got included. Fern is a Washoe Paiute, and generally speaking they didn't hang out with the student body. I was glad I finally got to ask "why me?" when she came for dinner.

She said, "You kept your head down, kept to yourself. Didn't trust anyone. You fit right in."

Dammit! I think I found someone else to love.

Over the next week, she whipped those yearbook-organizing and movie-making skills on us like a drill sargeant. She made diagrams and "scenarios." Assigned us jobs.

Complimented Paul Tingle's cooking. Went skinny dipping. And get this: She has a tattoo of a butterfly on her right butt-cheek! I've never seen a tattoo on a chick. Never even thought about it, but now . . .

And get this: I thought Rodney's eye was going to pop right out of his head when he saw her beautiful black hair spread out on the water, her sleek, brown body gliding like an otter. I might not be the only one in love with her!

Now, the day is here. As they say in the movies, "Action."

• • •

Victoria's place turned out not to really be Victoria's place after all. Paramount Pictures are the actual owners. She just happens to be crashing there. Some arrangement. Nothing in the mansion belongs to her except the clothes on her back, her wigs and baubles, and a yappie dog name Fauntleroy with a butt-scooting problem. The little fuzzball drags himself across the entryway rug like it's his way of saying hello. Now he's licking his pecker for all he wishes he was worth. The rhinestone bow holding up his bangs is not helping his case for being a proud descendent of wolves.

Victoria and I fumble through some small talk until we reach an uncomfortable silence.

Then there she is: Mona.

Top of the staircase. Resting her hot pink manicured fingers on the handrail. Dolled up like a movie star. Perfect Marilyn Monroe hair.

Her own conniving self. Looking all sorrowful and repentant. Looking for me to tell her it's all okay between us. We are still okay. She's going so far as to work up some

336

crocodile tears that I don't believe for one second. Keep it together, Flack. You're so close now. So close.

That fucking dog needs to shut the fuck up. Mona needs not to come near me. Victoria needs not to be so comically gracious.

"Are the boys getting along okay?" Mona asks as she glides – maybe oozes – down the stairs. "They seem to like each other."

I need to keep her backed off.

"They're fine."

She comes toward me. I cross my arms and look down. I don't know how much Victoria knows, but she can see enough to keep her mouth shut and let whatever's going to play out between me and Mona play out.

"I'm glad you're here," Mona says. "I almost miss you, stupid."

"Thanks." What the hell am I thanking her for her? Reflex.

Victoria says, "Would you like to see the house?"

Under ordinary circumstances? Yes. In extraordinary circumstances? Also yes. Gives me time to build my story. Gotta say the place is fucking great. I've always wanted to see it.

The Redfield Mansion inside is a fairytale dollhouse of flocked wallpaper and polished wood and wavy glass windows and crystal chandeliers and lace tablecloths and the heads of a whole bunch of wild animals on the rock walls. There are velvet chairs and couches and oriental carpets and brass candlesticks. Paramount Pictures can really set a stage. Far as I can tell, they got their history pretty doggone right. I can't tell what's real and what's fake. Doesn't matter. It's so cool I can actually appreciate it even in my stick-to-the-script frame of mind.

The rooms upstairs have TVs and phones. The tow-headed kid who walked Mona out the night we brought her here is watching Popeye in color in his own room. He hears us, waves over his shoulder, and keeps watching. Go away, grown-ups.

"Who is he?" I ask and couldn't care less.

Victoria says, "My grandson."

We come down into the kitchen by some back stairs. Gleaming copper pots and pans line the walls. A too-shiny wood cookstove sits next to a massive gas stove and subzero refrigerator. Dishwasher. All in as-new condition.

"The studio just renovated," Victoria says. "Not bad."

Fauntleroy finally quits yapping and bails on us to spend time with Junior. In the quiet, I can hear several clocks ticking and tocking without any kind of harmony. Our talk has been simple – general things about the house and all the goo-gaws. But the moment of truth gets closer and closer.

"Shall we do cocktails?" Victoria offers.

Well, of course.

Victoria passes through some swinging doors. I hear ice tumbling into glasses. Mona and I have finally locked eyes. This is my first chance to make a nasty impression. I smile. Just a tiny one. No teeth, barely a dimple. And I don't look away. There is a flash of – oh, we'll call it "concern" – in her eyes. She's not exactly on the ropes, but she's been given notice.

We settle at the fancy-schmancy, lace-covered table in the formal dining room. A dozen people could join us, and there would be space for plenty more.

"Like your new trailer space?" she asks. "Grady says it has lots of shade."

"It's a good one, thanks."

"Is everything as it was before the impound?"

"Tell you the truth, I haven't looked. Busy."

"Oh? What is my favorite private eye busy with these

days?"

"Living it up. You know: golf, tennis, massages, tropical vacations . . ."

"Business is good, then?"

"The best. Never been happier."

"I'm pleased to hear it."

Victoria looks like she's in the middle of the world's most confusing soap opera, but she keeps a cool smile plastered on her face. I'm not sure what she knows, but she seems to be waiting to see who cracks first.

Victoria brings our drinks in on a tray.

"These family portraits?" I ask her, pointing at the lineup on the wall.

"I'm not sure. You never know in the movie business what's real and what isn't."

"Good point. They sure look real, but I wouldn't know how to spot a fake."

Right at that moment, the clocks start chiming or ringing or singing or chirping the hour. Makes me jump. They're all different noises coming from all over the place. It's chaos. It's 7. I hope the ladies can't hear my scared shitless heart beating louder than all of it. This goes on and on before the sounds begin to fade out one by one. The last to quit is a cuckoo clock that gets off two more clucks before I hear it snap shut.

"Ha ha. Nothing like having the last word," I say. "Mind if I get a refill?"

I get up.

"No, no, allow me," Victoria says. She takes all of our glasses back through the swinging doors. There's a bar back there. A bar. I want a bar. If I ever get a place of my own that's not on wheels, it will have to have a bar.

Victoria left in a bit of a rush like she couldn't stand another minute of tension between me and Mona, who leans forward with her elbows on the table and her chin propped on her knuckles.

"Talk," is all she says.

"Love to." I mimic her body language. "First I have a present for you."

I take a big paper bag out of my purse and dump a pile of Betamax tapes on the table. The clatter makes Mona flinch, and I like that. Flinching is good.

I start to stack them into piles. Make shapes with them. Turn them into the plastic box equivalent of Lincoln Logs. Playing around.

I get a fortress going in front of me and sit back to admire my design.

"Remember Fern Howell from school?" I ask as I make minor adjustments to my wall of videotapes.

"Refresh my memory, please."

"Fern's dad was, is, an elder of the Pyramid Lake Paiutes. Been one for as long as I can remember. John Howell. Good guy. Done a lot for the tribe. You'd never know from the grief Fern got at school how important her family is. John Howell gets invited to speak at the legislature. He's even been called to Washington, D.C

"Really? How interesting. I still can't place her."

"Doesn't matter. Fern graduated UNR and works at KOLO TV news now. She works with filming machinery and shit. Knows those machines backwards and forwards. A real wiz when it comes to all this newfangled video crap. Like Betamax.

"I flashed on her the other day when I was wondering whatever became of the tape you gave me. I kind of lost track of it, you know, in all the running around I've been doing. A thing like that is easy to, oh, toss out by accident."

She hasn't moved a muscle, neither has Victoria

reappeared. She's keeping her distance but no doubt eavesdropping.

"I couldn't think where the damn thing disappeared to. Then, boom!, I found it under the couch at your place."

Not a sexy lie, but the truth about me giving it to Grady – and what I know about her showing it to the police commissioner – didn't need to come out. Yet.

"And I got to thinking who I might know that could tell me if you can make copies of Betamaxes. That's how I remembered Fern.

"Long story short, I went down to the TV studio to look her up. See if she could help."

Mona's got a squidge of an idea where I'm going with this, but you and I both know she doesn't know the half of it. Yet.

"I showed your tape to her. Watched it with her right there at a real goddam TV studio. With all those cameras and lights and stacks of equipment covered with dials and levers and lights. People running around doing all kinds of important TV newsy shit. We watched it, like, three times. She even backed up a few parts and watched them again."

I start playing with the tapes in front of me. Rearranging, re-stacking. This is fun.

Mona clears her throat. "What are you doing?"

"Playing."

"God DAMN it, Susan Anne!"

"Well, Sheryl – you don't mind it if I call you Sheryl for old time's sake? Of course you don't. Here goes: Grady told me he walked in on you and Vincent's little meeting with the police commissioner. Remember? You guys slammed the door on him when he saw the three of you watching the tape? I had already shown it to him."

No sense letting her know he was holding the one I gave him that day. I'm not putting him in more danger than I already have.

"He knew," I say.

Victoria reappears with our drinks, leaves ours on the table, and quickly excuses herself to go check on the grandkid.

"How could you, Sheryl? I started thinking back on how you came to me, how you used me – even to kill for your sorry ass. How you shipped your daughter off so you wouldn't be burdened with her anymore. How you took up with Johnny's brother so that whole racetrack thing doesn't fall apart and leave you broke again. I get it now. All that 'hate you/hate you more' crap that you never meant. How you will use anybody, any time, any way, for anything just for money. I'm an idiot for taking you back as a friend over and over, thinking every fucking time that you changed . . ."

She's hates the name Sheryl. I need it to put some distance between us to keep me from getting too emotional.

She says, "I don't know where this is coming from. How can you think such things about me? I love you like a sister. You know that. I would never . . ."

"Oh, shut the fuck up, Sheryl. I don't believe you anymore."

"You have the nerve to think I'd abandon my own child . . .?"

"Honey, I think you put Pio out of your mind the minute you handed her over to her drug-manufacturing father. That's all people like you can do: Squeeze work and favors and the life out of everyone around you until there's nothing left, and conveniently forget you ever knew them."

"What a horrible thing to say! How dare you! I love Pioche! She's the world to me!"

"Which world is that: The world of PTA meetings and braces and sleepovers and pimples? Or the world of yachts and diamonds and rich men to suck up to? You're too fucking lazy to be a mom. Too much commitment for too little payback."

"Wow. That's what you think of me."

"I do. It kills me, but I do.

"You're a gaping hole of greed that sucks in everything around you and gives not a goddam thing back. I love you and I'm sorry for you. Those are my problems, and I have to live with that. I'm glad you'll never have to know how I feel. You could not take this much pain.

"But, I'm positive you don't want to spend a nice long stretch in prison. Same clothes every day. Basic gray. Busted up fingernails. Your hair back to dirty blonde. You'll still have plenty of people to use. No time flat you'll be the queen of cigarettes and toilet hooch. That's where I'm sending you. With these." I spread my hands out over the tapes.

"Fern showed your tape to her father. We needed to know what to do, who to trust. Clearly no one on the tape, not the police commissioner. Mr. Howell gave us a list. Politicians, press, other tribal elders, casino owners. All of them got copies, courtesy of Fern and KOLO. Hand-delivered. It's amazing how large John Howell's circle of friends is. Washoe Paiutes will shut down that whole racetrack fiasco permanently. The press will have a field day with all the juicy bribery and extortion and scandal. The Ruggerios have such a crappy reputation with the other casino owners, they'll be glad to see their reputation go to hell and see them lose their licenses. The politicians will scatter like cockroaches for a while, but eventually lie, cheat, and steal their way back in. But you? Low, low, low man on the totem pole. You're nothing to them. But you are the sexy porno queen playing hide the salami with Johnny as the short feature on the tape. Who will come to your rescue? Um, no one. You're going down for a big, juicy chunk of your life behind this pile of shit."

"You wouldn't."

"Already done."

"You fucking bitch."

"Hate you more."

I finish my drink and stand up to leave.

"These?" I say, shoving the pile at her and watching the tapes clatter into a mess in front of her and onto her lap and onto the floor. "Blanks. I just used them for effect. Pretty classy, huh? Like the movies."

She looks tired. I'm tired, too. I lost a best friend who wasn't any such thing as a friend. Ever. That's really confusing. Don't know if I'll fully figure out why she happened to me. One thing I know: she was interesting.

Chapter 43

"Big" doesn't even begin to describe the scandal. Fingers were pointed. Heads rolled. Reputations crumbled. The whole thing was national news for a long while. KOLO won all kinds of fancy news awards. Fern got a huge promotion. First woman ever in her new position. First Indian, too.

I can't bring myself not to give a flying fuck about Mona. I try not to think about her. From the little bit of news I see, she's fighting for all she's worth, but it's less and less every day. She still doesn't get that money isn't everything.

Grady took retirement. Came to stay out here at Mona's for a bit. He's welcome as long as he wants. Hell, we're all basically squatters until we ain't. To this day, no one knows how much he knew, mainly because no one believes a word Mona says.

Officer Tingle got subpoenaed. Had to go back to San Francisco for hearings and crap about the guy he capped. Had to go. Hope things turn out okay for him. I got kind of used to having him around. I mean, really used to having him around.

And guess what else? Rodney and Fern did hit it off, poor things. Pretty tough in Nevada to be either black or Indian, but to be a couple who is both? They have their work cut out for them. They are absolutely adorable together. New love. Best feeling in the world. Even if it's happening to someone else. Make that especially if it's happening to someone else.

Me? Well, shit. Still got the trailer. Rockalee. The GTO. Still love Nevada. It'll take me a while to run through the money people threw at me all year, so I'm not looking for investigator work at the moment. I need to reset. From everything. Everything.

Paul Tingle. He says when he gets through with his trouble in San Francisco, he's coming back here to me. Wherever that might be. He says he doesn't care as long as we're together. Tempting as that is, there is a big part of me that wants to run far, far away. No forwarding address. No breadcrumbs.

Then there is that other part.

The part that makes me tingle.

THE END
. . . of this part . . .

Mitzi Miles is a US author whose work celebrates the West where she's lived all her life. She loves to explore the romance, humor, beauty, strength, and quirkiness of small towns and small town characters. She spent her "formative years" ('60s and '70s) in Nevada and draws much of her inspiration from those days of wide open spaces and rugged individualism.

Love to hear from you!
mitzimiles.author@gmail.com
mitzimileskubota.com

www.ingramcontent.com/pod-product-compliance
Lightning Source LLC
Chambersburg PA
CBHW022248020726
47496CB00004B/1112